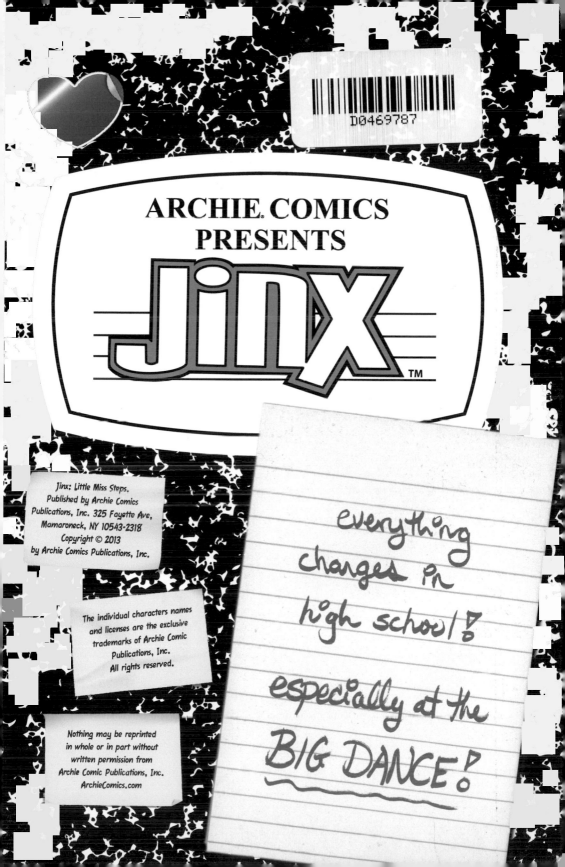

ARCHIE® COMICS
PRESENTS

JINX™

Jinx: Little Miss Steps.
Published by Archie Comics
Publications, Inc. 325 Fayette Ave,
Mamaroneck, NY 10543-2318
Copyright © 2013
by Archie Comics Publications, Inc.

everything
changes in
high school!

especially at the
BIG DANCE!

JINX

LITTLE MISS STEPS

Written by J. Torres

Pencils by Rick Burchett

Inks by Terry Austin

Letters by John Workman

Colors by Digikore Studios

Cover colors by Rosario "Tito" Pena

Publisher / Co-CEO: Jon Goldwater
Co-CEO: Nancy Silberkleit
President: Mike Pellerito
Co-President / Editor-In-Chief: Victor Gorelick
CFO: William Mooar
SVP - Sales & Business Devolpment: Jim Sokolowski
SVP - Publishing & Operations: Harold Buchholz
VP - Special Projects: Steve Mooar
Executive Director of Editorial: Paul Kaminski
Production Manager: Stephen Oswald
Director of Publicity & Marketing: Steven Scott
Editor / Book Design: Suzannah Rowntree
Editorial Assistant: Jamie Lee Rotante
Proofreader: Jon Mosley

Torres, J., 1969-
   Jinx. [2], Little Miss Steps / written by J. Torres ; pencils by Rick Burchett ; inks by Terry Austin ; letters by John Workman ; colors by Digikore Studios.
      p. : chiefly col. ill. ; cm.
   Summary: For most of her life Li'l Jinx has found life was easy to understand. Now that she's in high school, a more mature Jinx Holliday is discovering that growing up is complicated, especially when she's confronted with an absent mother, gender identity, and sexual preference. Jinx deals with the stuff that we all encounter when we reach high school.
      Interest age level: 010-014.
   ISBN: 978-1-936975-42-6 (hard cover)
   ISBN: 978-1-936975-41-9 (trade paper)

   1. High school girls--United States--Comic books, strips, etc. 2. High school girls--United States--Conduct of life--Comic books, strips, etc. 3. Teenage girls--United States--Comic books, strips, etc. 4. Graphic novels. 5. Young adult fiction, American. I. Burchett, Rick. II. Austin, Terry, 1952- III. Workman, John, 1950- IV. Digikore Studios. V. Title. VI. Title: Little Miss Steps VII. Title: Archie comics presents Jinx
   PN6727.T67 J562 2013
   813/.6 [Fic]

CONTENTS

CAST OF JINX

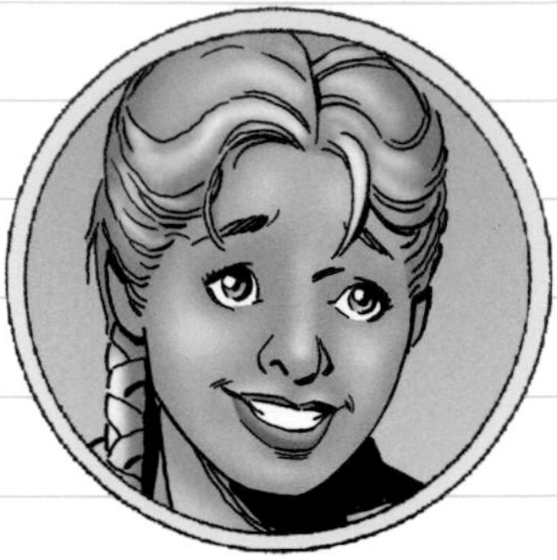

jinx
your hero

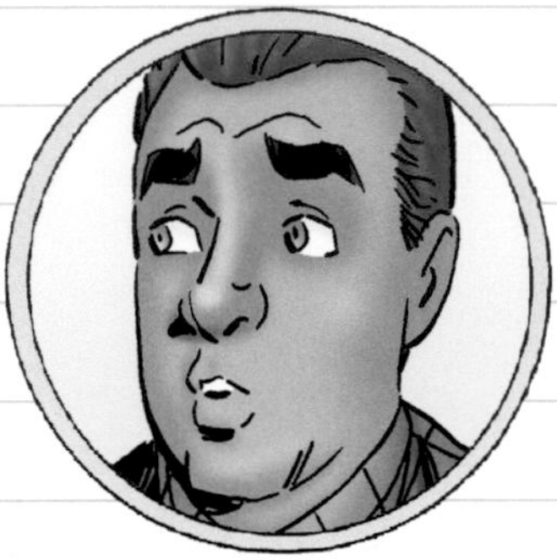

hap
her father

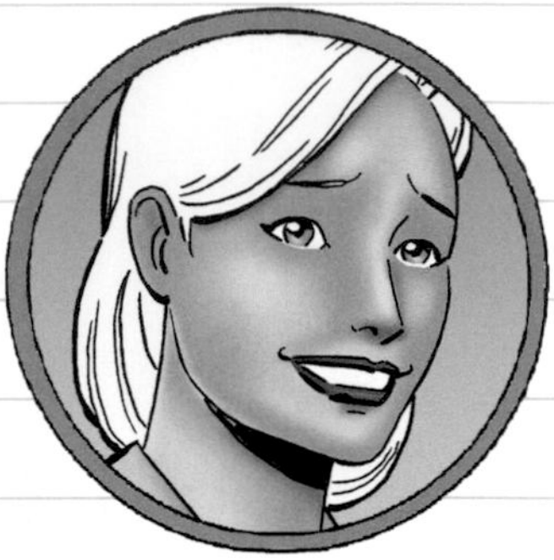

mery
absentee mom

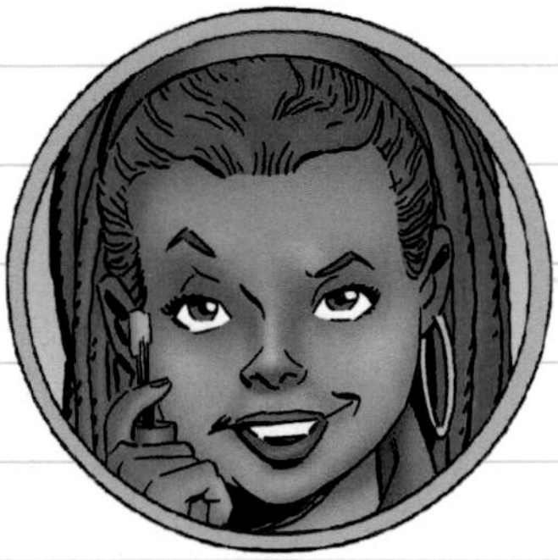

roz
friend, optimist

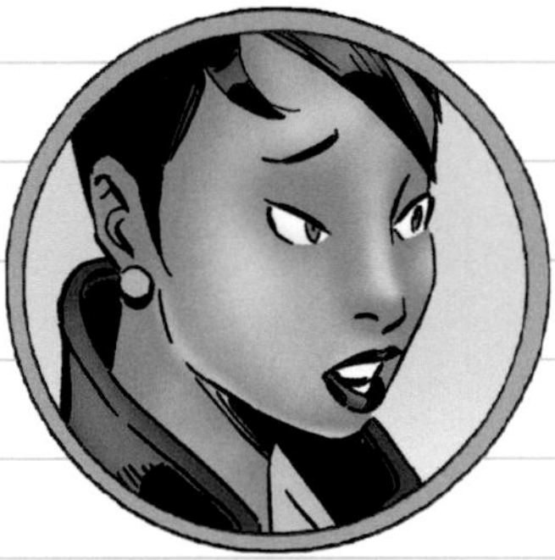

gigi
frenemy, glam queen

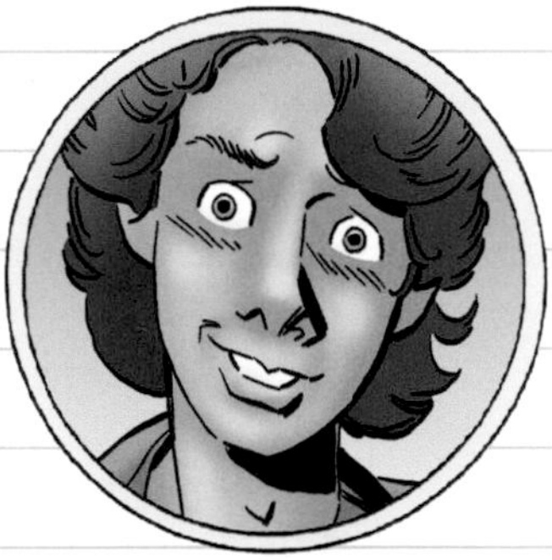

greg
friend, skater

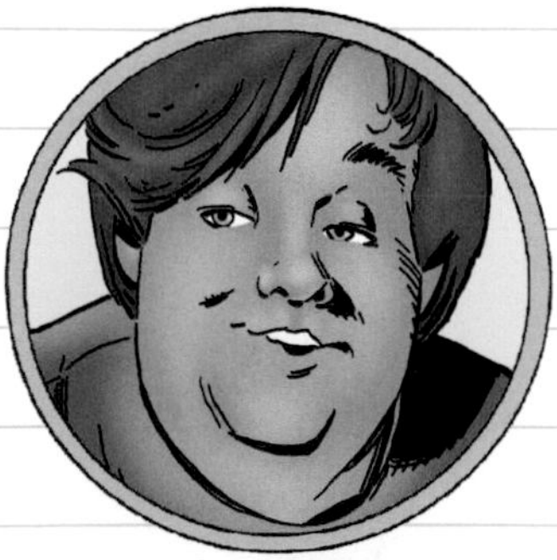

charley
frenemy, rival

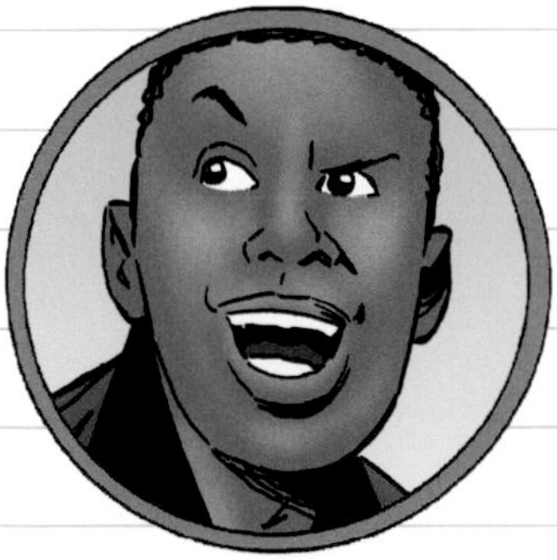

russ
friend, jock

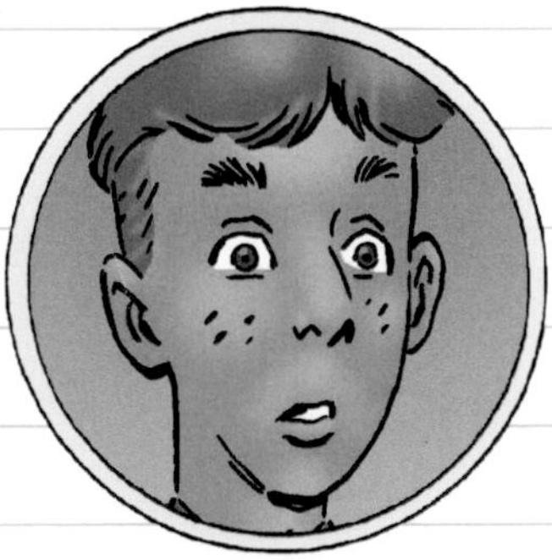

mort
friend, pessimist

JINX™

CHAPTER 1

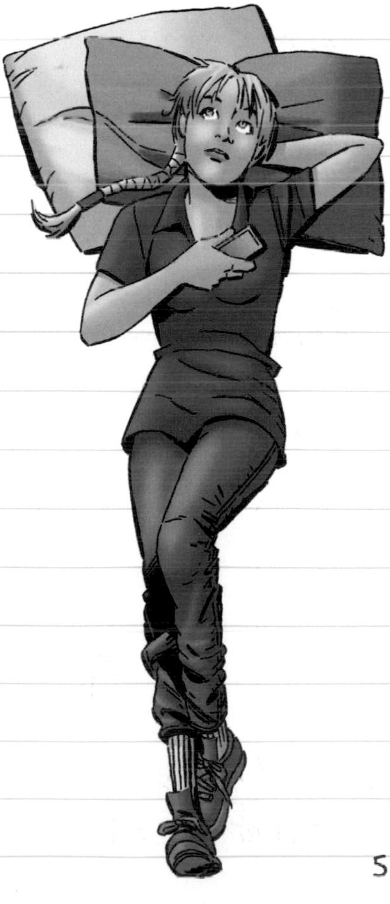

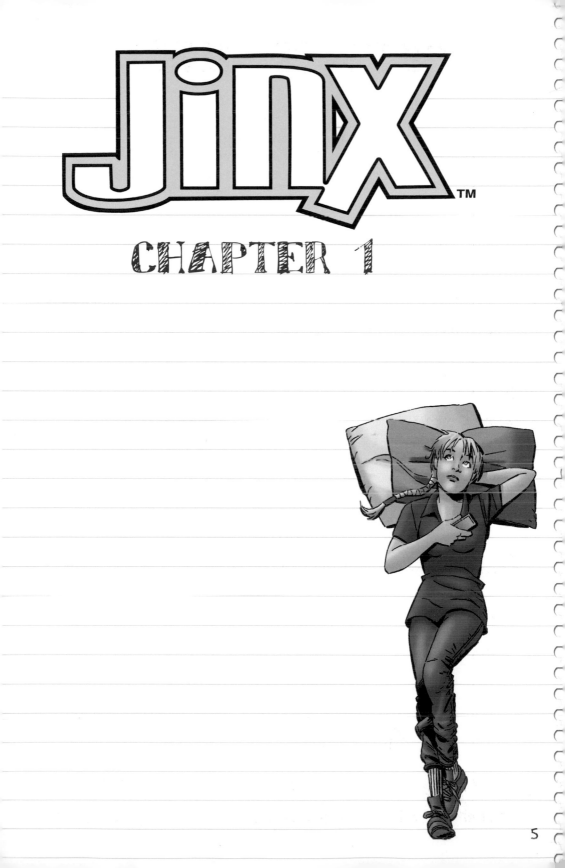

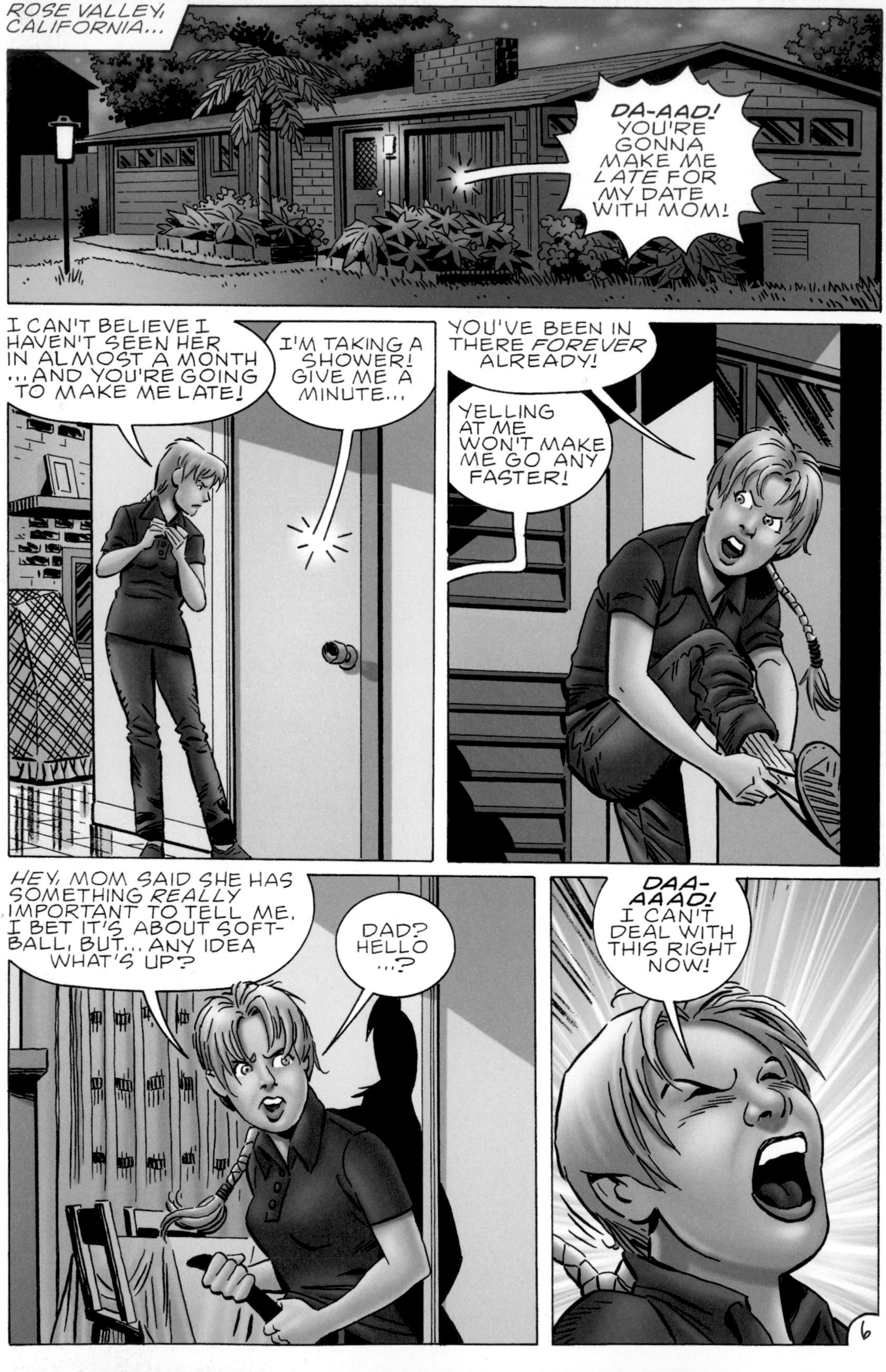
ROSE VALLEY, CALIFORNIA...
DA-AAD! YOU'RE GONNA MAKE ME LATE FOR MY DATE WITH MOM!
I CAN'T BELIEVE I HAVEN'T SEEN HER IN ALMOST A MONTH ...AND YOU'RE GOING TO MAKE ME LATE!
I'M TAKING A SHOWER! GIVE ME A MINUTE...
YOU'VE BEEN IN THERE FOREVER ALREADY!
YELLING AT ME WON'T MAKE ME GO ANY FASTER!
HEY, MOM SAID SHE HAS SOMETHING REALLY IMPORTANT TO TELL ME. I BET IT'S ABOUT SOFT-BALL, BUT... ANY IDEA WHAT'S UP?
DAD? HELLO ...?
DAA-AAAD! I CAN'T DEAL WITH THIS RIGHT NOW!
6

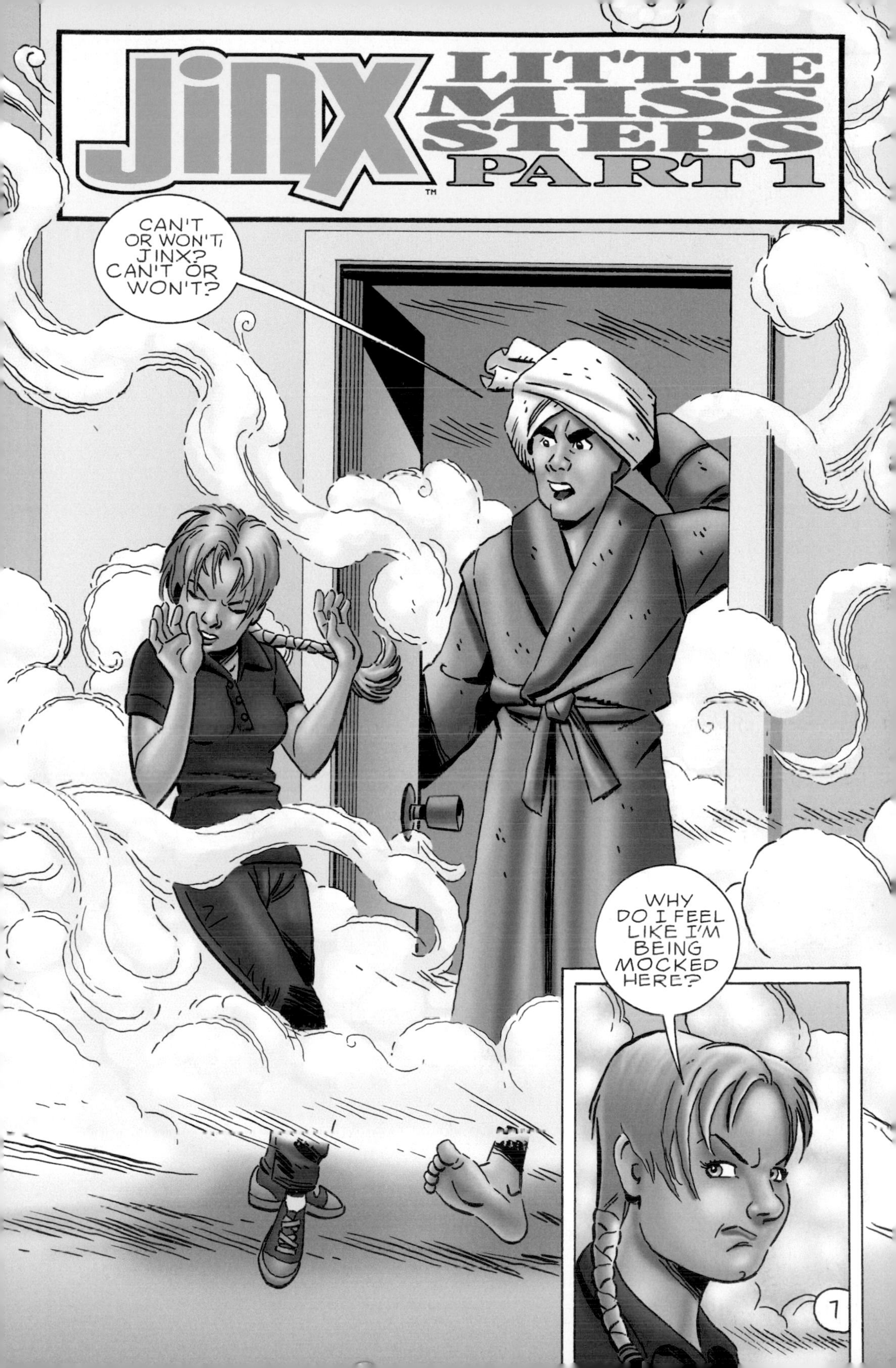
JINX™
LITTLE MISS STEPS PART 1
CAN'T OR WON'T, JINX? CAN'T OR WON'T?
WHY DO I FEEL LIKE I'M BEING MOCKED HERE?

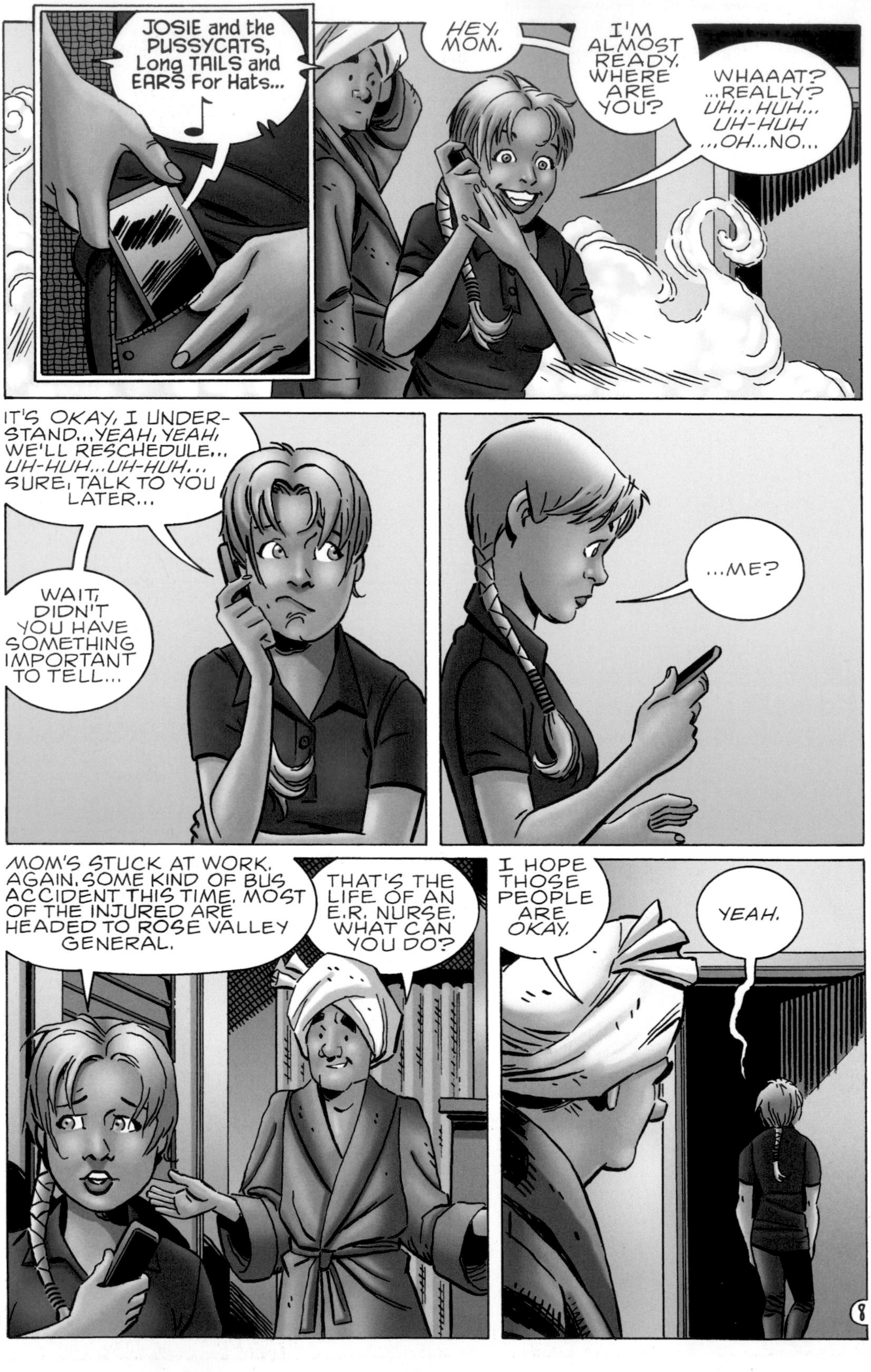
JOSIE and the PUSSYCATS, Long TAILS and EARS For Hats...
HEY, MOM.
I'M ALMOST READY. WHERE ARE YOU?
WHAAAT? ...REALLY? UH... HUH... UH-HUH ...OH...NO...
IT'S OKAY, I UNDERSTAND... YEAH, YEAH, WE'LL RESCHEDULE... UH-HUH...UH-HUH... SURE, TALK TO YOU LATER...
WAIT, DIDN'T YOU HAVE SOMETHING IMPORTANT TO TELL...
...ME?
MOM'S STUCK AT WORK. AGAIN. SOME KIND OF BUS ACCIDENT THIS TIME. MOST OF THE INJURED ARE HEADED TO ROSE VALLEY GENERAL.
THAT'S THE LIFE OF AN E.R. NURSE. WHAT CAN YOU DO?
I HOPE THOSE PEOPLE ARE OKAY.
YEAH.
8

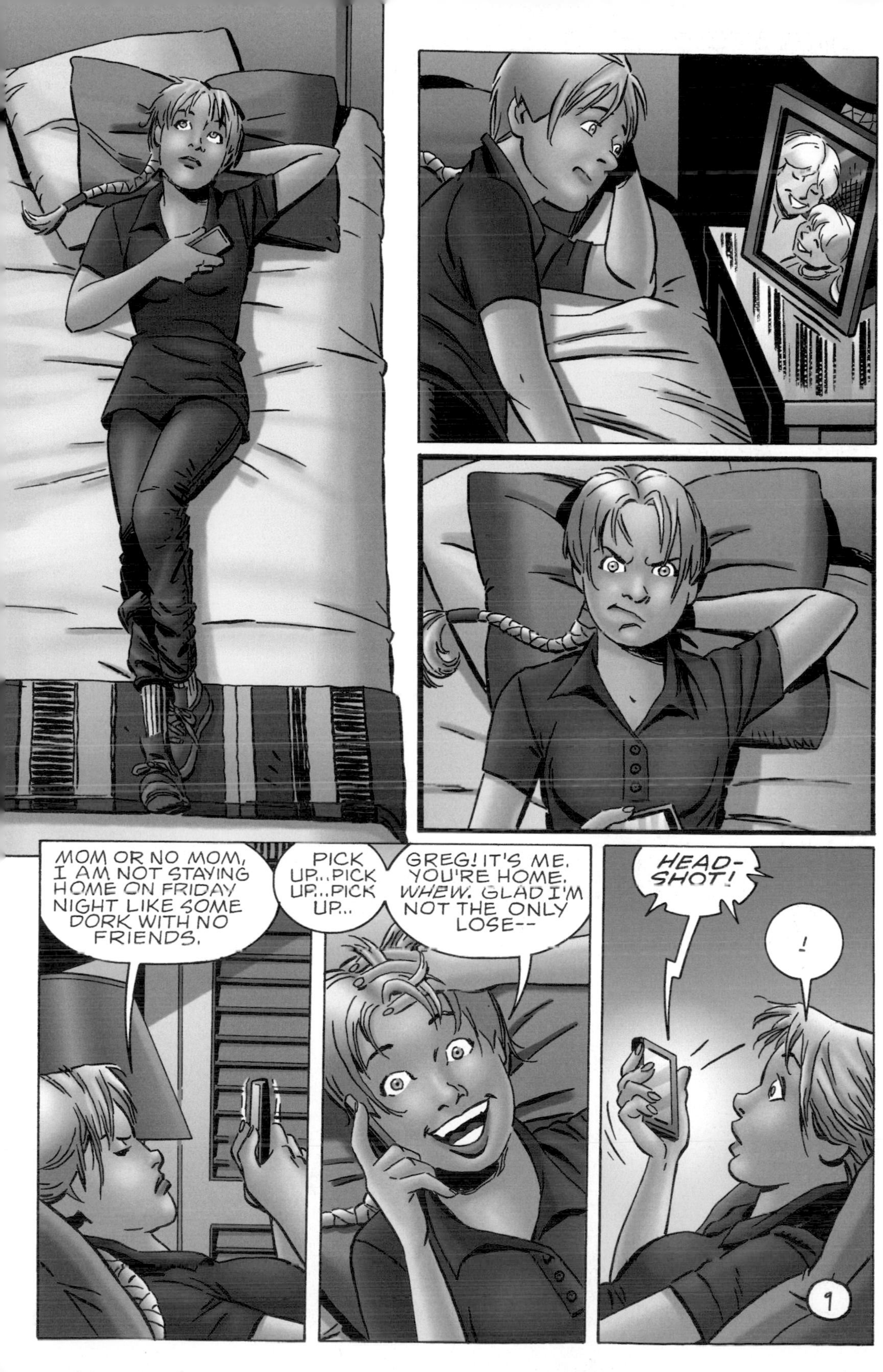
MOM OR NO MOM, I AM NOT STAYING HOME ON FRIDAY NIGHT LIKE SOME DORK WITH NO FRIENDS.
PICK UP...PICK UP...PICK UP...
GREG! IT'S ME. YOU'RE HOME. WHEW. GLAD I'M NOT THE ONLY LOSE--
HEAD-SHOT!
!

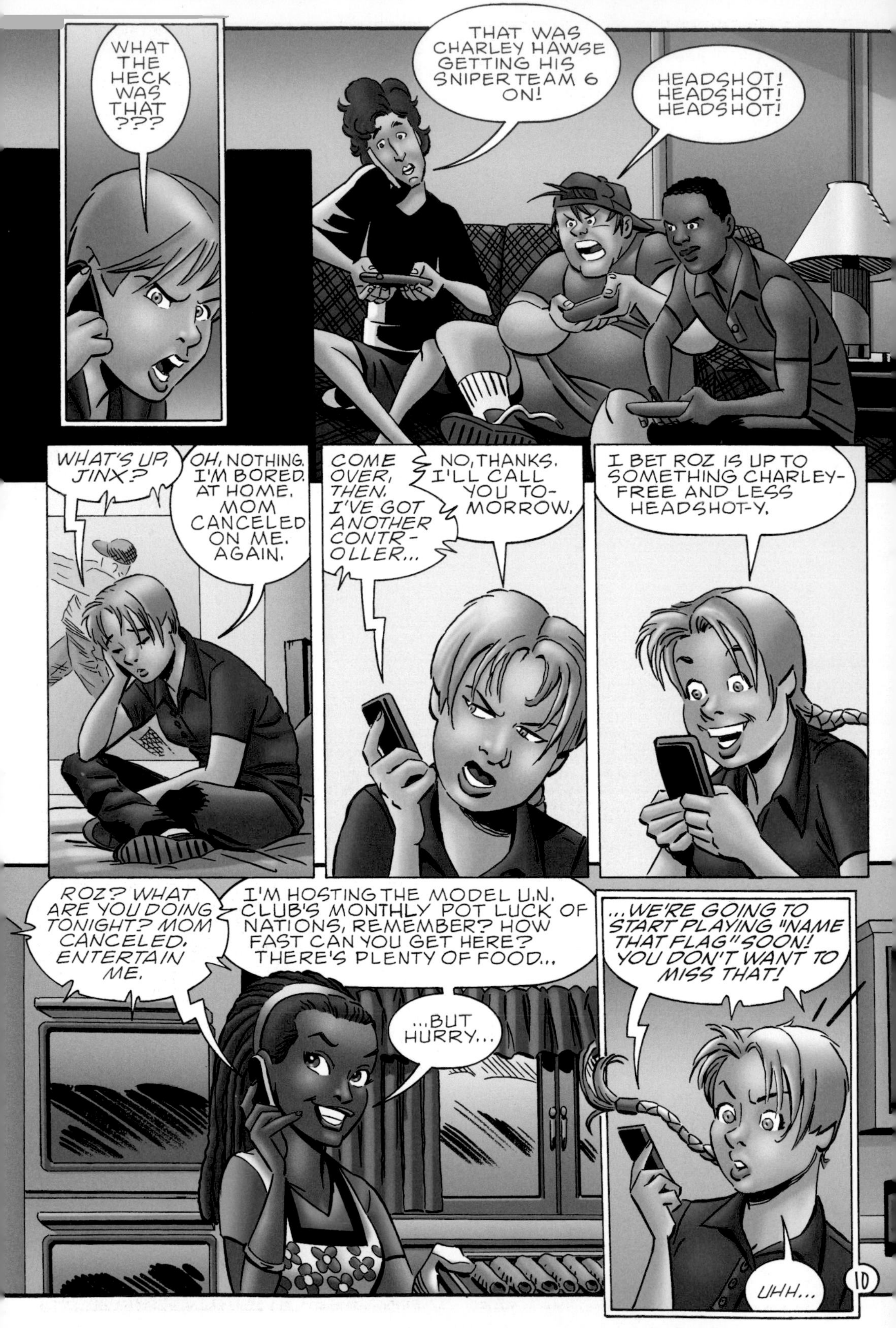
WHAT THE HECK WAS THAT???
THAT WAS CHARLEY HAWSE GETTING HIS SNIPER TEAM 6 ON!
HEADSHOT! HEADSHOT! HEADSHOT!
WHAT'S UP, JINX?
OH, NOTHING. I'M BORED. AT HOME. MOM CANCELED ON ME. AGAIN.
COME OVER, THEN. I'VE GOT ANOTHER CONTR-OLLER...
NO, THANKS. I'LL CALL YOU TO-MORROW.
I BET ROZ IS UP TO SOMETHING CHARLEY-FREE AND LESS HEADSHOT-Y.
ROZ? WHAT ARE YOU DOING TONIGHT? MOM CANCELED. ENTERTAIN ME.
I'M HOSTING THE MODEL U.N. CLUB'S MONTHLY POT LUCK OF NATIONS, REMEMBER? HOW FAST CAN YOU GET HERE? THERE'S PLENTY OF FOOD...
...BUT HURRY...
...WE'RE GOING TO START PLAYING "NAME THAT FLAG" SOON! YOU DON'T WANT TO MISS THAT!
UHH...
10

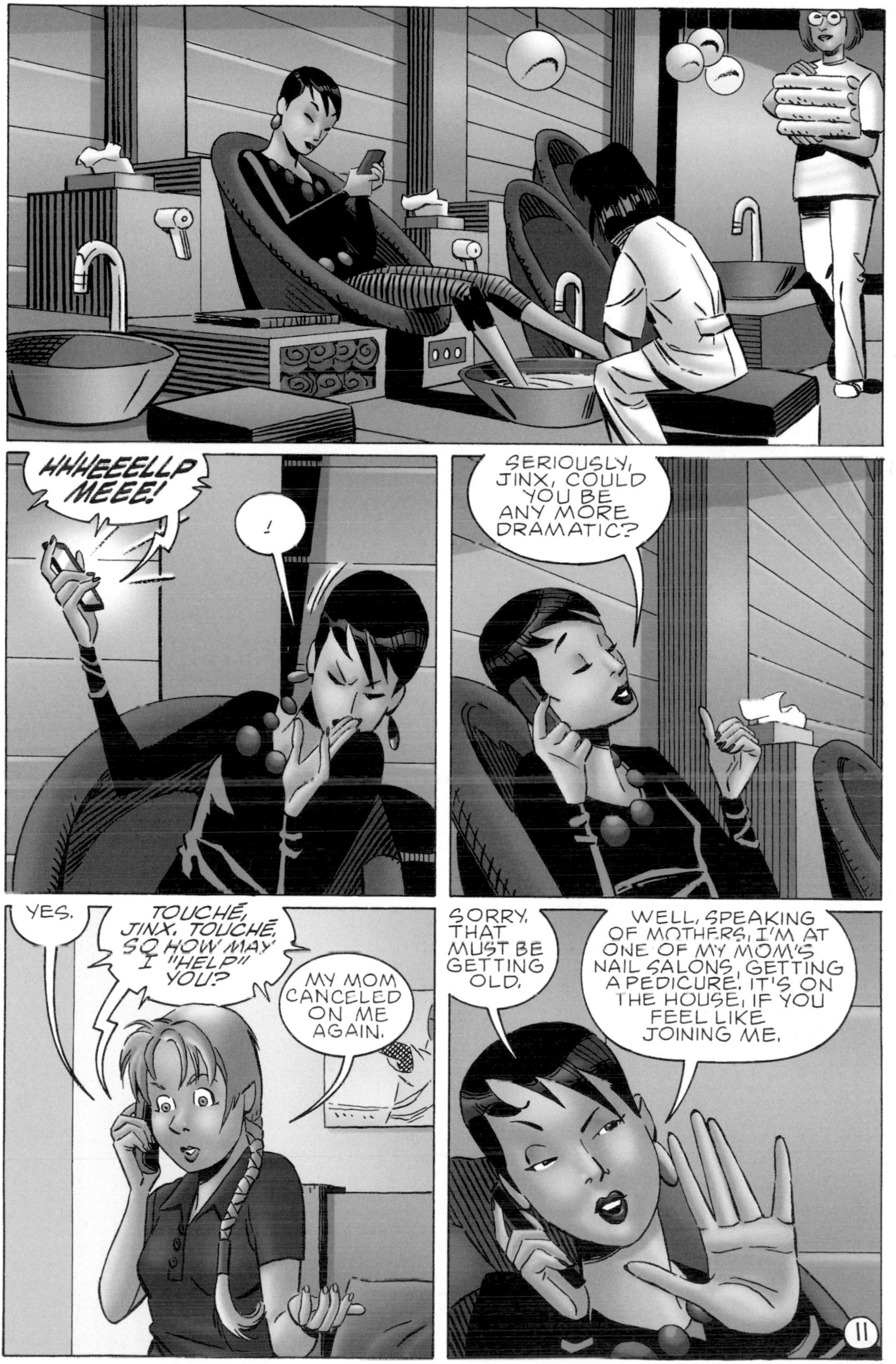

HHHEEELLP MEEE!
!
SERIOUSLY, JINX, COULD YOU BE ANY MORE DRAMATIC?
YES.
TOUCHÉ, JINX. TOUCHÉ. SO HOW MAY I "HELP" YOU?
MY MOM CANCELED ON ME AGAIN.
SORRY. THAT MUST BE GETTING OLD.
WELL, SPEAKING OF MOTHERS, I'M AT ONE OF MY MOM'S NAIL SALONS, GETTING A PEDICURE. IT'S ON THE HOUSE, IF YOU FEEL LIKE JOINING ME.

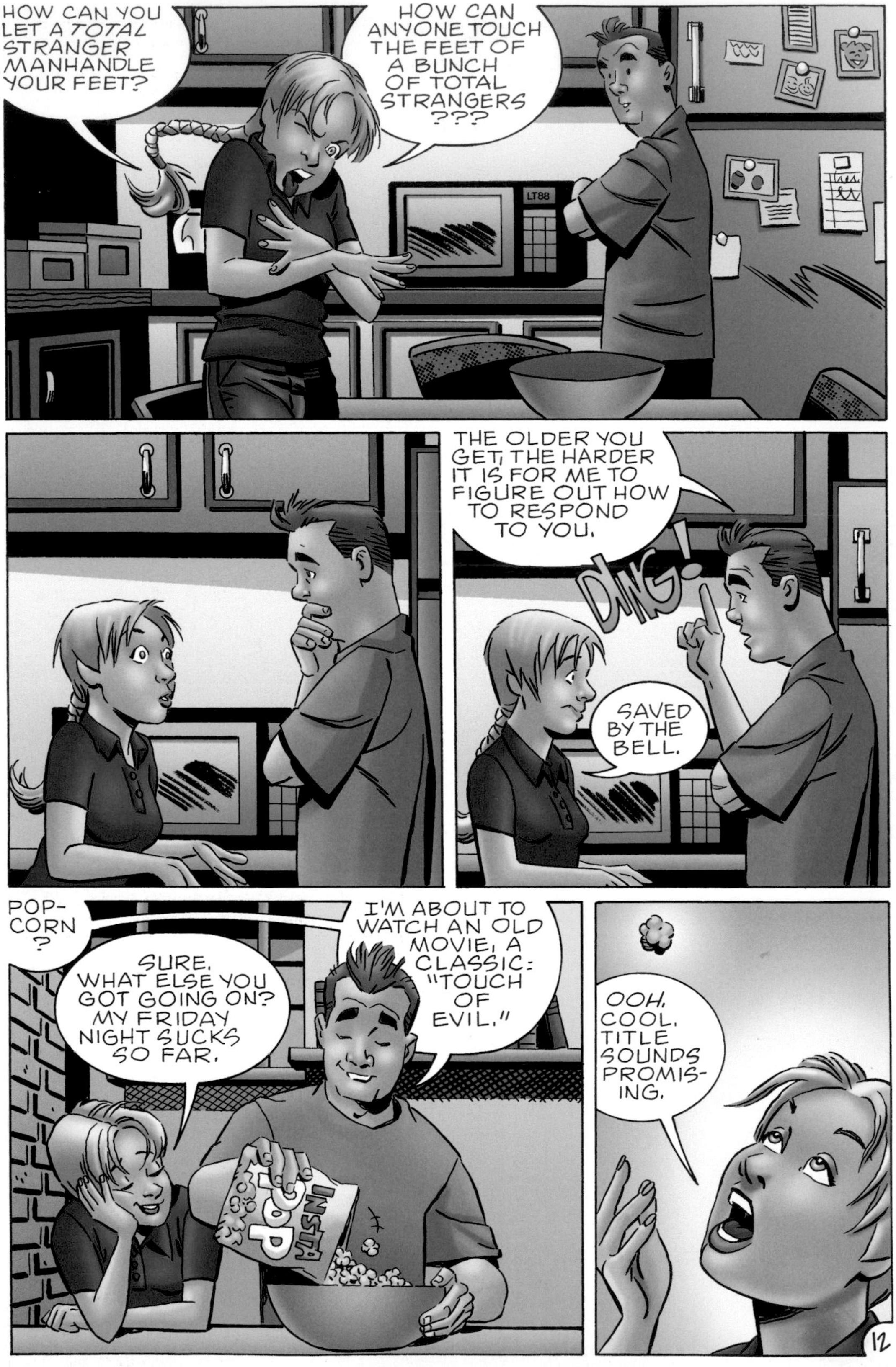
HOW CAN YOU LET A *TOTAL* STRANGER MANHANDLE YOUR FEET?
HOW CAN ANYONE TOUCH THE FEET OF A BUNCH OF TOTAL STRANGERS ???
LT88
THE OLDER YOU GET, THE HARDER IT IS FOR ME TO FIGURE OUT HOW TO RESPOND TO YOU.
DING!
SAVED BY THE BELL.
POP-CORN ?
SURE. WHAT ELSE YOU GOT GOING ON? MY FRIDAY NIGHT SUCKS SO FAR.
I'M ABOUT TO WATCH AN OLD MOVIE, A CLASSIC: "TOUCH OF EVIL."
INSTA POP
OOH. COOL. TITLE SOUNDS PROMIS-ING.

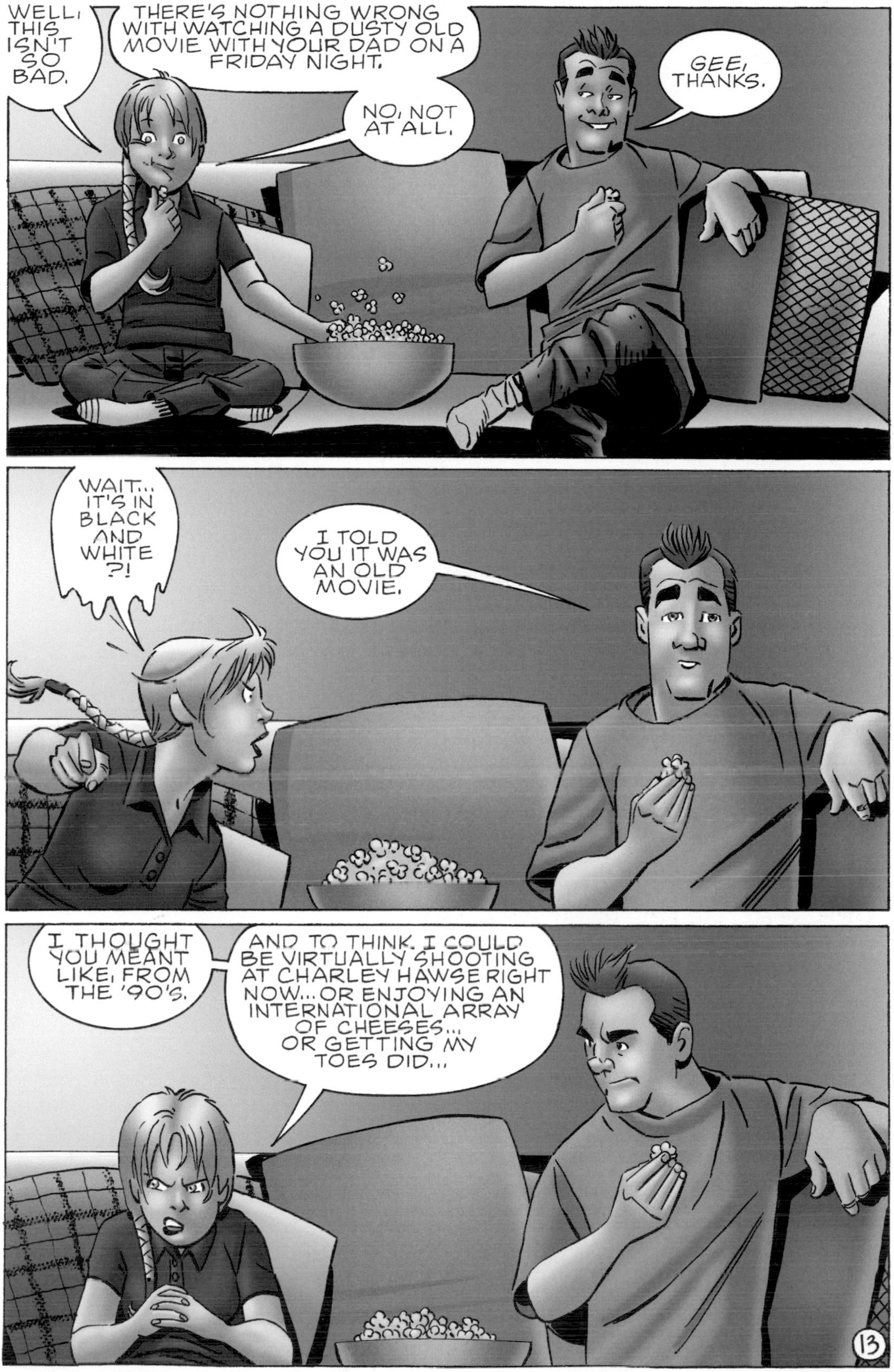
WELL, THIS ISN'T SO BAD.
THERE'S NOTHING WRONG WITH WATCHING A DUSTY OLD MOVIE WITH YOUR DAD ON A FRIDAY NIGHT.
NO, NOT AT ALL.
GEE, THANKS.
WAIT... IT'S IN BLACK AND WHITE ?!
I TOLD YOU IT WAS AN OLD MOVIE.
I THOUGHT YOU MEANT LIKE, FROM THE '90'S.
AND TO THINK. I COULD BE VIRTUALLY SHOOTING AT CHARLEY HAWSE RIGHT NOW...OR ENJOYING AN INTERNATIONAL ARRAY OF CHEESES... OR GETTING MY TOES DID...

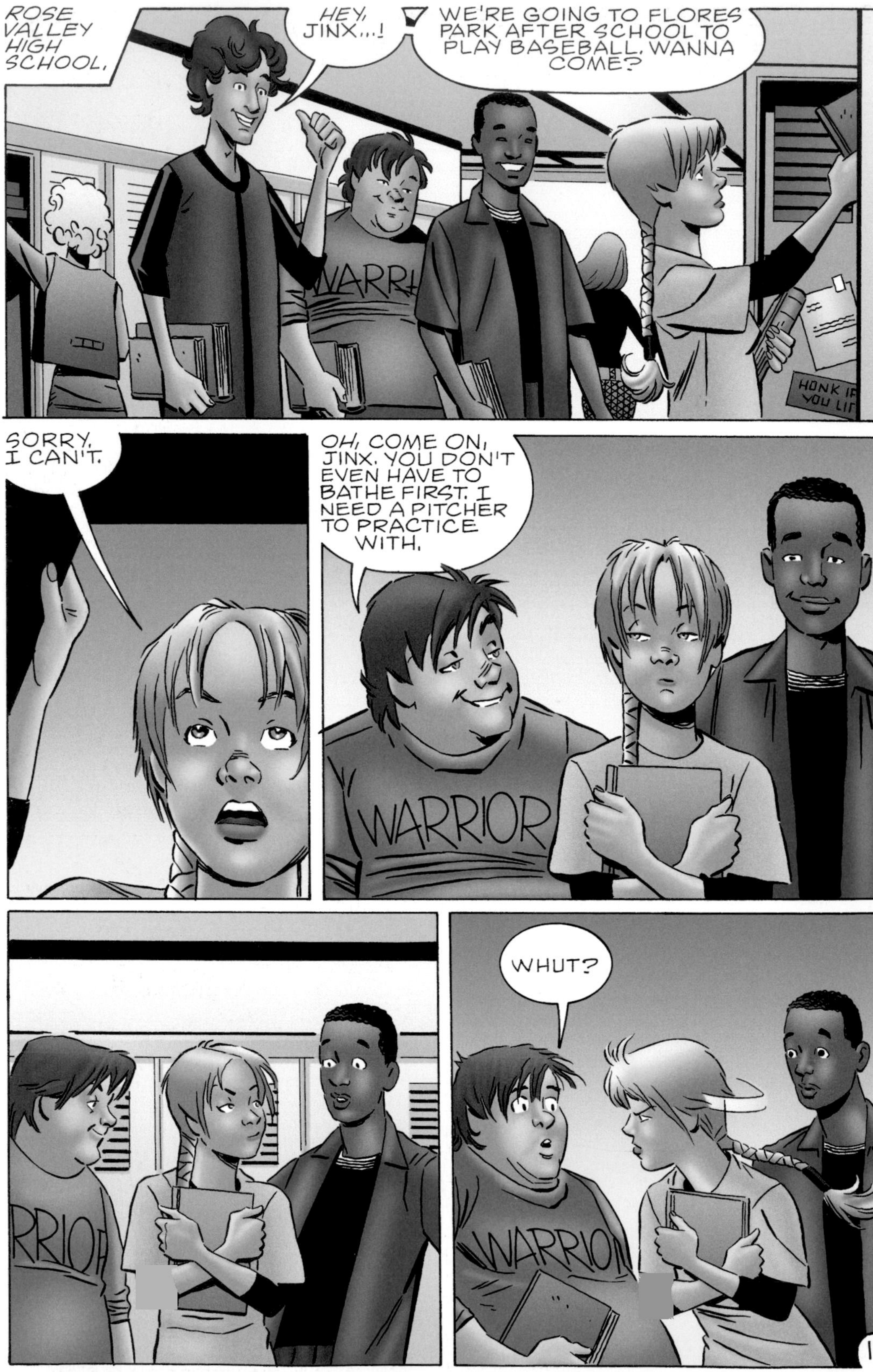
ROSE VALLEY HIGH SCHOOL.
HEY, JINX...!
WE'RE GOING TO FLORES PARK AFTER SCHOOL TO PLAY BASEBALL. WANNA COME?
WARRI
HONK IF YOU LI
SORRY, I CAN'T.
OH, COME ON, JINX. YOU DON'T EVEN HAVE TO BATHE FIRST. I NEED A PITCHER TO PRACTICE WITH.
WARRIOR
RRIOR
WHUT?
WARRIO

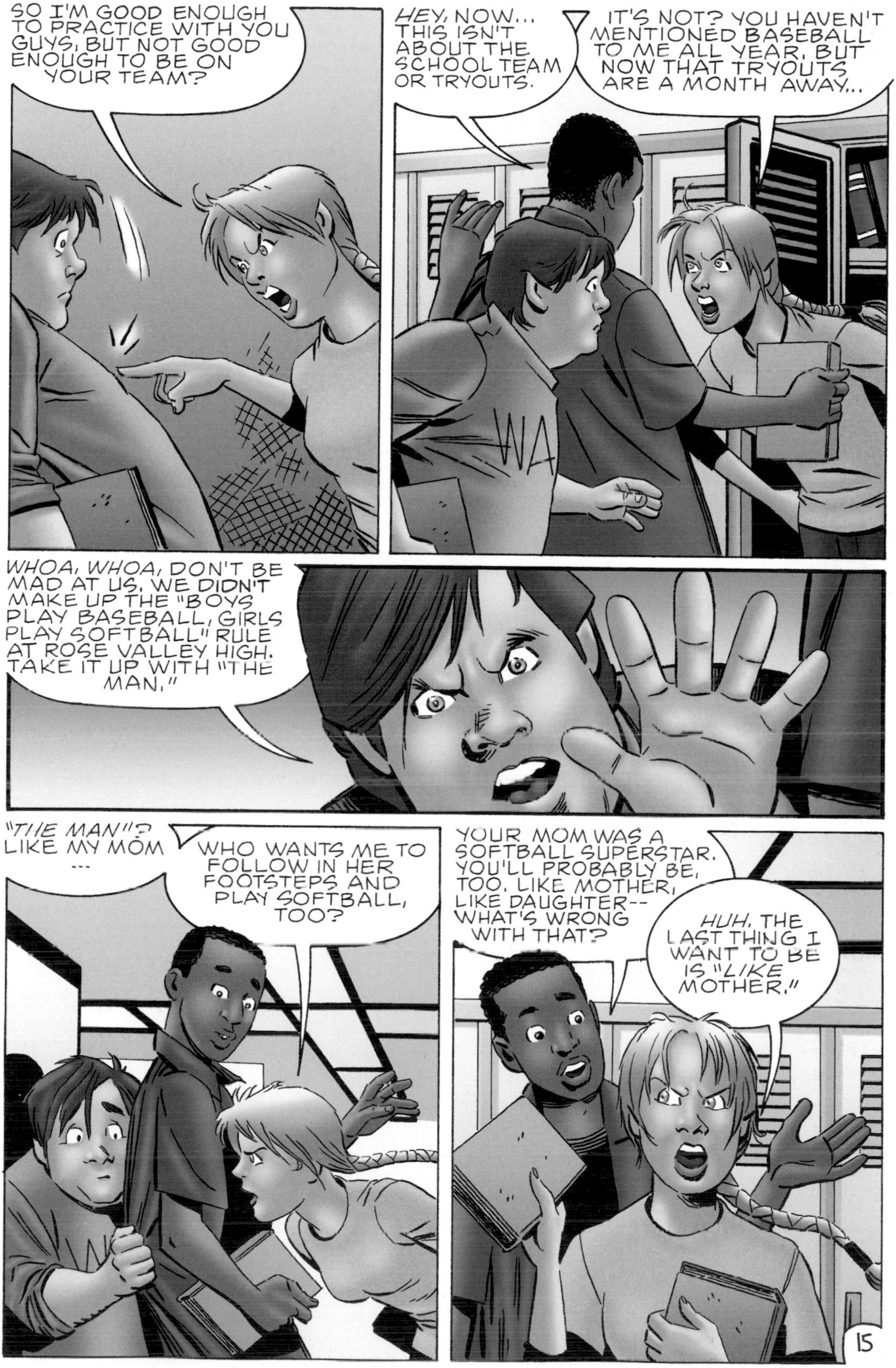
SO I'M GOOD ENOUGH TO PRACTICE WITH YOU GUYS, BUT NOT GOOD ENOUGH TO BE ON YOUR TEAM?
HEY, NOW... THIS ISN'T ABOUT THE SCHOOL TEAM OR TRYOUTS.
IT'S NOT? YOU HAVEN'T MENTIONED BASEBALL TO ME ALL YEAR, BUT NOW THAT TRYOUTS ARE A MONTH AWAY...
WHOA, WHOA, DON'T BE MAD AT US. WE DIDN'T MAKE UP THE "BOYS PLAY BASEBALL, GIRLS PLAY SOFTBALL" RULE AT ROSE VALLEY HIGH. TAKE IT UP WITH "THE MAN."
"THE MAN"? LIKE MY MOM ---
WHO WANTS ME TO FOLLOW IN HER FOOTSTEPS AND PLAY SOFTBALL, TOO?
YOUR MOM WAS A SOFTBALL SUPERSTAR. YOU'LL PROBABLY BE, TOO. LIKE MOTHER, LIKE DAUGHTER-- WHAT'S WRONG WITH THAT?
HUH. THE LAST THING I WANT TO BE IS "LIKE MOTHER."
15

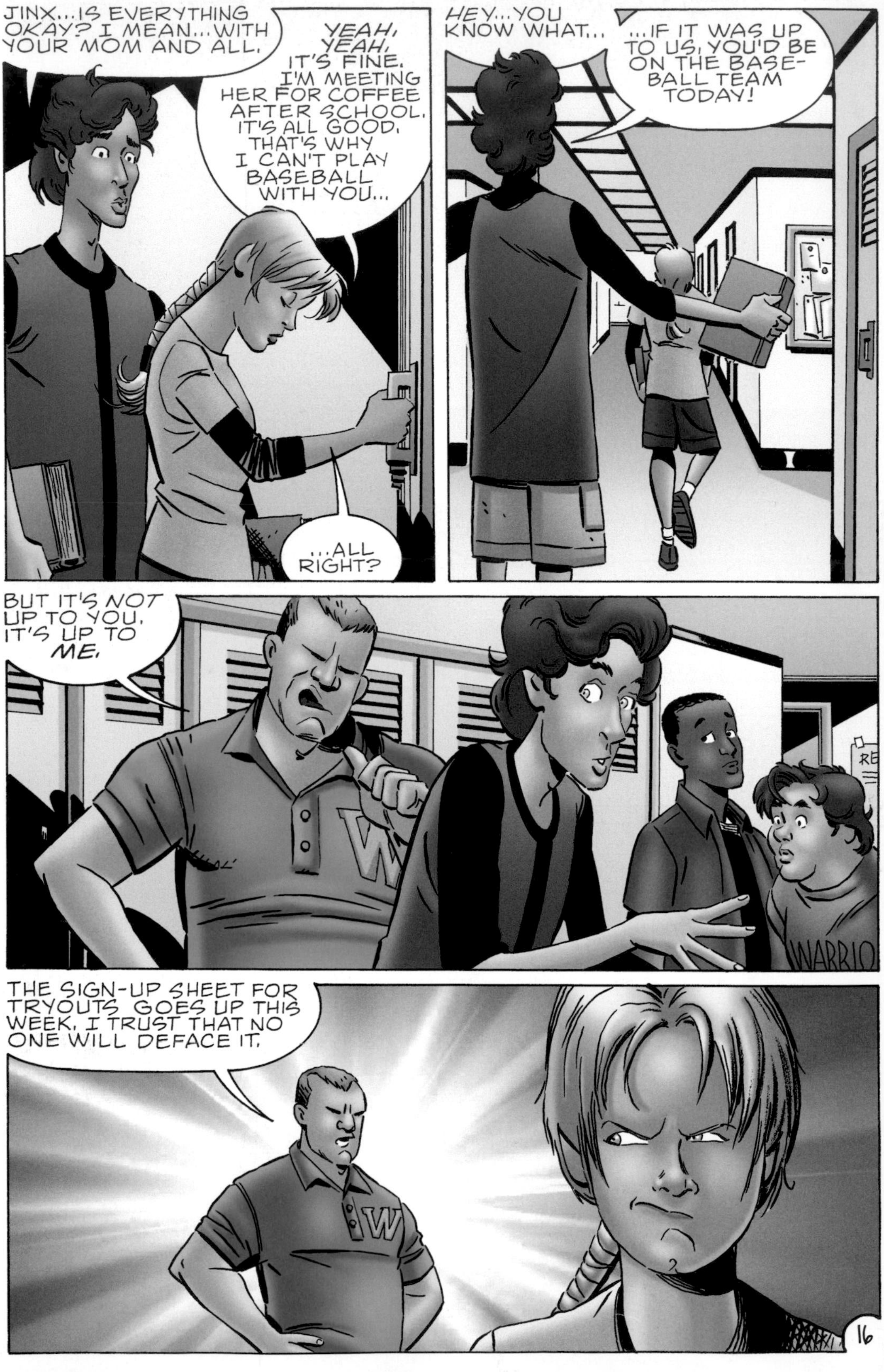

JINX... IS EVERYTHING OKAY? I MEAN... WITH YOUR MOM AND ALL.
YEAH, YEAH, IT'S FINE. I'M MEETING HER FOR COFFEE AFTER SCHOOL. IT'S ALL GOOD. THAT'S WHY I CAN'T PLAY BASEBALL WITH YOU...
...ALL RIGHT?
HEY... YOU KNOW WHAT...
...IF IT WAS UP TO US, YOU'D BE ON THE BASE-BALL TEAM TODAY!
BUT IT'S NOT UP TO YOU. IT'S UP TO ME.
THE SIGN-UP SHEET FOR TRYOUTS GOES UP THIS WEEK. I TRUST THAT NO ONE WILL DEFACE IT.

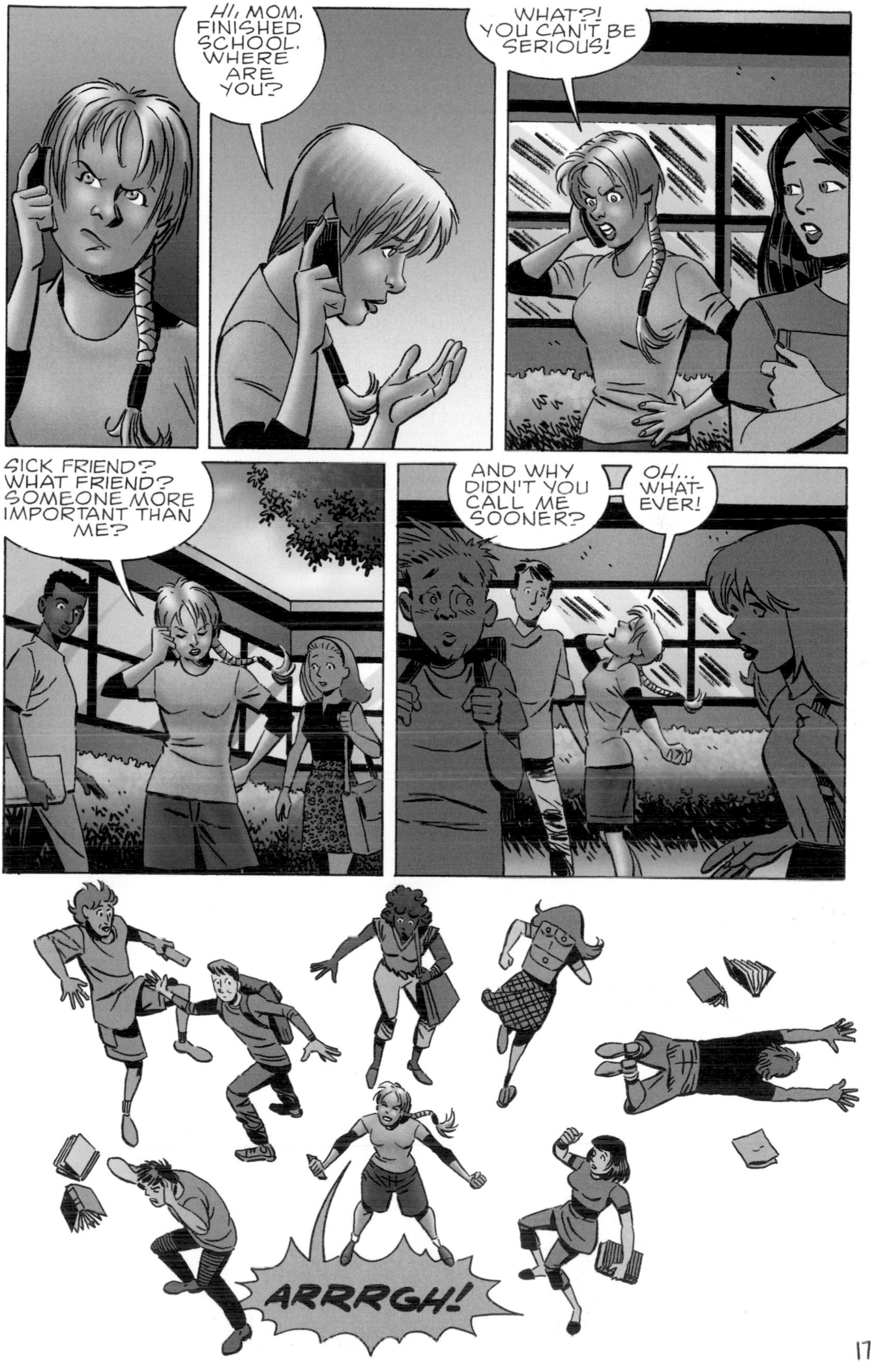
HI, MOM. FINISHED SCHOOL. WHERE ARE YOU?
WHAT?! YOU CAN'T BE SERIOUS!
SICK FRIEND? WHAT FRIEND? SOMEONE MORE IMPORTANT THAN ME?
AND WHY DIDN'T YOU CALL ME SOONER?
OH... WHAT-EVER!
ARRRGH!

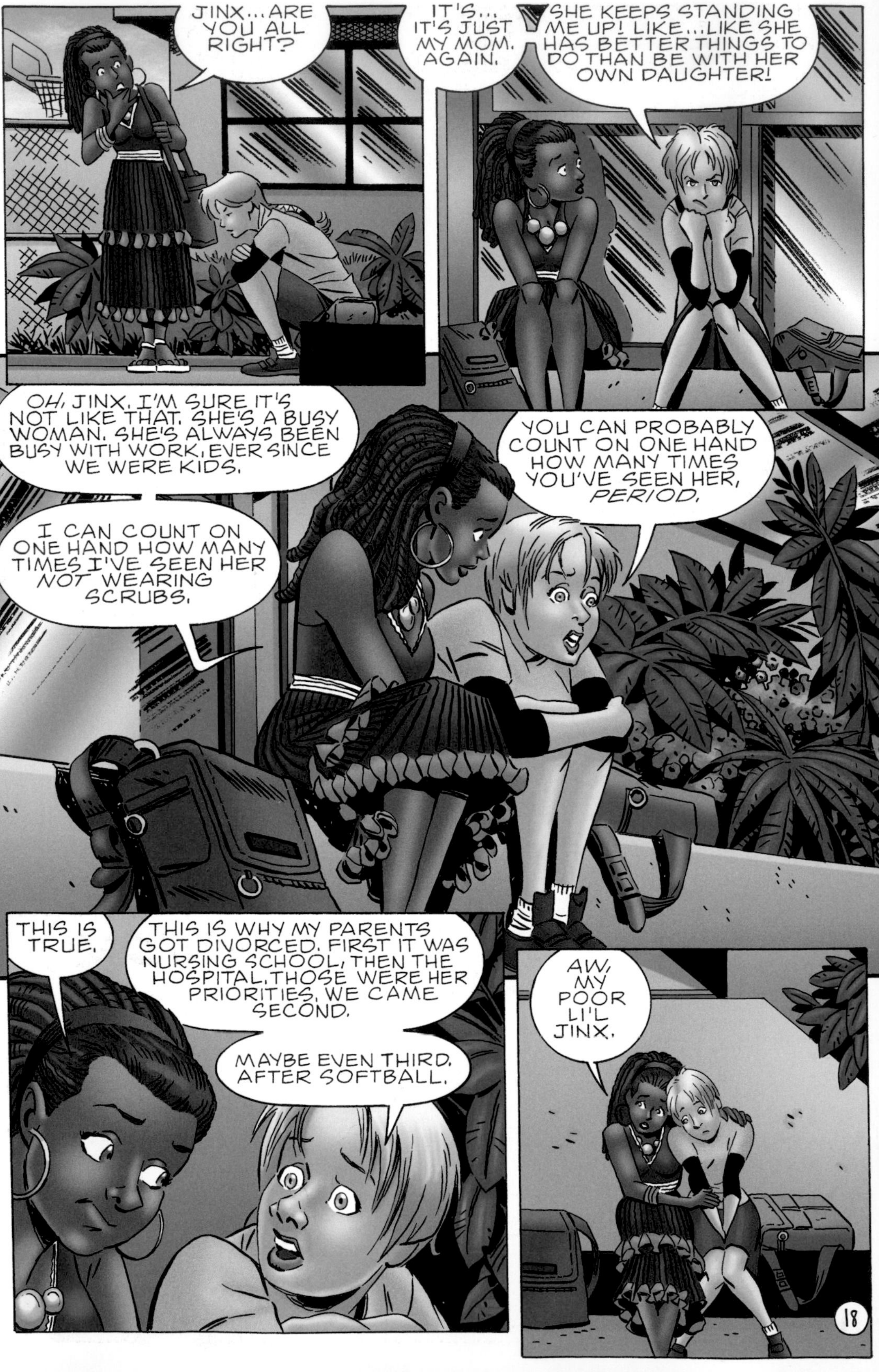
JINX...ARE YOU ALL RIGHT?
IT'S... IT'S JUST MY MOM. AGAIN.
SHE KEEPS STANDING ME UP! LIKE...LIKE SHE HAS BETTER THINGS TO DO THAN BE WITH HER OWN DAUGHTER!
OH, JINX. I'M SURE IT'S NOT LIKE THAT. SHE'S A BUSY WOMAN. SHE'S ALWAYS BEEN BUSY WITH WORK, EVER SINCE WE WERE KIDS.
I CAN COUNT ON ONE HAND HOW MANY TIMES I'VE SEEN HER NOT WEARING SCRUBS.
YOU CAN PROBABLY COUNT ON ONE HAND HOW MANY TIMES YOU'VE SEEN HER, PERIOD.
THIS IS TRUE.
THIS IS WHY MY PARENTS GOT DIVORCED. FIRST IT WAS NURSING SCHOOL, THEN THE HOSPITAL. THOSE WERE HER PRIORITIES. WE CAME SECOND.
MAYBE EVEN THIRD. AFTER SOFTBALL.
AW, MY POOR LI'L JINX.

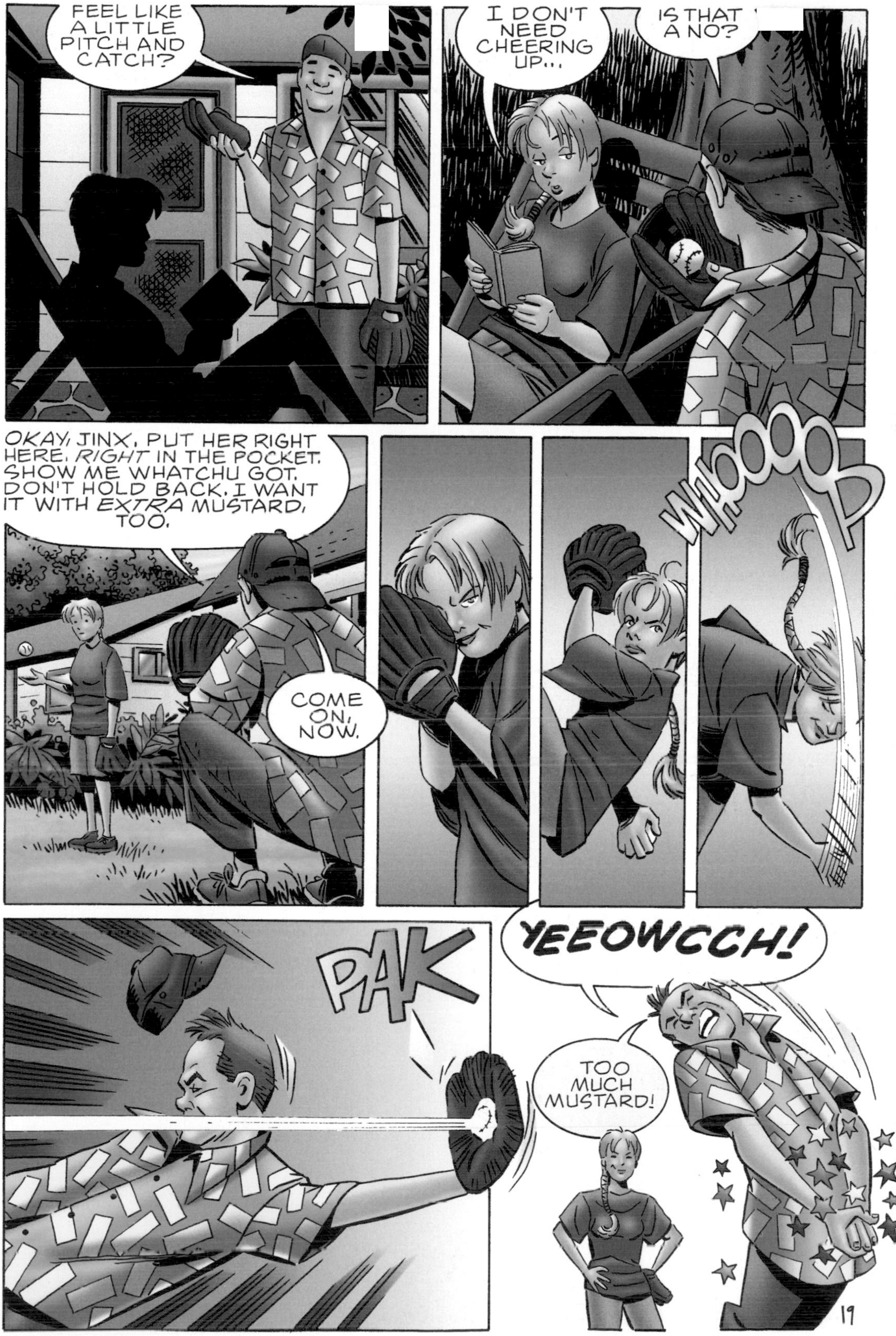
FEEL LIKE A LITTLE PITCH AND CATCH?
I DON'T NEED CHEERING UP...
IS THAT A NO?
OKAY, JINX. PUT HER RIGHT HERE. *RIGHT* IN THE POCKET. SHOW ME WHATCHU GOT. DON'T HOLD BACK. I WANT IT WITH *EXTRA* MUSTARD, TOO.
COME ON, NOW.
WHOOOP
PAK
YEEOWCCH!
TOO MUCH MUSTARD!

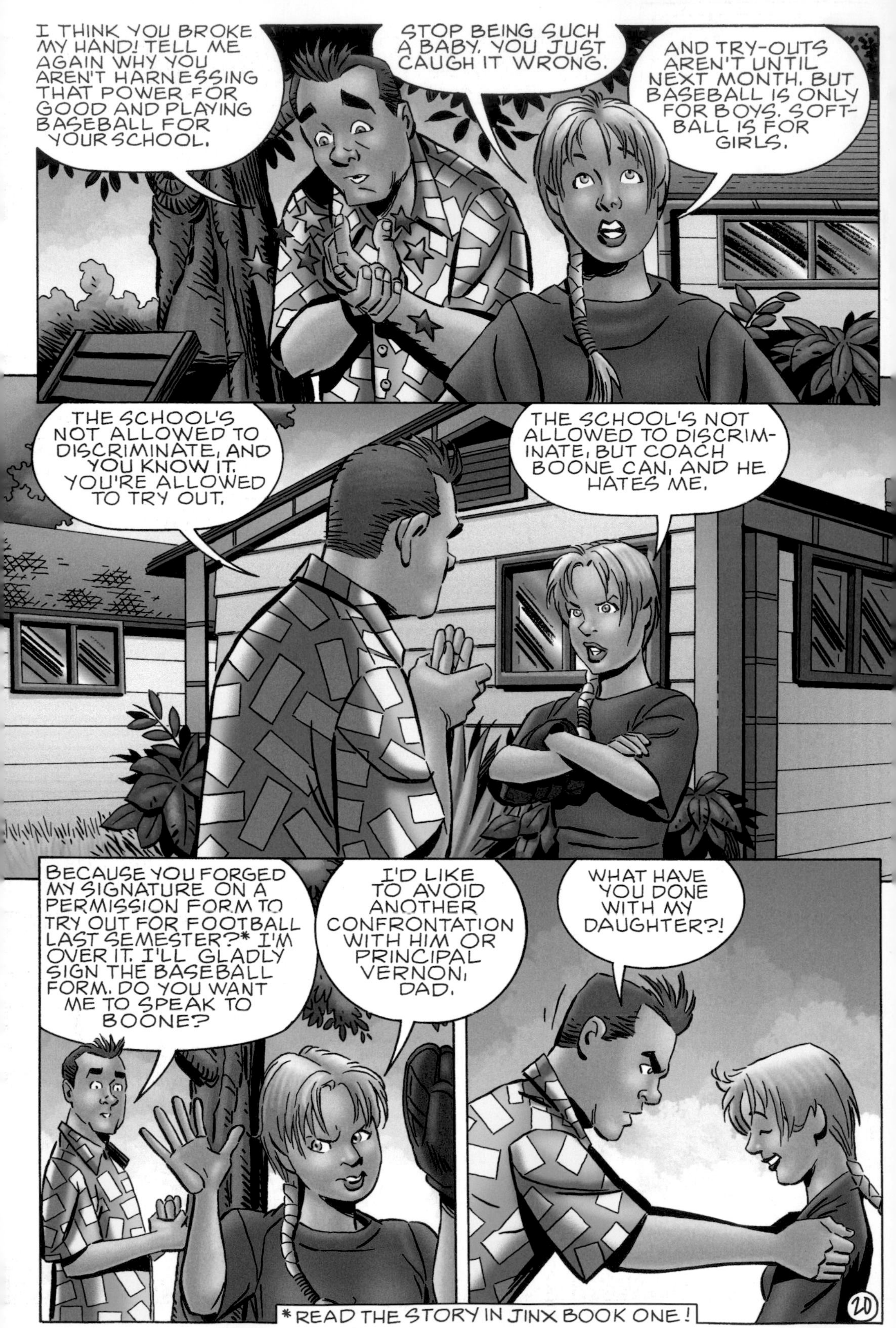
I THINK YOU BROKE MY HAND! TELL ME AGAIN WHY YOU AREN'T HARNESSING THAT POWER FOR GOOD AND PLAYING BASEBALL FOR YOUR SCHOOL.
STOP BEING SUCH A BABY. YOU JUST CAUGHT IT WRONG.
AND TRY-OUTS AREN'T UNTIL NEXT MONTH. BUT BASEBALL IS ONLY FOR BOYS. SOFT-BALL IS FOR GIRLS.
THE SCHOOL'S NOT ALLOWED TO DISCRIMINATE, AND YOU KNOW IT. YOU'RE ALLOWED TO TRY OUT.
THE SCHOOL'S NOT ALLOWED TO DISCRIM-INATE, BUT COACH BOONE CAN, AND HE HATES ME.
BECAUSE YOU FORGED MY SIGNATURE ON A PERMISSION FORM TO TRY OUT FOR FOOTBALL LAST SEMESTER?* I'M OVER IT. I'LL GLADLY SIGN THE BASEBALL FORM. DO YOU WANT ME TO SPEAK TO BOONE?
I'D LIKE TO AVOID ANOTHER CONFRONTATION WITH HIM OR PRINCIPAL VERNON, DAD.
WHAT HAVE YOU DONE WITH MY DAUGHTER?!

* READ THE STORY IN JINX BOOK ONE!

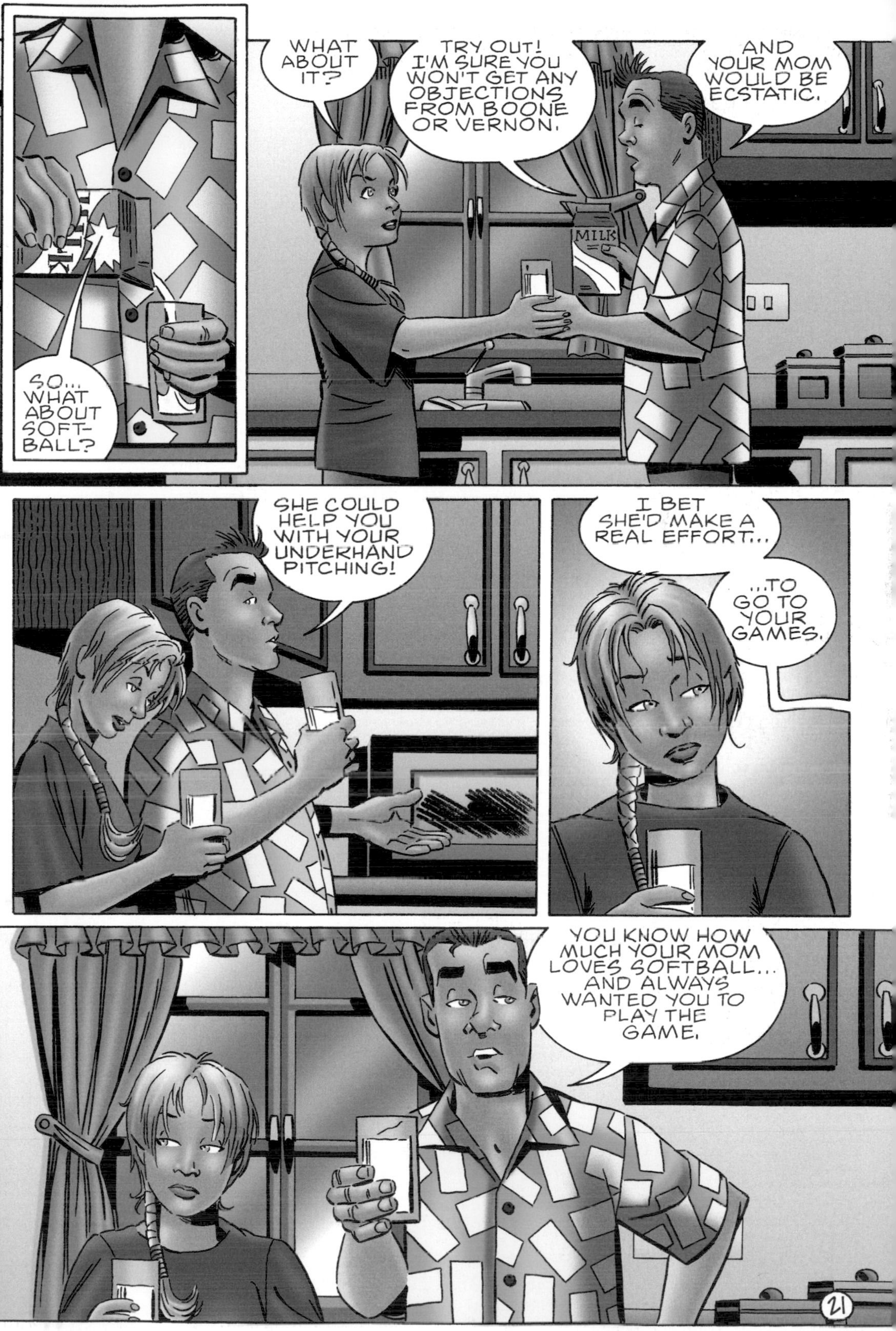
SO... WHAT ABOUT SOFT-BALL?
WHAT ABOUT IT?
TRY OUT! I'M SURE YOU WON'T GET ANY OBJECTIONS FROM BOONE OR VERNON.
AND YOUR MOM WOULD BE ECSTATIC.
MILK
SHE COULD HELP YOU WITH YOUR UNDERHAND PITCHING!
I BET SHE'D MAKE A REAL EFFORT...
...TO GO TO YOUR GAMES.
YOU KNOW HOW MUCH YOUR MOM LOVES SOFTBALL... AND ALWAYS WANTED YOU TO PLAY THE GAME.

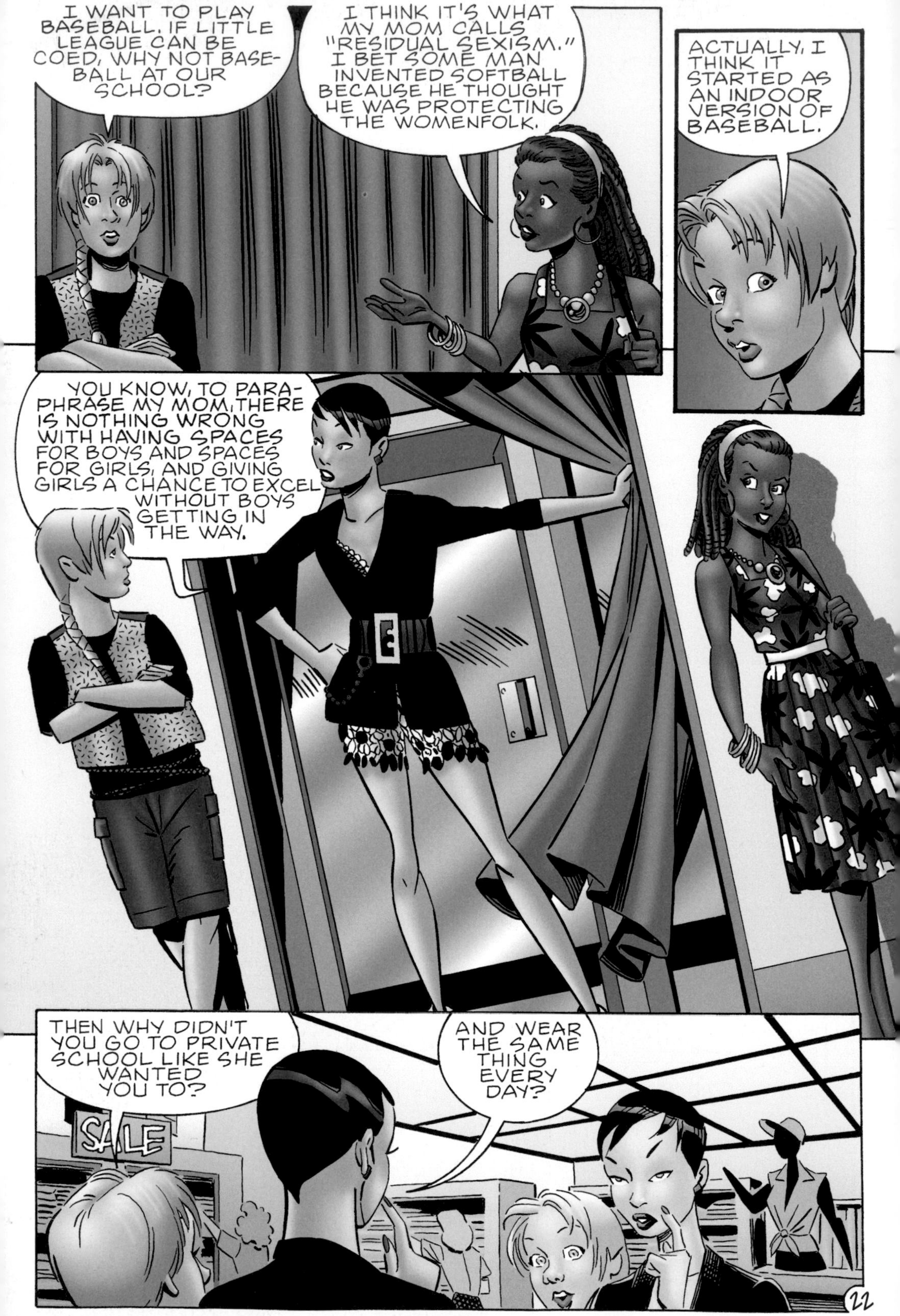

I WANT TO PLAY BASEBALL. IF LITTLE LEAGUE CAN BE COED, WHY NOT BASE-BALL AT OUR SCHOOL?
I THINK IT'S WHAT MY MOM CALLS "RESIDUAL SEXISM." I BET SOME MAN INVENTED SOFTBALL BECAUSE HE THOUGHT HE WAS PROTECTING THE WOMENFOLK.
ACTUALLY, I THINK IT STARTED AS AN INDOOR VERSION OF BASEBALL.
YOU KNOW, TO PARA-PHRASE MY MOM, THERE IS NOTHING WRONG WITH HAVING SPACES FOR BOYS AND SPACES FOR GIRLS, AND GIVING GIRLS A CHANCE TO EXCEL WITHOUT BOYS GETTING IN THE WAY.
THEN WHY DIDN'T YOU GO TO PRIVATE SCHOOL LIKE SHE WANTED YOU TO?
AND WEAR THE SAME THING EVERY DAY?
SALE

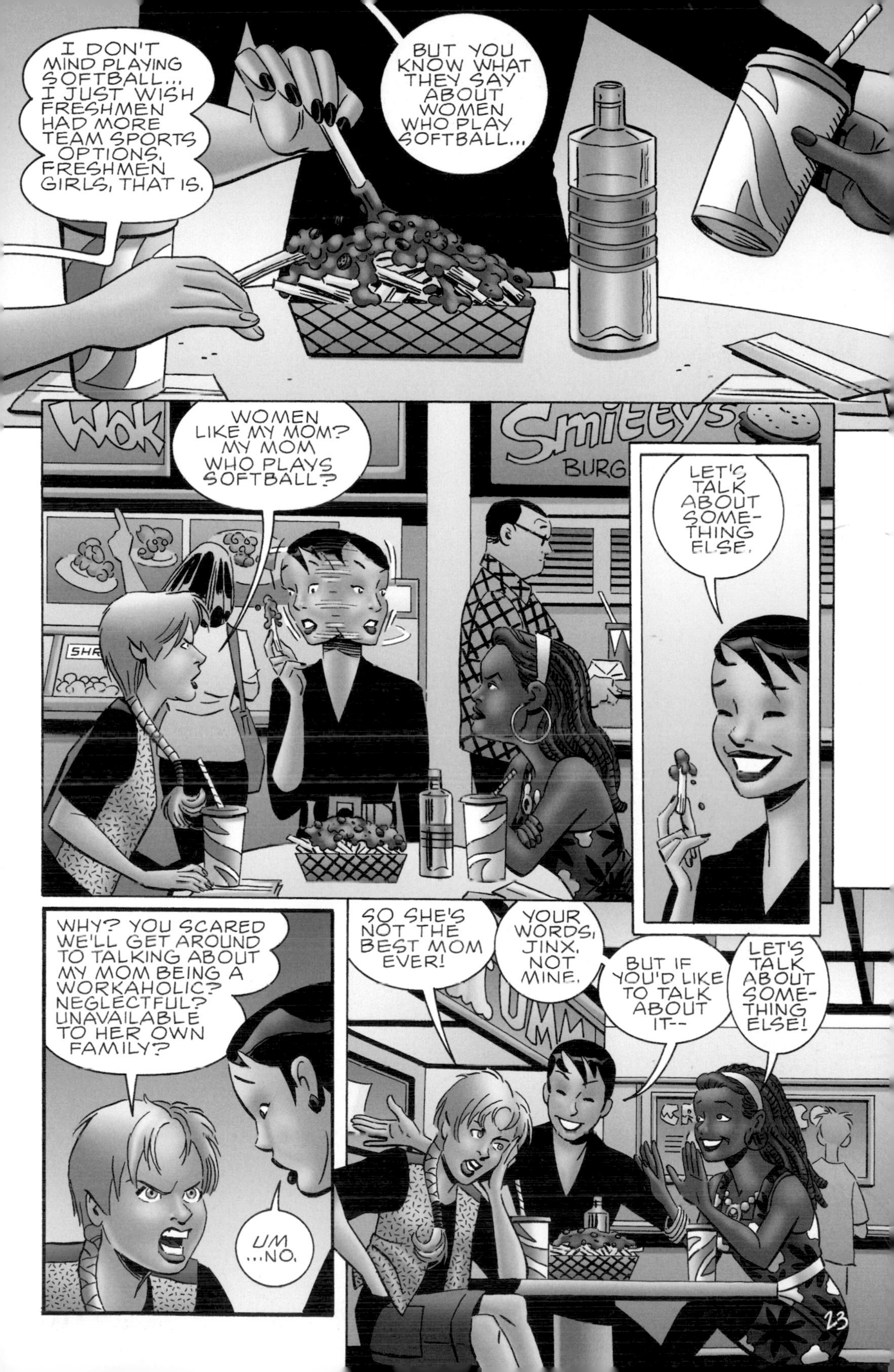
I DON'T MIND PLAYING SOFTBALL... I JUST WISH FRESHMEN HAD MORE TEAM SPORTS OPTIONS. FRESHMEN GIRLS, THAT IS.
BUT YOU KNOW WHAT THEY SAY ABOUT WOMEN WHO PLAY SOFTBALL...
WOK
WOMEN LIKE MY MOM? MY MOM WHO PLAYS SOFTBALL?
SMITTYS
BURG
LET'S TALK ABOUT SOME-THING ELSE.
WHY? YOU SCARED WE'LL GET AROUND TO TALKING ABOUT MY MOM BEING A WORKAHOLIC? NEGLECTFUL? UNAVAILABLE TO HER OWN FAMILY?
UM ...NO.
SO SHE'S NOT THE BEST MOM EVER!
YOUR WORDS, JINX, NOT MINE.
BUT IF YOU'D LIKE TO TALK ABOUT IT--
LET'S TALK ABOUT SOME-THING ELSE!

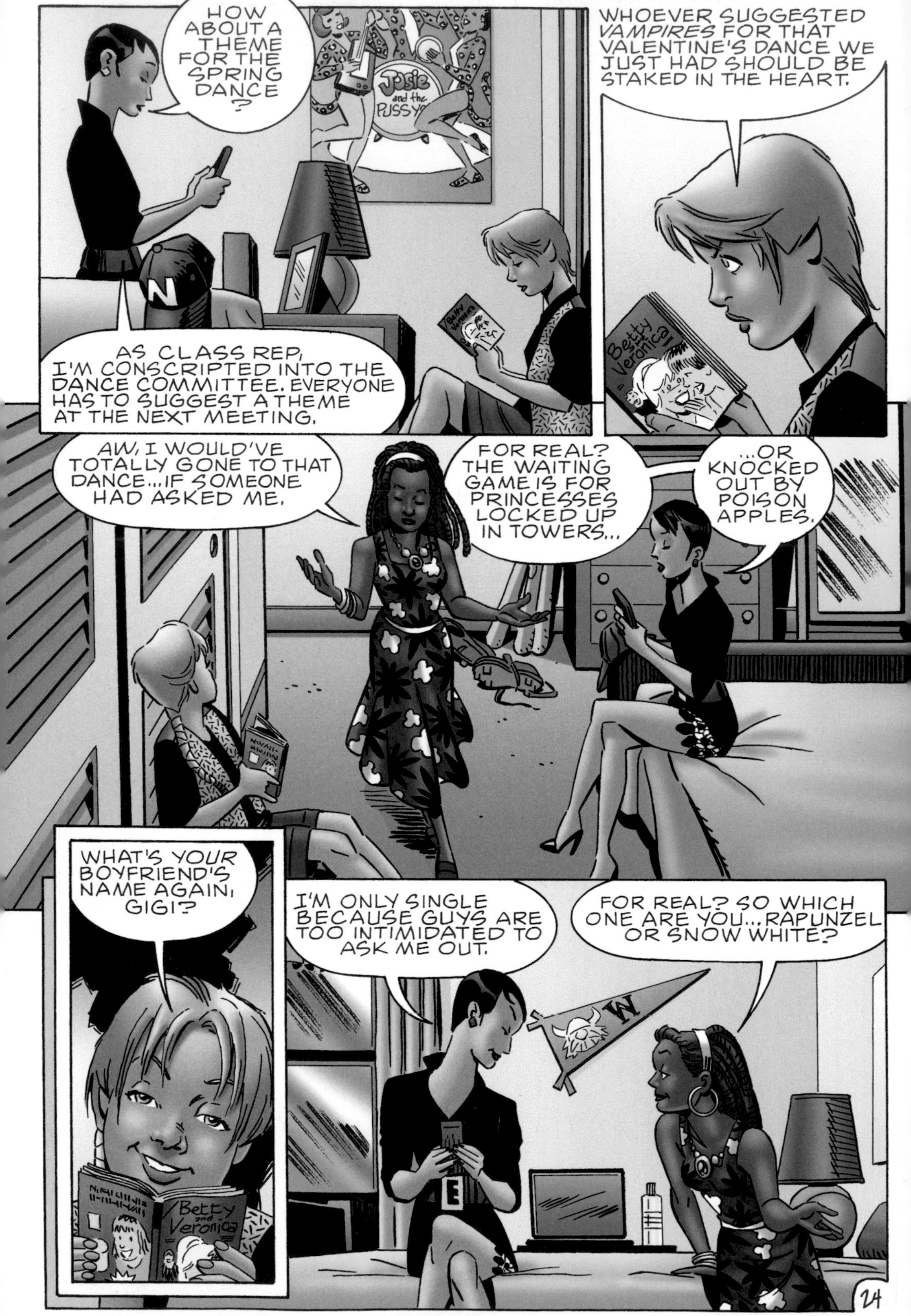
HOW ABOUT A THEME FOR THE SPRING DANCE ?
AS CLASS REP, I'M CONSCRIPTED INTO THE DANCE COMMITTEE. EVERYONE HAS TO SUGGEST A THEME AT THE NEXT MEETING.
Josie and the PUSSY
WHOEVER SUGGESTED *VAMPIRES* FOR THAT VALENTINE'S DANCE WE JUST HAD SHOULD BE STAKED IN THE HEART.
Betty and Veronica
AW, I WOULD'VE TOTALLY GONE TO THAT DANCE...IF SOMEONE HAD ASKED ME.
FOR REAL? THE WAITING GAME IS FOR PRINCESSES LOCKED UP IN TOWERS...
...OR KNOCKED OUT BY POISON APPLES.
WHAT'S *YOUR* BOYFRIEND'S NAME AGAIN, GIGI?
I'M ONLY SINGLE BECAUSE GUYS ARE TOO INTIMIDATED TO ASK ME OUT.
FOR REAL? SO WHICH ONE ARE YOU...RAPUNZEL OR SNOW WHITE?
Betty and Veronica

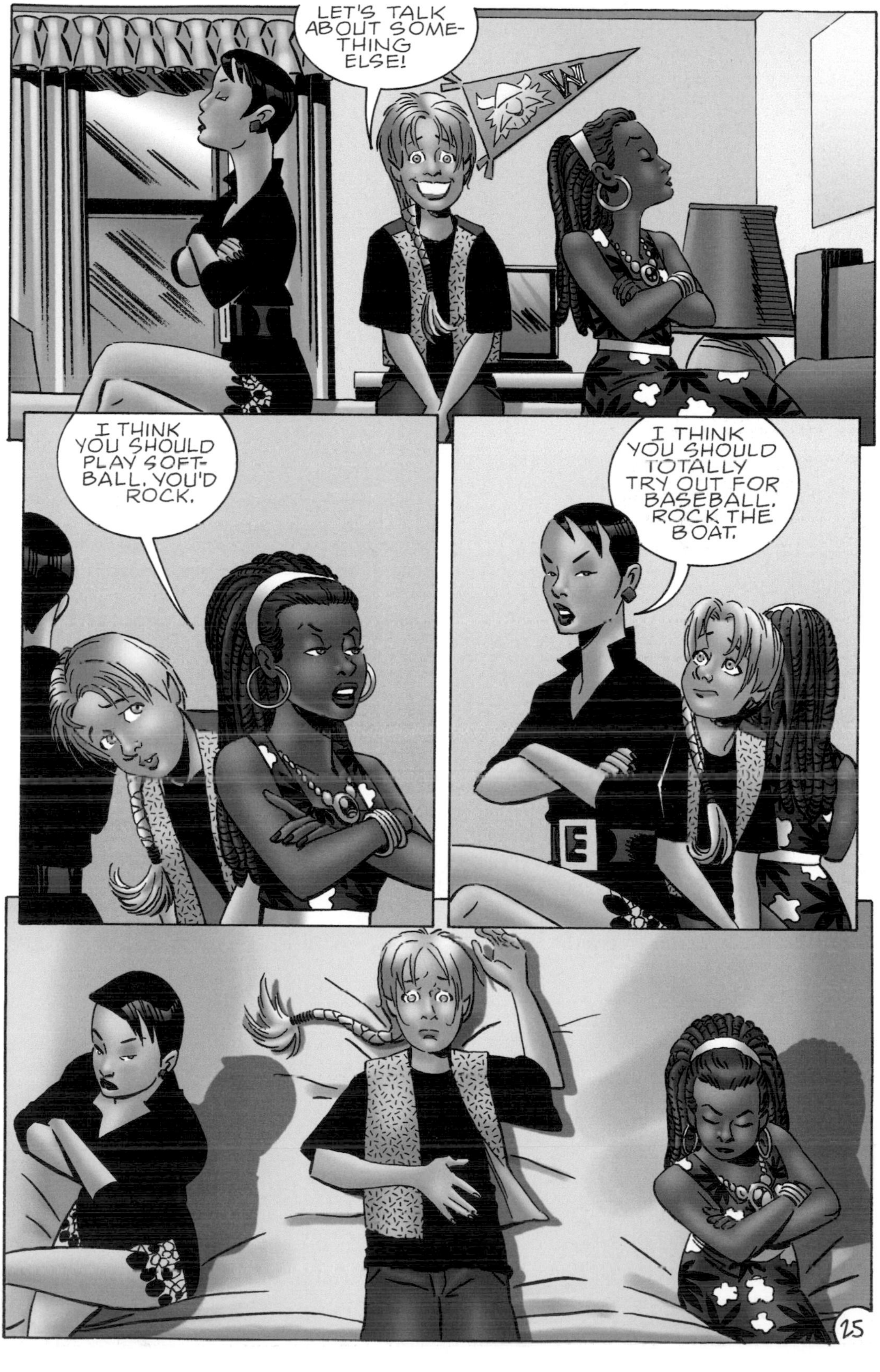
LET'S TALK ABOUT SOME-THING ELSE!
I THINK YOU SHOULD PLAY SOFT-BALL. YOU'D ROCK.
I THINK YOU SHOULD TOTALLY TRY OUT FOR BASEBALL. ROCK THE BOAT.

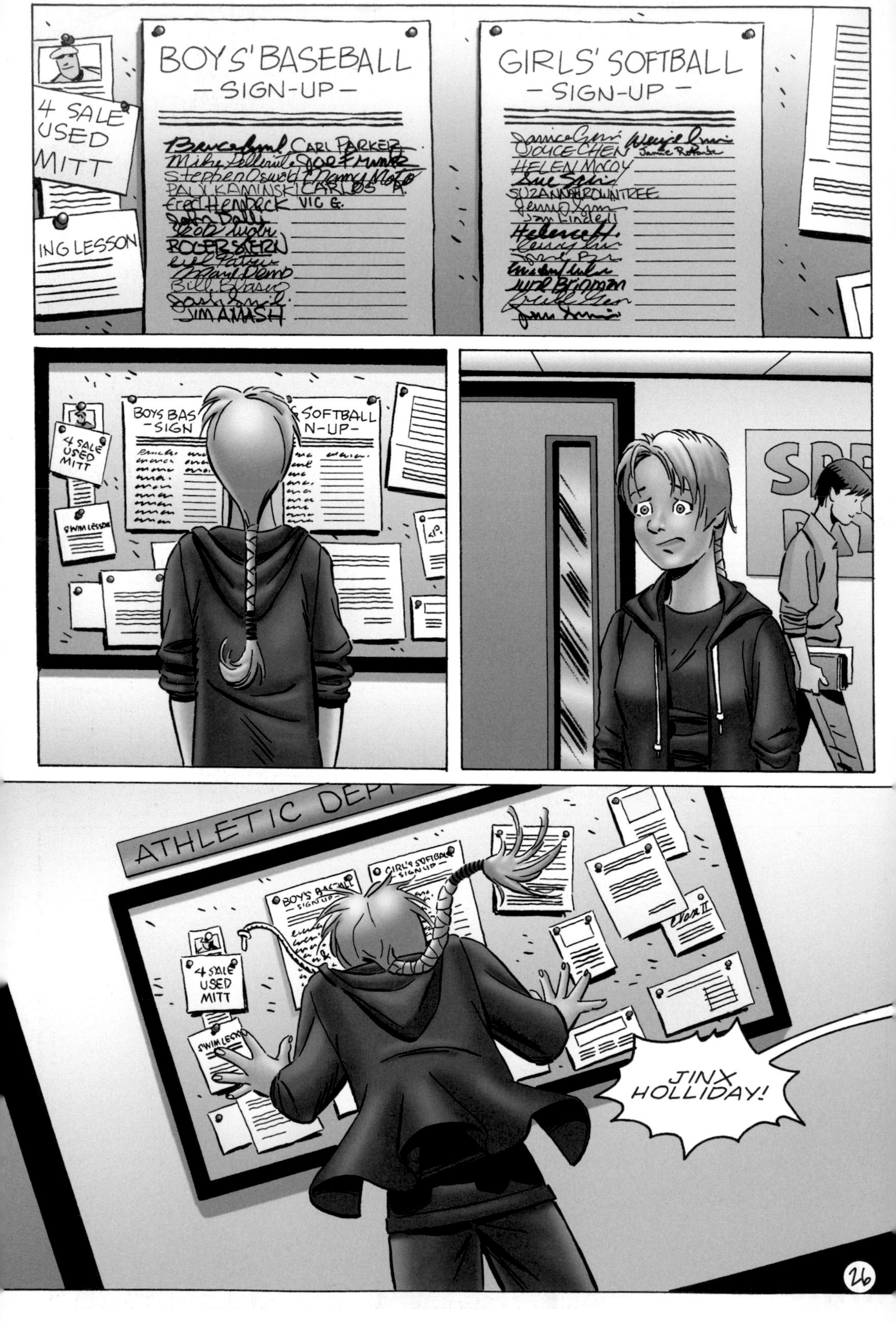

BOY'S BASEBALL
– SIGN-UP –
CARL PARKER
Stephen Oswald
PAUL KAMINSKI
CARLOS A.
VIC G.
ROGER STERN
JIM AMASH
GIRLS' SOFTBALL
– SIGN-UP –
JOYCE CHEN
HELEN McCOY
SUZANNAH ROWNTREE
4 SALE USED MITT
ING LESSON
ATHLETIC DEPT
JINX HOLLIDAY!

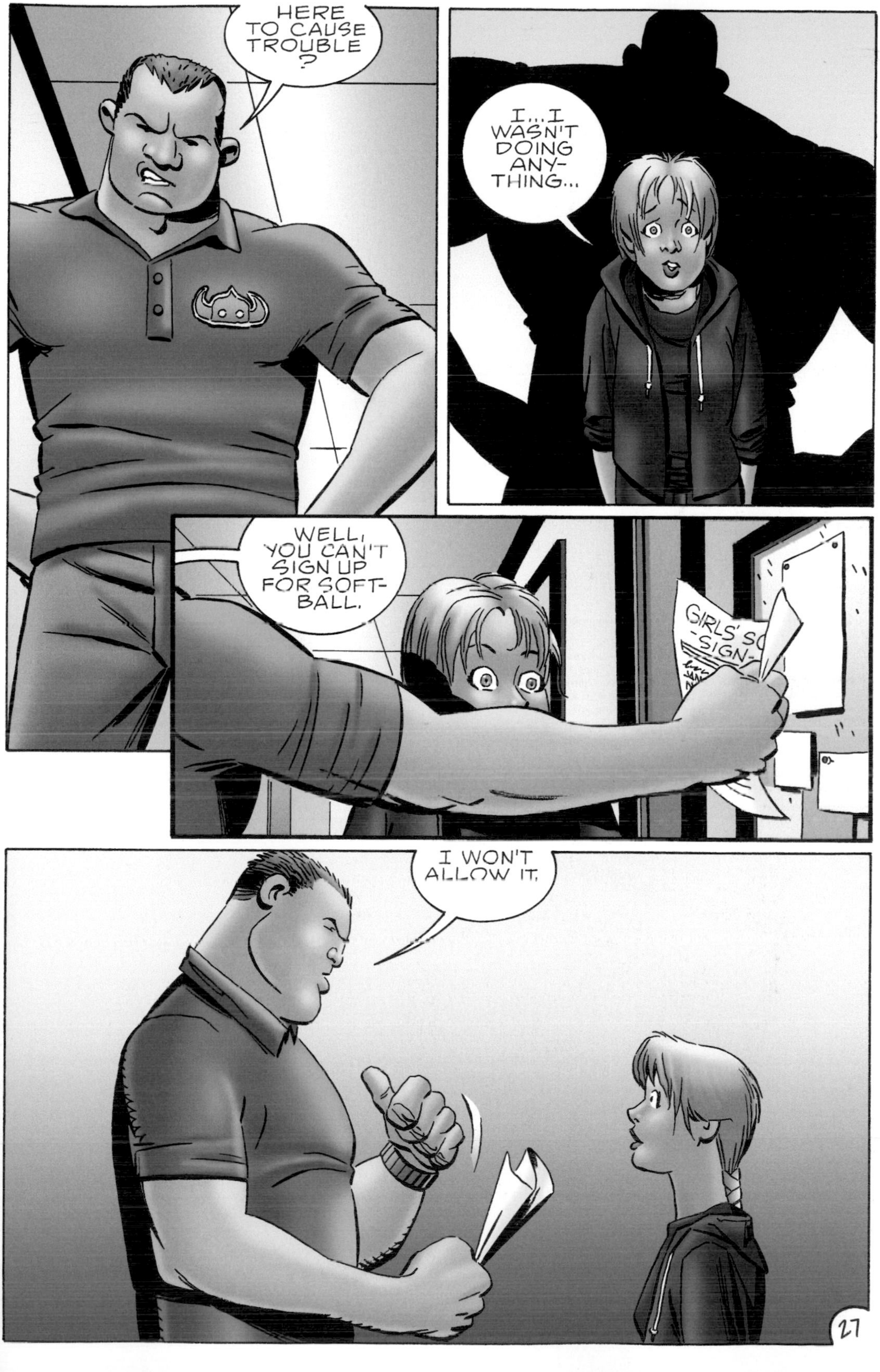
HERE TO CAUSE TROUBLE?
I... I WASN'T DOING ANY-THING...
WELL, YOU CAN'T SIGN UP FOR SOFT-BALL.
GIRLS' SO -SIGN-
I WON'T ALLOW IT.

JINX™

CHAPTER 2

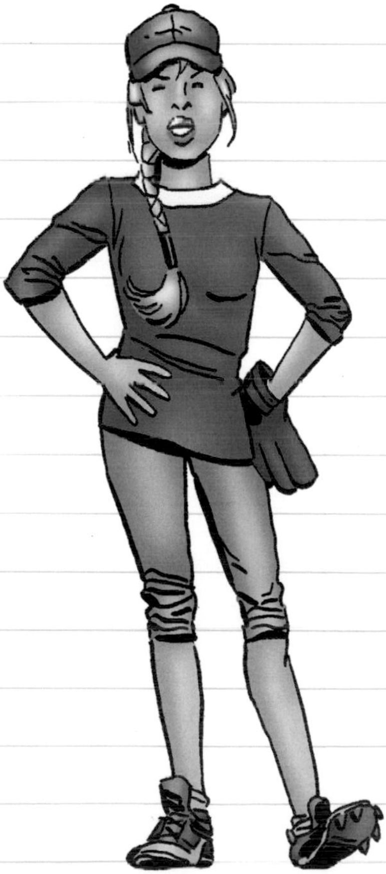

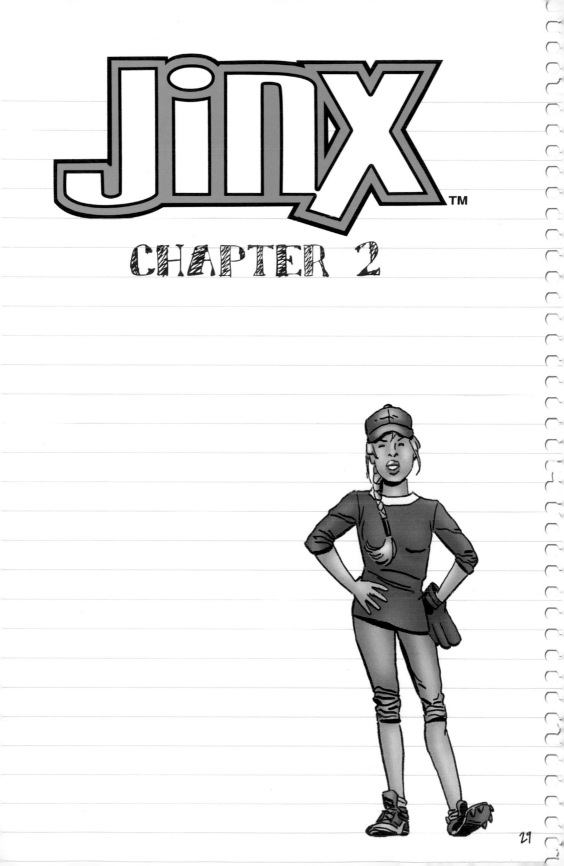

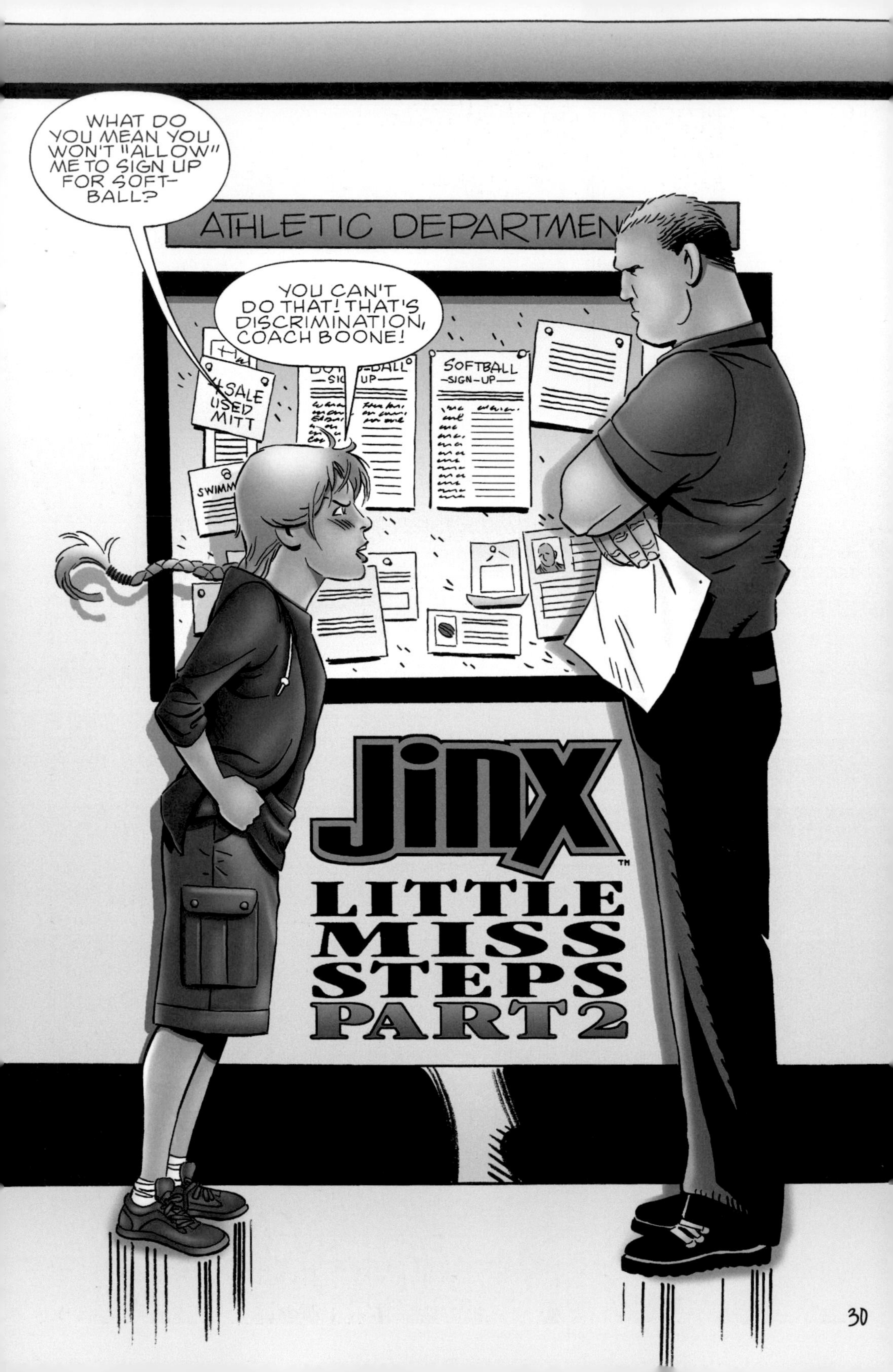
WHAT DO YOU MEAN YOU WON'T "ALLOW" ME TO SIGN UP FOR SOFT-BALL?
YOU CAN'T DO THAT! THAT'S DISCRIMINATION, COACH BOONE!
ATHLETIC DEPARTMEN
SOFTBALL -SIGN-UP-
4SALE USED MITT
SWIMM
JINX™
LITTLE MISS STEPS PART 2

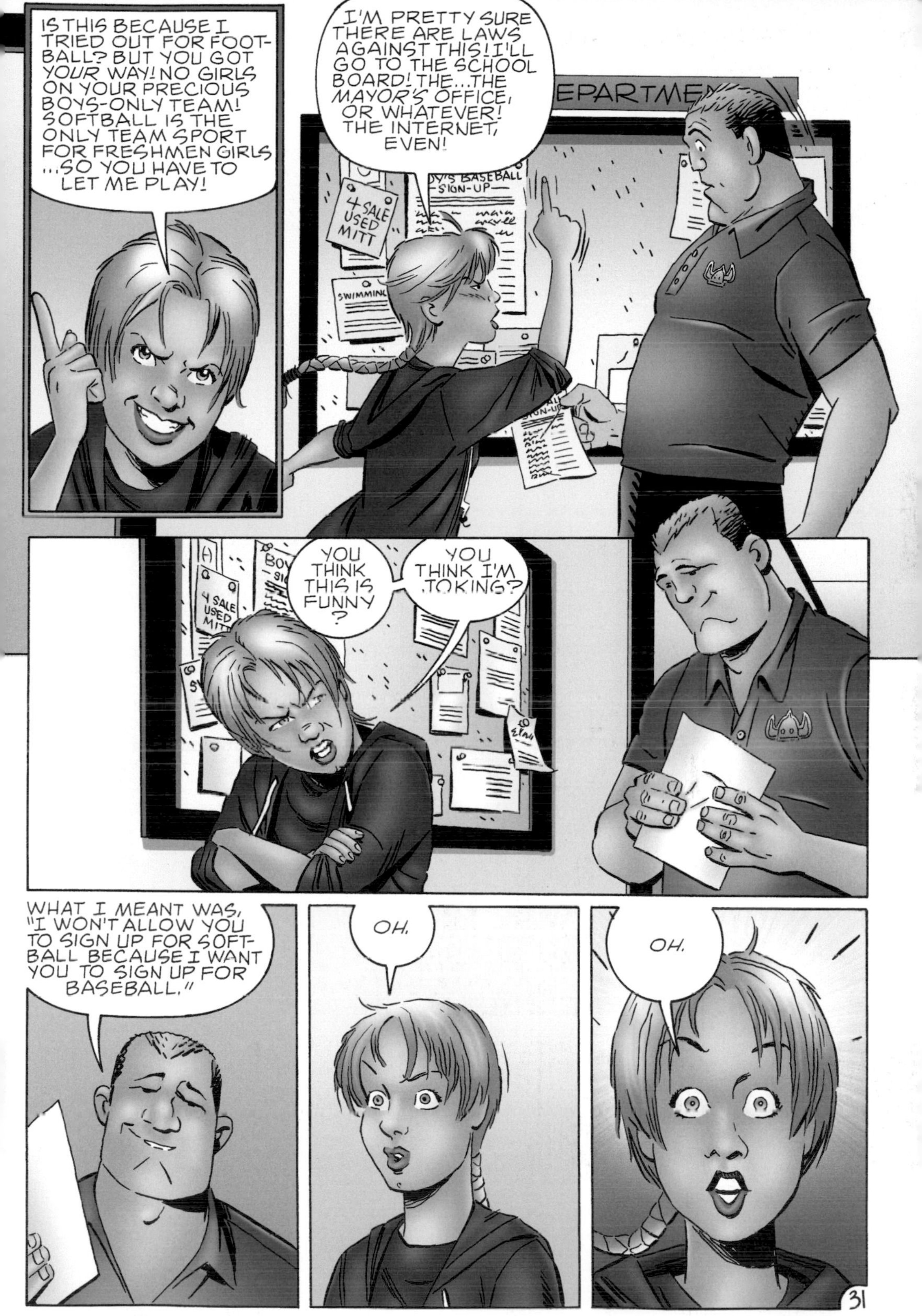
IS THIS BECAUSE I TRIED OUT FOR FOOT-BALL? BUT YOU GOT *YOUR* WAY! NO GIRLS ON YOUR PRECIOUS BOYS-ONLY TEAM! SOFTBALL IS THE ONLY TEAM SPORT FOR FRESHMEN GIRLS ...SO YOU HAVE TO LET ME PLAY!
I'M PRETTY SURE THERE ARE LAWS AGAINST THIS! I'LL GO TO THE SCHOOL BOARD! THE...THE *MAYOR'S* OFFICE, OR WHATEVER! THE INTERNET, EVEN!
EPARTMEN
4 SALE USED MITT
SIGN-UP
SWIMMING
YOU THINK THIS IS FUNNY?
YOU THINK I'M JOKING?
4 SALE USED MITT
WHAT I MEANT WAS, "I WON'T ALLOW YOU TO SIGN UP FOR SOFT-BALL BECAUSE I WANT YOU TO SIGN UP FOR BASEBALL."
OH.
OH.

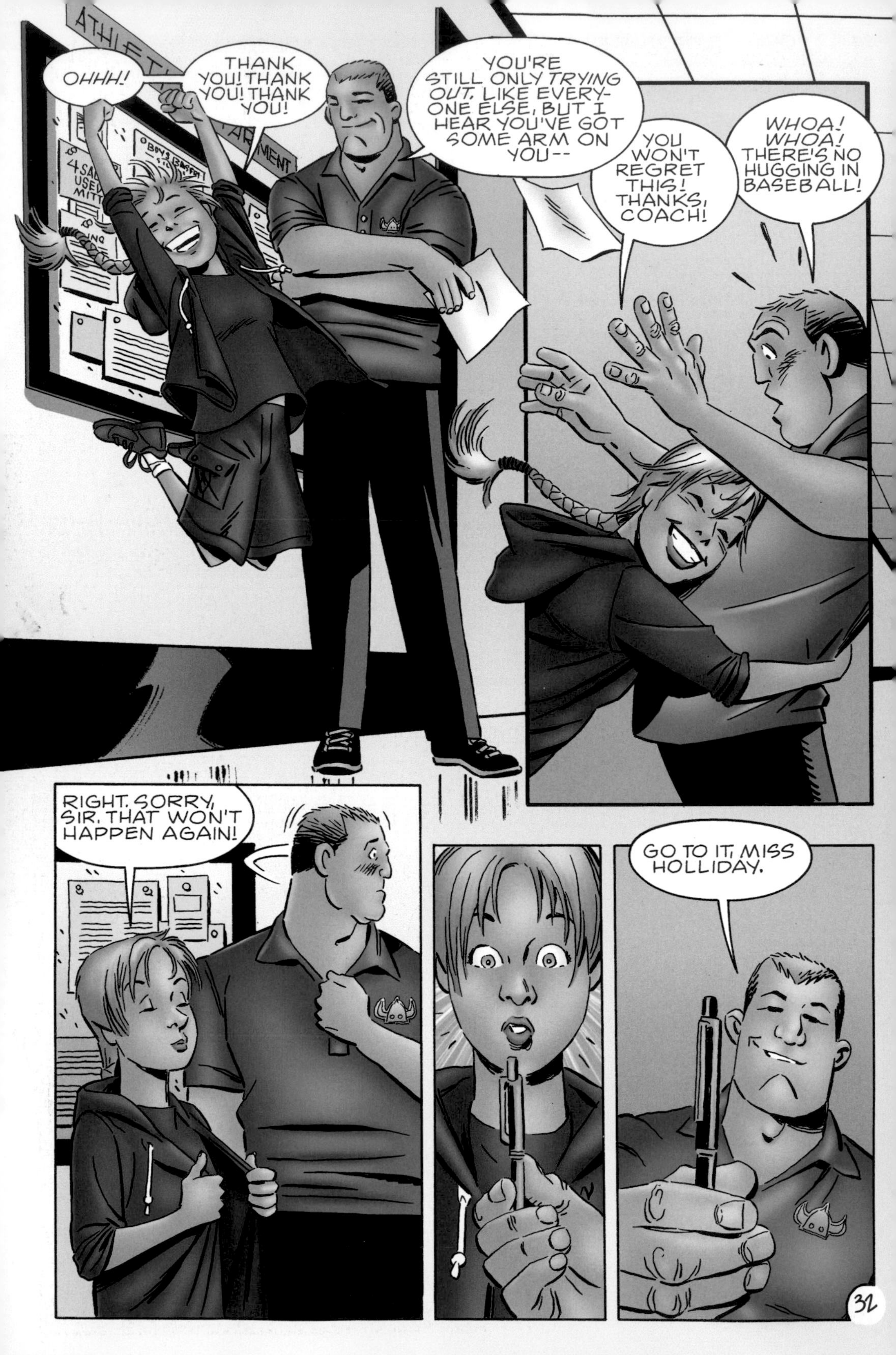
ATHLETIC DEPARTMENT
OHHH!
THANK YOU! THANK YOU! THANK YOU!
YOU'RE STILL ONLY *TRYING OUT*, LIKE EVERY-ONE ELSE, BUT I HEAR YOU'VE GOT SOME ARM ON YOU--
YOU WON'T REGRET THIS! THANKS, COACH!
WHOA! WHOA! THERE'S NO HUGGING IN BASEBALL!
RIGHT. SORRY, SIR. THAT WON'T HAPPEN AGAIN!
GO TO IT, MISS HOLLIDAY.

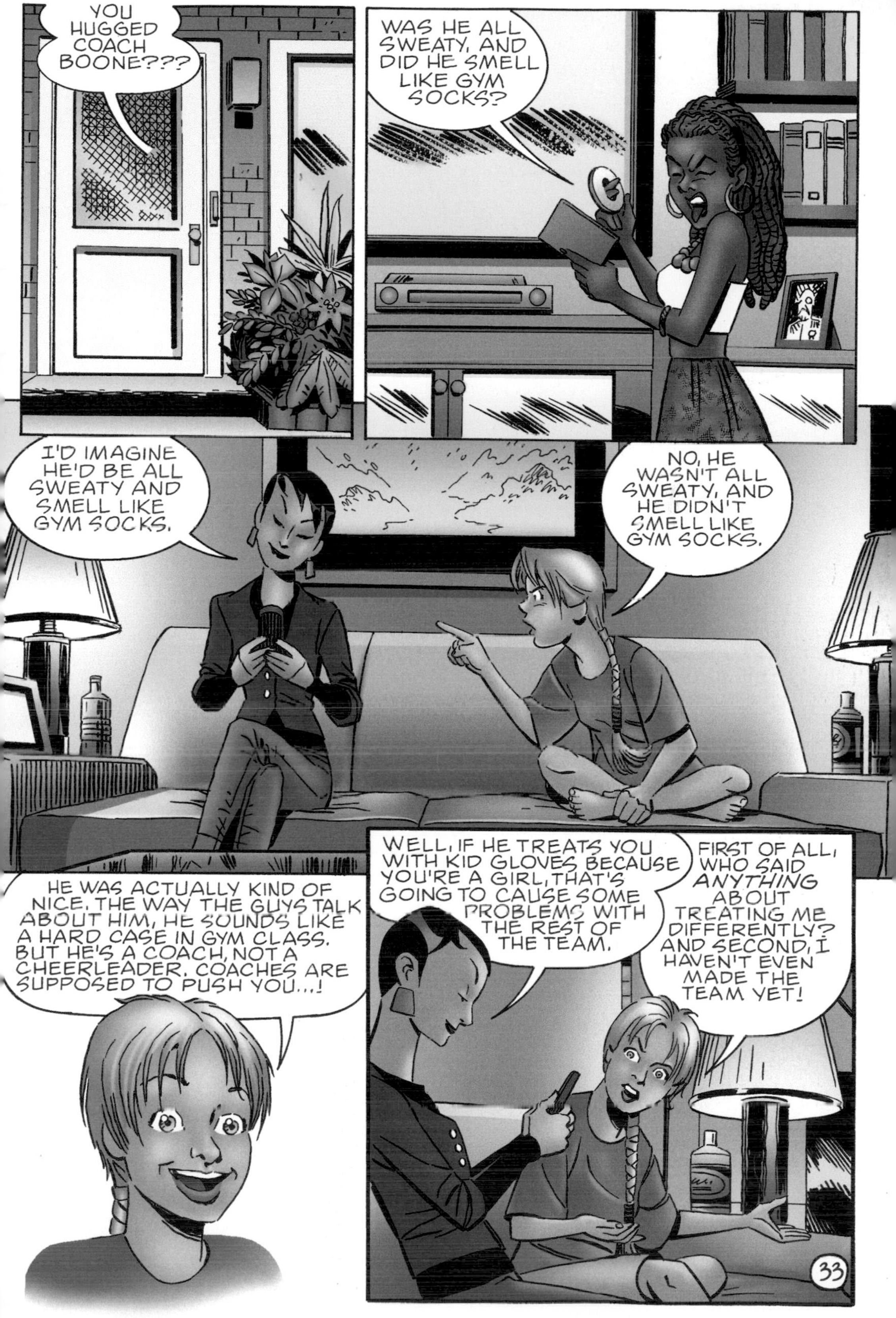
YOU HUGGED COACH BOONE???
WAS HE ALL SWEATY, AND DID HE SMELL LIKE GYM SOCKS?
I'D IMAGINE HE'D BE ALL SWEATY AND SMELL LIKE GYM SOCKS.
NO, HE WASN'T ALL SWEATY, AND HE DIDN'T SMELL LIKE GYM SOCKS.
HE WAS ACTUALLY KIND OF NICE. THE WAY THE GUYS TALK ABOUT HIM, HE SOUNDS LIKE A HARD CASE IN GYM CLASS. BUT HE'S A COACH, NOT A CHEERLEADER. COACHES ARE SUPPOSED TO PUSH YOU...!
WELL, IF HE TREATS YOU WITH KID GLOVES BECAUSE YOU'RE A GIRL, THAT'S GOING TO CAUSE SOME PROBLEMS WITH THE REST OF THE TEAM.
FIRST OF ALL, WHO SAID *ANYTHING* ABOUT TREATING ME DIFFERENTLY? AND SECOND, I HAVEN'T EVEN MADE THE TEAM YET!
33

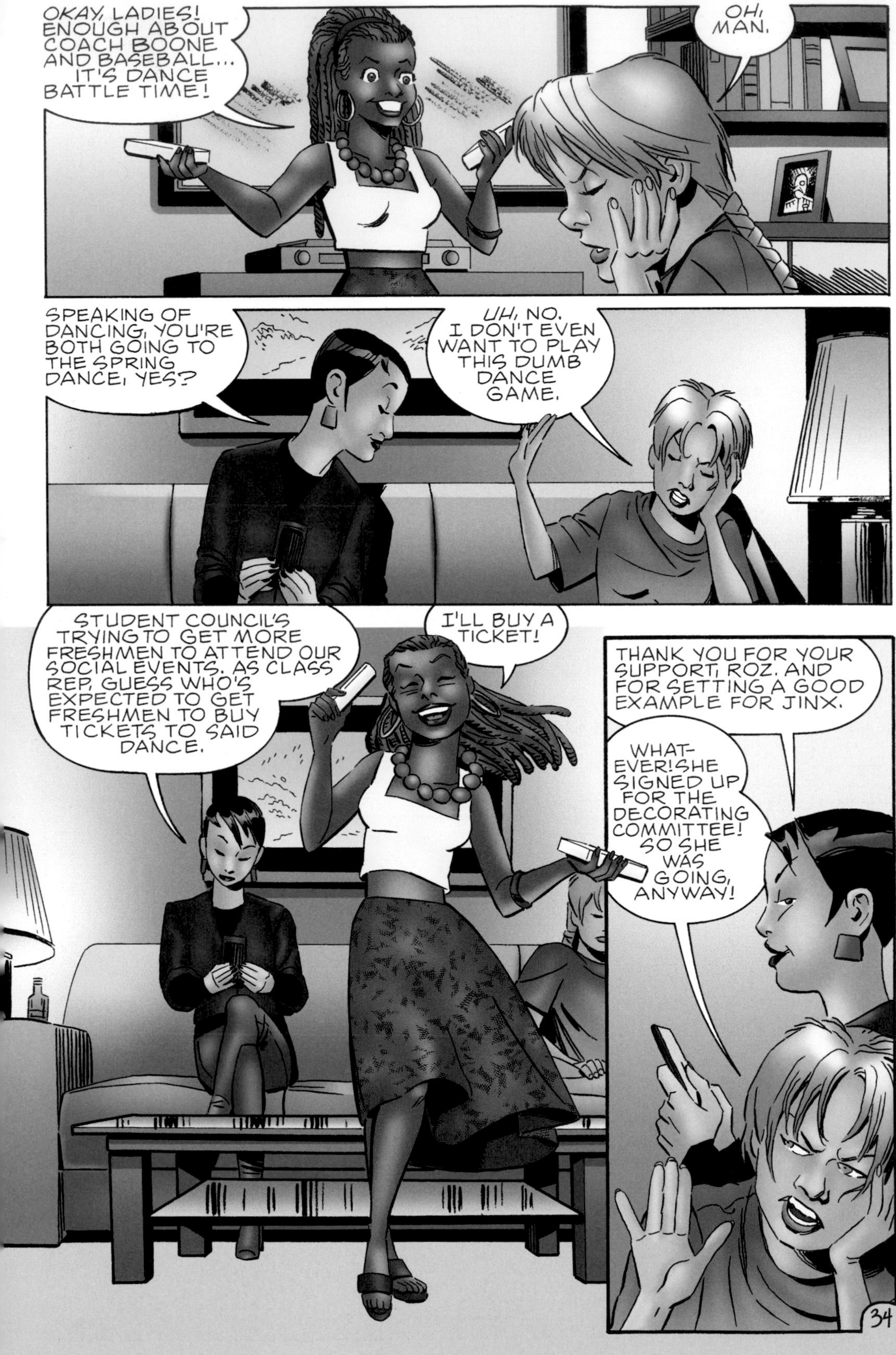
OKAY, LADIES! ENOUGH ABOUT COACH BOONE AND BASEBALL... IT'S DANCE BATTLE TIME!
OH, MAN.
SPEAKING OF DANCING, YOU'RE BOTH GOING TO THE SPRING DANCE, YES?
UH, NO. I DON'T EVEN WANT TO PLAY THIS DUMB DANCE GAME.
STUDENT COUNCIL'S TRYING TO GET MORE FRESHMEN TO ATTEND OUR SOCIAL EVENTS. AS CLASS REP, GUESS WHO'S EXPECTED TO GET FRESHMEN TO BUY TICKETS TO SAID DANCE.
I'LL BUY A TICKET!
THANK YOU FOR YOUR SUPPORT, ROZ. AND FOR SETTING A GOOD EXAMPLE FOR JINX.
WHAT-EVER! SHE SIGNED UP FOR THE DECORATING COMMITTEE! SO SHE WAS GOING, ANYWAY!

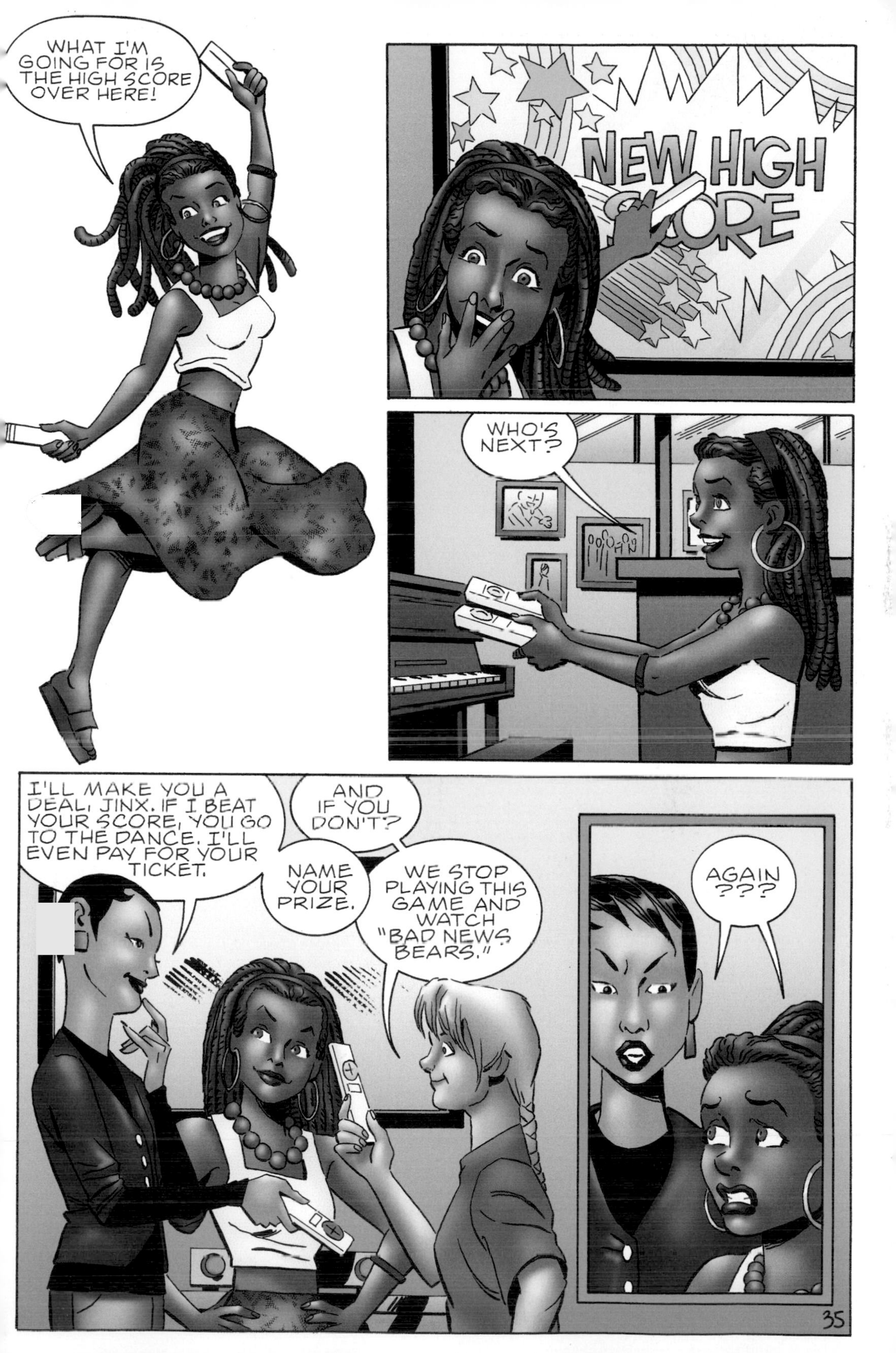

WHAT I'M GOING FOR IS THE HIGH SCORE OVER HERE!
NEW HIGH SCORE
WHO'S NEXT?
I'LL MAKE YOU A DEAL, JINX. IF I BEAT YOUR SCORE, YOU GO TO THE DANCE. I'LL EVEN PAY FOR YOUR TICKET.
AND IF YOU DON'T?
NAME YOUR PRIZE.
WE STOP PLAYING THIS GAME AND WATCH "BAD NEWS BEARS."
AGAIN ???

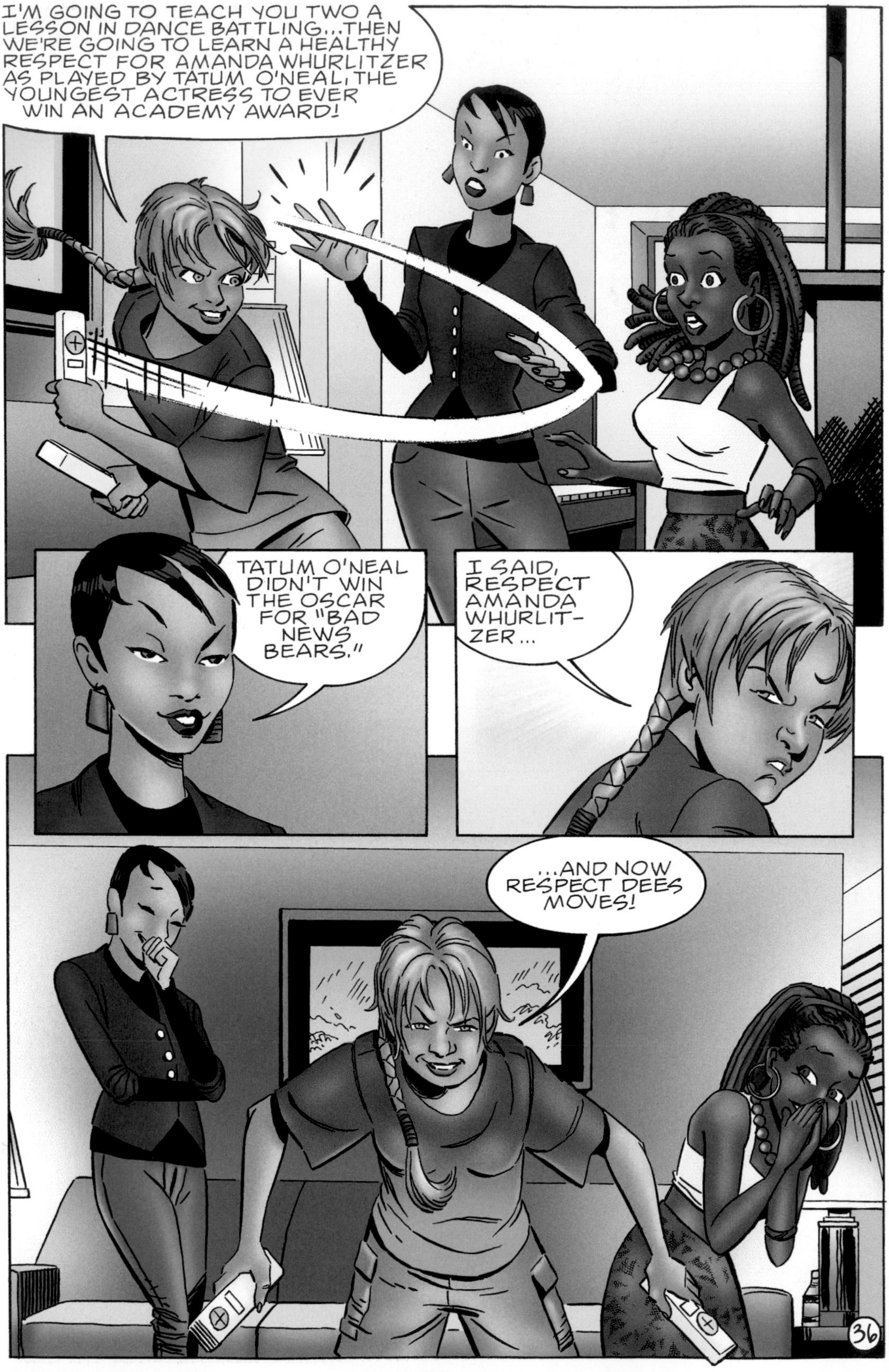
I'M GOING TO TEACH YOU TWO A LESSON IN DANCE BATTLING...THEN WE'RE GOING TO LEARN A HEALTHY RESPECT FOR AMANDA WHURLITZER AS PLAYED BY TATUM O'NEAL, THE YOUNGEST ACTRESS TO EVER WIN AN ACADEMY AWARD!
TATUM O'NEAL DIDN'T WIN THE OSCAR FOR "BAD NEWS BEARS."
I SAID, RESPECT AMANDA WHURLIT-ZER...
...AND NOW RESPECT DEES MOVES!
36

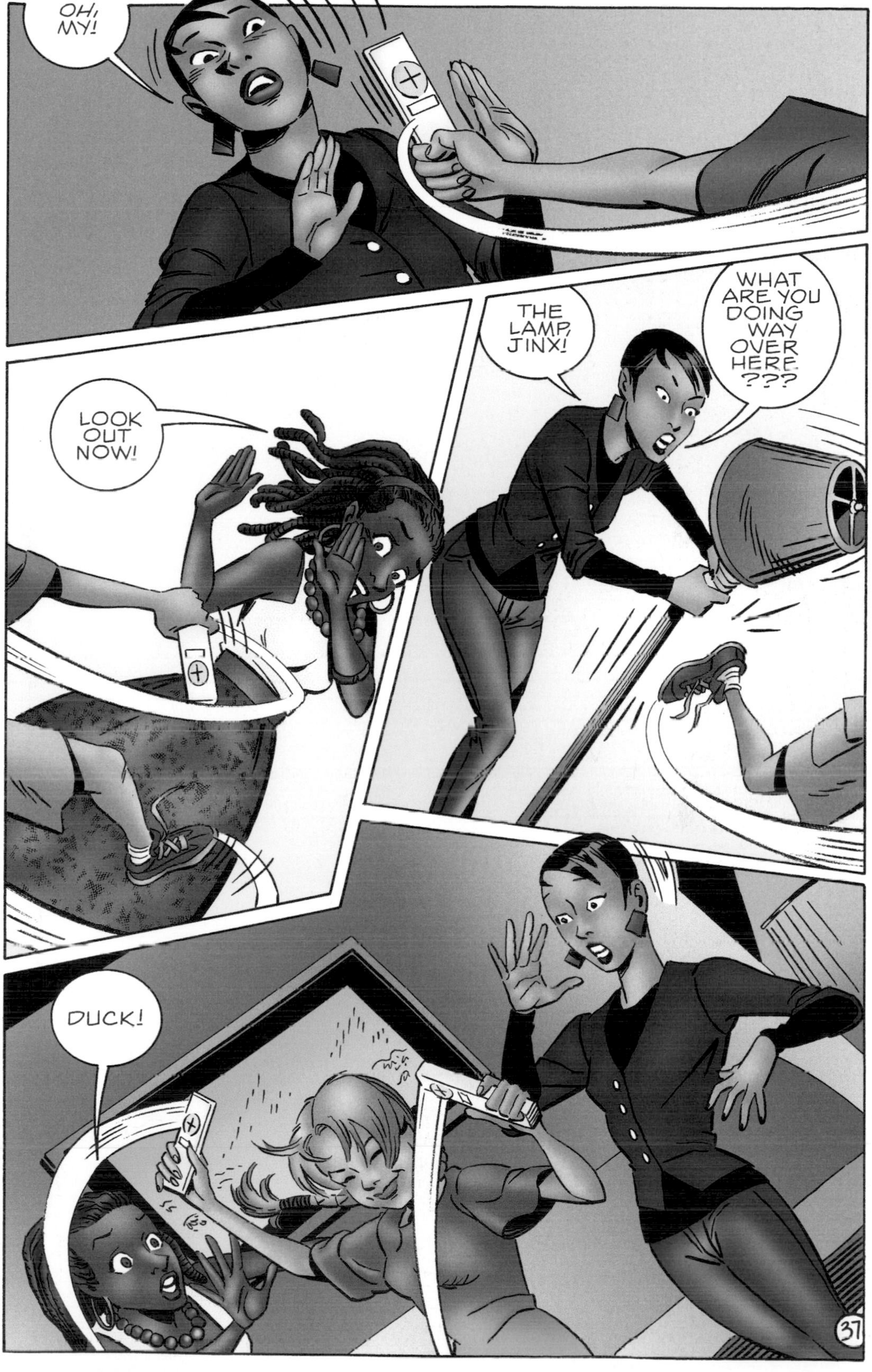
OH, MY!
LOOK OUT NOW!
THE LAMP, JINX!
WHAT ARE YOU DOING WAY OVER HERE???
DUCK!

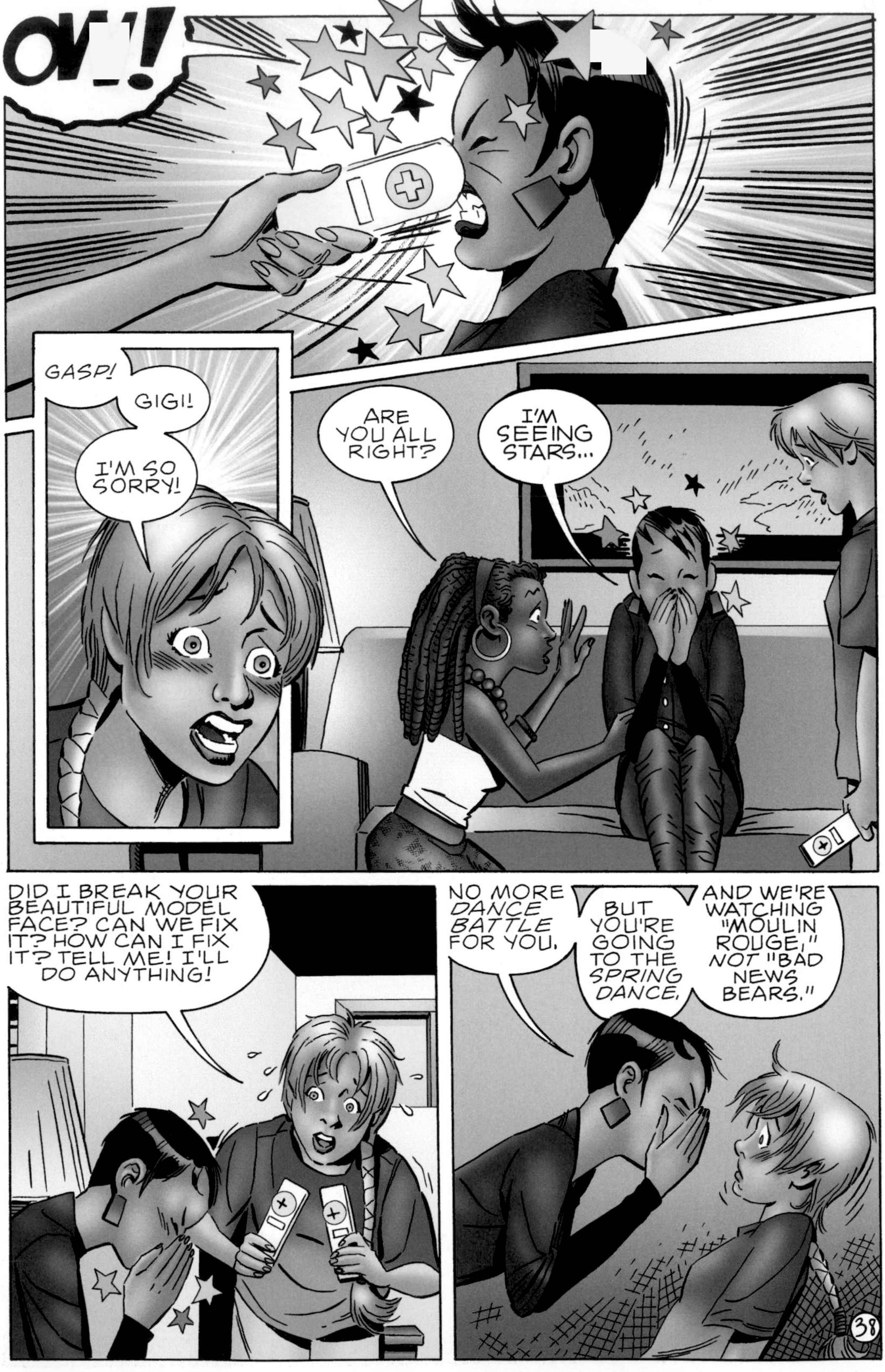
GASP!
GIGI!
I'M SO SORRY!
ARE YOU ALL RIGHT?
I'M SEEING STARS...
DID I BREAK YOUR BEAUTIFUL MODEL FACE? CAN WE FIX IT? HOW CAN I FIX IT? TELL ME! I'LL DO ANYTHING!
NO MORE *DANCE BATTLE* FOR YOU,
BUT YOU'RE GOING TO THE *SPRING DANCE,*
AND WE'RE WATCHING "MOULIN ROUGE," *NOT* "BAD NEWS BEARS."

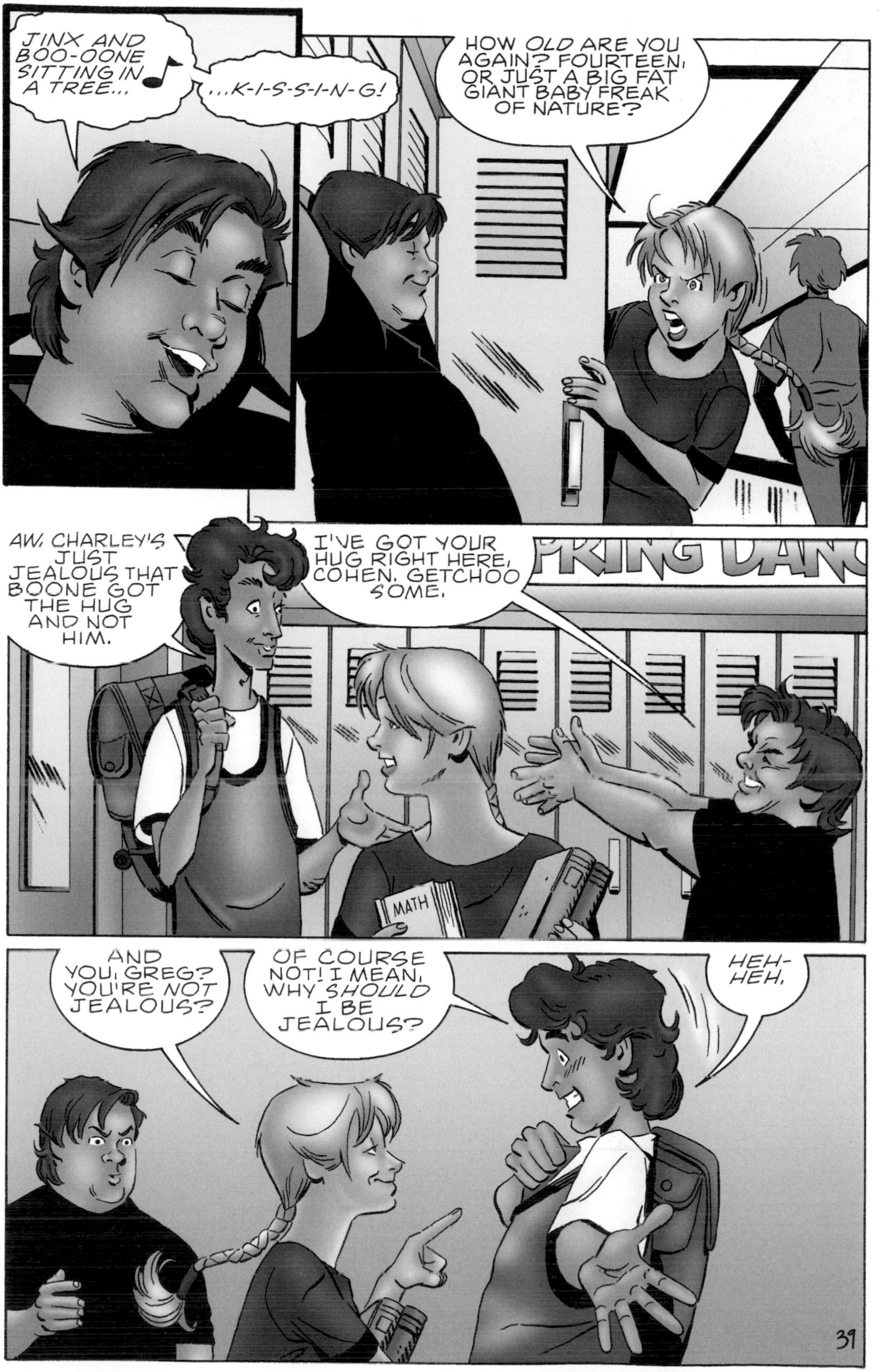
JINX AND BOO-OONE SITTING IN A TREE...
...K-I-S-S-I-N-G!
HOW OLD ARE YOU AGAIN? FOURTEEN, OR JUST A BIG FAT GIANT BABY FREAK OF NATURE?
AW, CHARLEY'S JUST JEALOUS THAT BOONE GOT THE HUG AND NOT HIM.
I'VE GOT YOUR HUG RIGHT HERE, COHEN. GETCHOO SOME.
PRING DAN
MATH
AND YOU, GREG? YOU'RE NOT JEALOUS?
OF COURSE NOT! I MEAN, WHY SHOULD I BE JEALOUS?
HEH-HEH.

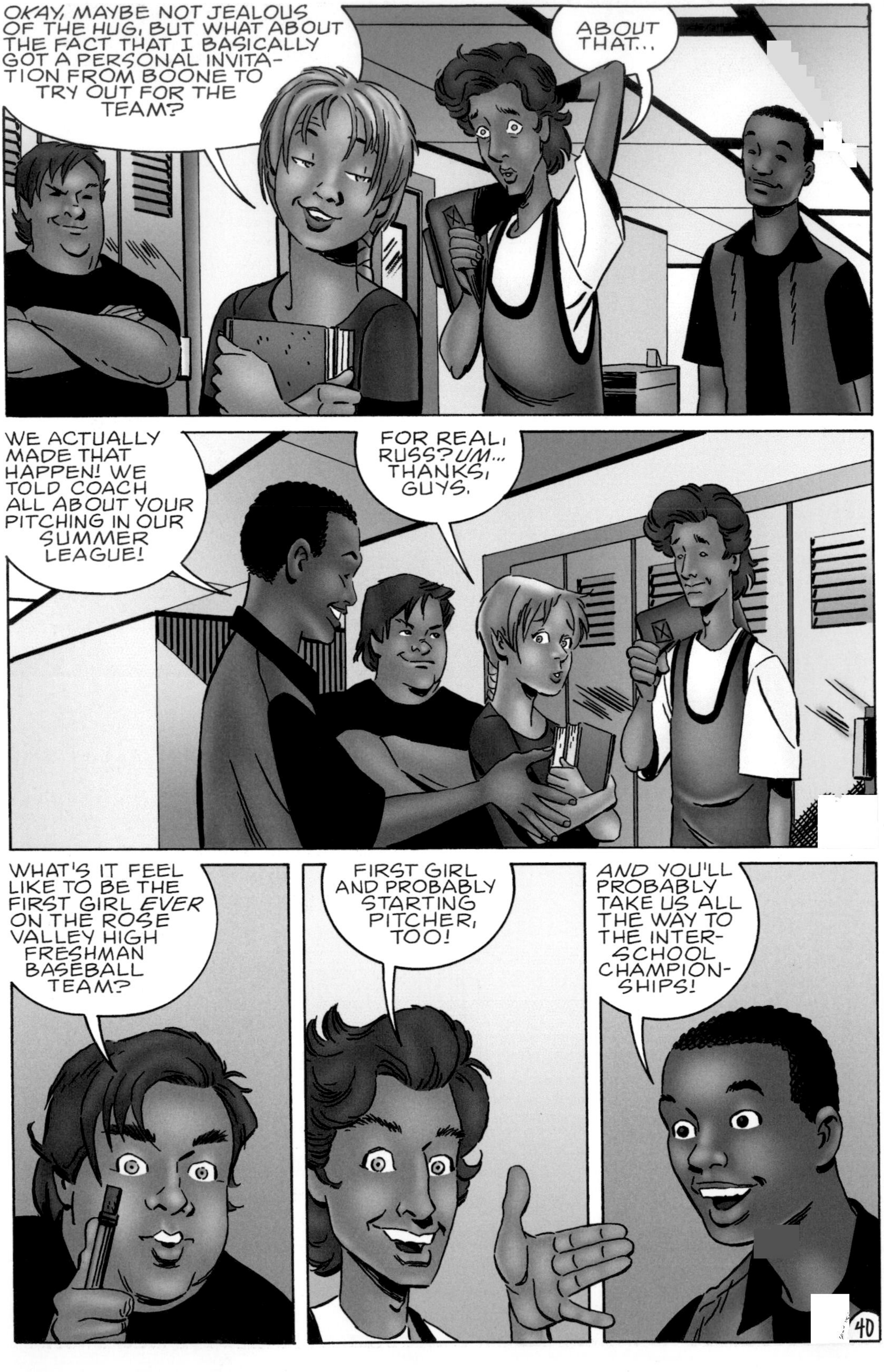
OKAY, MAYBE NOT JEALOUS OF THE HUG, BUT WHAT ABOUT THE FACT THAT I BASICALLY GOT A PERSONAL INVITATION FROM BOONE TO TRY OUT FOR THE TEAM?
ABOUT THAT...
WE ACTUALLY MADE THAT HAPPEN! WE TOLD COACH ALL ABOUT YOUR PITCHING IN OUR SUMMER LEAGUE!
FOR REAL, RUSS? *UM*... THANKS, GUYS.
WHAT'S IT FEEL LIKE TO BE THE FIRST GIRL *EVER* ON THE ROSE VALLEY HIGH FRESHMAN BASEBALL TEAM?
FIRST GIRL AND PROBABLY STARTING PITCHER, TOO!
AND YOU'LL PROBABLY TAKE US ALL THE WAY TO THE INTER-SCHOOL CHAMPIONSHIPS!
40

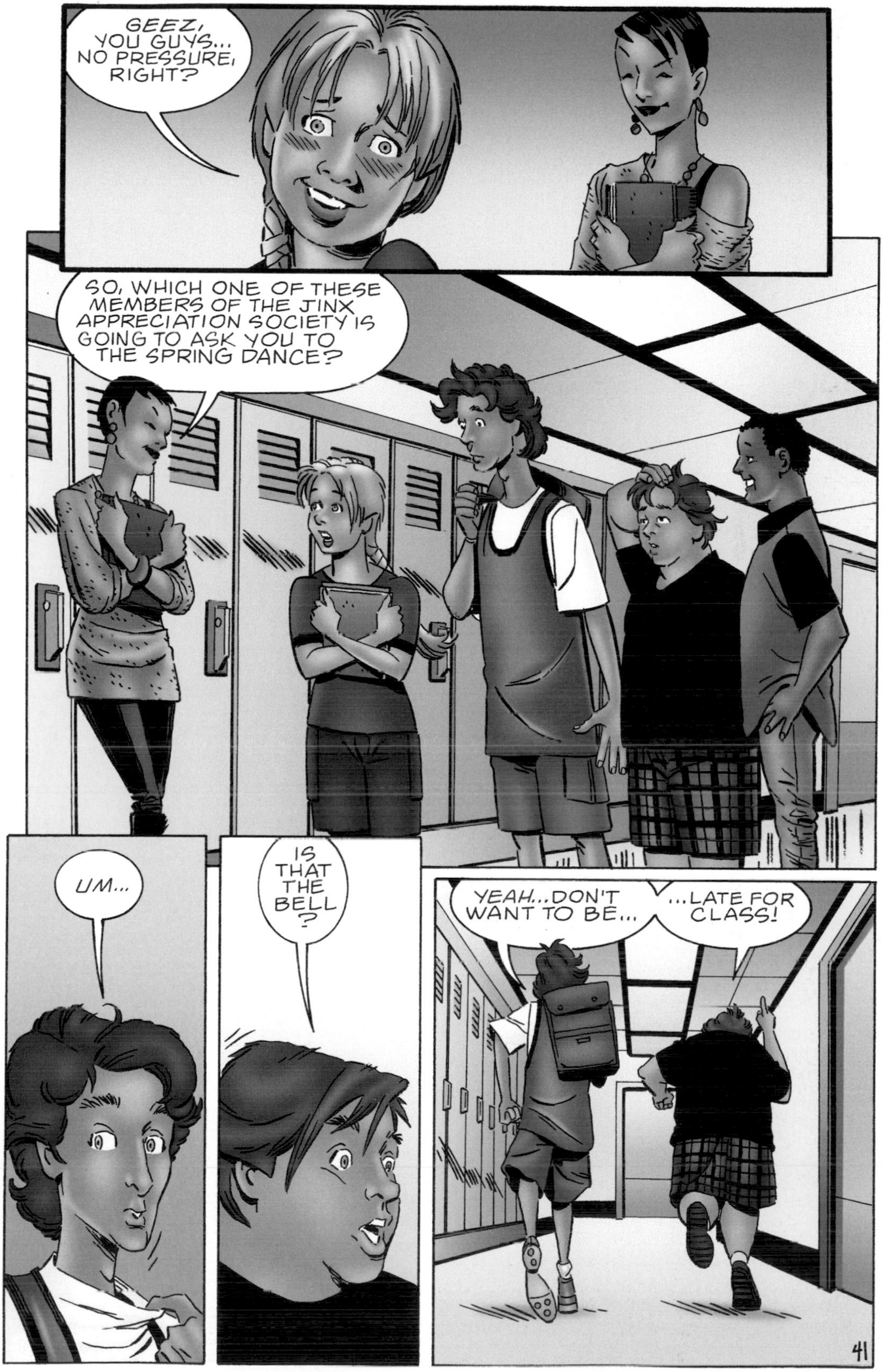
GEEZ, YOU GUYS... NO PRESSURE, RIGHT?
SO, WHICH ONE OF THESE MEMBERS OF THE JINX APPRECIATION SOCIETY IS GOING TO ASK YOU TO THE SPRING DANCE?
UM...
IS THAT THE BELL?
YEAH...DON'T WANT TO BE...
...LATE FOR CLASS!

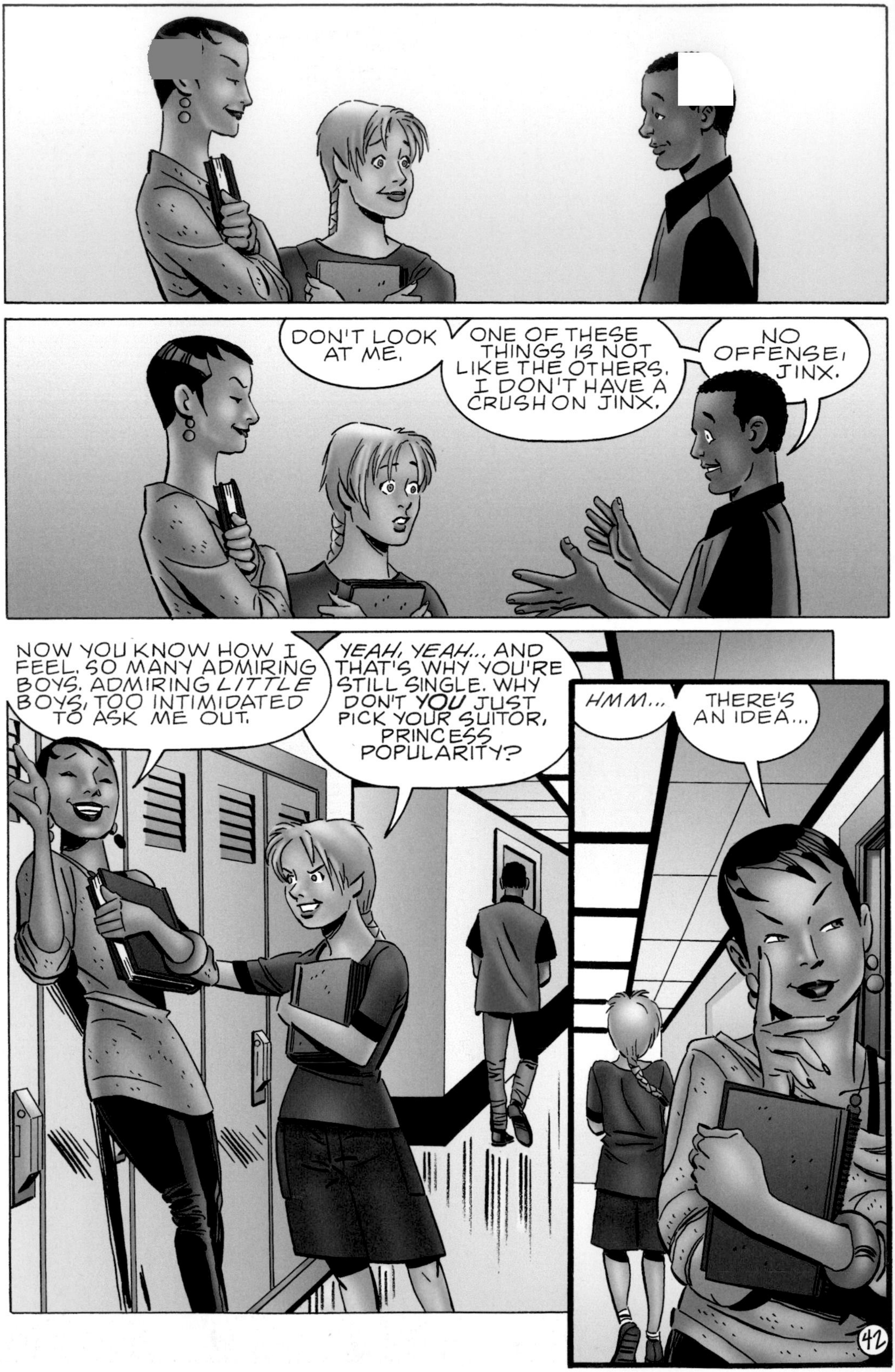
DON'T LOOK AT ME.
ONE OF THESE THINGS IS NOT LIKE THE OTHERS. I DON'T HAVE A CRUSH ON JINX.
NO OFFENSE, JINX.
NOW YOU KNOW HOW I FEEL. SO MANY ADMIRING BOYS. ADMIRING *LITTLE* BOYS, TOO INTIMIDATED TO ASK ME OUT.
YEAH, YEAH... AND THAT'S WHY YOU'RE STILL SINGLE. WHY DON'T ***YOU*** JUST PICK YOUR SUITOR, PRINCESS POPULARITY?
HMM...
THERE'S AN IDEA...

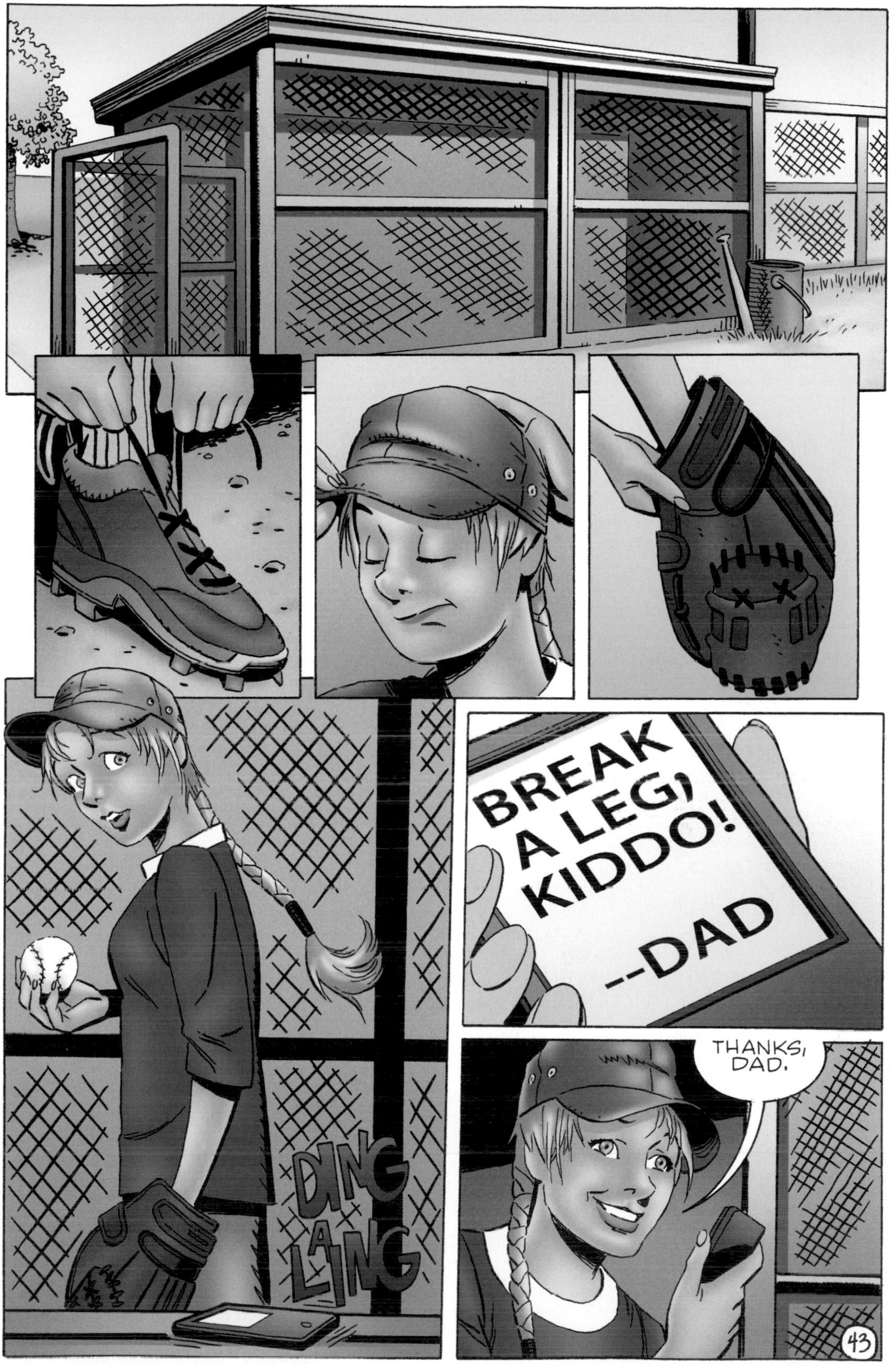
BREAK A LEG, KIDDO!
--DAD
DING A LING
THANKS, DAD.

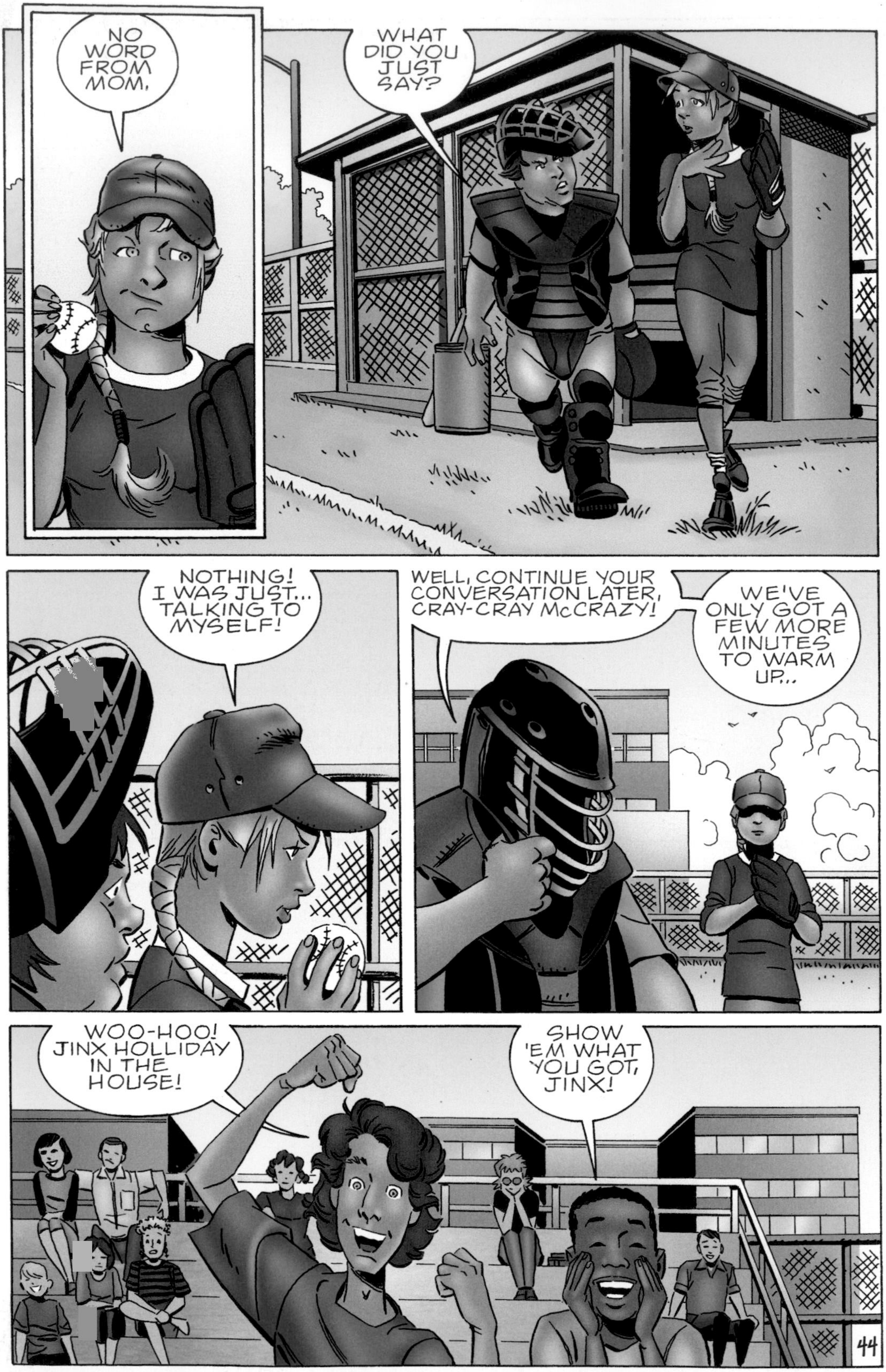

NO WORD FROM MOM,
WHAT DID YOU JUST SAY?
NOTHING! I WAS JUST... TALKING TO MYSELF!
WELL, CONTINUE YOUR CONVERSATION LATER, CRAY-CRAY McCRAZY!
WE'VE ONLY GOT A FEW MORE MINUTES TO WARM UP...
WOO-HOO! JINX HOLLIDAY IN THE HOUSE!
SHOW 'EM WHAT YOU GOT, JINX!

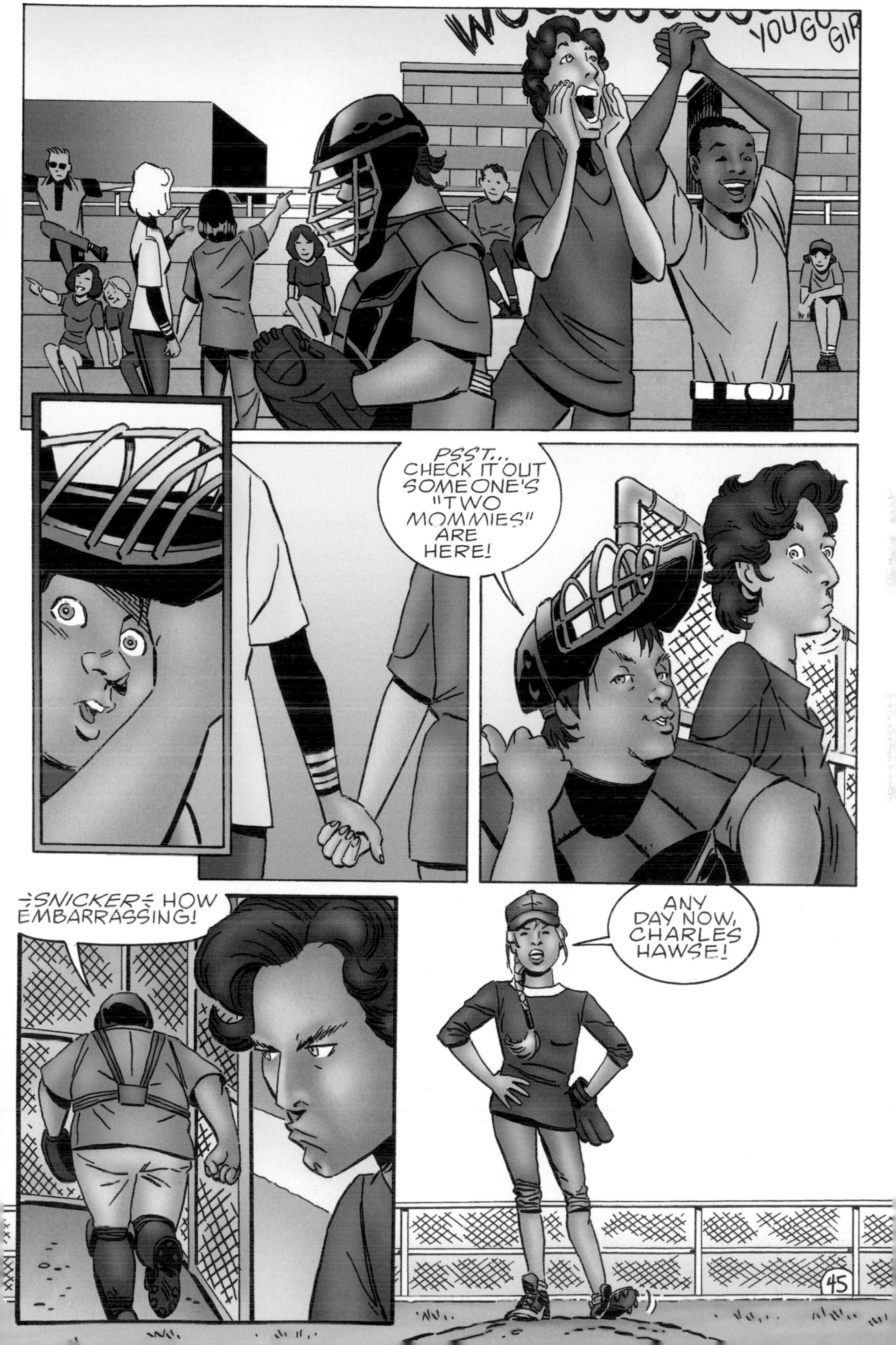
WOOOOOOOO
YOU GO GIR
PSST... CHECK IT OUT SOMEONE'S "TWO MOMMIES" ARE HERE!
=SNICKER= HOW EMBARRASSING!
ANY DAY NOW, CHARLES HAWSE!

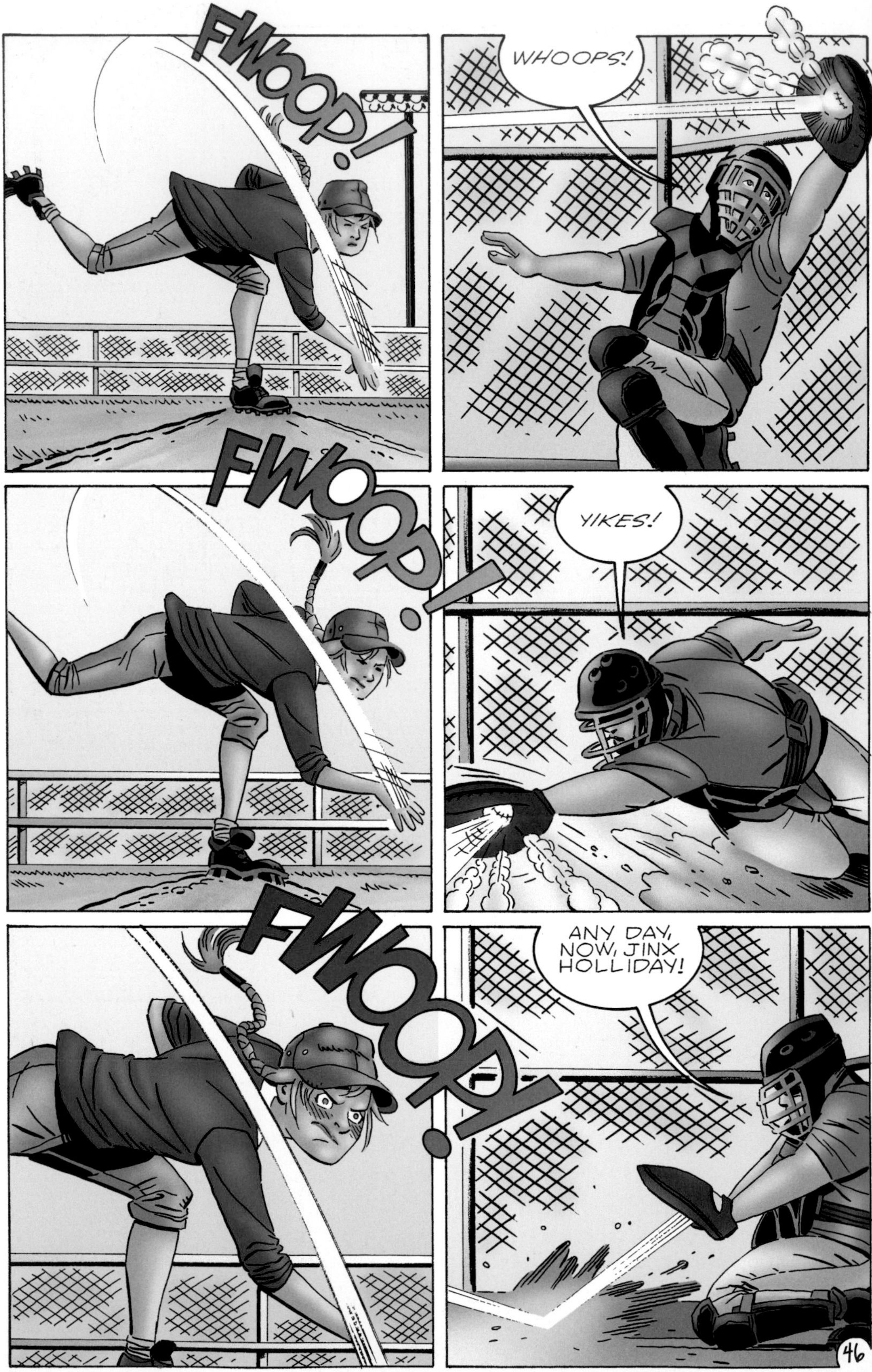
FWOOP!
WHOOPS!
FWOOP!
YIKES!
FWOOP!
ANY DAY, NOW, JINX HOLLIDAY!

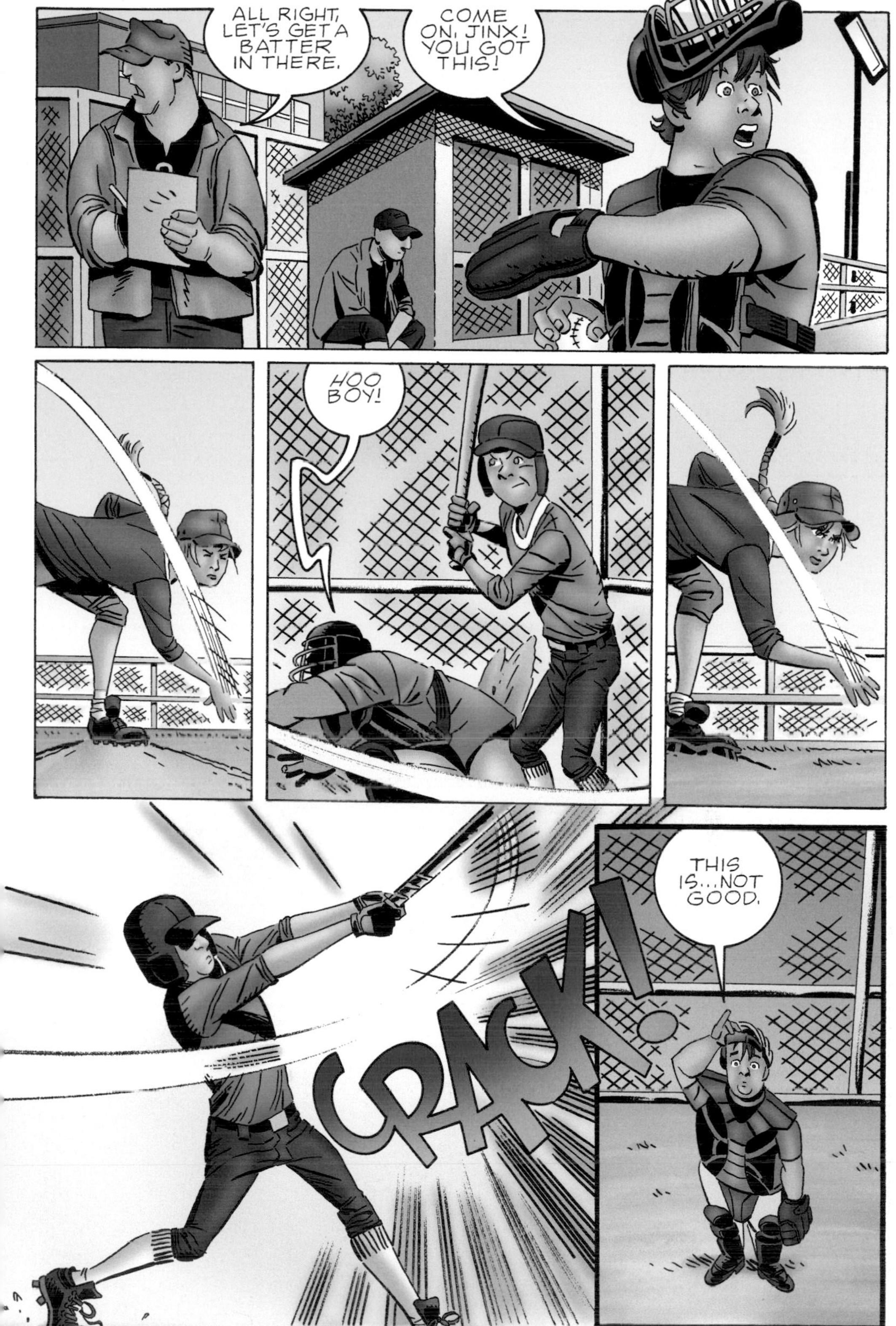
ALL RIGHT, LET'S GET A BATTER IN THERE.
COME ON, JINX! YOU GOT THIS!
HOO BOY!
THIS IS...NOT GOOD.
CRACK!

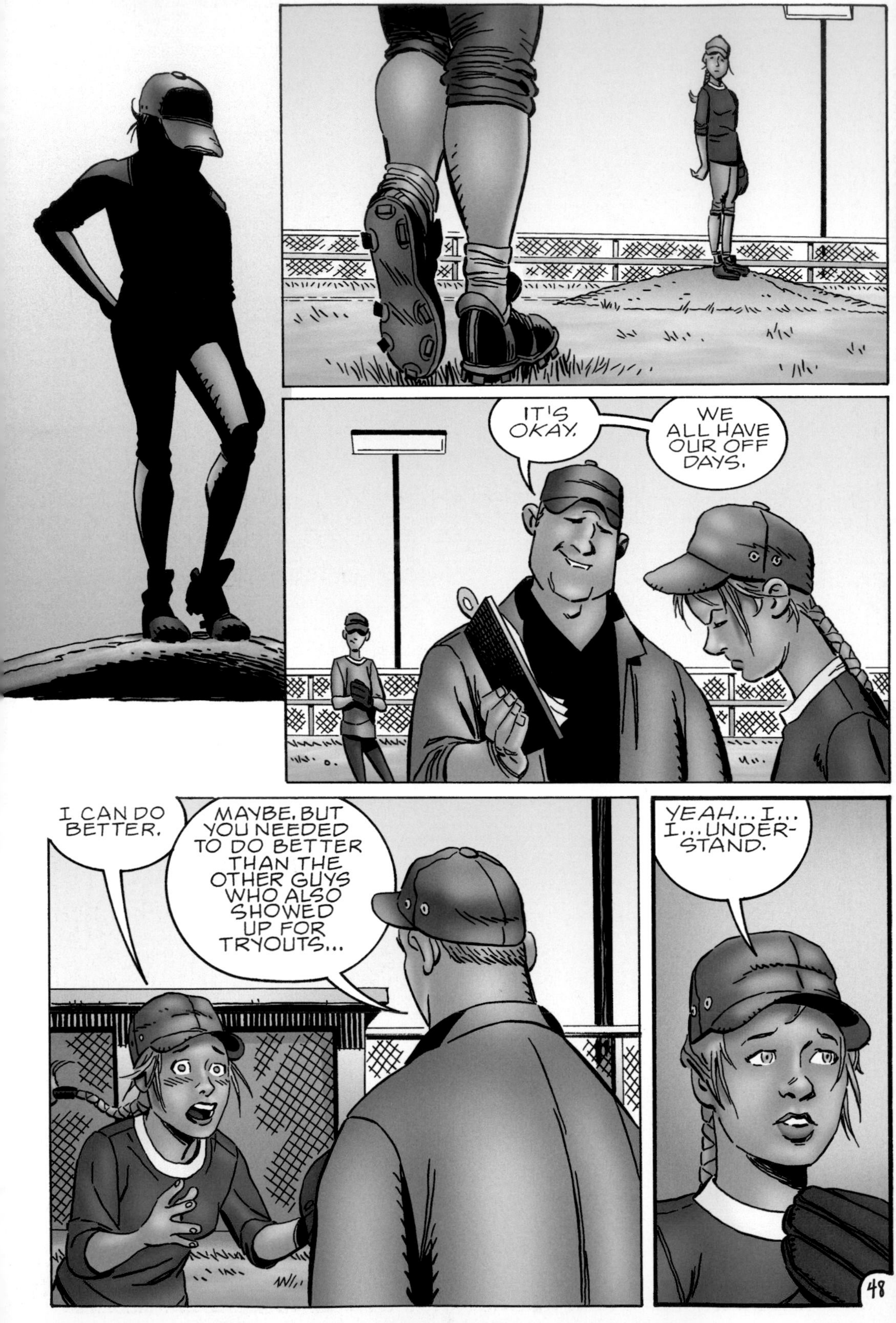

IT'S OKAY.
WE ALL HAVE OUR OFF DAYS.
I CAN DO BETTER.
MAYBE. BUT YOU NEEDED TO DO BETTER THAN THE OTHER GUYS WHO ALSO SHOWED UP FOR TRYOUTS...
YEAH... I... I... UNDER-STAND.

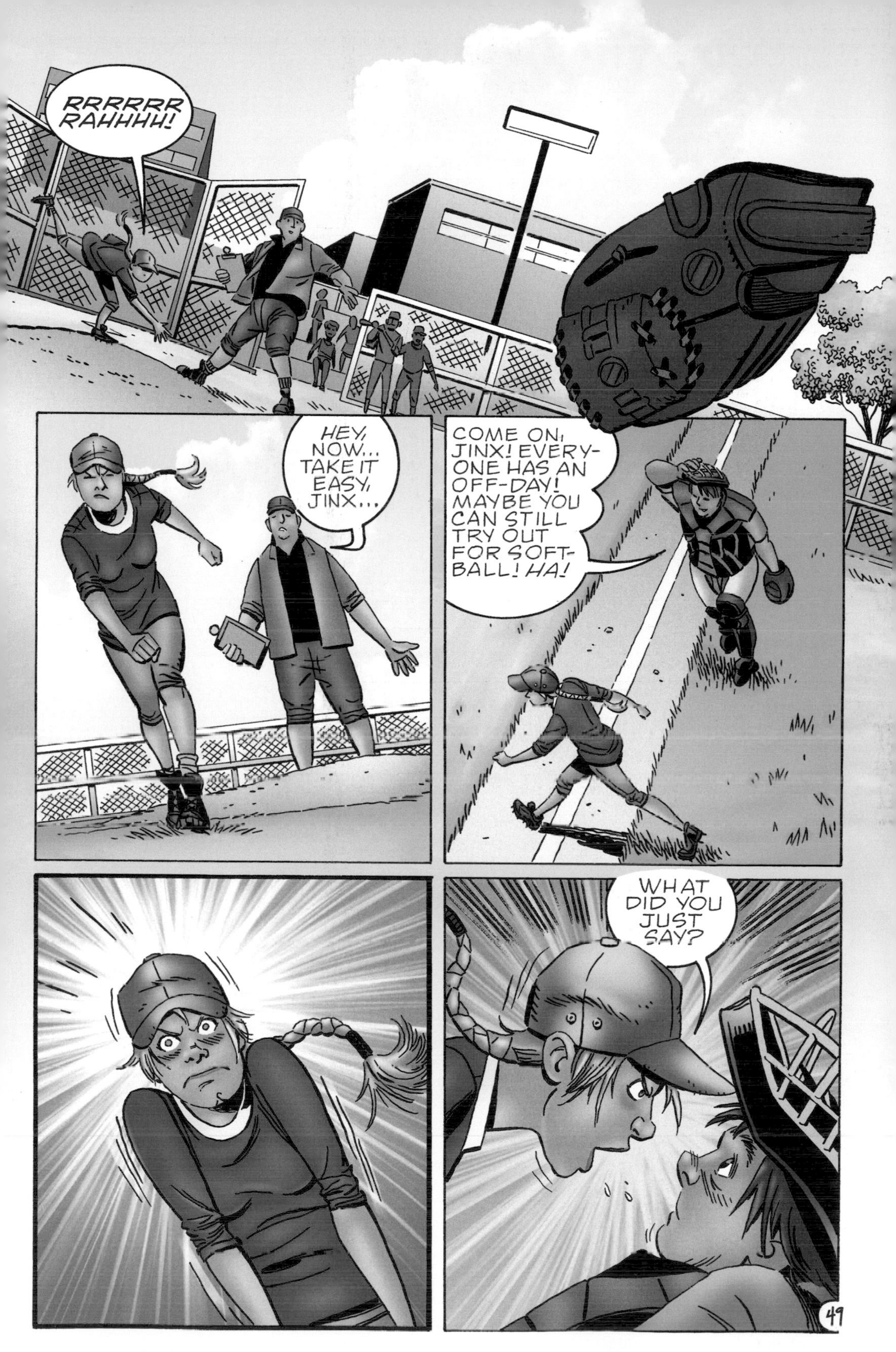
RRRRRR RAHHHH!
HEY, NOW... TAKE IT EASY, JINX...
COME ON, JINX! EVERY-ONE HAS AN OFF-DAY! MAYBE YOU CAN STILL TRY OUT FOR SOFT-BALL! HA!
WHAT DID YOU JUST SAY?

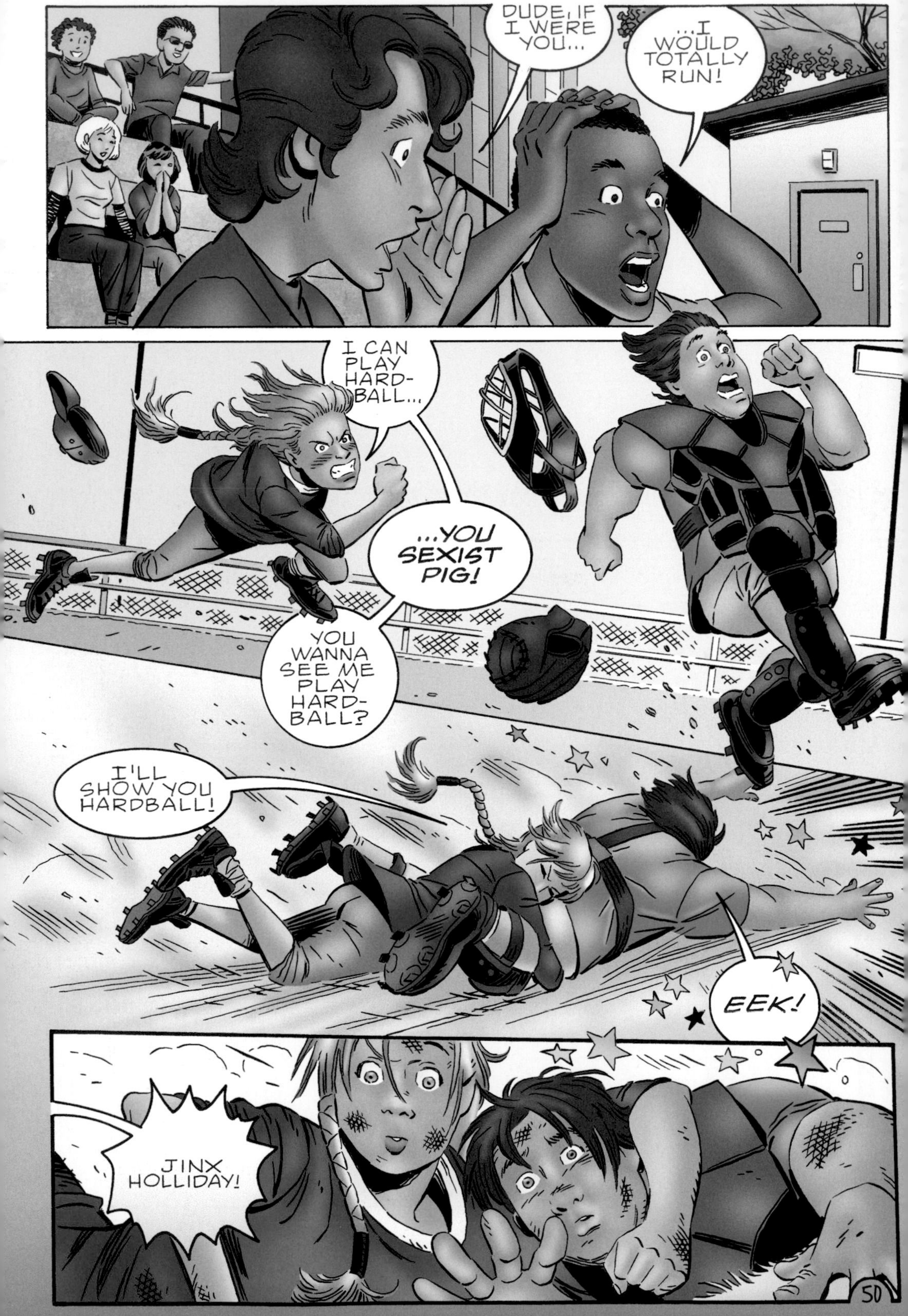

DUDE, IF I WERE YOU...
...I WOULD TOTALLY RUN!
I CAN PLAY HARD-BALL...
...YOU SEXIST PIG!
YOU WANNA SEE ME PLAY HARD-BALL?
I'LL SHOW YOU HARDBALL!
EEK!
JINX HOLLIDAY!

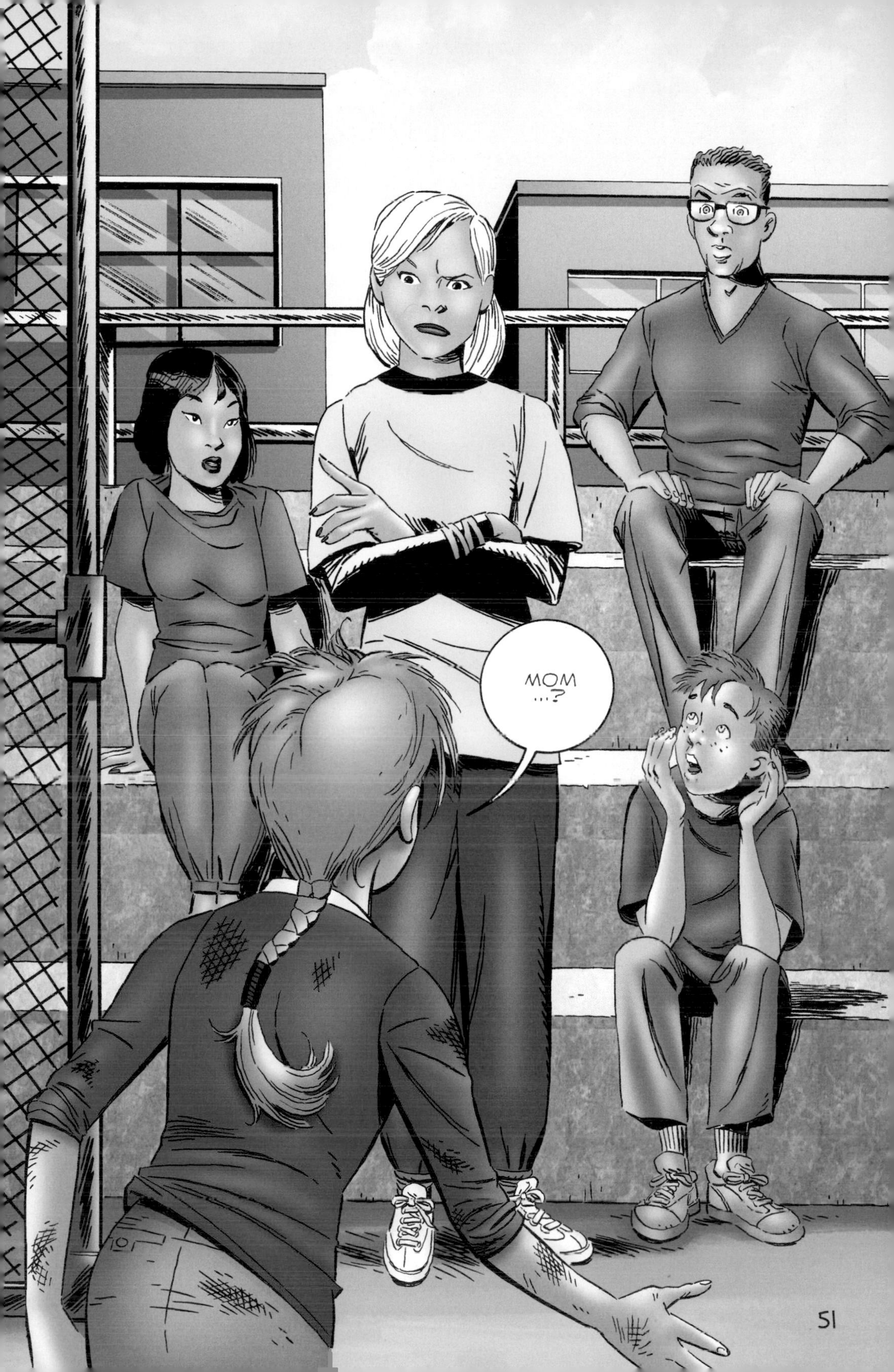
MOM ...?

JINX™

CHAPTER 3

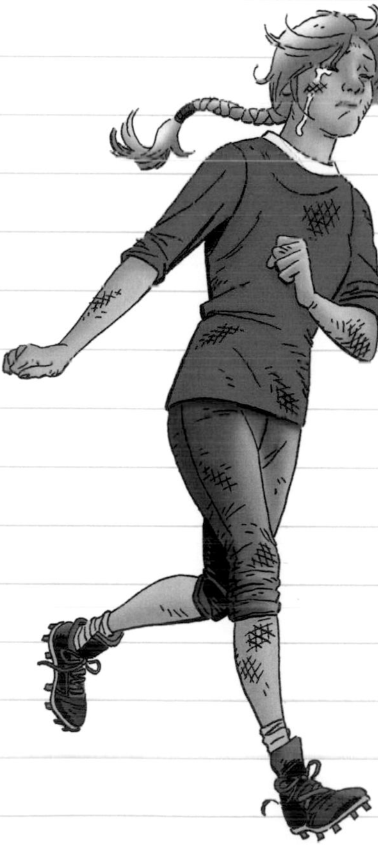

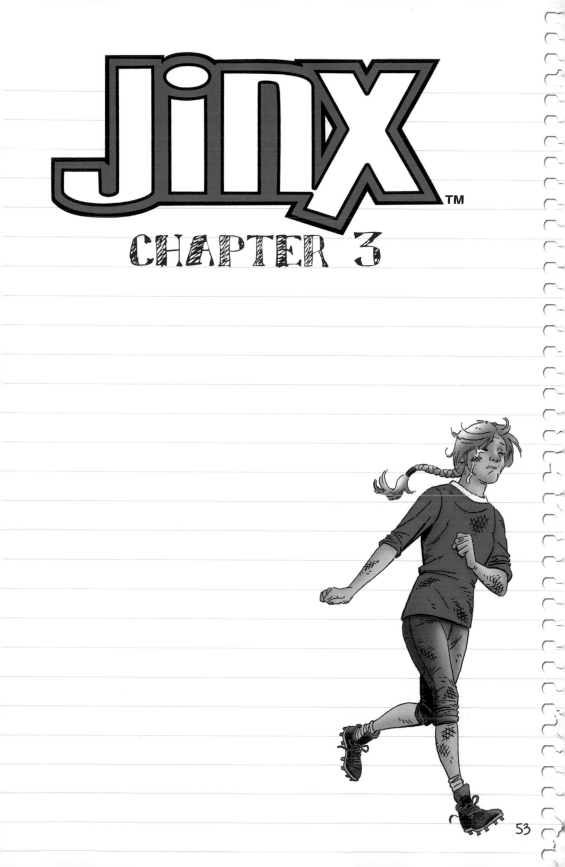

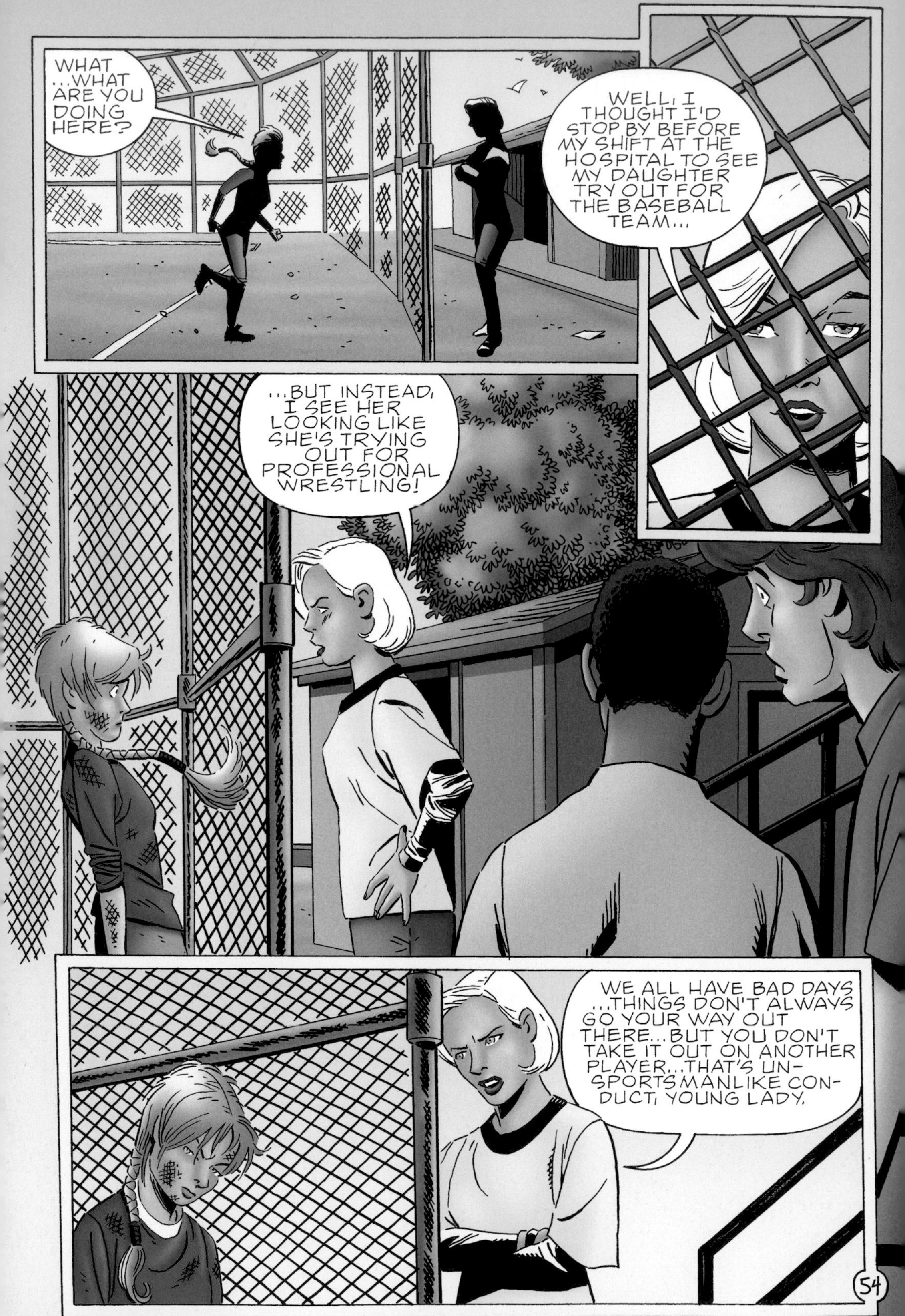
WHAT ...WHAT ARE YOU DOING HERE?
WELL, I THOUGHT I'D STOP BY BEFORE MY SHIFT AT THE HOSPITAL TO SEE MY DAUGHTER TRY OUT FOR THE BASEBALL TEAM...
...BUT INSTEAD, I SEE HER LOOKING LIKE SHE'S TRYING OUT FOR PROFESSIONAL WRESTLING!
WE ALL HAVE BAD DAYS ...THINGS DON'T ALWAYS GO YOUR WAY OUT THERE...BUT YOU DON'T TAKE IT OUT ON ANOTHER PLAYER...THAT'S UN-SPORTSMANLIKE CON-DUCT, YOUNG LADY.
54

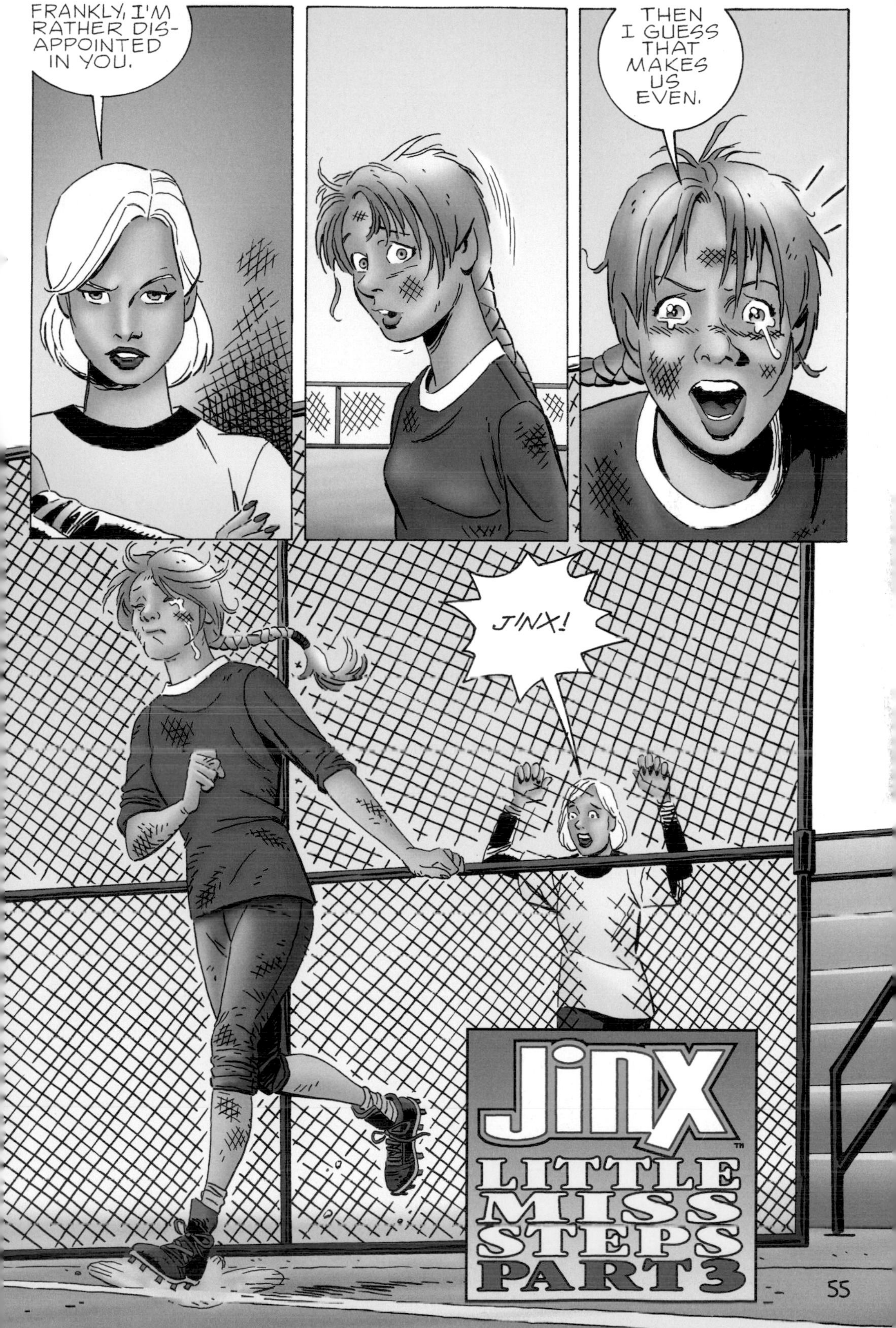
FRANKLY, I'M RATHER DIS-APPOINTED IN YOU.
THEN I GUESS THAT MAKES US EVEN.
JINX!
JINX
LITTLE MISS STEPS PART 3

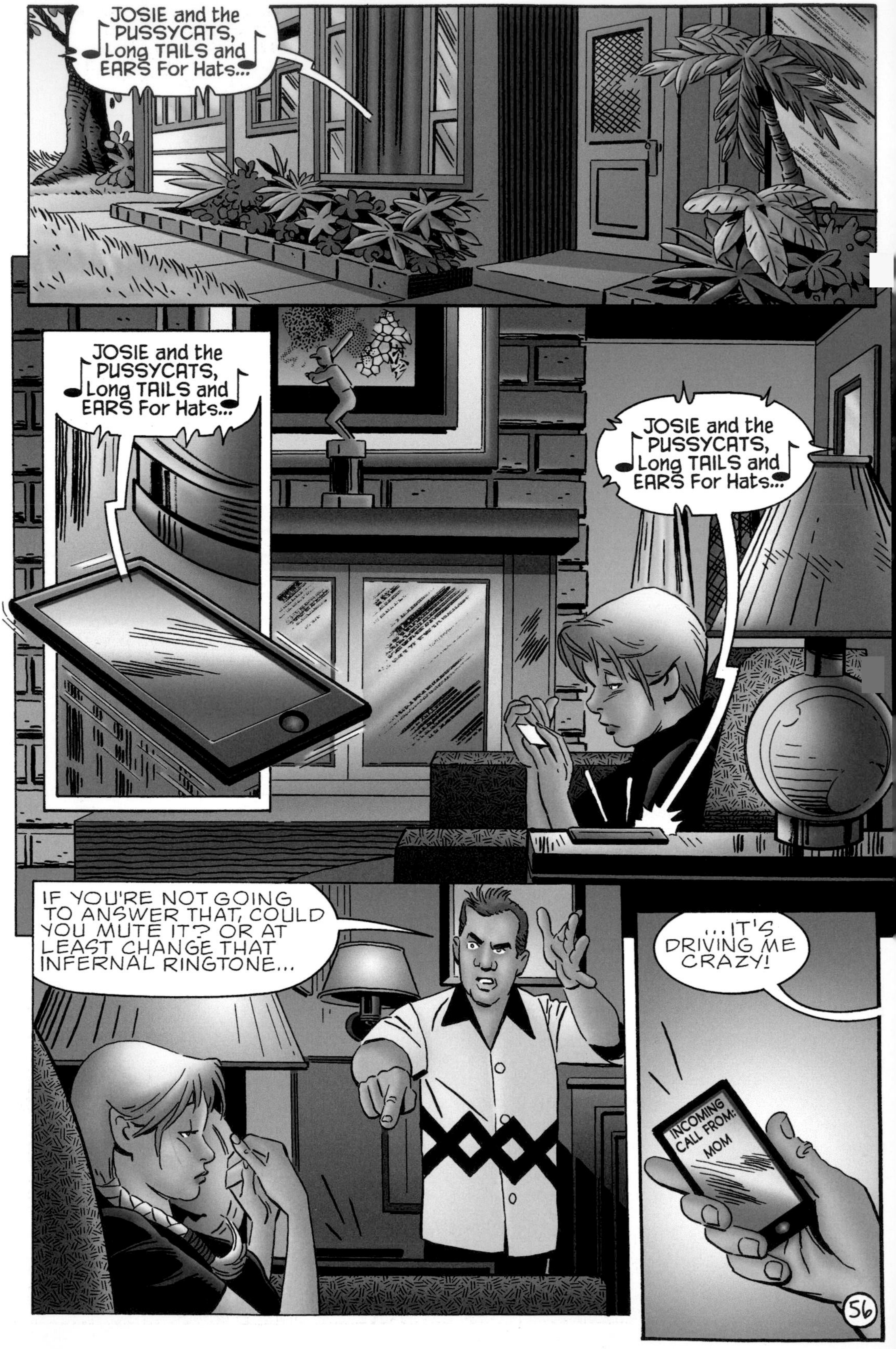
JOSIE and the PUSSYCATS, Long TAILS and EARS For Hats...
JOSIE and the PUSSYCATS, Long TAILS and EARS For Hats...
JOSIE and the PUSSYCATS, Long TAILS and EARS For Hats...
IF YOU'RE NOT GOING TO ANSWER THAT, COULD YOU MUTE IT? OR AT LEAST CHANGE THAT INFERNAL RINGTONE...
...IT'S DRIVING ME CRAZY!
INCOMING CALL FROM: MOM

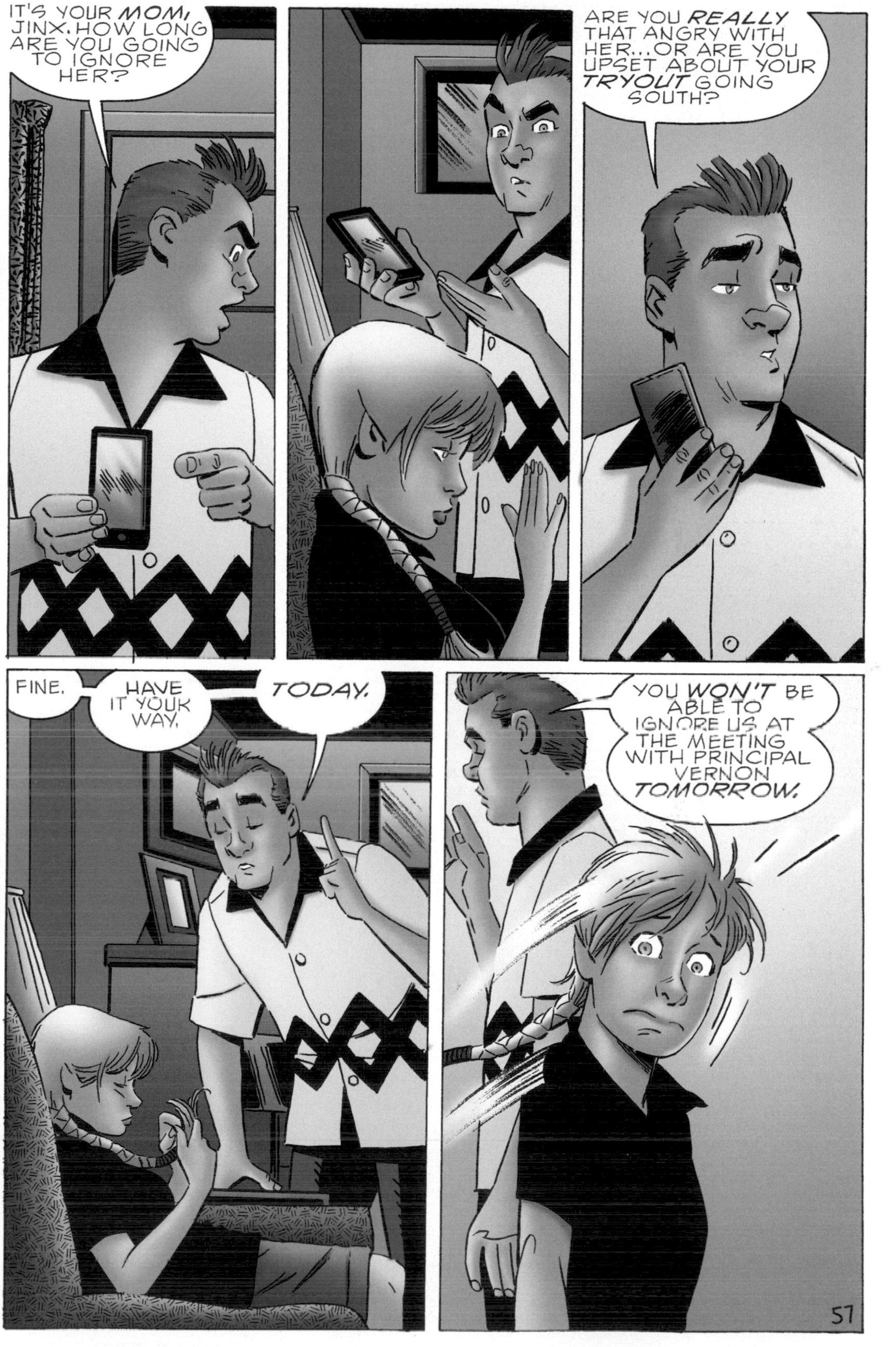
IT'S YOUR MOM, JINX. HOW LONG ARE YOU GOING TO IGNORE HER?
ARE YOU REALLY THAT ANGRY WITH HER...OR ARE YOU UPSET ABOUT YOUR TRYOUT GOING SOUTH?
FINE.
HAVE IT YOUR WAY.
TODAY.
YOU WON'T BE ABLE TO IGNORE US AT THE MEETING WITH PRINCIPAL VERNON TOMORROW.

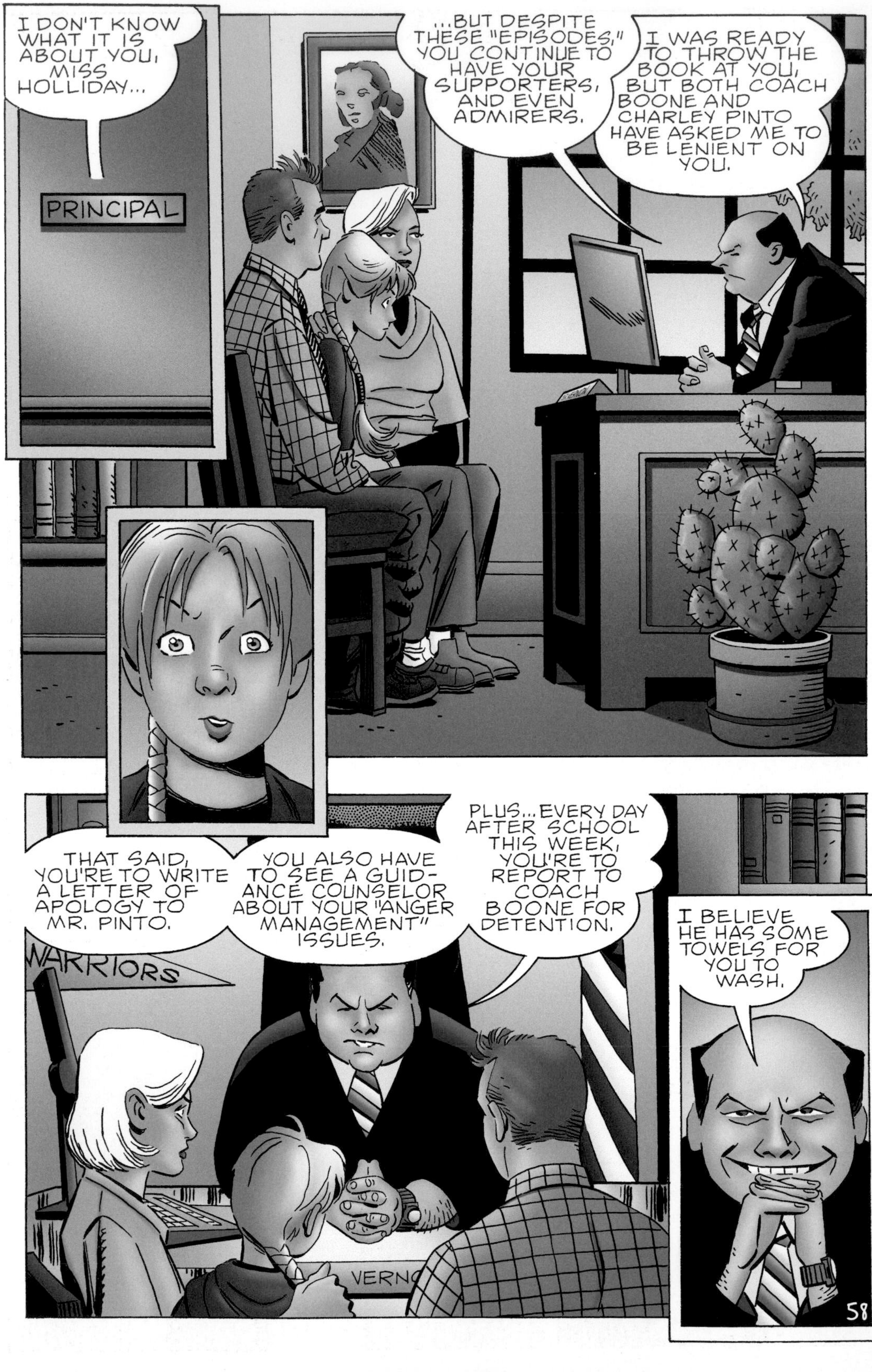
I DON'T KNOW WHAT IT IS ABOUT YOU, MISS HOLLIDAY...
...BUT DESPITE THESE "EPISODES," YOU CONTINUE TO HAVE YOUR SUPPORTERS, AND EVEN ADMIRERS.
I WAS READY TO THROW THE BOOK AT YOU, BUT BOTH COACH BOONE AND CHARLEY PINTO HAVE ASKED ME TO BE LENIENT ON YOU.
PRINCIPAL
THAT SAID, YOU'RE TO WRITE A LETTER OF APOLOGY TO MR. PINTO.
YOU ALSO HAVE TO SEE A GUIDANCE COUNSELOR ABOUT YOUR "ANGER MANAGEMENT" ISSUES.
PLUS... EVERY DAY AFTER SCHOOL THIS WEEK, YOU'RE TO REPORT TO COACH BOONE FOR DETENTION.
I BELIEVE HE HAS SOME TOWELS FOR YOU TO WASH.
WARRIORS
VERNO

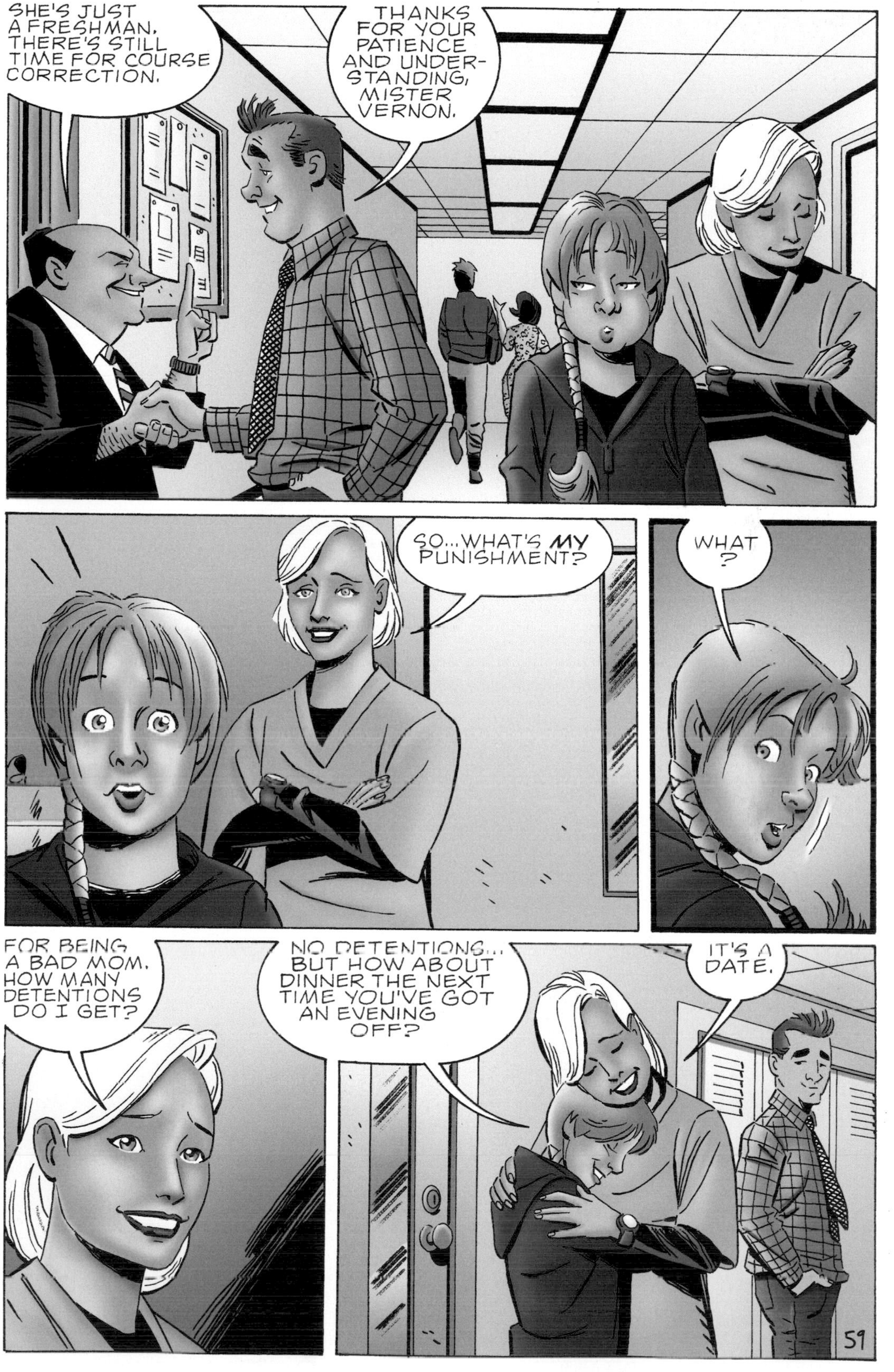
SHE'S JUST A FRESHMAN. THERE'S STILL TIME FOR COURSE CORRECTION.
THANKS FOR YOUR PATIENCE AND UNDER-STANDING, MISTER VERNON.
SO...WHAT'S MY PUNISHMENT?
WHAT?
FOR BEING A BAD MOM. HOW MANY DETENTIONS DO I GET?
NO DETENTIONS... BUT HOW ABOUT DINNER THE NEXT TIME YOU'VE GOT AN EVENING OFF?
IT'S A DATE.

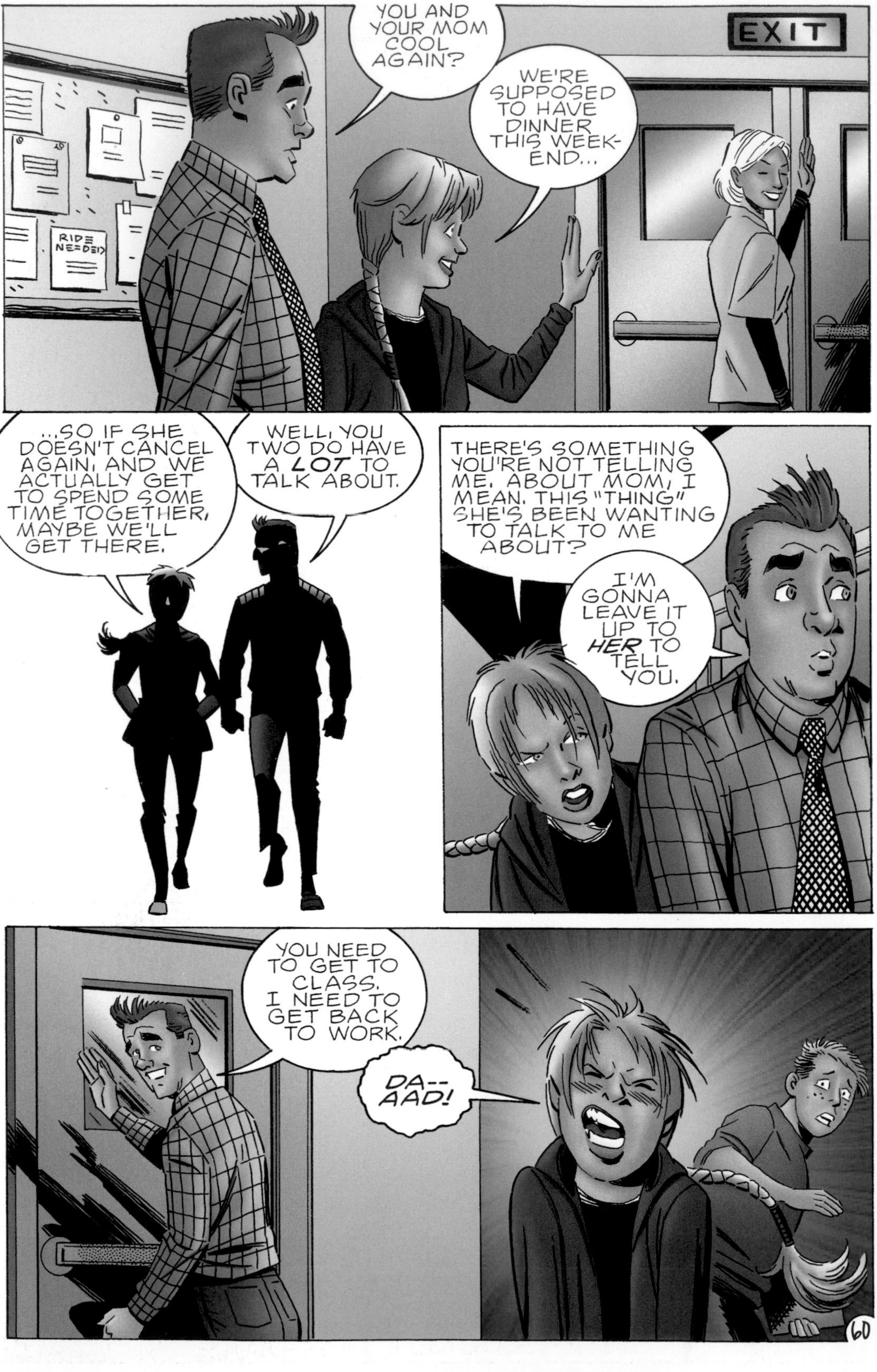
EXIT
YOU AND YOUR MOM COOL AGAIN?
WE'RE SUPPOSED TO HAVE DINNER THIS WEEK-END...
RIDE NEEDED
...SO IF SHE DOESN'T CANCEL AGAIN, AND WE ACTUALLY GET TO SPEND SOME TIME TOGETHER, MAYBE WE'LL GET THERE.
WELL, YOU TWO DO HAVE A LOT TO TALK ABOUT.
THERE'S SOMETHING YOU'RE NOT TELLING ME. ABOUT MOM, I MEAN. THIS "THING" SHE'S BEEN WANTING TO TALK TO ME ABOUT?
I'M GONNA LEAVE IT UP TO HER TO TELL YOU.
YOU NEED TO GET TO CLASS. I NEED TO GET BACK TO WORK.
DA--AAD!

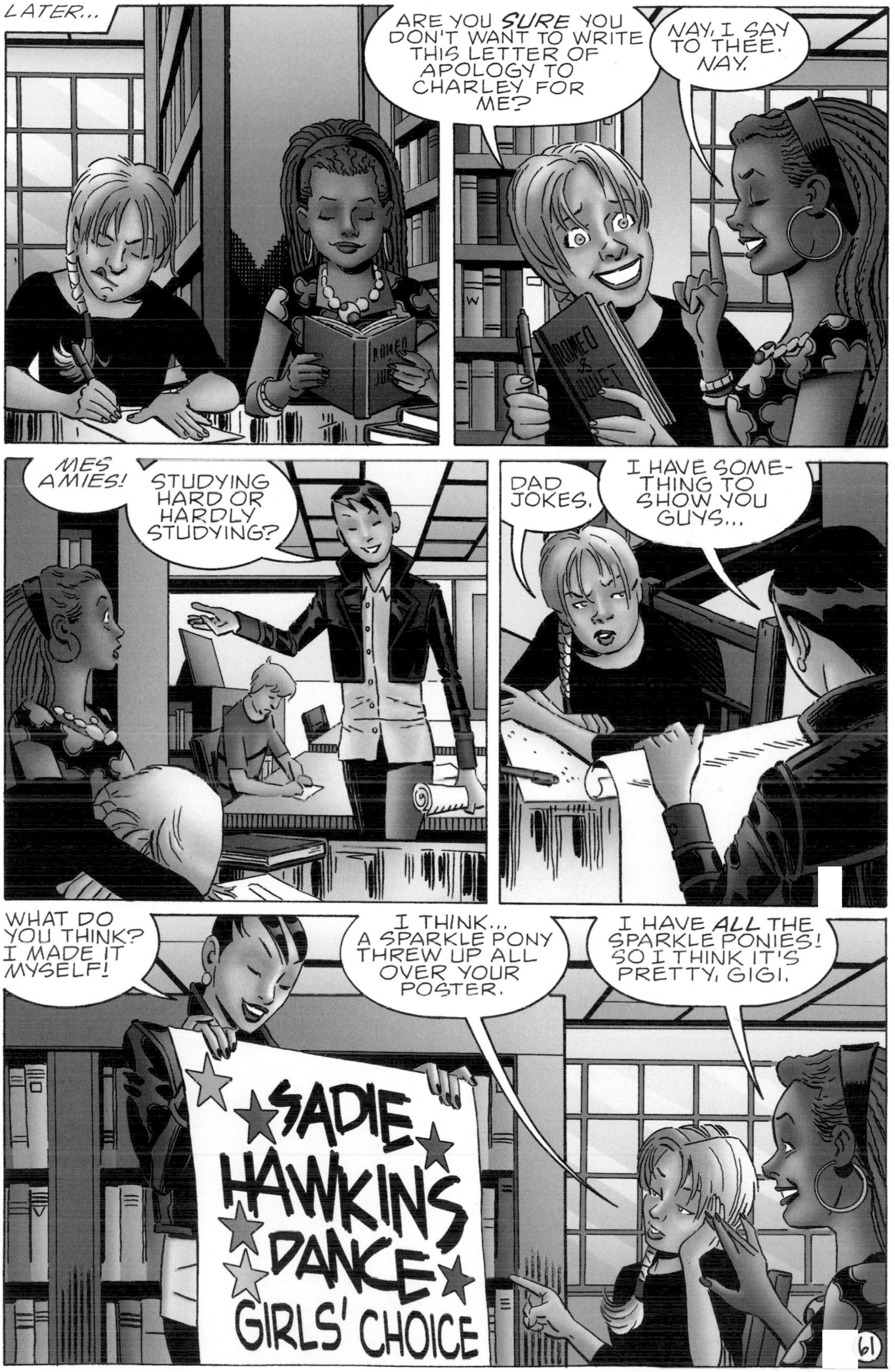
LATER...
ARE YOU SURE YOU DON'T WANT TO WRITE THIS LETTER OF APOLOGY TO CHARLEY FOR ME?
NAY, I SAY TO THEE. NAY.
ROMEO & JULIET
MES AMIES!
STUDYING HARD OR HARDLY STUDYING?
DAD JOKES.
I HAVE SOMETHING TO SHOW YOU GUYS...
WHAT DO YOU THINK? I MADE IT MYSELF!
I THINK... A SPARKLE PONY THREW UP ALL OVER YOUR POSTER.
I HAVE ALL THE SPARKLE PONIES! SO I THINK IT'S PRETTY, GIGI.
SADIE HAWKINS DANCE
GIRLS' CHOICE

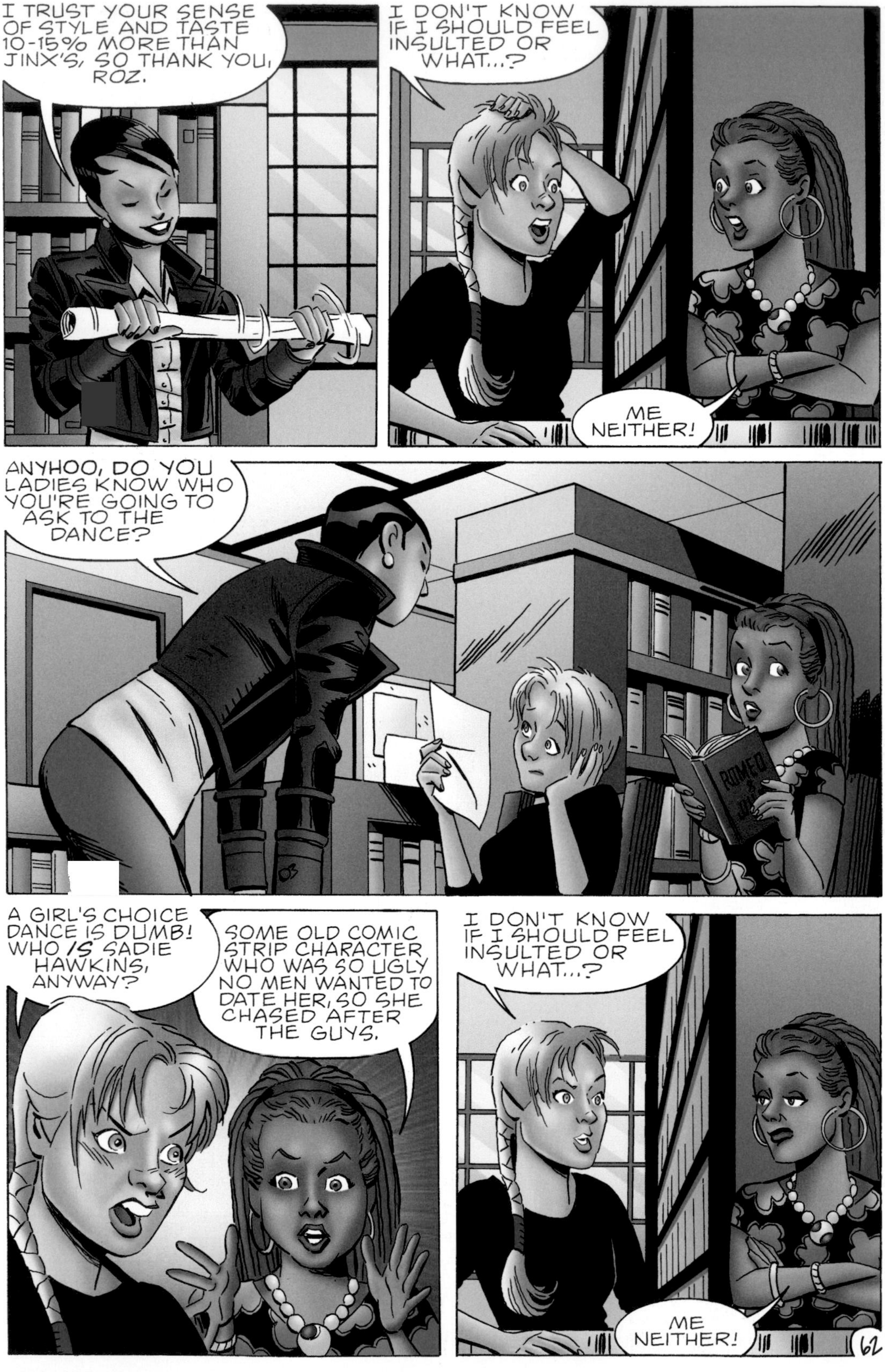
I TRUST YOUR SENSE OF STYLE AND TASTE 10-15% MORE THAN JINX'S, SO THANK YOU, ROZ.
I DON'T KNOW IF I SHOULD FEEL INSULTED OR WHAT...?
ME NEITHER!
ANYHOO, DO YOU LADIES KNOW WHO YOU'RE GOING TO ASK TO THE DANCE?
ROMEO & JU
A GIRL'S CHOICE DANCE IS DUMB! WHO *IS* SADIE HAWKINS, ANYWAY?
SOME OLD COMIC STRIP CHARACTER WHO WAS SO UGLY NO MEN WANTED TO DATE HER, SO SHE CHASED AFTER THE GUYS.
I DON'T KNOW IF I SHOULD FEEL INSULTED OR WHAT...?
ME NEITHER!

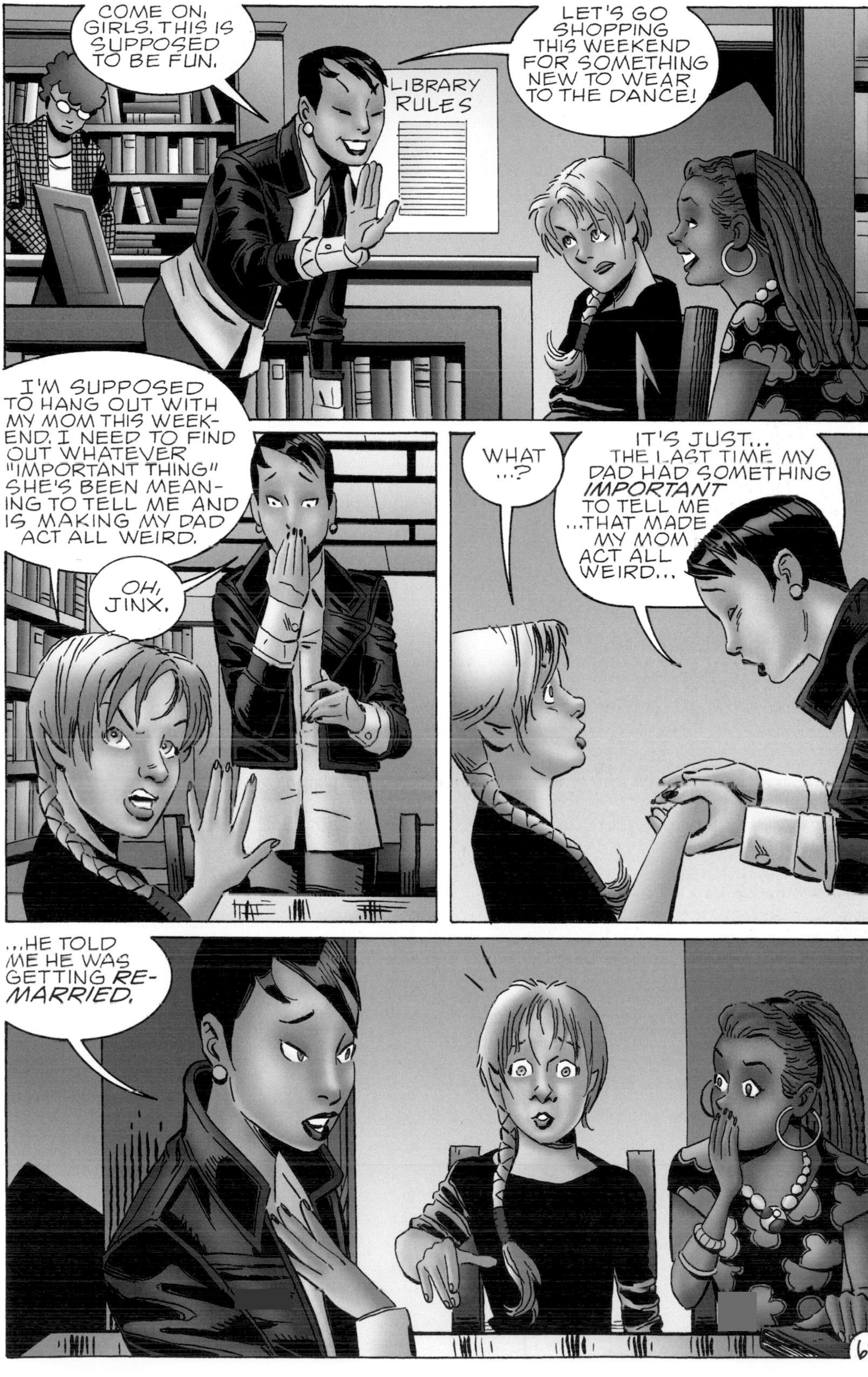
COME ON, GIRLS. THIS IS SUPPOSED TO BE FUN.
LET'S GO SHOPPING THIS WEEKEND FOR SOMETHING NEW TO WEAR TO THE DANCE!
LIBRARY RULES
I'M SUPPOSED TO HANG OUT WITH MY MOM THIS WEEK-END. I NEED TO FIND OUT WHATEVER "IMPORTANT THING" SHE'S BEEN MEAN-ING TO TELL ME AND IS MAKING MY DAD ACT ALL WEIRD.
OH, JINX.
WHAT ...?
IT'S JUST... THE LAST TIME MY DAD HAD SOMETHING *IMPORTANT* TO TELL ME ...THAT MADE MY MOM ACT ALL WEIRD...
...HE TOLD ME HE WAS GETTING *RE-MARRIED*.

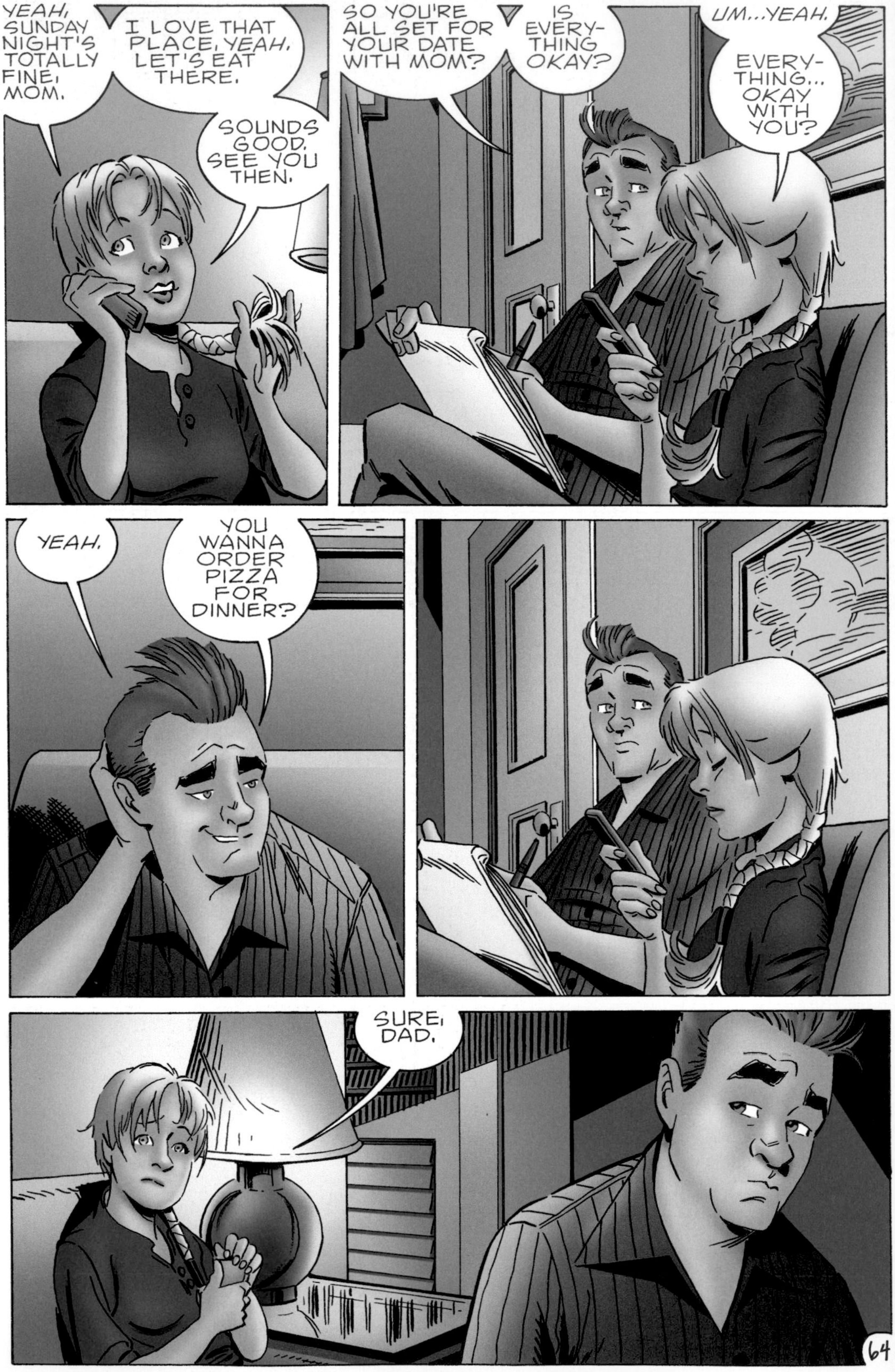
YEAH, SUNDAY NIGHT'S TOTALLY FINE, MOM.
I LOVE THAT PLACE, YEAH, LET'S EAT THERE.
SOUNDS GOOD. SEE YOU THEN.
SO YOU'RE ALL SET FOR YOUR DATE WITH MOM?
IS EVERY-THING OKAY?
UM...YEAH.
EVERY-THING... OKAY WITH YOU?
YEAH.
YOU WANNA ORDER PIZZA FOR DINNER?
SURE, DAD.

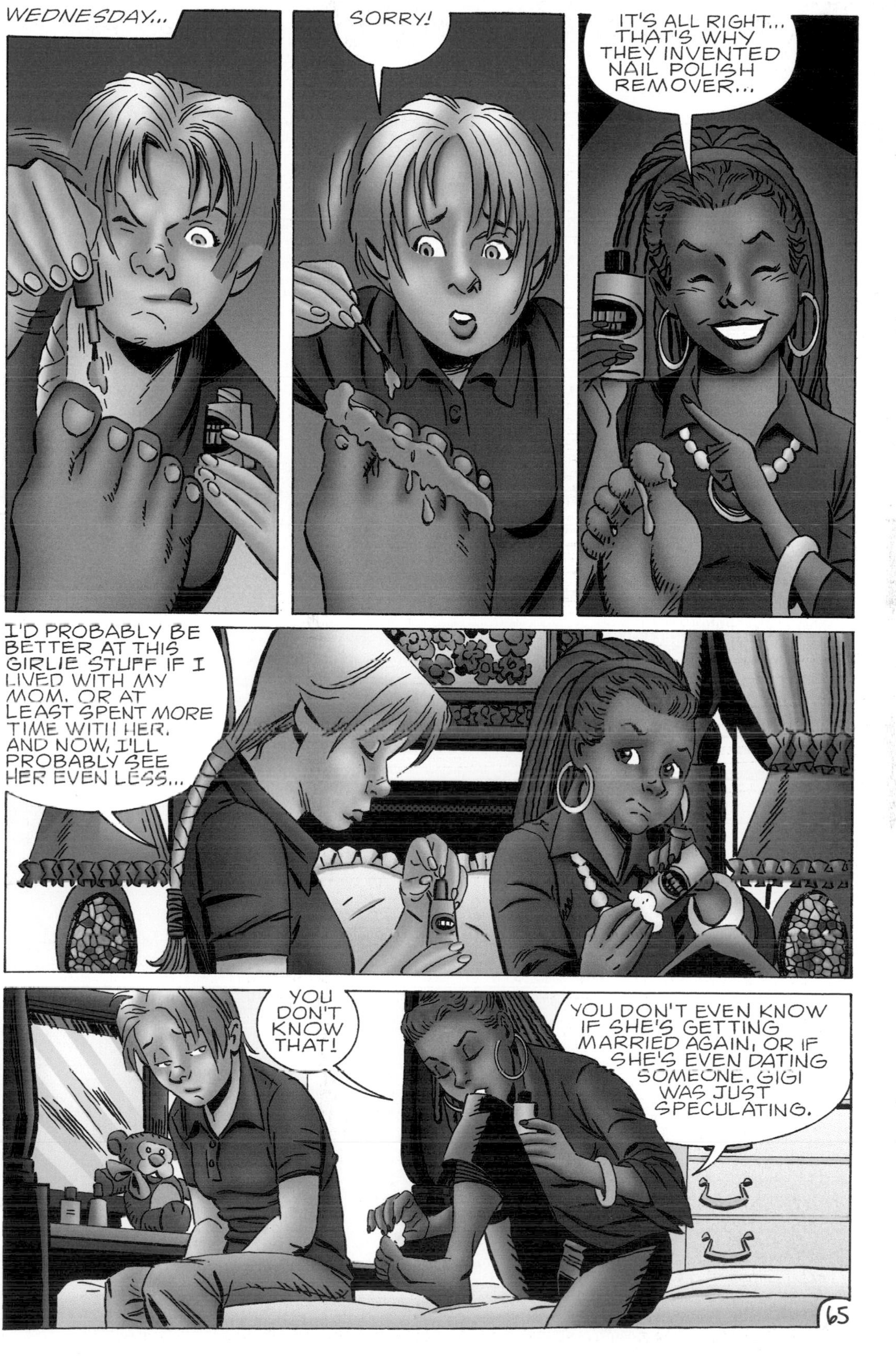
WEDNESDAY...
SORRY!
IT'S ALL RIGHT... THAT'S WHY THEY INVENTED NAIL POLISH REMOVER...
I'D PROBABLY BE BETTER AT THIS GIRLIE STUFF IF I LIVED WITH MY MOM. OR AT LEAST SPENT MORE TIME WITH HER. AND NOW, I'LL PROBABLY SEE HER EVEN LESS...
YOU DON'T KNOW THAT!
YOU DON'T EVEN KNOW IF SHE'S GETTING MARRIED AGAIN, OR IF SHE'S EVEN DATING SOMEONE. GIGI WAS JUST SPECULATING.

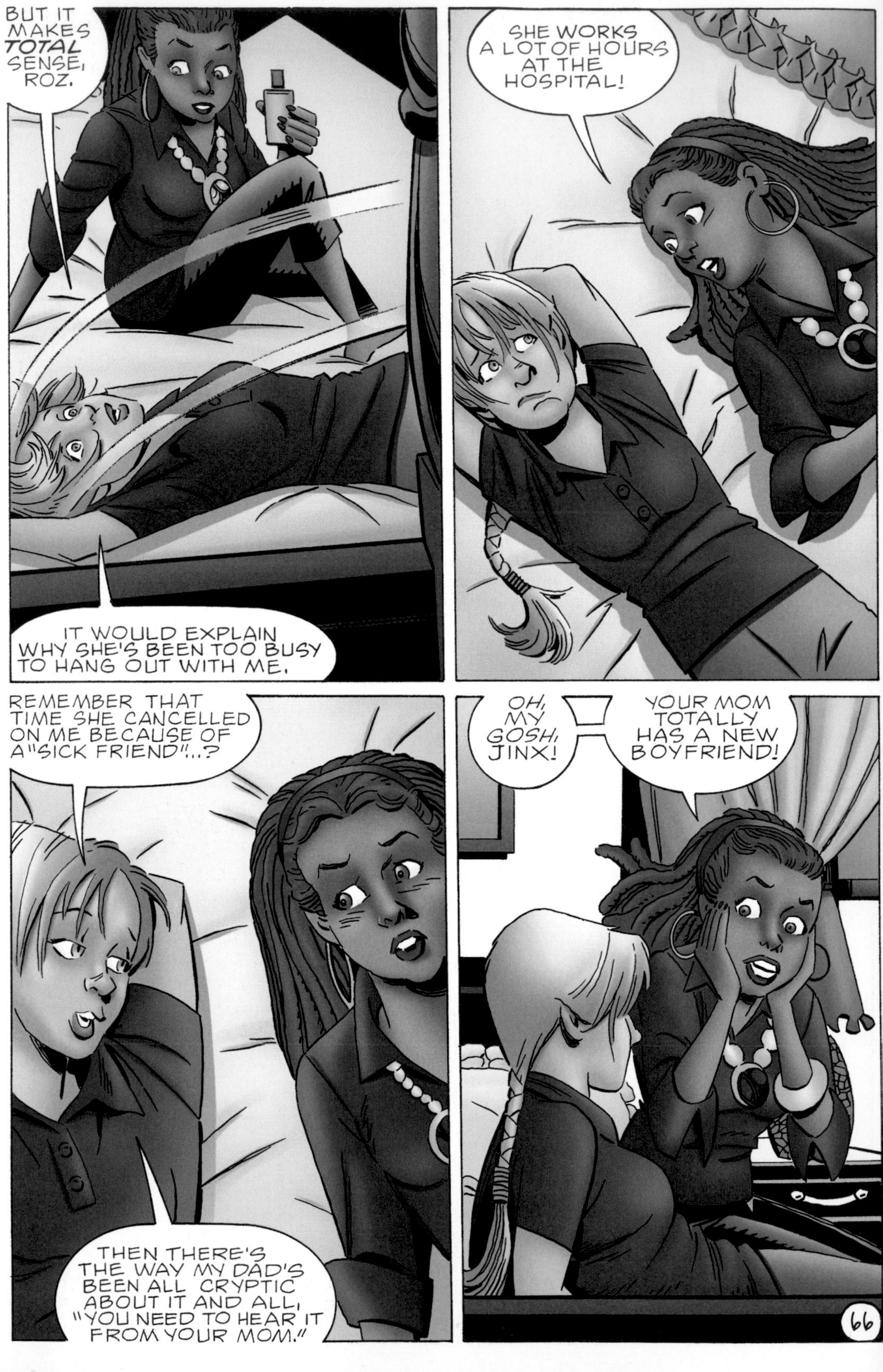
BUT IT MAKES **TOTAL** SENSE, ROZ.
IT WOULD EXPLAIN WHY SHE'S BEEN TOO BUSY TO HANG OUT WITH ME.
SHE WORKS A LOT OF HOURS AT THE HOSPITAL!
REMEMBER THAT TIME SHE CANCELLED ON ME BECAUSE OF A "SICK FRIEND"...?
THEN THERE'S THE WAY MY DAD'S BEEN ALL CRYPTIC ABOUT IT AND ALL, "YOU NEED TO HEAR IT FROM YOUR MOM."
OH, MY GOSH, JINX!
YOUR MOM TOTALLY HAS A NEW BOYFRIEND!

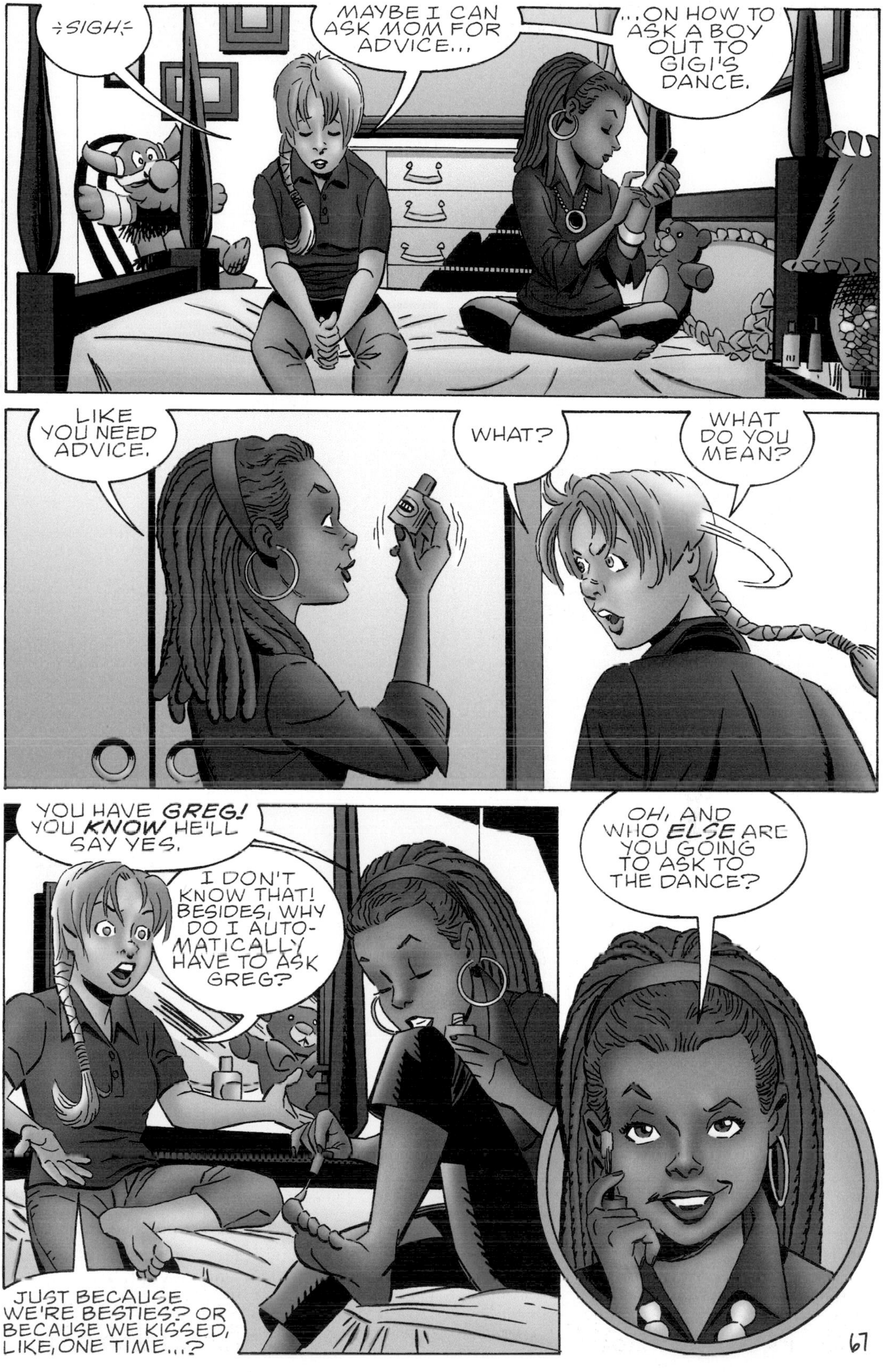

÷SIGH÷
MAYBE I CAN ASK MOM FOR ADVICE...
...ON HOW TO ASK A BOY OUT TO GIGI'S DANCE.
LIKE YOU NEED ADVICE.
WHAT?
WHAT DO YOU MEAN?
YOU HAVE GREG! YOU KNOW HE'LL SAY YES.
I DON'T KNOW THAT! BESIDES, WHY DO I AUTO-MATICALLY HAVE TO ASK GREG?
JUST BECAUSE WE'RE BESTIES? OR BECAUSE WE KISSED, LIKE, ONE TIME...?
OH, AND WHO ELSE ARE YOU GOING TO ASK TO THE DANCE?

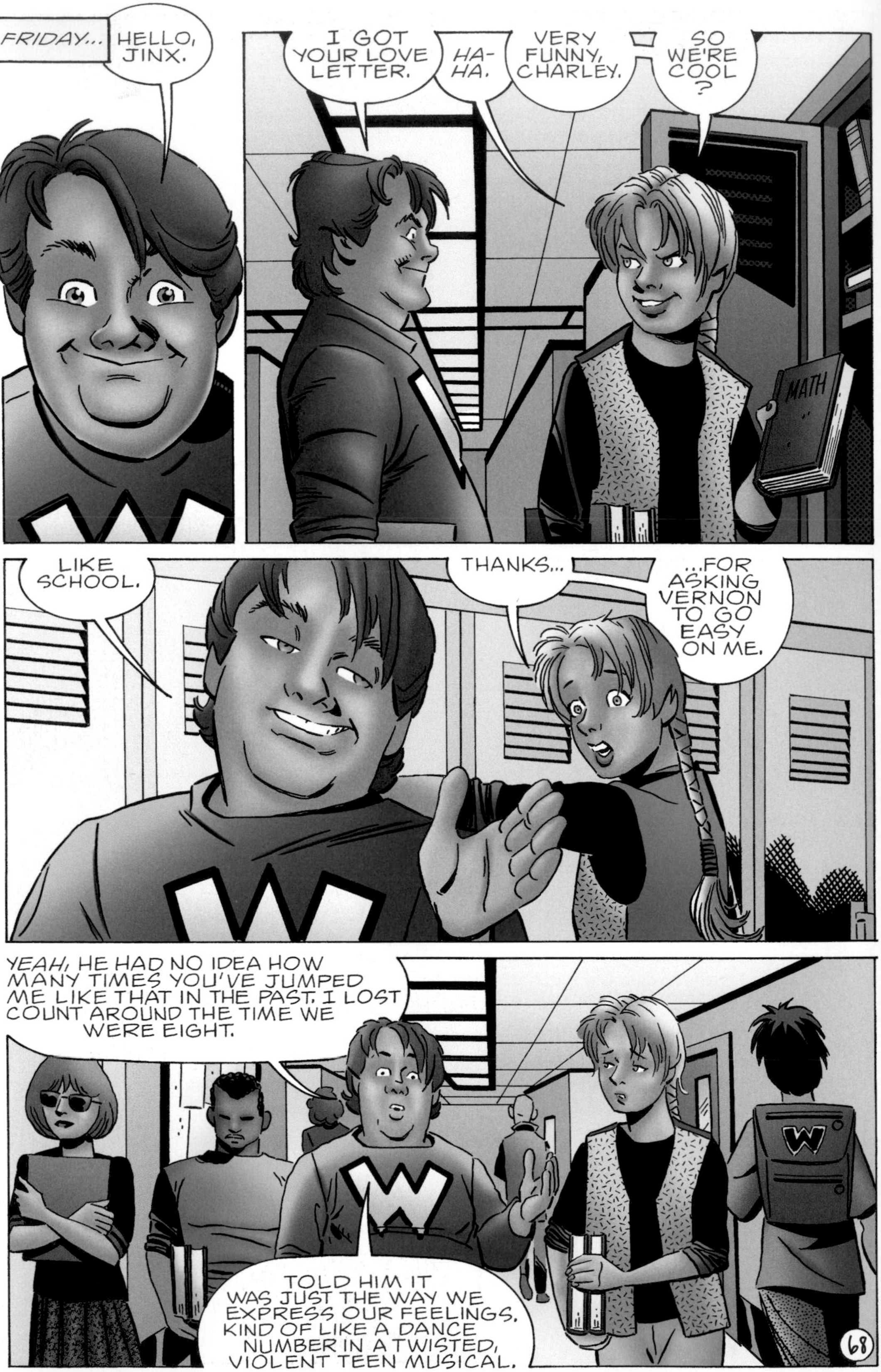
FRIDAY...
HELLO, JINX.
I GOT YOUR LOVE LETTER.
HA-HA.
VERY FUNNY, CHARLEY.
SO WE'RE COOL?
MATH
LIKE SCHOOL.
THANKS...
...FOR ASKING VERNON TO GO EASY ON ME.
YEAH, HE HAD NO IDEA HOW MANY TIMES YOU'VE JUMPED ME LIKE THAT IN THE PAST. I LOST COUNT AROUND THE TIME WE WERE EIGHT.
TOLD HIM IT WAS JUST THE WAY WE EXPRESS OUR FEELINGS. KIND OF LIKE A DANCE NUMBER IN A TWISTED, VIOLENT TEEN MUSICAL.

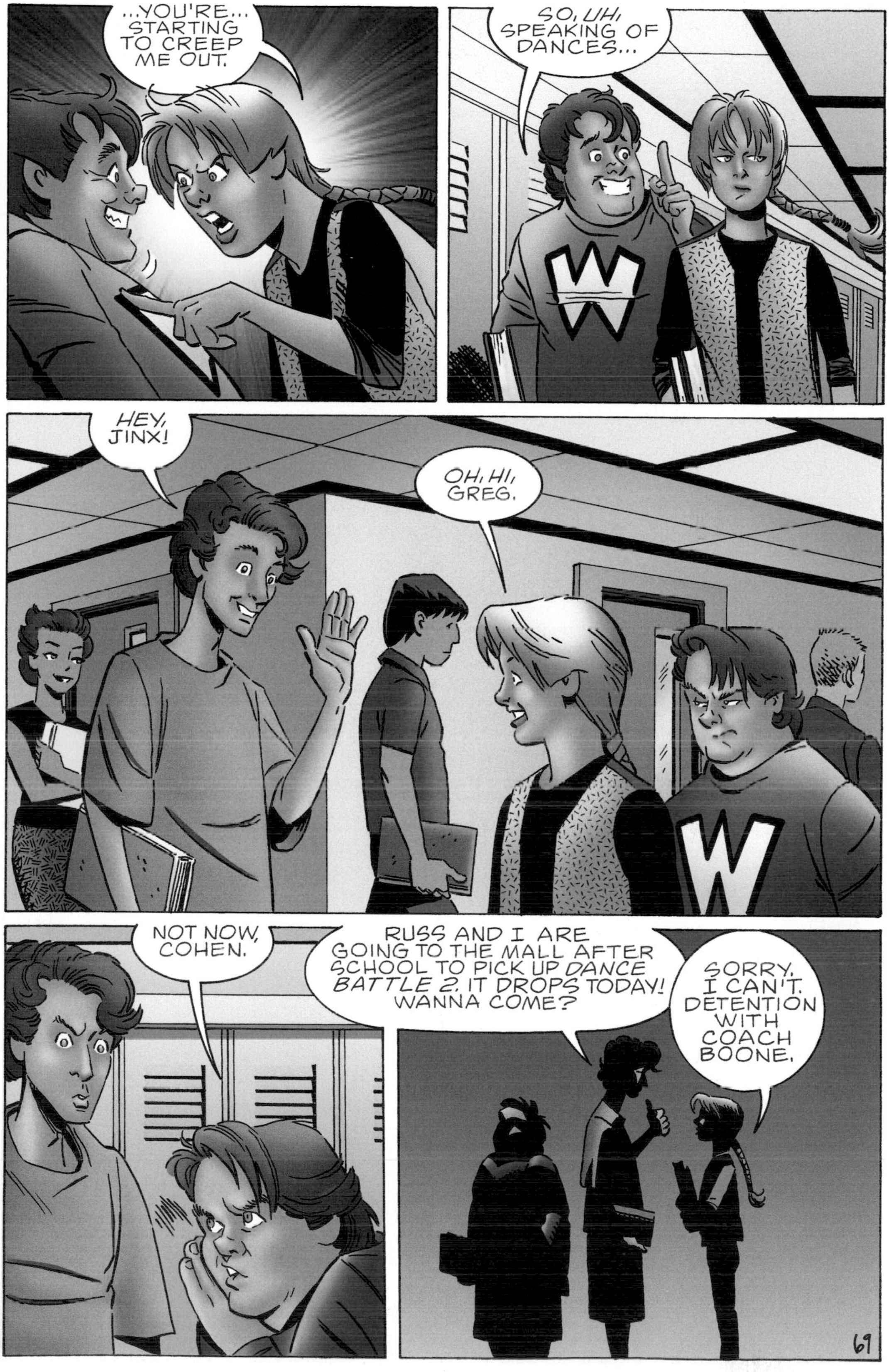
...YOU'RE... STARTING TO CREEP ME OUT.
SO, UH, SPEAKING OF DANCES...
HEY, JINX!
OH, HI, GREG.
NOT NOW, COHEN.
RUSS AND I ARE GOING TO THE MALL AFTER SCHOOL TO PICK UP DANCE BATTLE 2. IT DROPS TODAY! WANNA COME?
SORRY. I CAN'T. DETENTION WITH COACH BOONE.

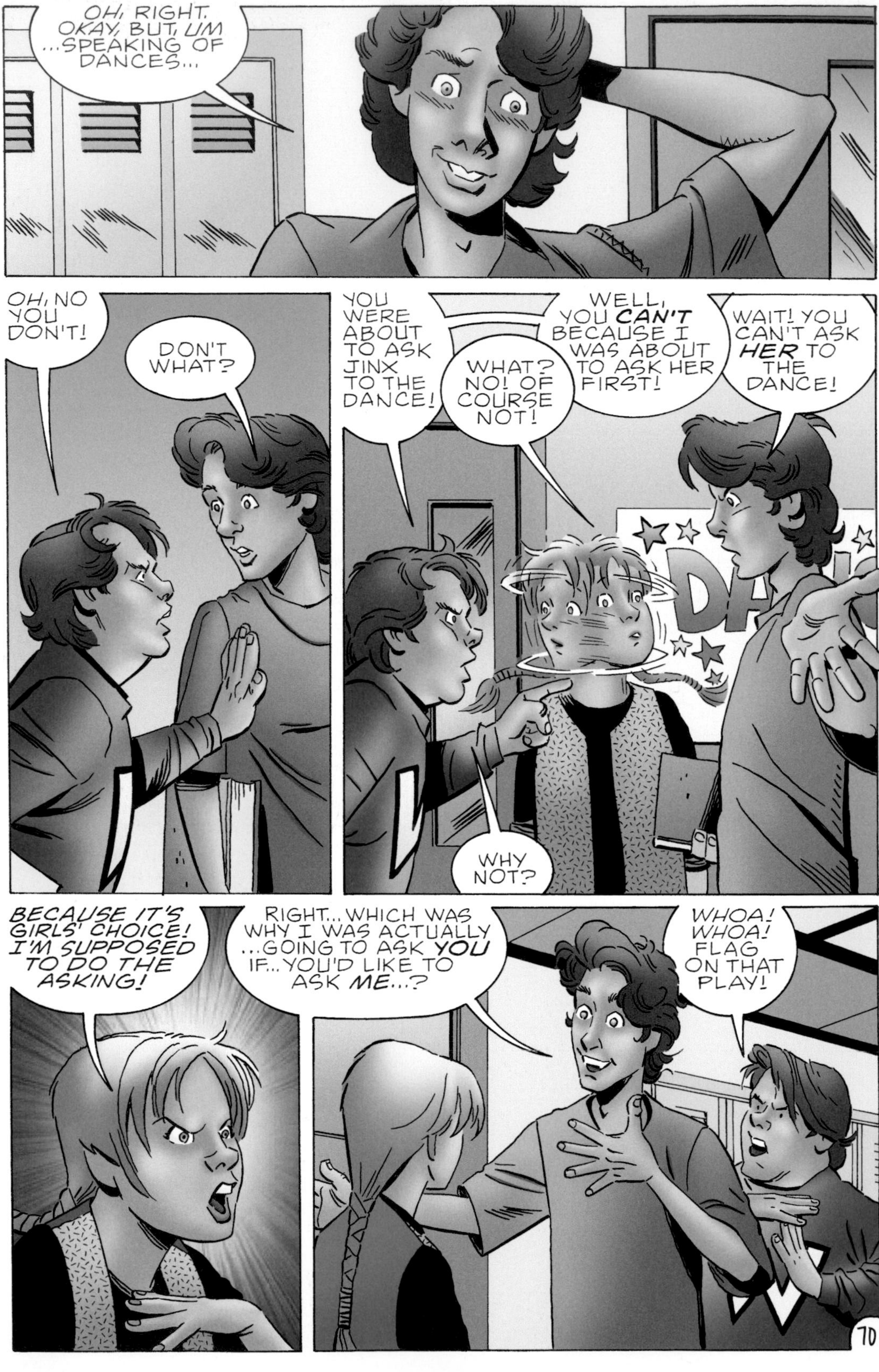
OH, RIGHT. OKAY, BUT, UM ...SPEAKING OF DANCES...
OH, NO YOU DON'T!
DON'T WHAT?
YOU WERE ABOUT TO ASK JINX TO THE DANCE!
WHAT? NO! OF COURSE NOT!
WELL, YOU CAN'T BECAUSE I WAS ABOUT TO ASK HER FIRST!
WAIT! YOU CAN'T ASK HER TO THE DANCE!
WHY NOT?
BECAUSE IT'S GIRLS' CHOICE! I'M SUPPOSED TO DO THE ASKING!
RIGHT... WHICH WAS WHY I WAS ACTUALLY ...GOING TO ASK YOU IF... YOU'D LIKE TO ASK ME...?
WHOA! WHOA! FLAG ON THAT PLAY!

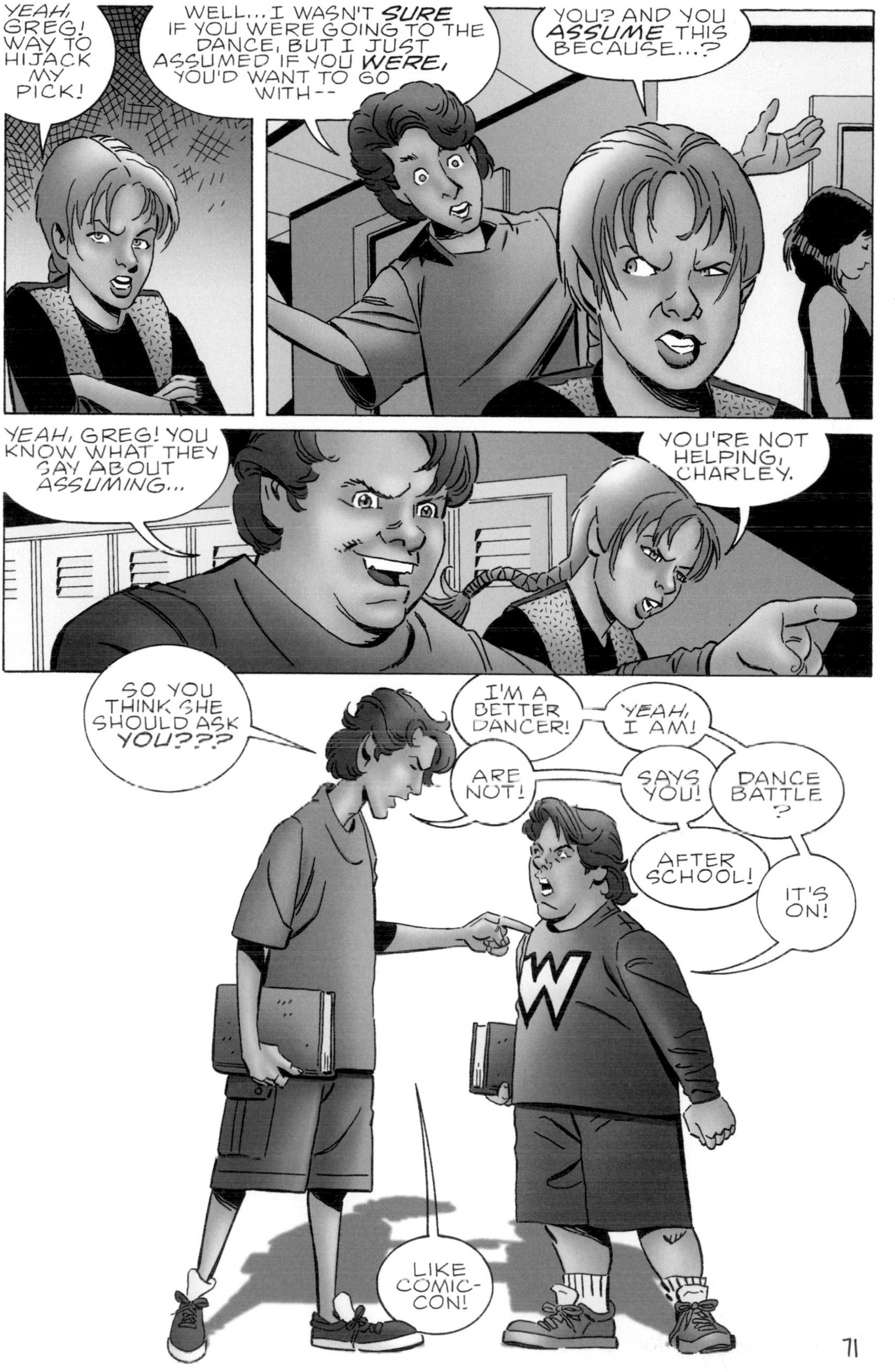
YEAH, GREG! WAY TO HIJACK MY PICK!
WELL... I WASN'T SURE IF YOU WERE GOING TO THE DANCE, BUT I JUST ASSUMED IF YOU WERE, YOU'D WANT TO GO WITH--
YOU? AND YOU ASSUME THIS BECAUSE...?
YEAH, GREG! YOU KNOW WHAT THEY SAY ABOUT ASSUMING...
YOU'RE NOT HELPING, CHARLEY.
SO YOU THINK SHE SHOULD ASK YOU???
I'M A BETTER DANCER!
ARE NOT!
YEAH, I AM!
SAYS YOU!
DANCE BATTLE?
AFTER SCHOOL!
IT'S ON!
LIKE COMIC-CON!

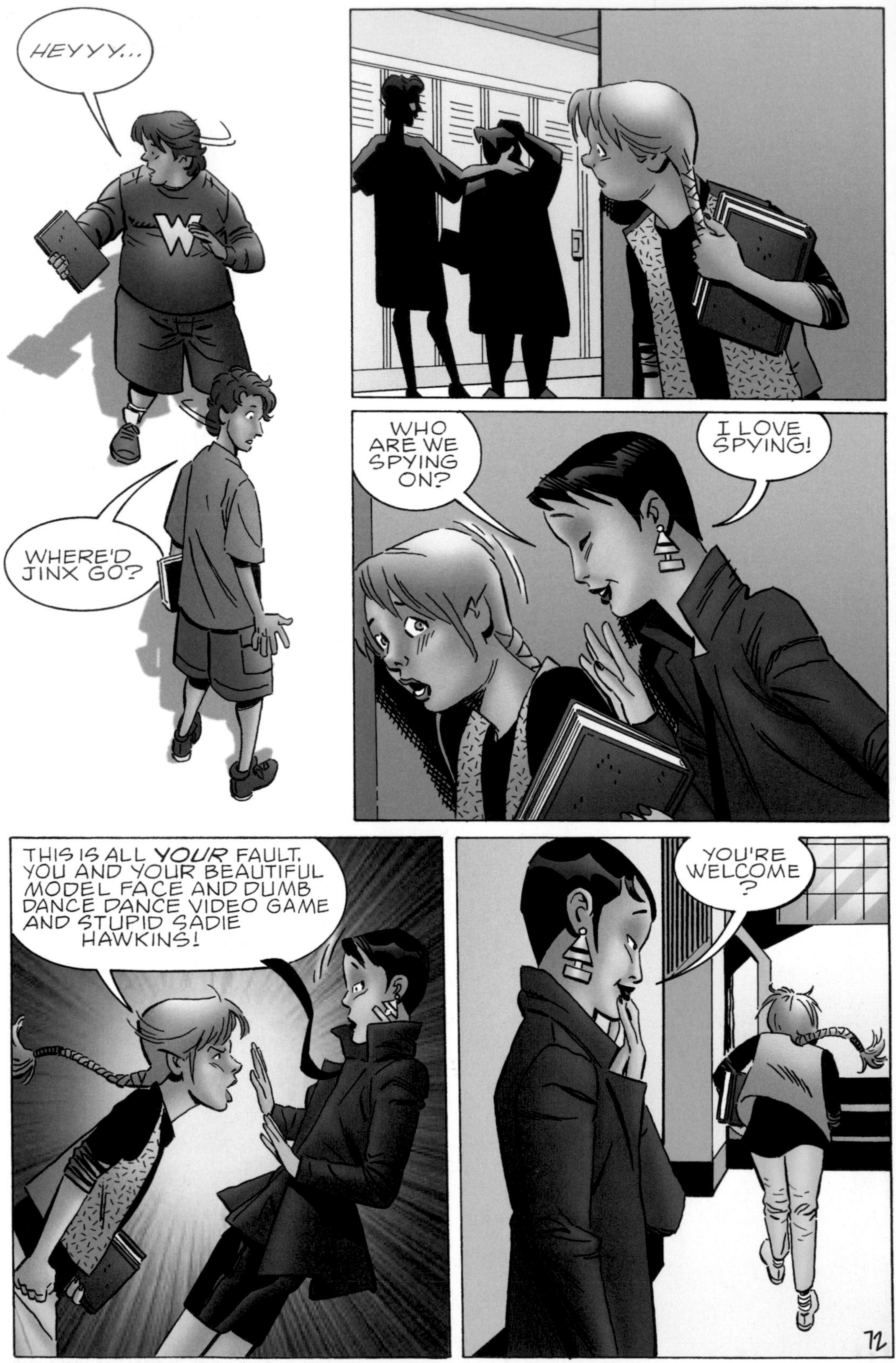
HEYYY...
WHERE'D JINX GO?
WHO ARE WE SPYING ON?
I LOVE SPYING!
THIS IS ALL YOUR FAULT. YOU AND YOUR BEAUTIFUL MODEL FACE AND DUMB DANCE DANCE VIDEO GAME AND STUPID SADIE HAWKINS!
YOU'RE WELCOME?
72

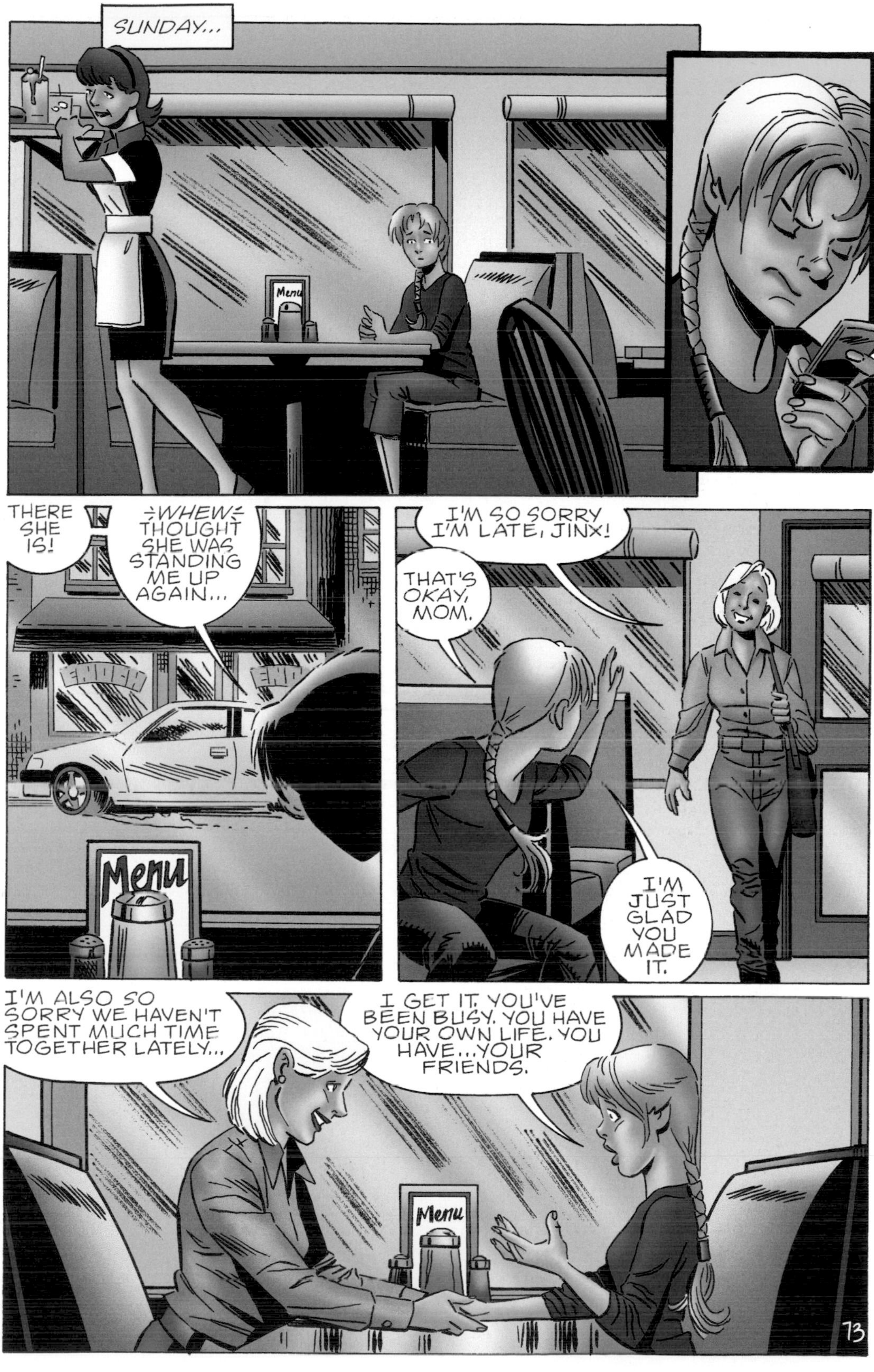
SUNDAY...
THERE SHE IS!
WHEW THOUGHT SHE WAS STANDING ME UP AGAIN...
Menu
I'M SO SORRY I'M LATE, JINX!
THAT'S OKAY, MOM.
I'M JUST GLAD YOU MADE IT.
I'M ALSO SO SORRY WE HAVEN'T SPENT MUCH TIME TOGETHER LATELY...
I GET IT. YOU'VE BEEN BUSY. YOU HAVE YOUR OWN LIFE. YOU HAVE...YOUR FRIENDS.
Menu

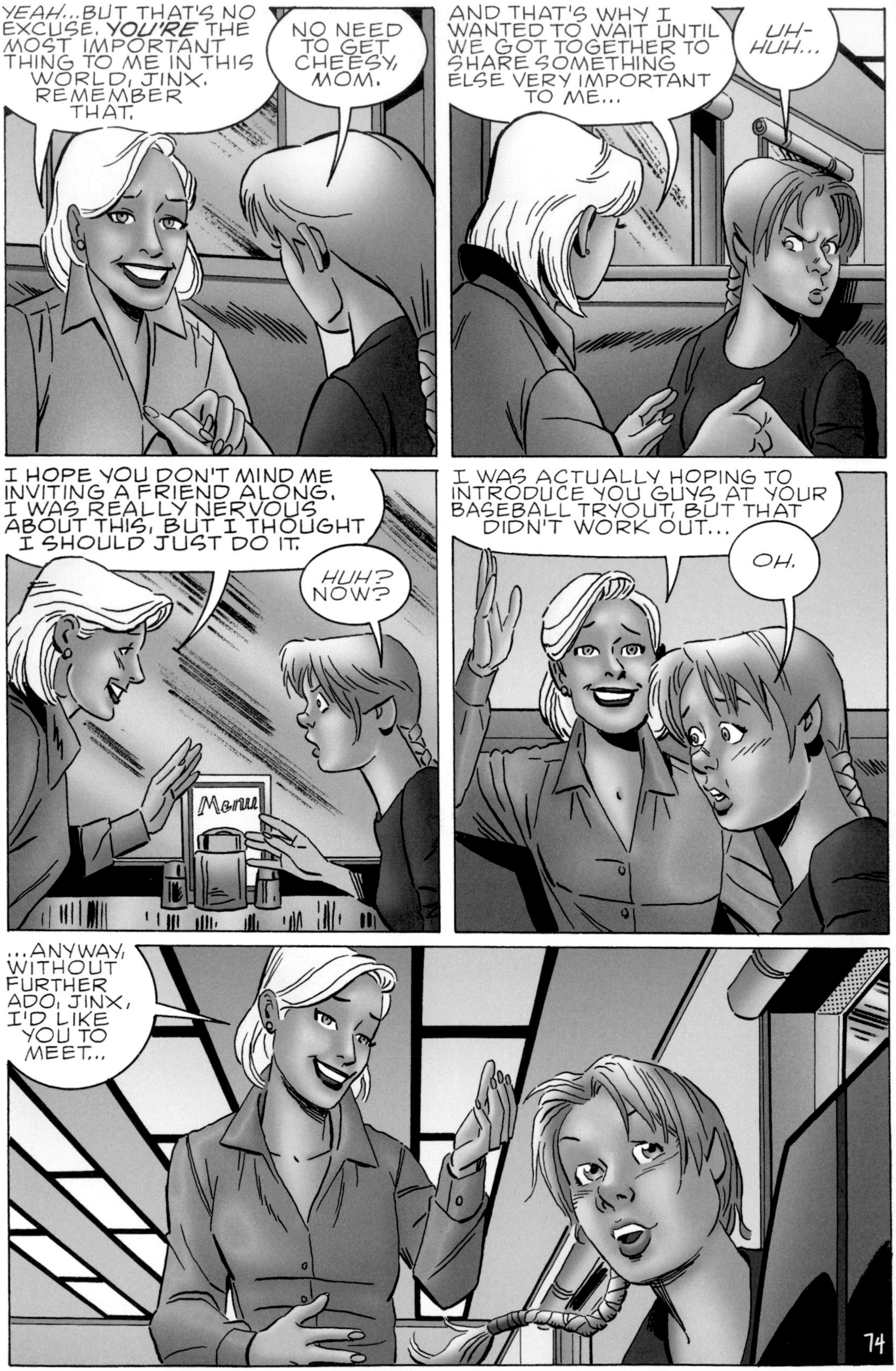

YEAH...BUT THAT'S NO EXCUSE. **YOU'RE** THE MOST IMPORTANT THING TO ME IN THIS WORLD, JINX. REMEMBER THAT.
NO NEED TO GET CHEESY, MOM.
AND THAT'S WHY I WANTED TO WAIT UNTIL WE GOT TOGETHER TO SHARE SOMETHING ELSE VERY IMPORTANT TO ME...
UH-HUH...
I HOPE YOU DON'T MIND ME INVITING A FRIEND ALONG. I WAS REALLY NERVOUS ABOUT THIS, BUT I THOUGHT I SHOULD JUST DO IT.
HUH? NOW?
Menu
I WAS ACTUALLY HOPING TO INTRODUCE YOU GUYS AT YOUR BASEBALL TRYOUT, BUT THAT DIDN'T WORK OUT...
OH.
...ANYWAY, WITHOUT FURTHER ADO, JINX, I'D LIKE YOU TO MEET...

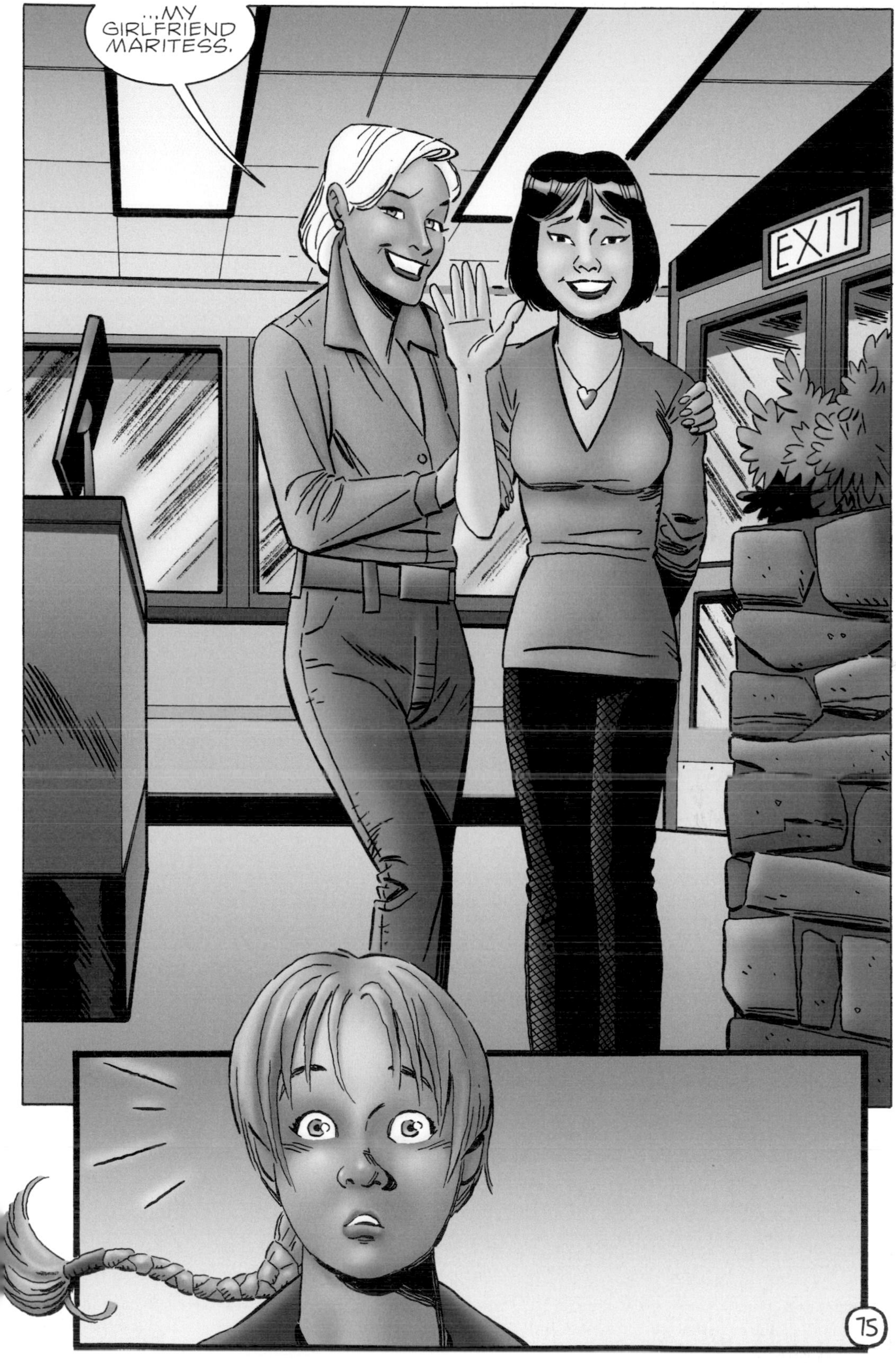
...MY GIRLFRIEND MARITESS.
EXIT

Jinx™

CHAPTER 4

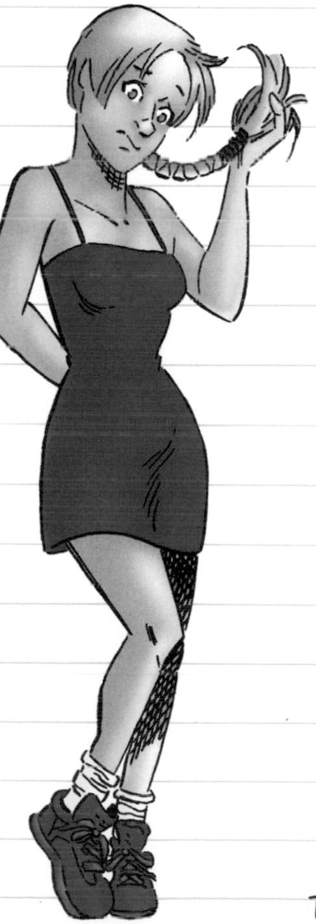

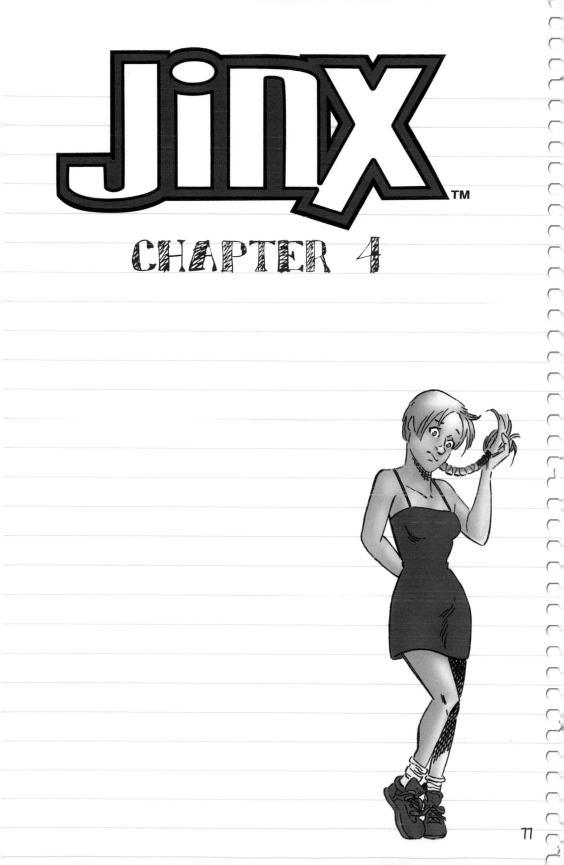

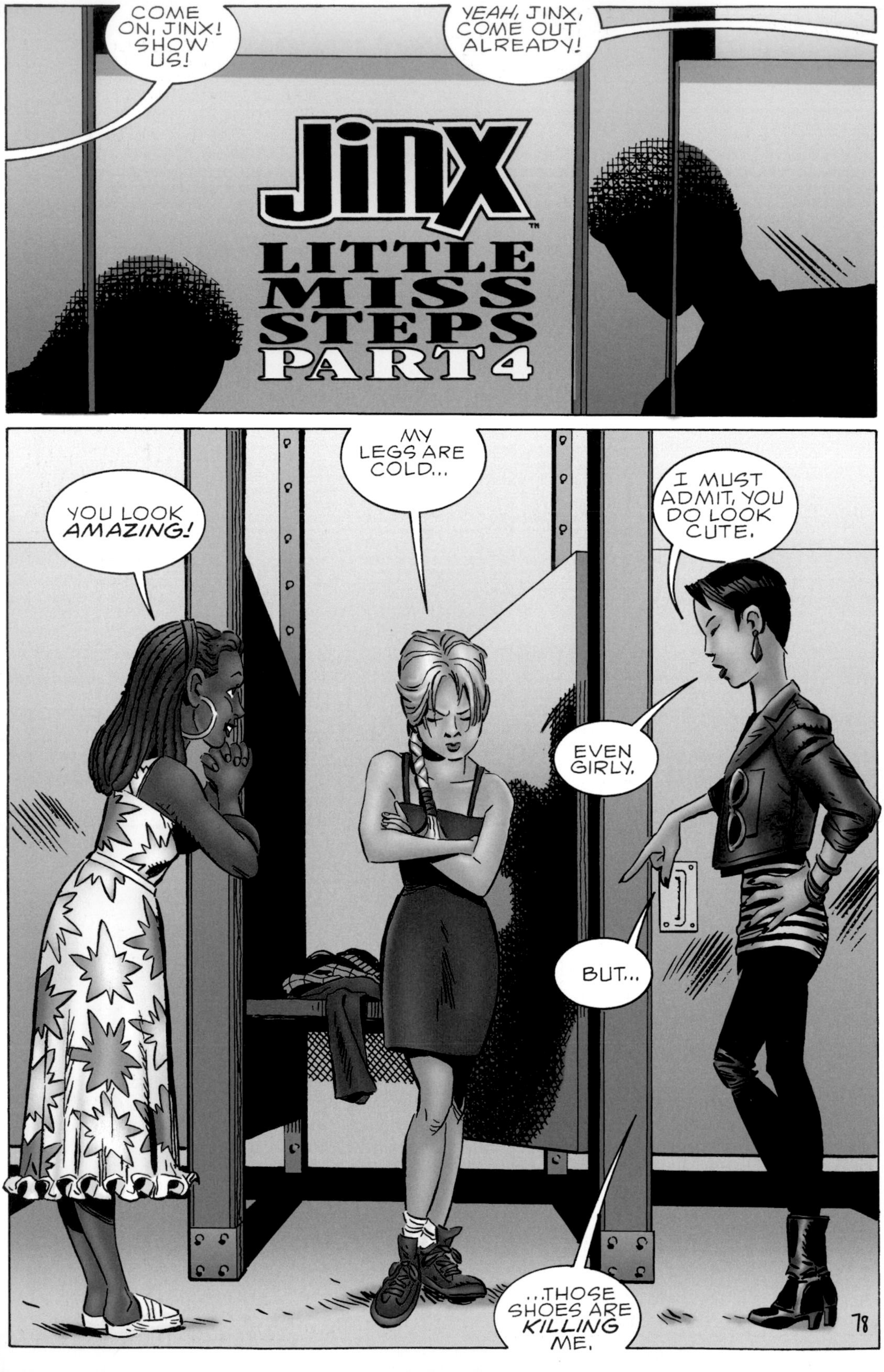

COME ON, JINX! SHOW US!
YEAH, JINX, COME OUT ALREADY!
JINX™
LITTLE MISS STEPS PART 4
YOU LOOK AMAZING!
MY LEGS ARE COLD...
I MUST ADMIT, YOU DO LOOK CUTE.
EVEN GIRLY.
BUT...
...THOSE SHOES ARE KILLING ME.

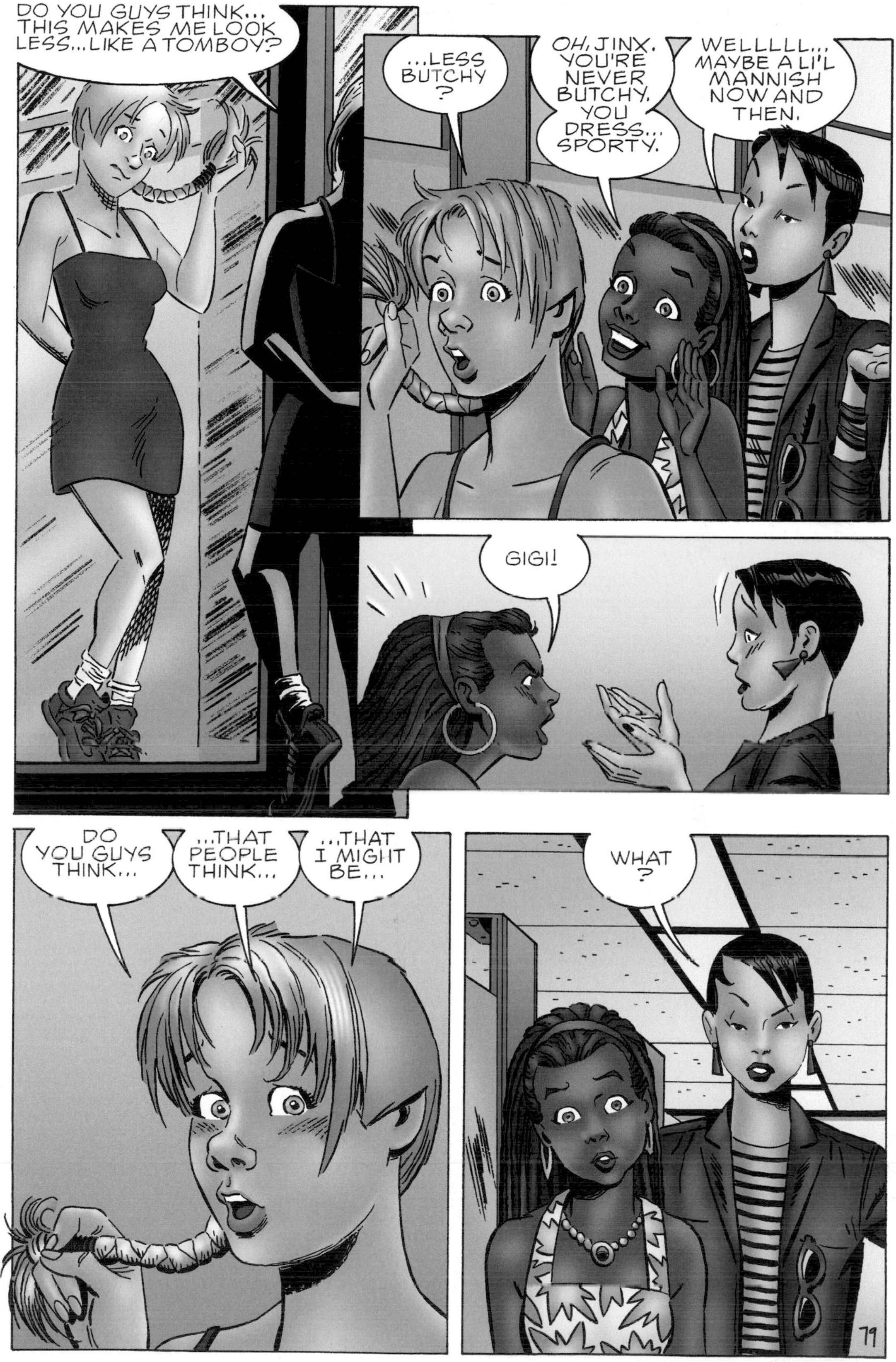
DO YOU GUYS THINK... THIS MAKES ME LOOK LESS...LIKE A TOMBOY?
...LESS BUTCHY?
OH, JINX. YOU'RE NEVER BUTCHY. YOU DRESS... SPORTY.
WELLLLL... MAYBE A LI'L MANNISH NOW AND THEN.
GIGI!
DO YOU GUYS THINK...
...THAT PEOPLE THINK...
...THAT I MIGHT BE...
WHAT?

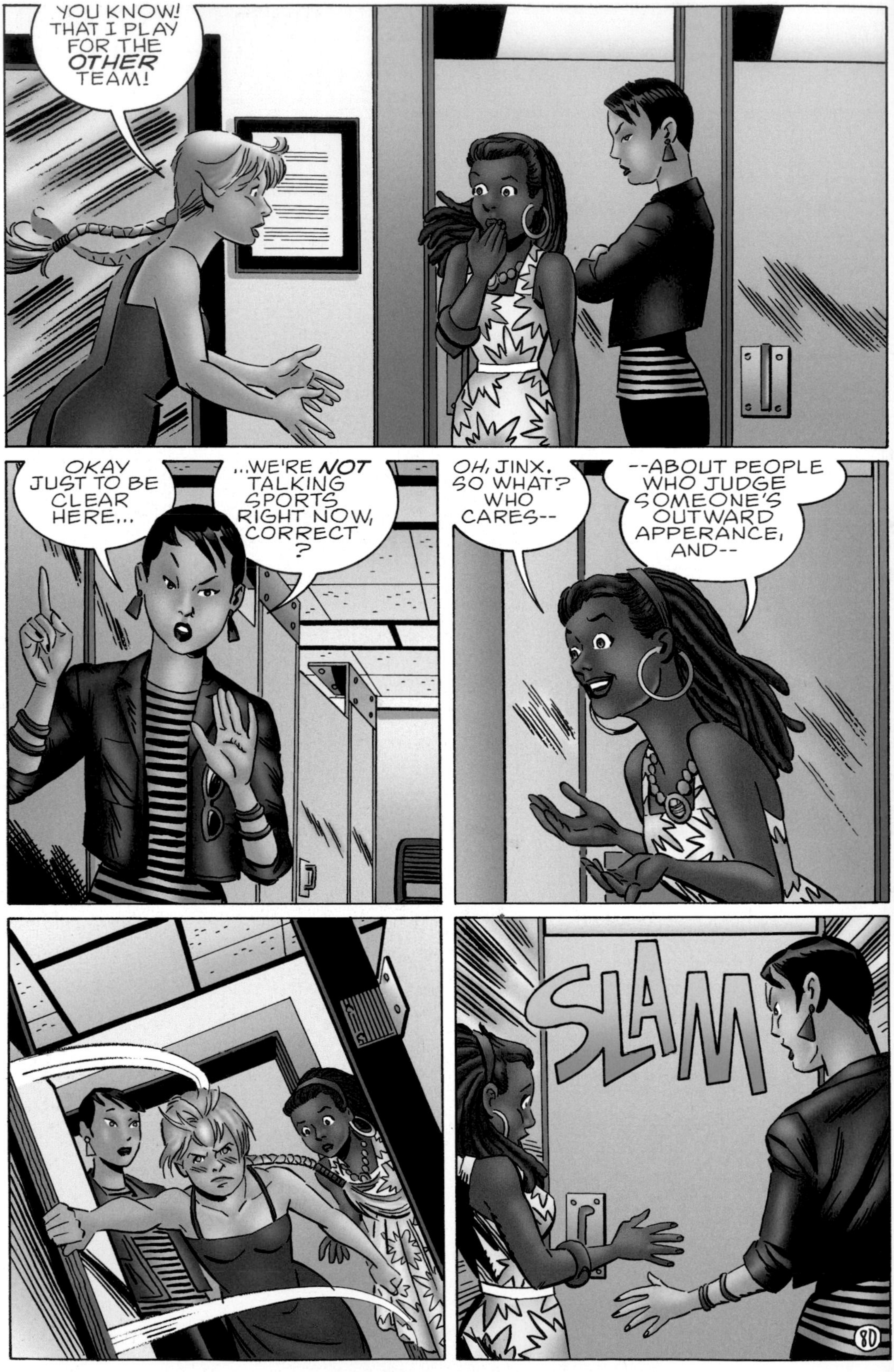
YOU KNOW! THAT I PLAY FOR THE OTHER TEAM!
OKAY JUST TO BE CLEAR HERE...
...WE'RE NOT TALKING SPORTS RIGHT NOW, CORRECT?
OH, JINX. SO WHAT? WHO CARES--
--ABOUT PEOPLE WHO JUDGE SOMEONE'S OUTWARD APPERANCE, AND--
SLAM

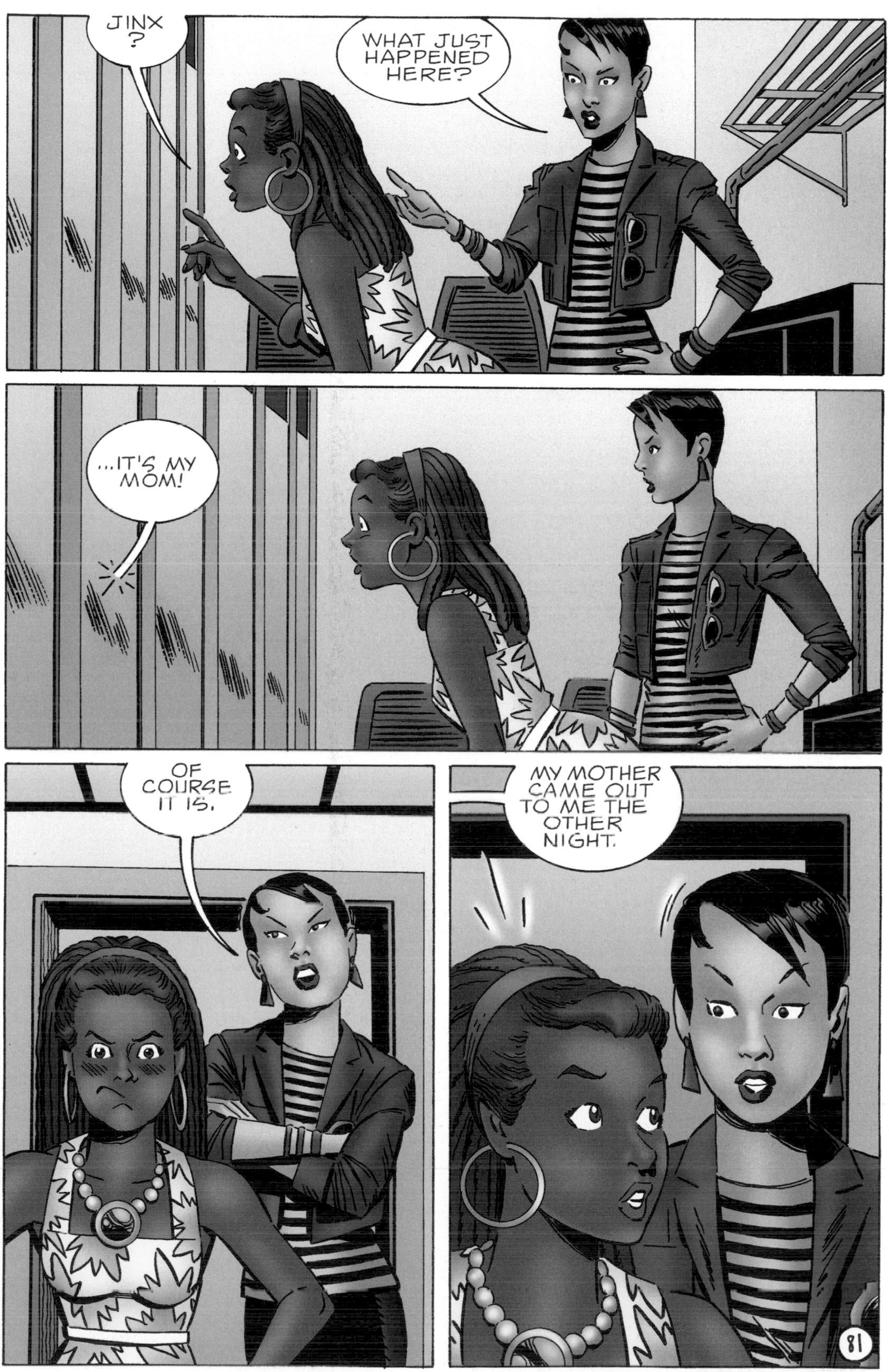

JINX?
WHAT JUST HAPPENED HERE?
...IT'S MY MOM!
OF COURSE IT IS.
MY MOTHER CAME OUT TO ME THE OTHER NIGHT.

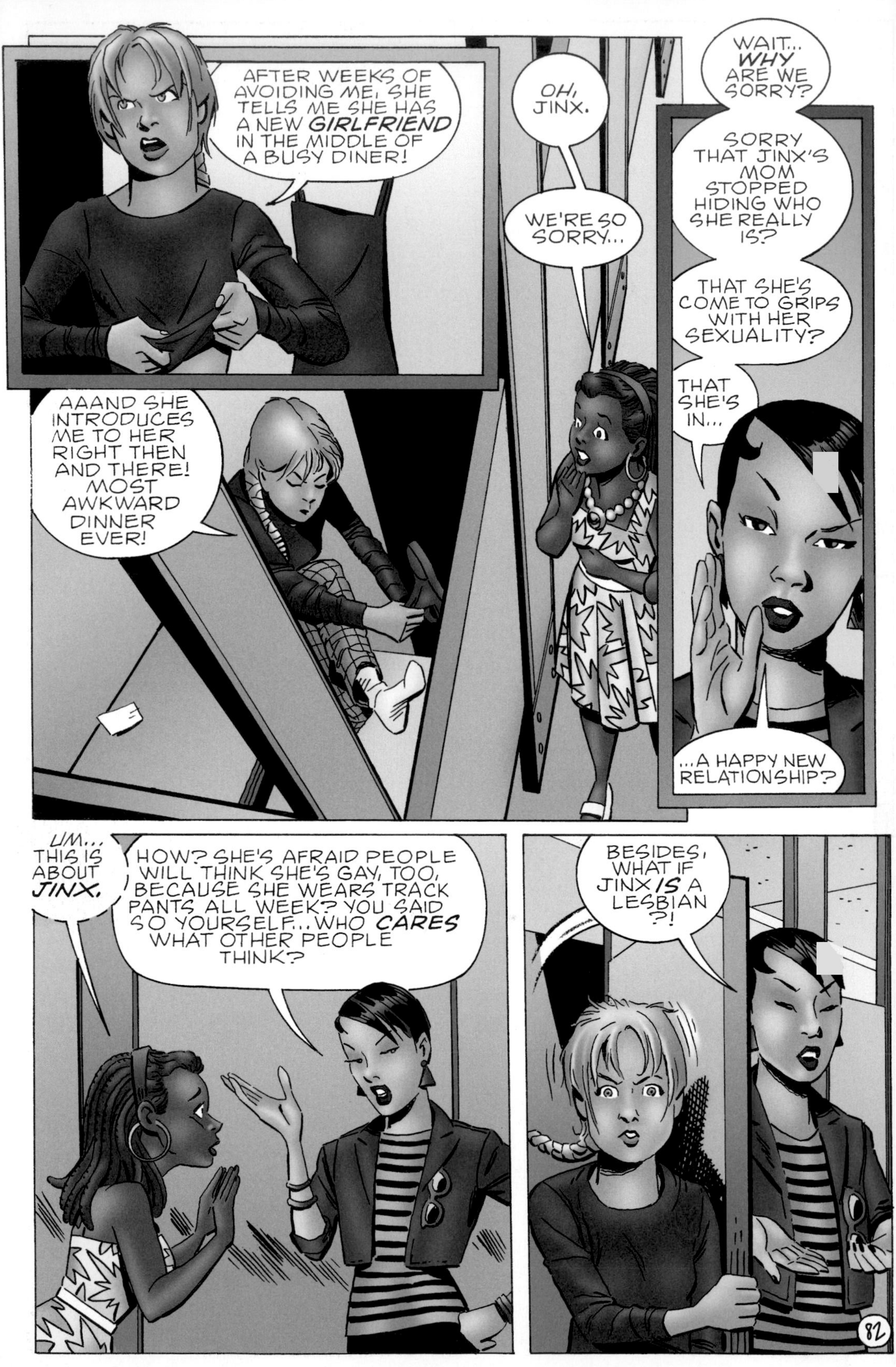
AFTER WEEKS OF AVOIDING ME, SHE TELLS ME SHE HAS A NEW GIRLFRIEND IN THE MIDDLE OF A BUSY DINER!
OH, JINX.
WE'RE SO SORRY...
WAIT... WHY ARE WE SORRY?
SORRY THAT JINX'S MOM STOPPED HIDING WHO SHE REALLY IS?
THAT SHE'S COME TO GRIPS WITH HER SEXUALITY?
THAT SHE'S IN...
...A HAPPY NEW RELATIONSHIP?
AAAND SHE INTRODUCES ME TO HER RIGHT THEN AND THERE! MOST AWKWARD DINNER EVER!
UM... THIS IS ABOUT JINX.
HOW? SHE'S AFRAID PEOPLE WILL THINK SHE'S GAY, TOO, BECAUSE SHE WEARS TRACK PANTS ALL WEEK? YOU SAID SO YOURSELF... WHO CARES WHAT OTHER PEOPLE THINK?
BESIDES, WHAT IF JINX IS A LESBIAN ?!
82

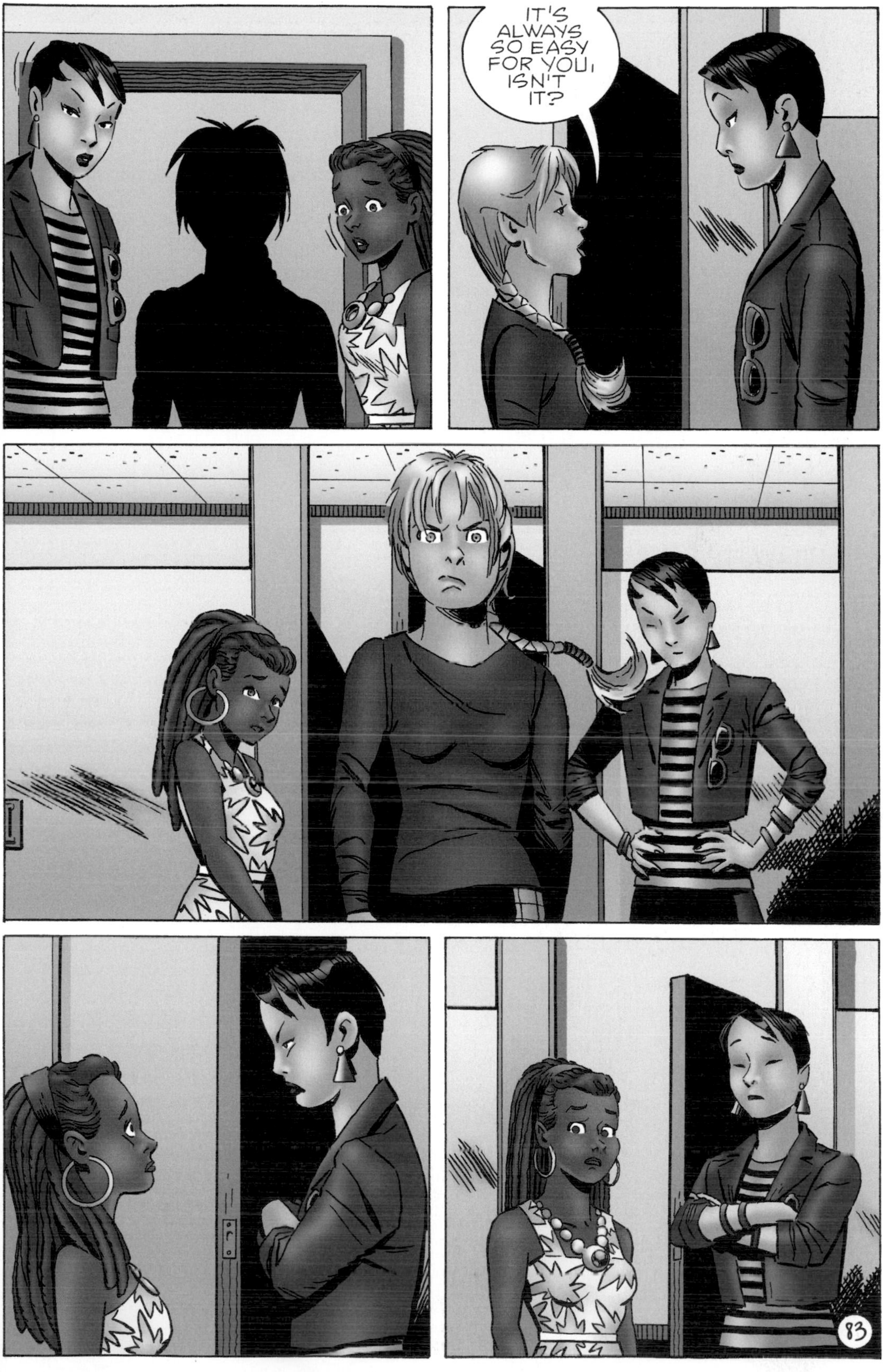
IT'S ALWAYS SO EASY FOR YOU, ISN'T IT?

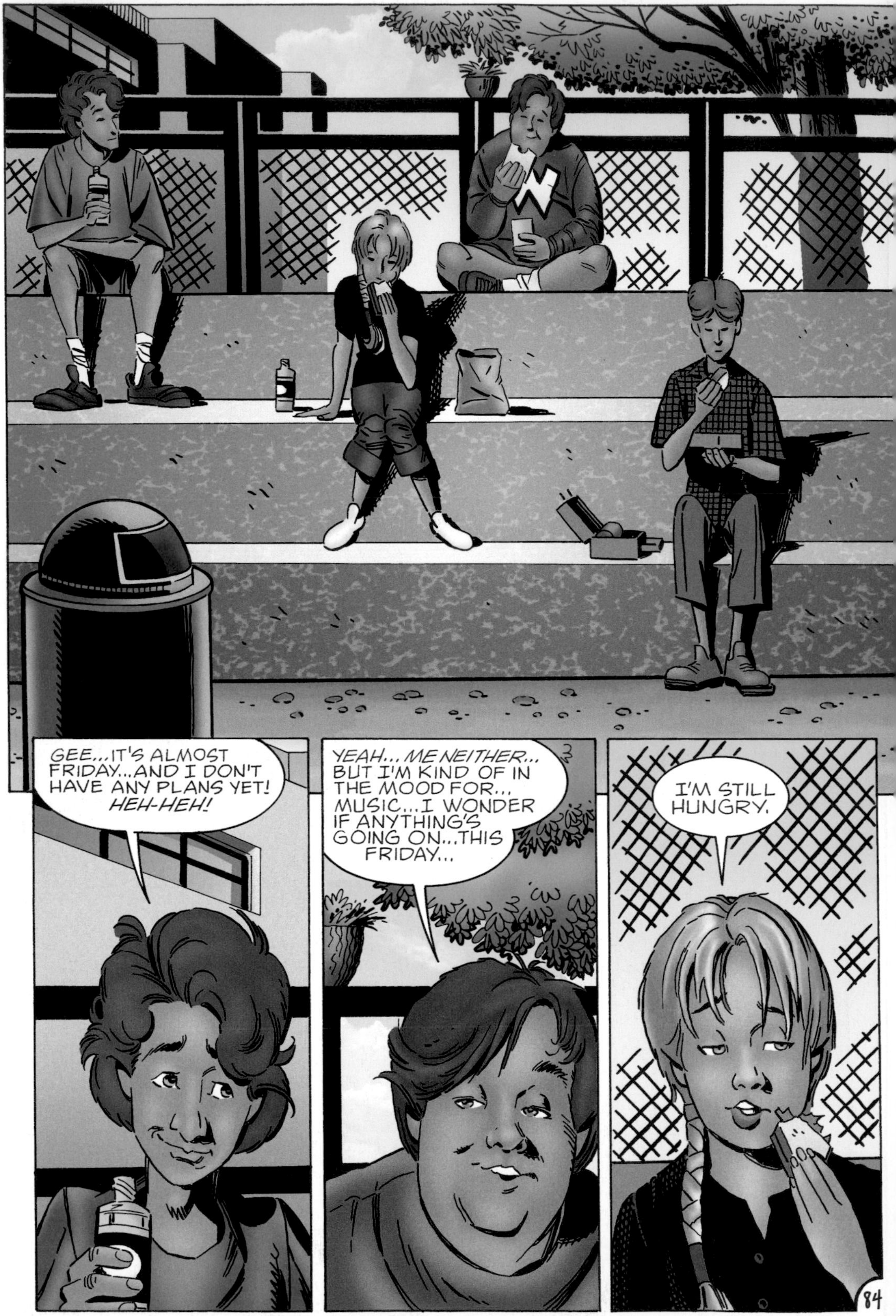
GEE... IT'S ALMOST FRIDAY... AND I DON'T HAVE ANY PLANS YET! HEH-HEH!
YEAH... ME NEITHER... BUT I'M KIND OF IN THE MOOD FOR... MUSIC... I WONDER IF ANYTHING'S GOING ON... THIS FRIDAY...
I'M STILL HUNGRY.

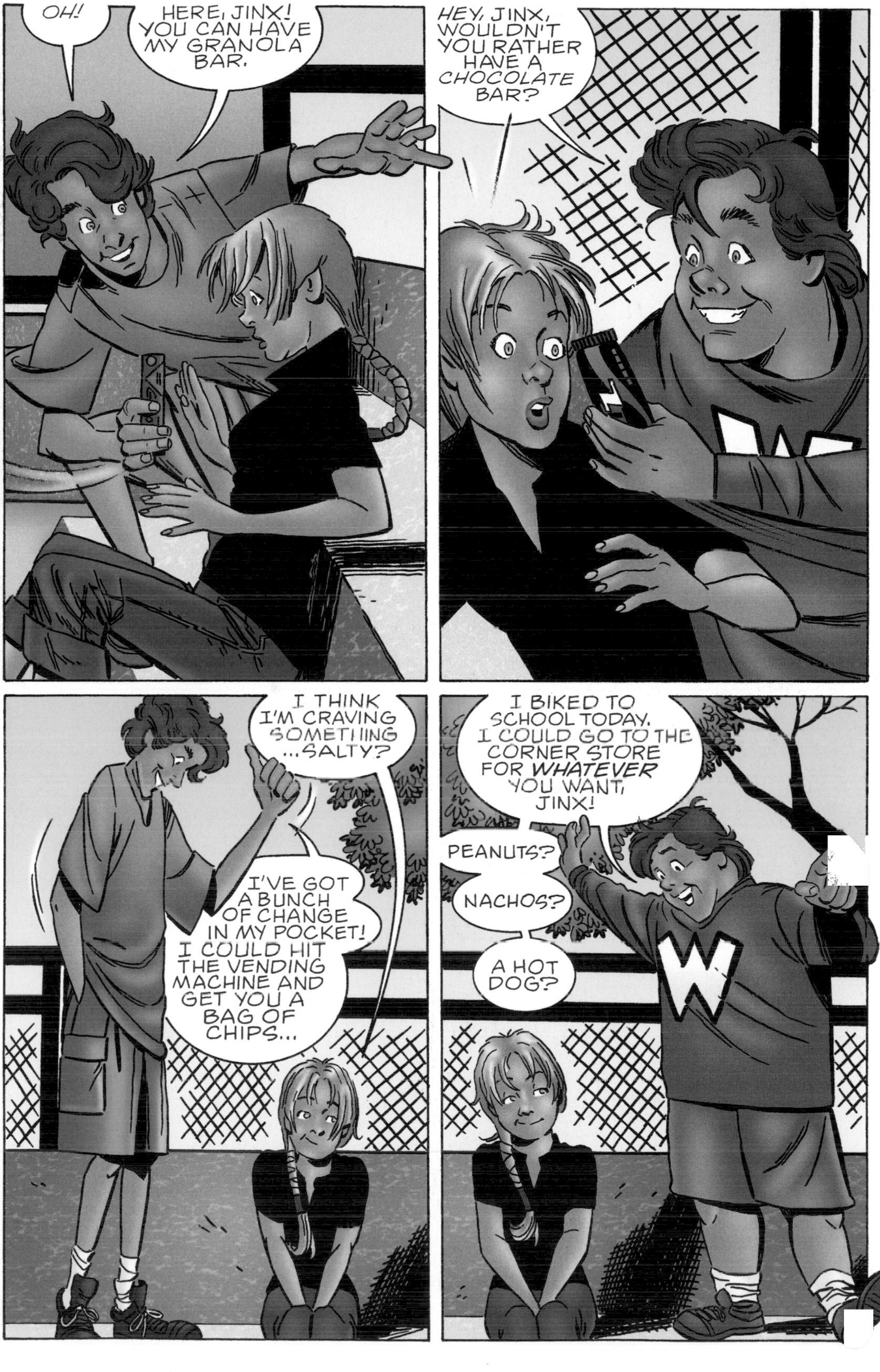
OH!
HERE, JINX! YOU CAN HAVE MY GRANOLA BAR.
HEY, JINX, WOULDN'T YOU RATHER HAVE A CHOCOLATE BAR?
I THINK I'M CRAVING SOMETHING ...SALTY?
I'VE GOT A BUNCH OF CHANGE IN MY POCKET! I COULD HIT THE VENDING MACHINE AND GET YOU A BAG OF CHIPS...
I BIKED TO SCHOOL TODAY. I COULD GO TO THE CORNER STORE FOR WHATEVER YOU WANT, JINX!
PEANUTS?
NACHOS?
A HOT DOG?

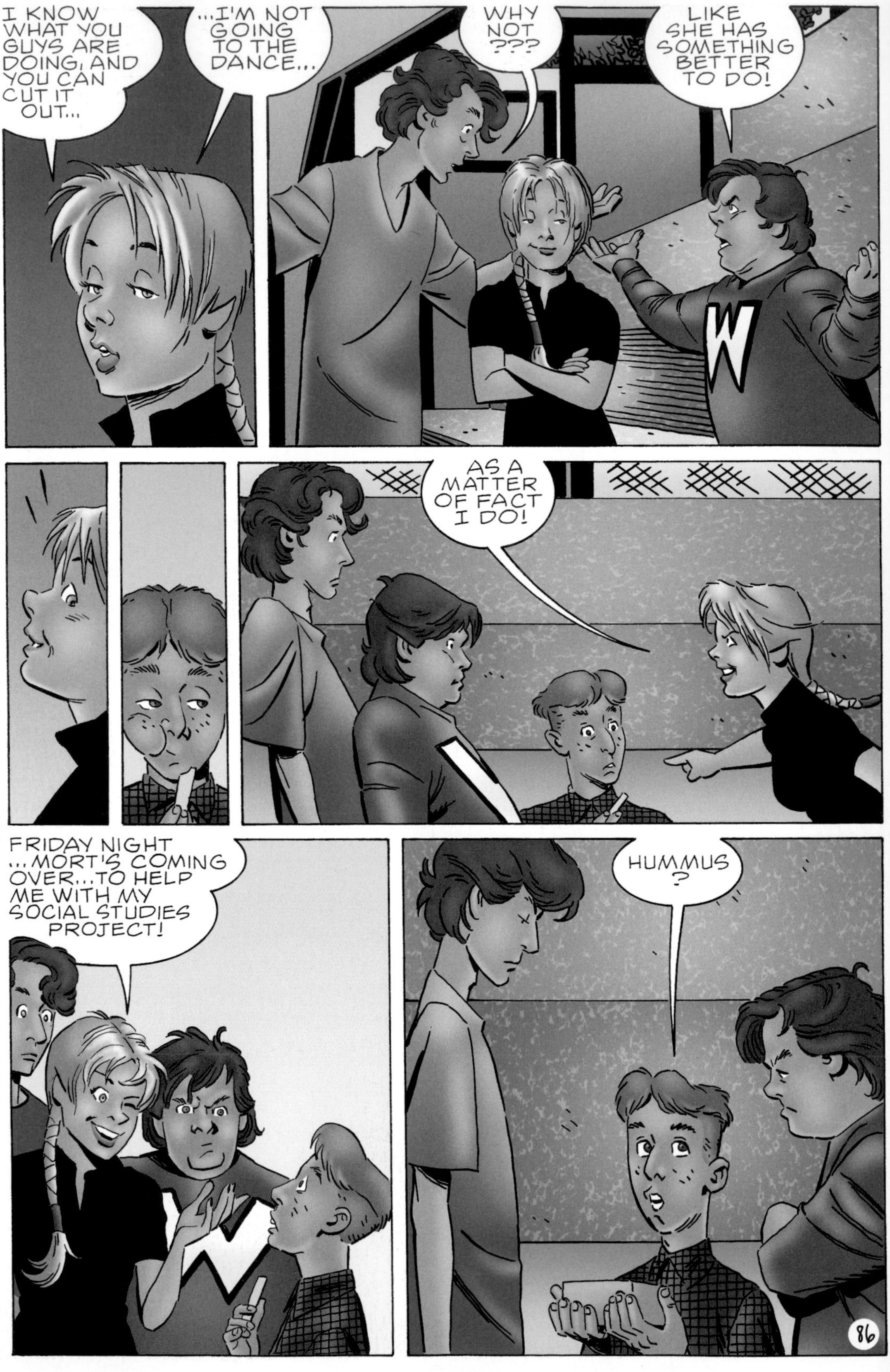
I KNOW WHAT YOU GUYS ARE DOING, AND YOU CAN CUT IT OUT...
...I'M NOT GOING TO THE DANCE...
WHY NOT ???
LIKE SHE HAS SOMETHING BETTER TO DO!
AS A MATTER OF FACT I DO!
FRIDAY NIGHT ...MORT'S COMING OVER...TO HELP ME WITH MY SOCIAL STUDIES PROJECT!
HUMMUS ?

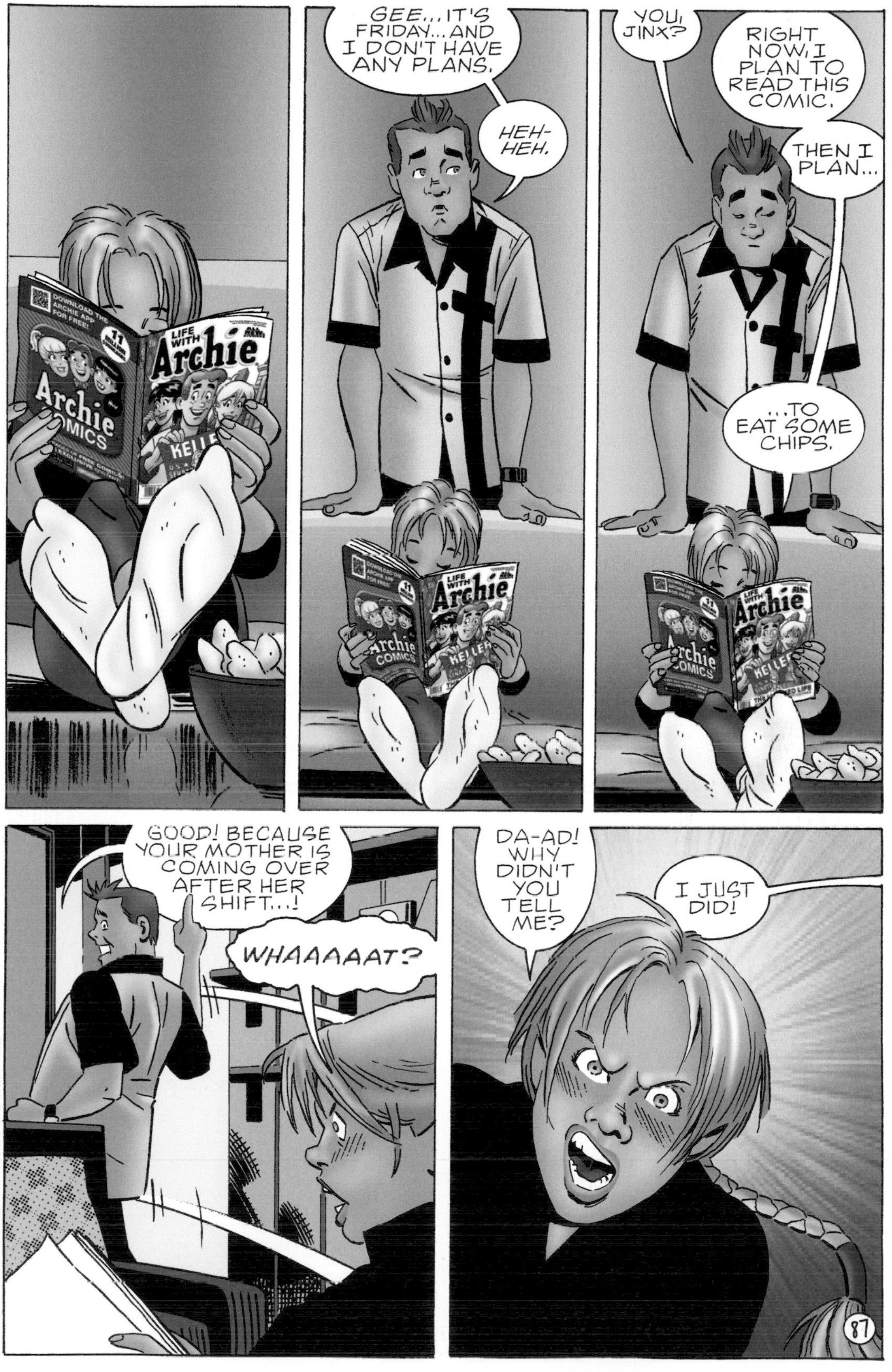

DOWNLOAD THE ARCHIE APP FOR FREE!
LIFE WITH Archie
Archie COMICS
GEE... IT'S FRIDAY... AND I DON'T HAVE ANY PLANS.
HEH-HEH.
YOU, JINX?
RIGHT NOW, I PLAN TO READ THIS COMIC.
THEN I PLAN...
...TO EAT SOME CHIPS.
GOOD! BECAUSE YOUR MOTHER IS COMING OVER AFTER HER SHIFT...!
WHAAAAAT?
DA-AD! WHY DIDN'T YOU TELL ME?
I JUST DID!

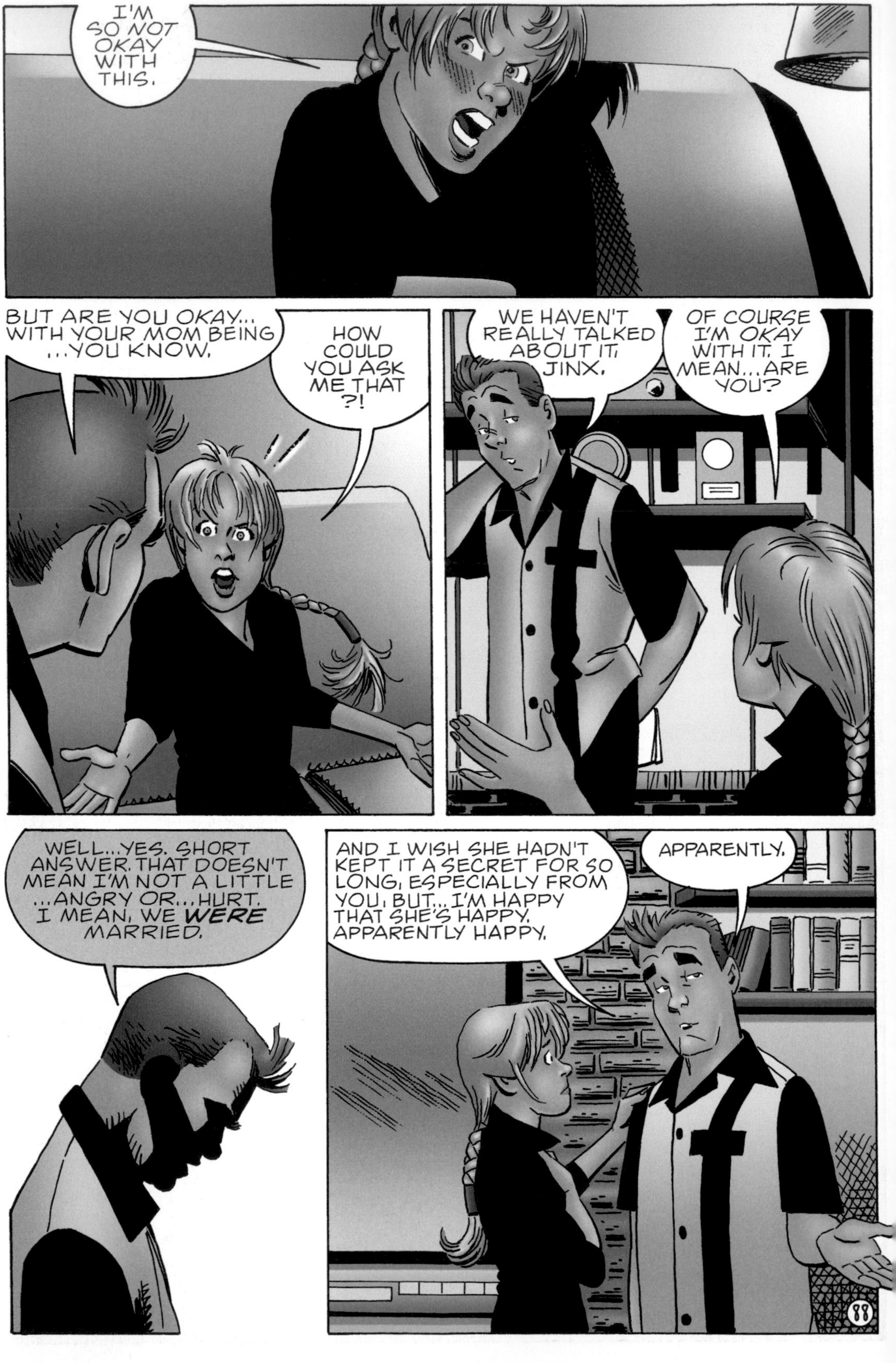
I'M SO NOT OKAY WITH THIS.
BUT ARE YOU OKAY... WITH YOUR MOM BEING ...YOU KNOW.
HOW COULD YOU ASK ME THAT ?!
WE HAVEN'T REALLY TALKED ABOUT IT, JINX.
OF COURSE I'M OKAY WITH IT. I MEAN... ARE YOU?
WELL... YES. SHORT ANSWER. THAT DOESN'T MEAN I'M NOT A LITTLE ...ANGRY OR... HURT. I MEAN, WE WERE MARRIED.
AND I WISH SHE HADN'T KEPT IT A SECRET FOR SO LONG, ESPECIALLY FROM YOU, BUT... I'M HAPPY THAT SHE'S HAPPY. APPARENTLY HAPPY.
APPARENTLY.

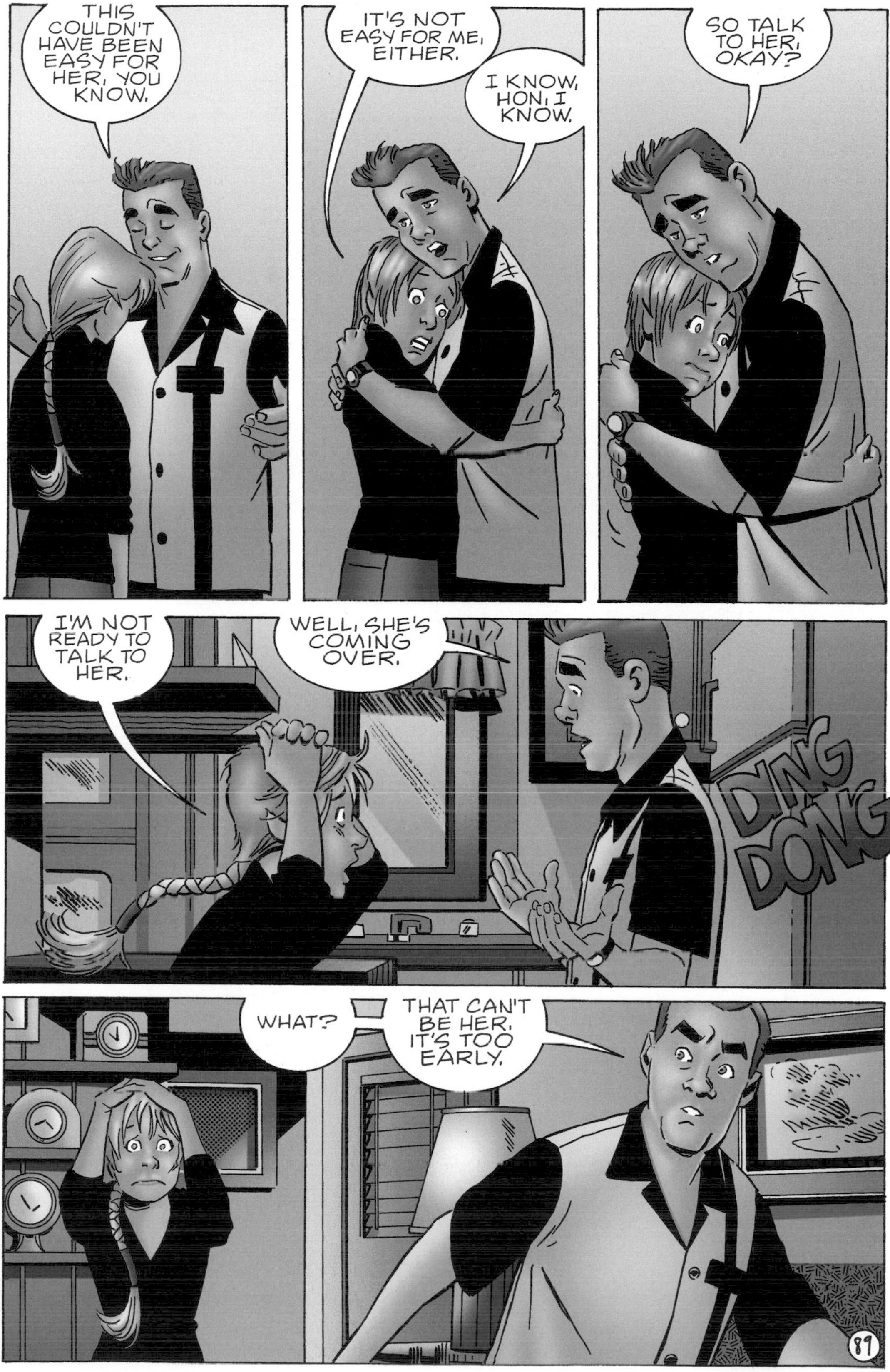
THIS COULDN'T HAVE BEEN EASY FOR HER, YOU KNOW.
IT'S NOT EASY FOR ME, EITHER.
I KNOW, HON, I KNOW.
SO TALK TO HER, OKAY?
I'M NOT READY TO TALK TO HER.
WELL, SHE'S COMING OVER.
DING DONG
WHAT?
THAT CAN'T BE HER. IT'S TOO EARLY.

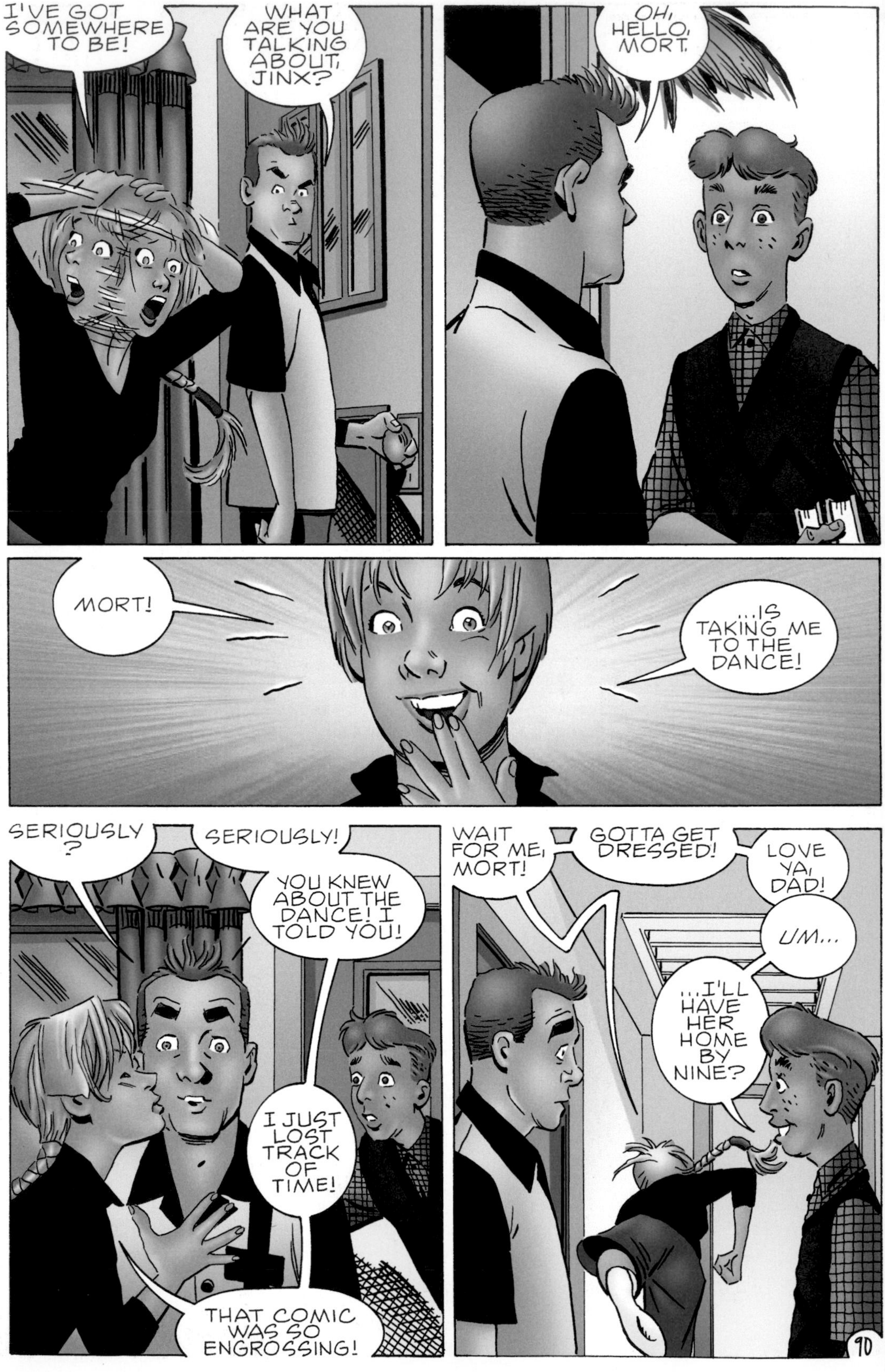
I'VE GOT SOMEWHERE TO BE!
WHAT ARE YOU TALKING ABOUT, JINX?
OH, HELLO, MORT.
MORT!
...IS TAKING ME TO THE DANCE!
SERIOUSLY?
SERIOUSLY!
YOU KNEW ABOUT THE DANCE! I TOLD YOU!
I JUST LOST TRACK OF TIME!
THAT COMIC WAS SO ENGROSSING!
WAIT FOR ME, MORT!
GOTTA GET DRESSED!
LOVE YA, DAD!
UM...
...I'LL HAVE HER HOME BY NINE?

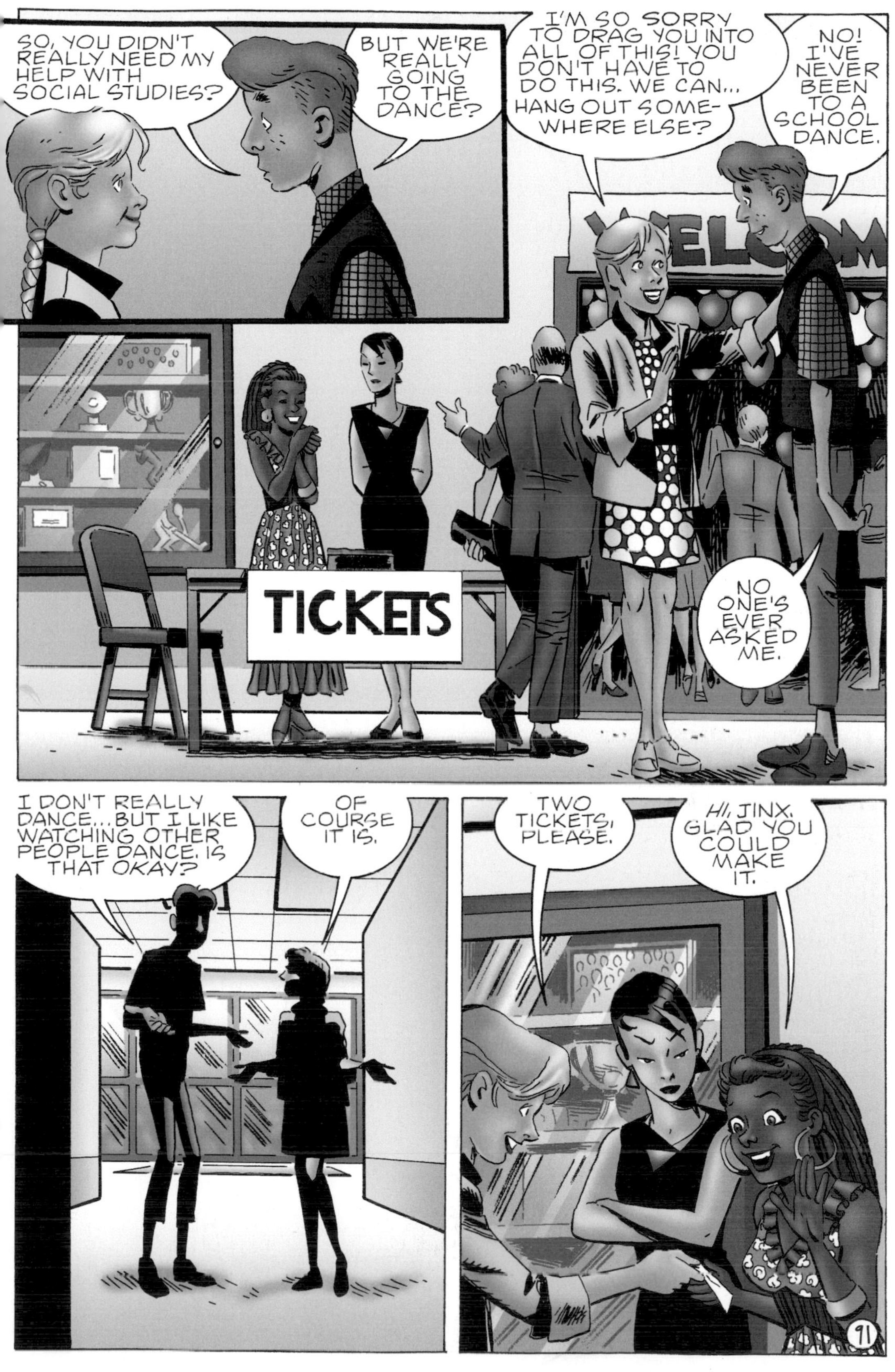

SO, YOU DIDN'T REALLY NEED MY HELP WITH SOCIAL STUDIES?
BUT WE'RE REALLY GOING TO THE DANCE?
I'M SO SORRY TO DRAG YOU INTO ALL OF THIS! YOU DON'T HAVE TO DO THIS. WE CAN... HANG OUT SOME-WHERE ELSE?
NO! I'VE NEVER BEEN TO A SCHOOL DANCE.
WELCOM
TICKETS
NO ONE'S EVER ASKED ME.
I DON'T REALLY DANCE... BUT I LIKE WATCHING OTHER PEOPLE DANCE. IS THAT OKAY?
OF COURSE IT IS.
TWO TICKETS, PLEASE.
HI, JINX. GLAD YOU COULD MAKE IT.

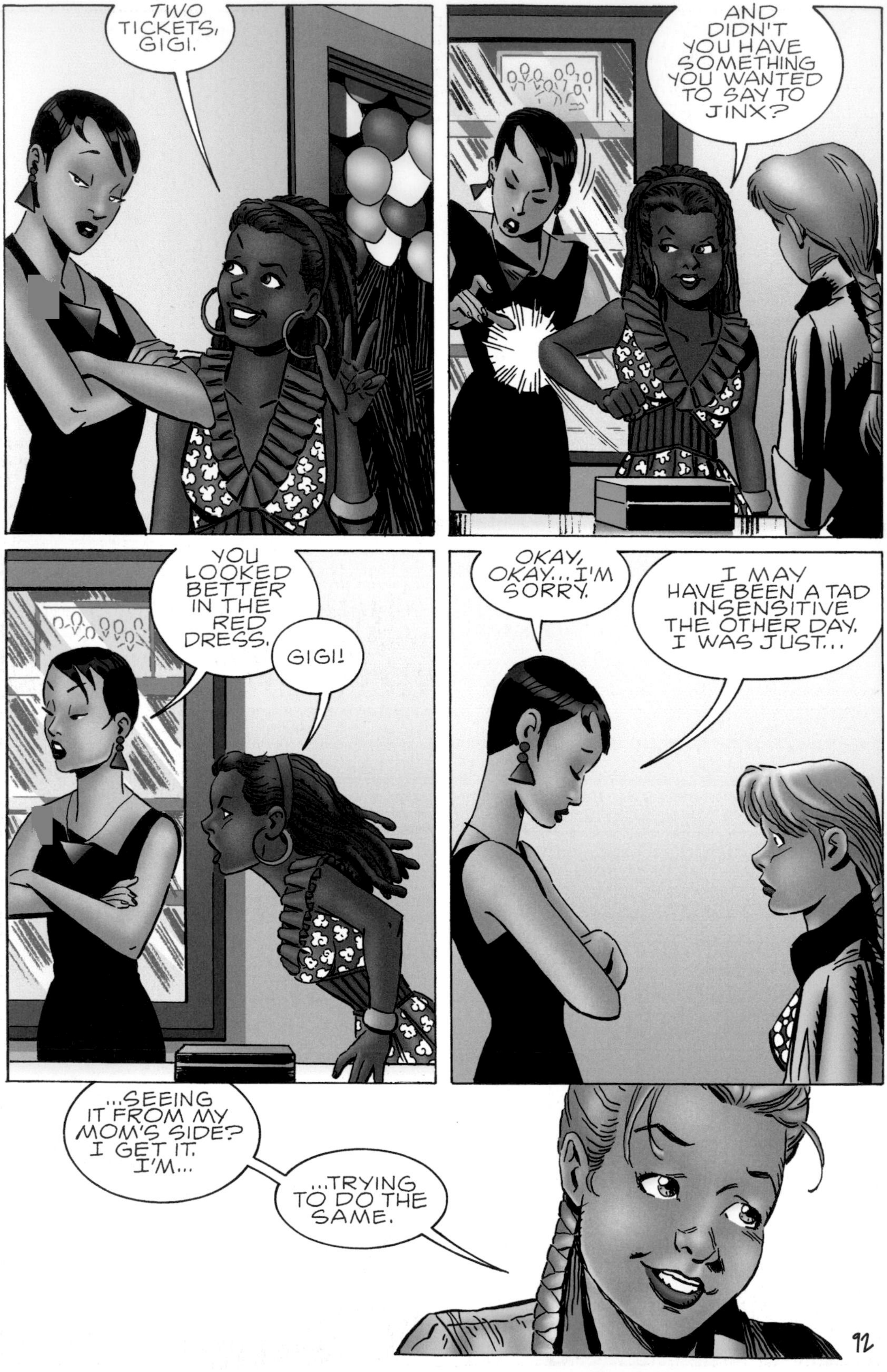

TWO TICKETS, GIGI.
AND DIDN'T YOU HAVE SOMETHING YOU WANTED TO SAY TO JINX?
YOU LOOKED BETTER IN THE RED DRESS.
GIGI!
OKAY, OKAY... I'M SORRY.
I MAY HAVE BEEN A TAD INSENSITIVE THE OTHER DAY. I WAS JUST...
...SEEING IT FROM MY MOM'S SIDE? I GET IT. I'M...
...TRYING TO DO THE SAME.

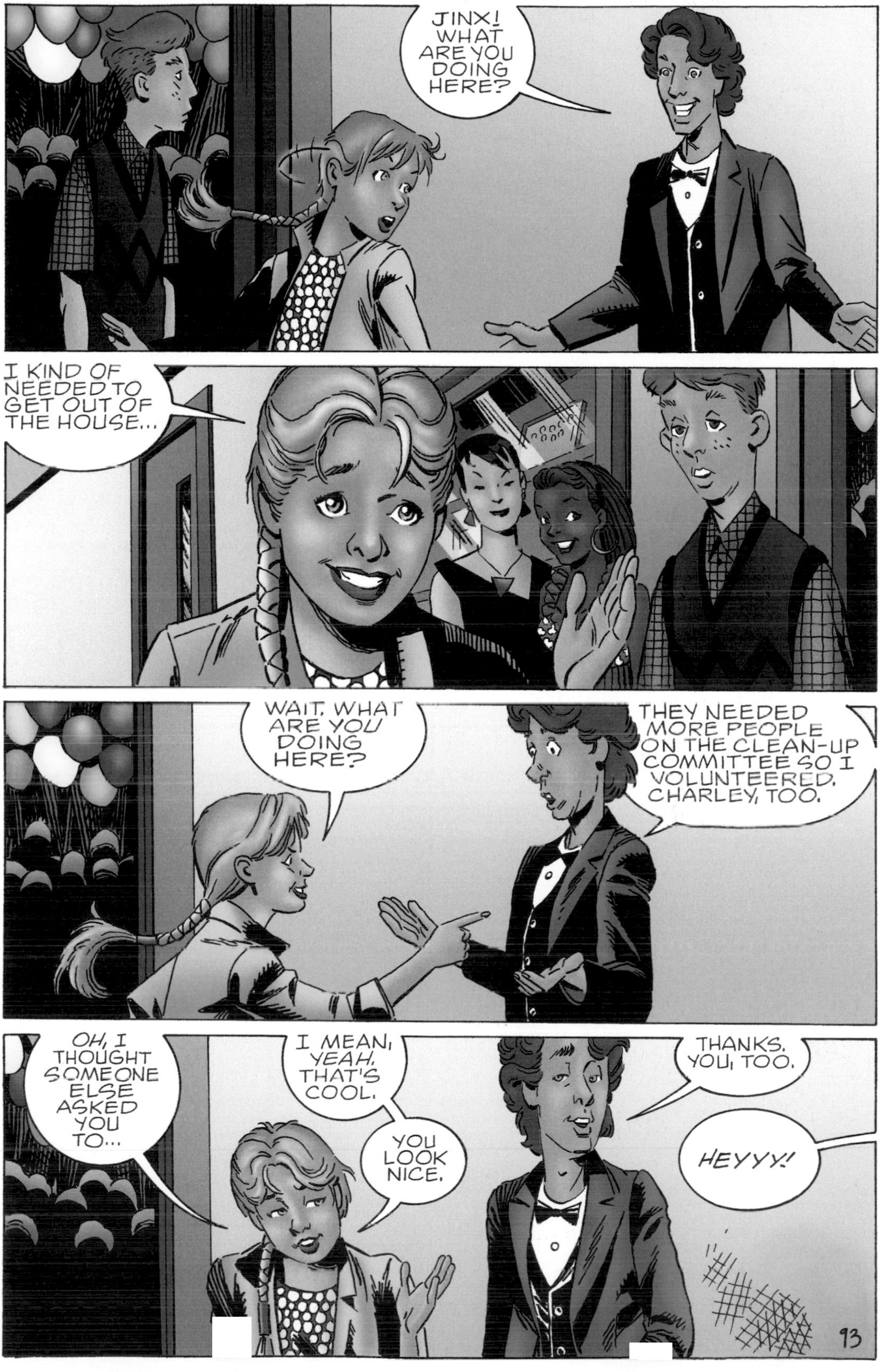
JINX! WHAT ARE YOU DOING HERE?
I KIND OF NEEDED TO GET OUT OF THE HOUSE...
WAIT. WHAT ARE *YOU* DOING HERE?
THEY NEEDED MORE PEOPLE ON THE CLEAN-UP COMMITTEE SO I VOLUNTEERED. CHARLEY, TOO.
OH, I THOUGHT SOMEONE ELSE ASKED YOU TO...
I MEAN, *YEAH*. THAT'S COOL.
YOU LOOK NICE.
THANKS. YOU, TOO.
HEYYY!

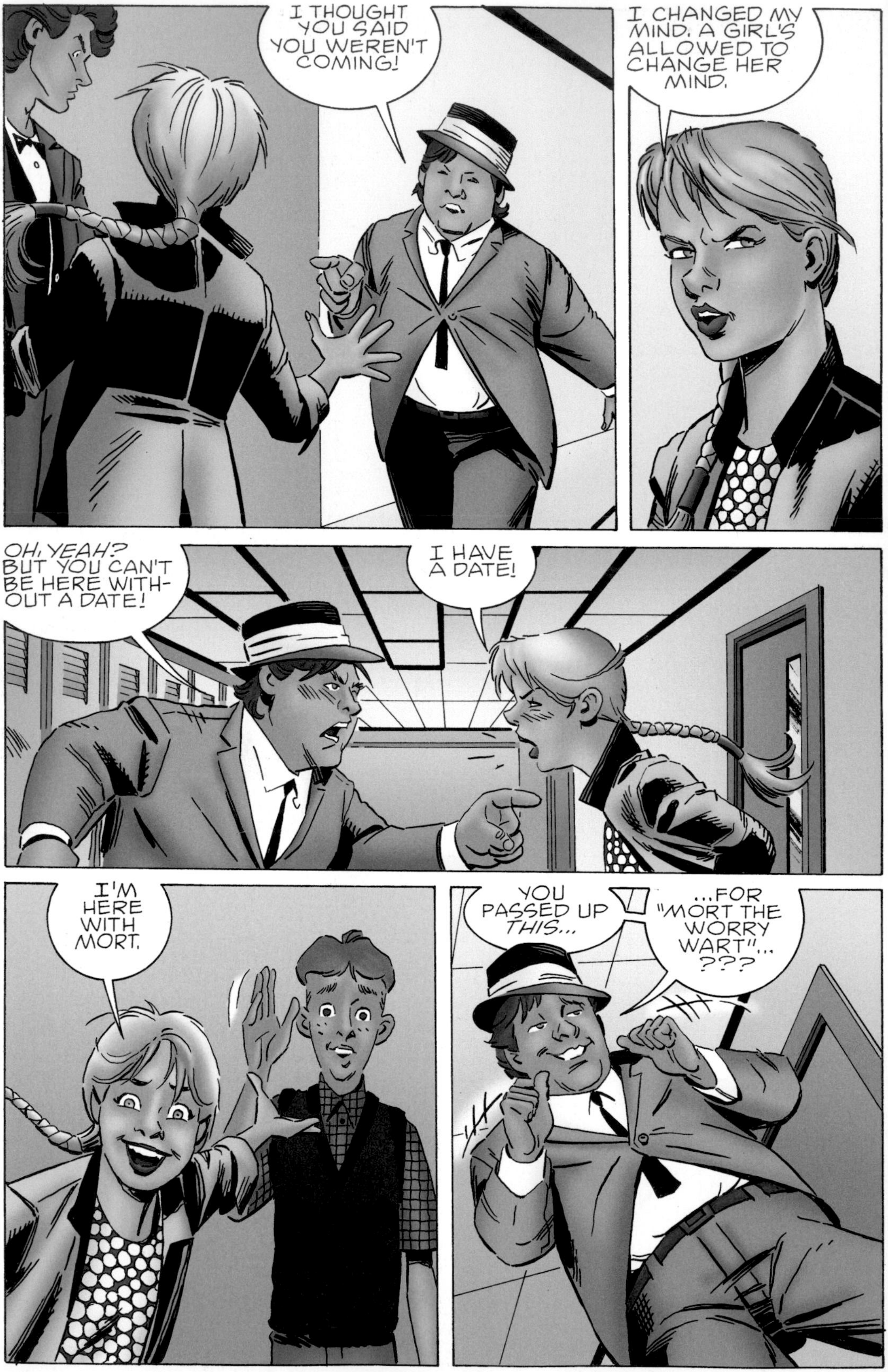
I THOUGHT YOU SAID YOU WEREN'T COMING!
I CHANGED MY MIND. A GIRL'S ALLOWED TO CHANGE HER MIND.
OH, YEAH? BUT YOU CAN'T BE HERE WITH-OUT A DATE!
I HAVE A DATE!
I'M HERE WITH MORT.
YOU PASSED UP THIS...
...FOR "MORT THE WORRY WART"... ???

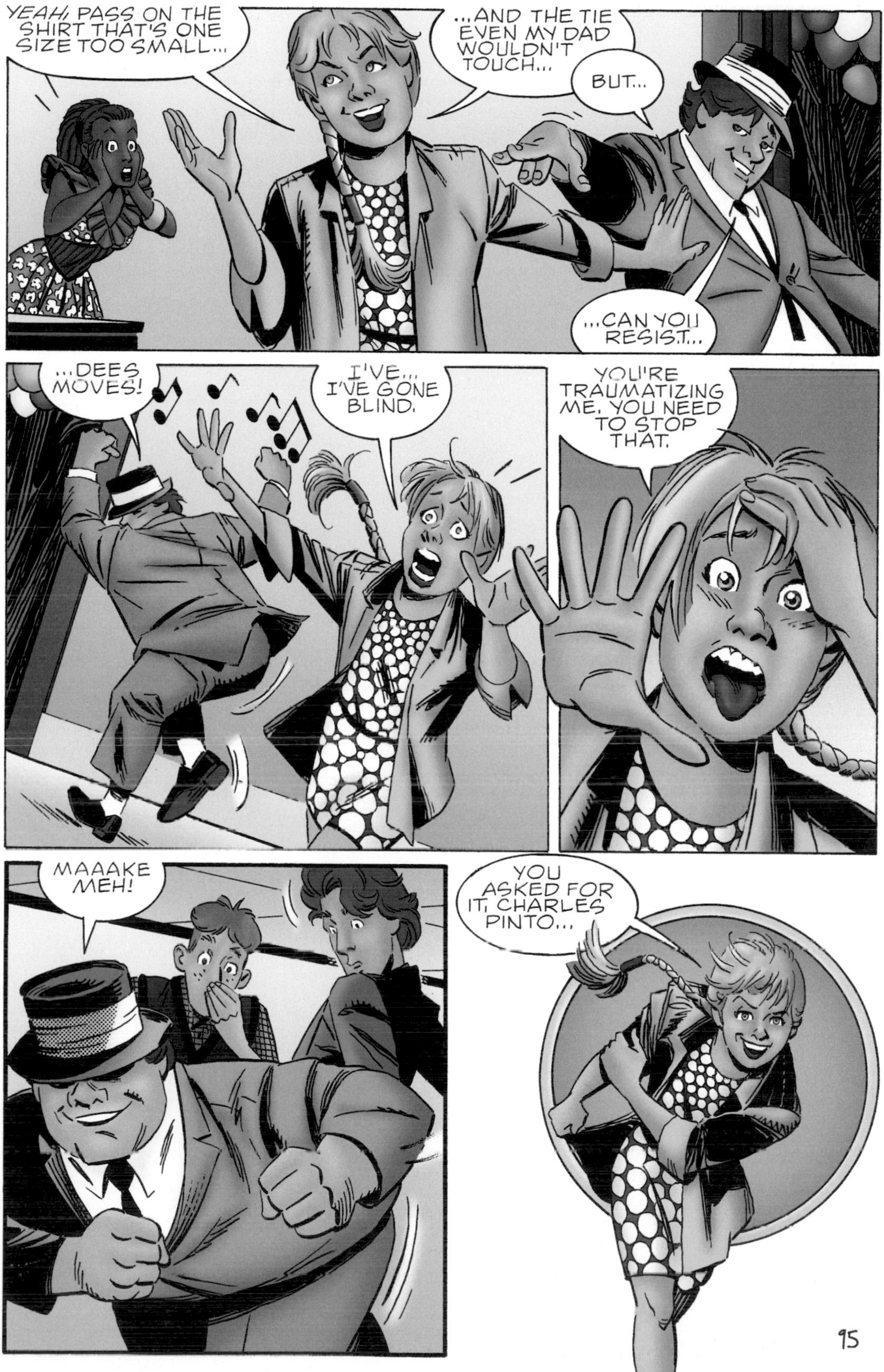
YEAH, PASS ON THE SHIRT THAT'S ONE SIZE TOO SMALL...
...AND THE TIE EVEN MY DAD WOULDN'T TOUCH...
BUT...
...CAN YOU RESIST...
...DEES MOVES!
I'VE... I'VE GONE BLIND.
YOU'RE TRAUMATIZING ME. YOU NEED TO STOP THAT.
MAAAKE MEH!
YOU ASKED FOR IT, CHARLES PINTO...

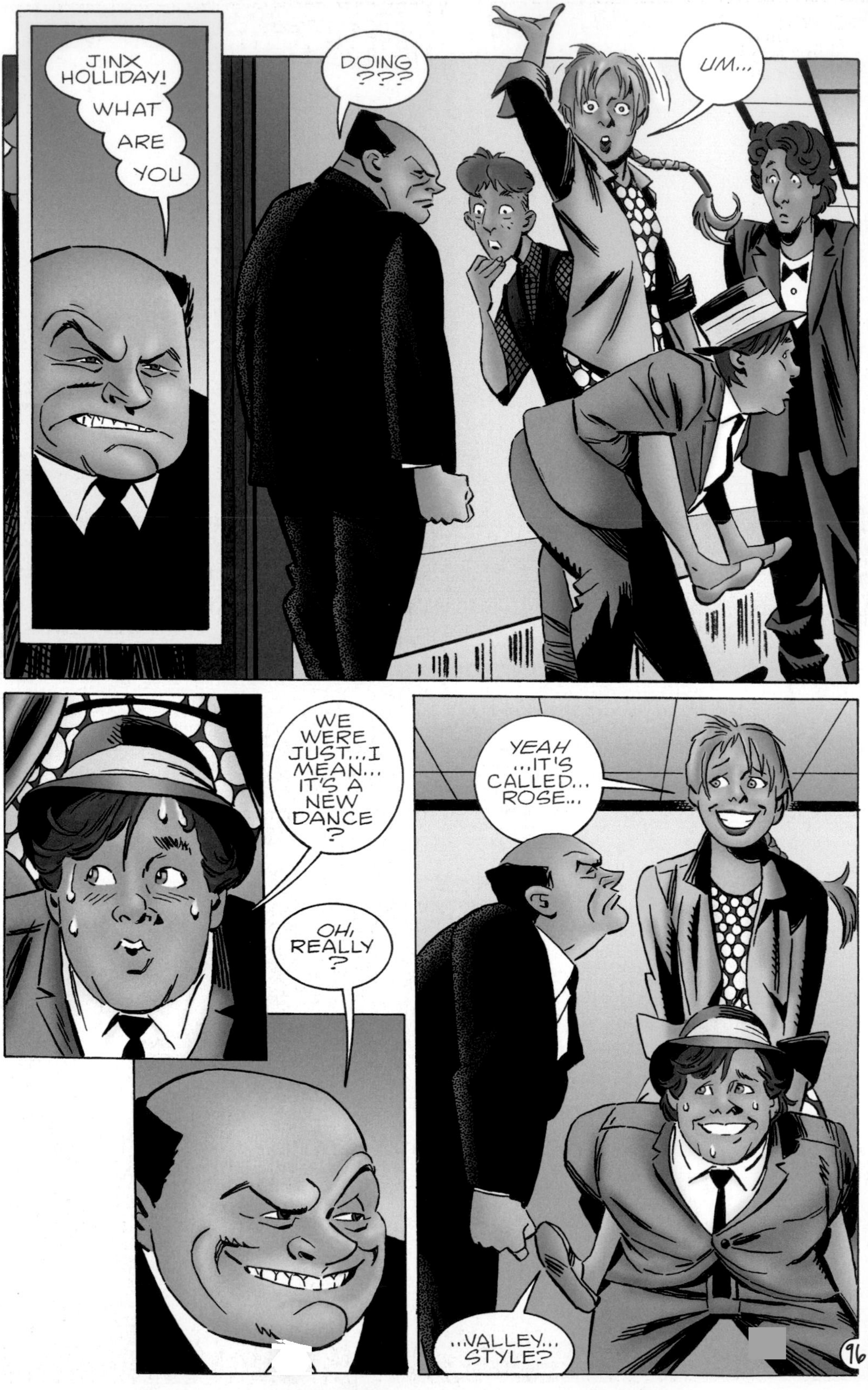

JINX HOLLIDAY! WHAT ARE YOU
DOING ???
UM...
WE WERE JUST...I MEAN... IT'S A NEW DANCE?
OH, REALLY?
YEAH ...IT'S CALLED... ROSE...
...VALLEY... STYLE?

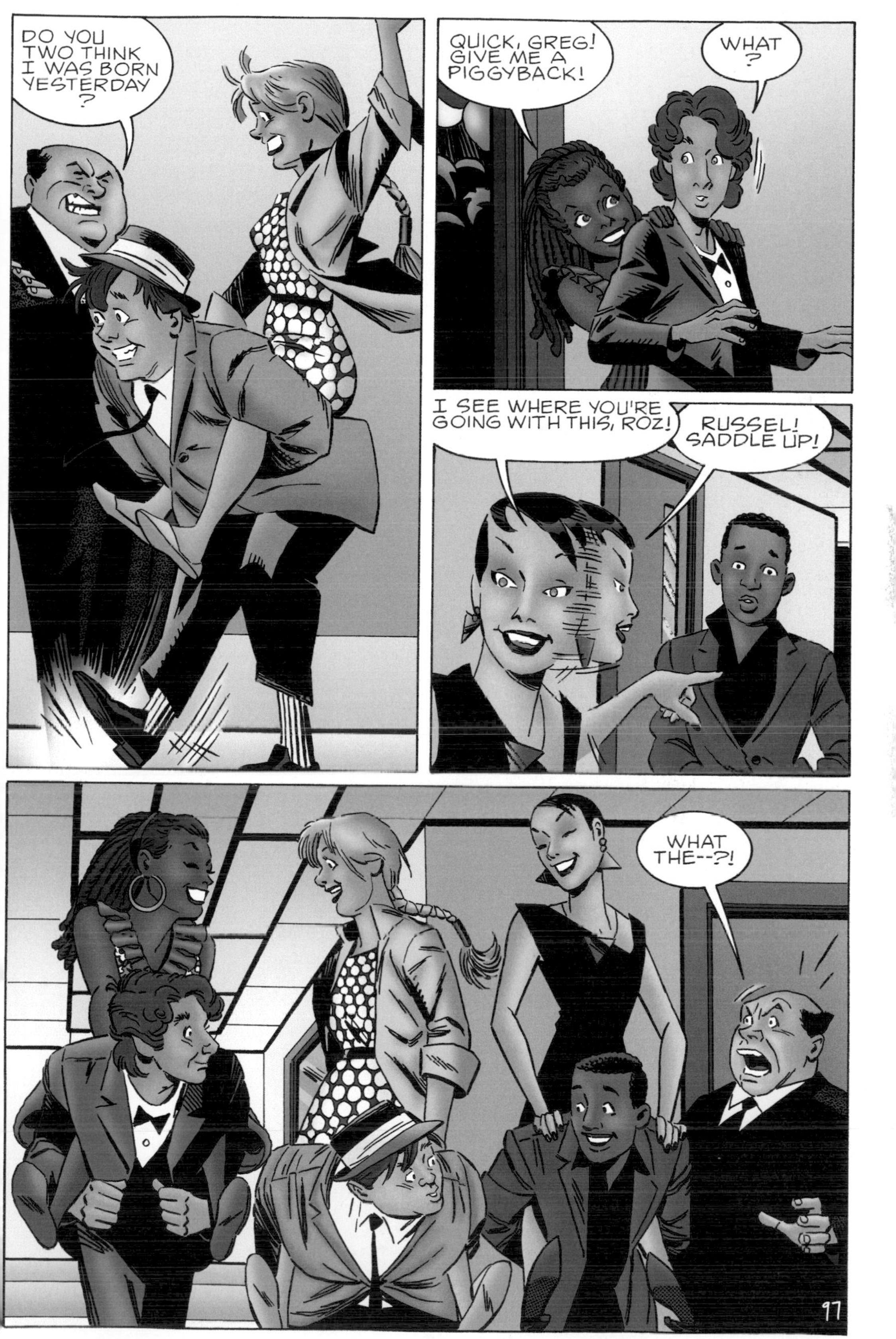
DO YOU TWO THINK I WAS BORN YESTERDAY ?
QUICK, GREG! GIVE ME A PIGGYBACK!
WHAT ?
I SEE WHERE YOU'RE GOING WITH THIS, ROZ!
RUSSEL! SADDLE UP!
WHAT THE--?!

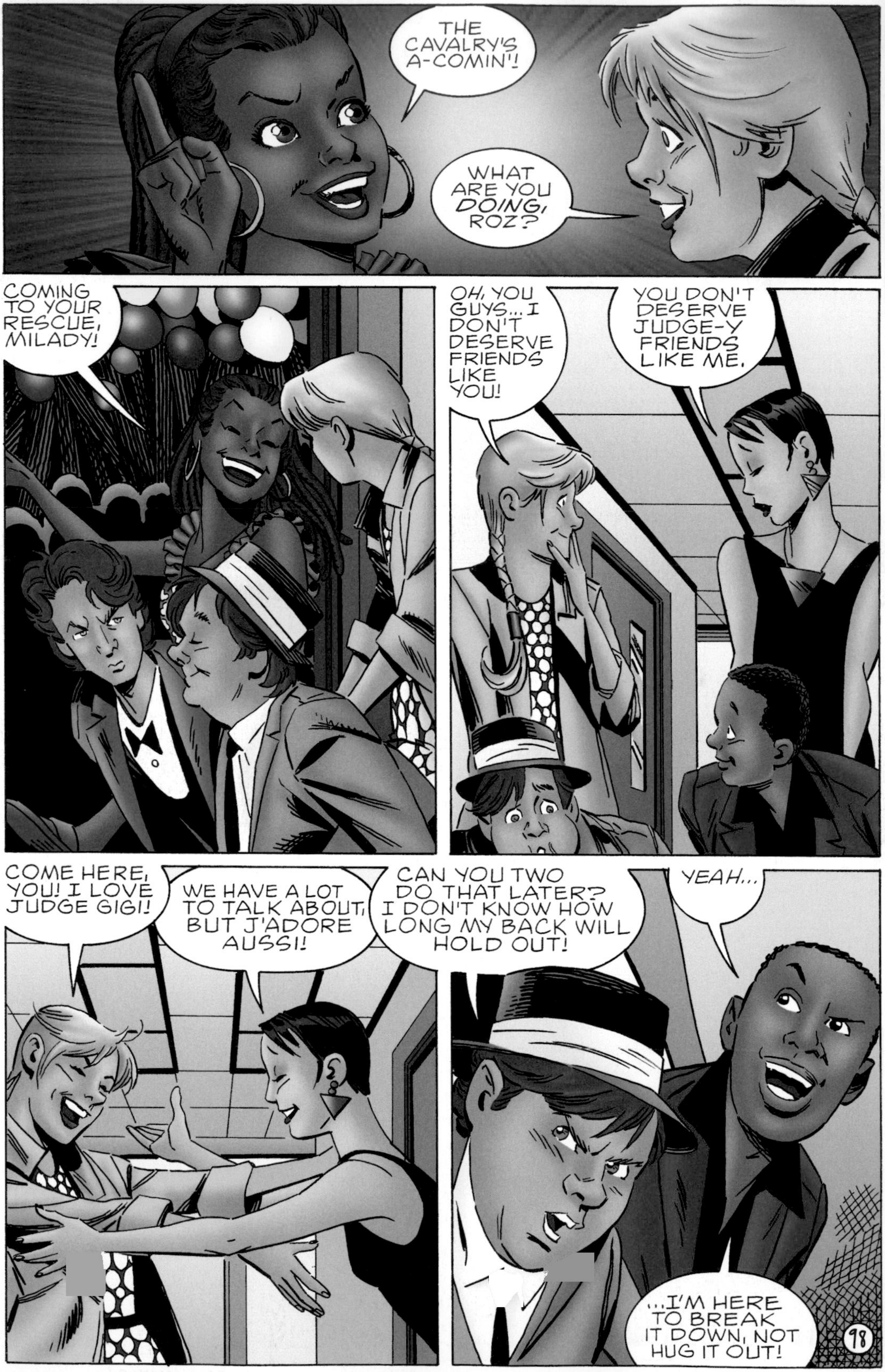

THE CAVALRY'S A-COMIN'!
WHAT ARE YOU DOING, ROZ?
COMING TO YOUR RESCUE, MILADY!
OH, YOU GUYS... I DON'T DESERVE FRIENDS LIKE YOU!
YOU DON'T DESERVE JUDGE-Y FRIENDS LIKE ME.
COME HERE, YOU! I LOVE JUDGE GIGI!
WE HAVE A LOT TO TALK ABOUT, BUT J'ADORE AUSSI!
CAN YOU TWO DO THAT LATER? I DON'T KNOW HOW LONG MY BACK WILL HOLD OUT!
YEAH...
...I'M HERE TO BREAK IT DOWN, NOT HUG IT OUT!

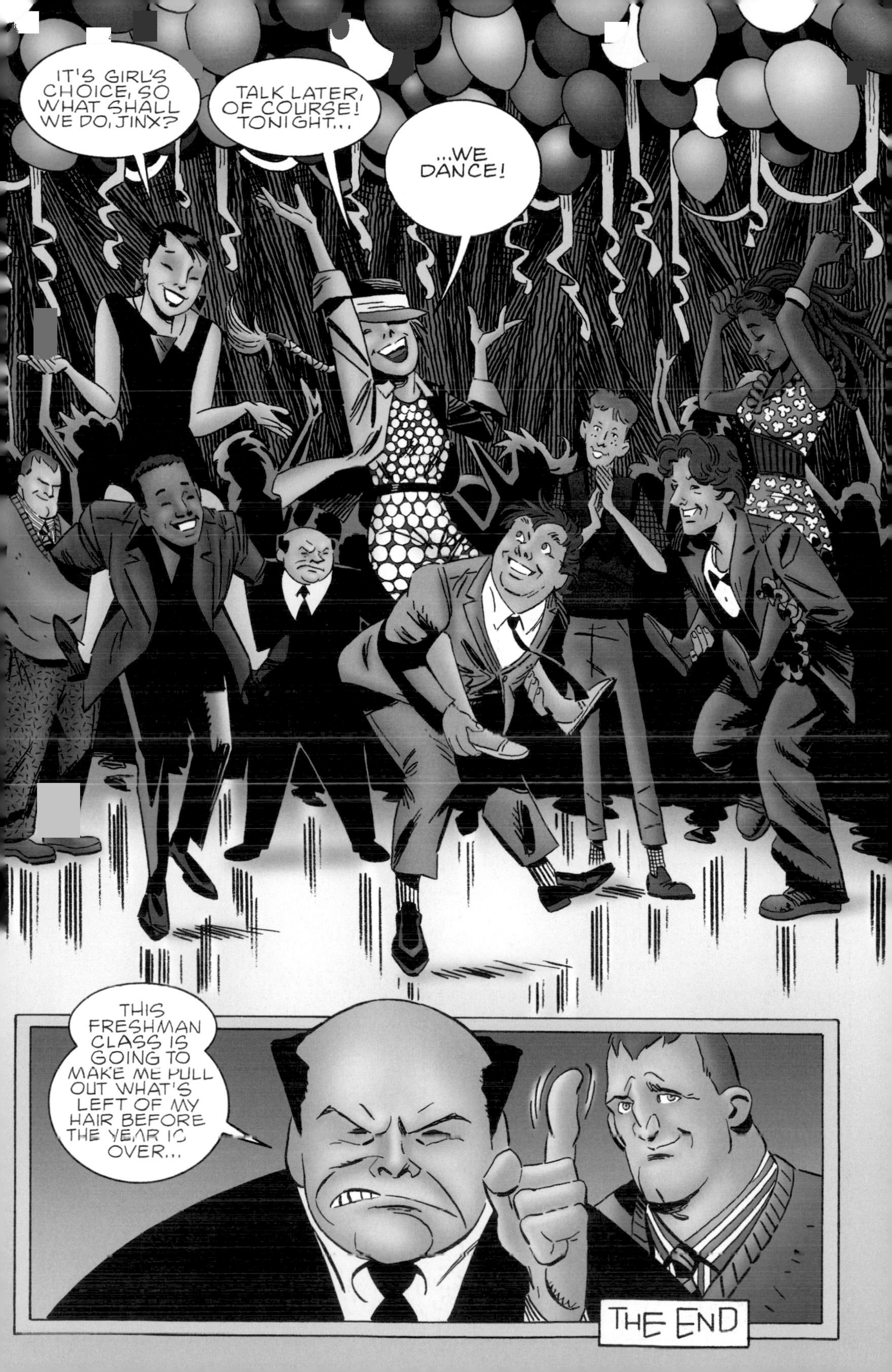
IT'S GIRL'S CHOICE, SO WHAT SHALL WE DO, JINX?
TALK LATER, OF COURSE! TONIGHT...
...WE DANCE!
THIS FRESHMAN CLASS IS GOING TO MAKE ME PULL OUT WHAT'S LEFT OF MY HAIR BEFORE THE YEAR IS OVER...
THE END

jinx

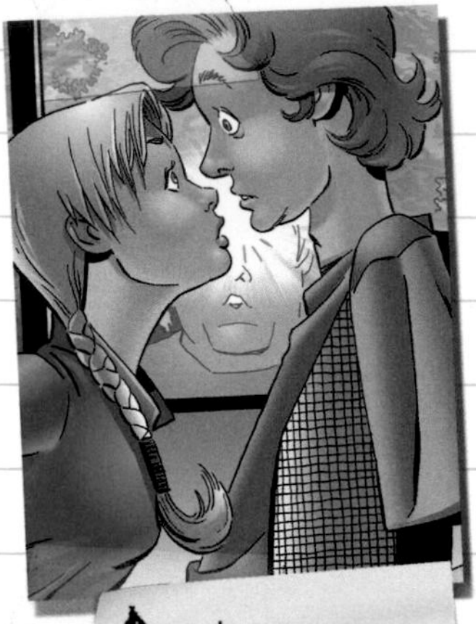

Since her first appearance in Pep Comics #8 in 1947, Jinx has charmed readers with her misadventures. While her pigtails and dresses may not be around anymore, her appeal is timeless, and her relationships with her friends and family have grown up too!

Jinx has been wearing red t-shirts for most of her life, but there's one thing thats been around for almost as long: Jinx loves baseball! She's got a great arm, and if she hadn't had such a bad tryout for the high school team -- a bad day -- she would have definitely been able to hold her own with the boys!

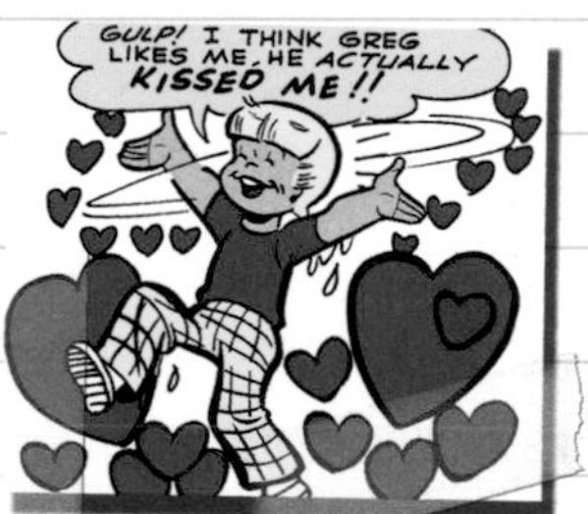
GULP! I THINK GREG LIKES ME. HE ACTUALLY KISSED ME!!

the more things change ....

jinx & her dad

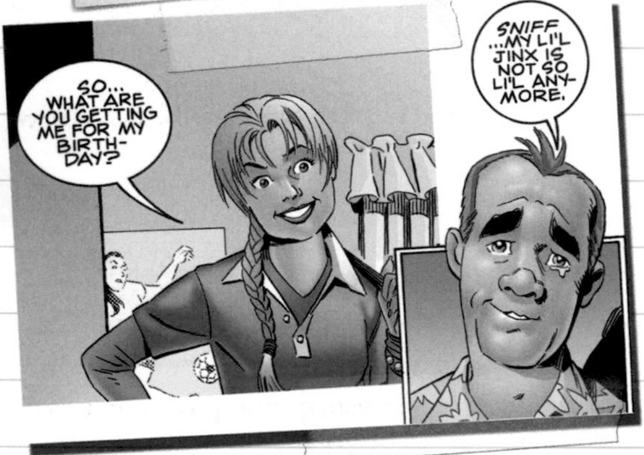
SO... WHAT ARE YOU GETTING ME FOR MY BIRTH-DAY?
SNIFF ...MY LI'L JINX IS NOT SO LI'L ANY-MORE.

Hap seems to have a hard time grasping the fact that his little girl isn't so li'l anymore! Jinx may be a teenager now, but she'll always be daddy's darling -- and eternal frustration! There's still plenty of time for Jinx to learn from dear old dad -- and for Hap to learn a thing or two from her!

jinx & gigi

Jinx and Gigi have been friends for a long time, but sometimes it seems that Jinx might be getting tired of Gigi's refusal to ride her drama-train. Gigi's seen her fair share of it -- after all she's been performing for broadway and television for most of her life! At least it hasn't all gone to her head ...

Despite a layer of sarcasm and a refusal to act like she cares about anything, Gigi tries to be there for Jinx in her own tough-love kind of a way!

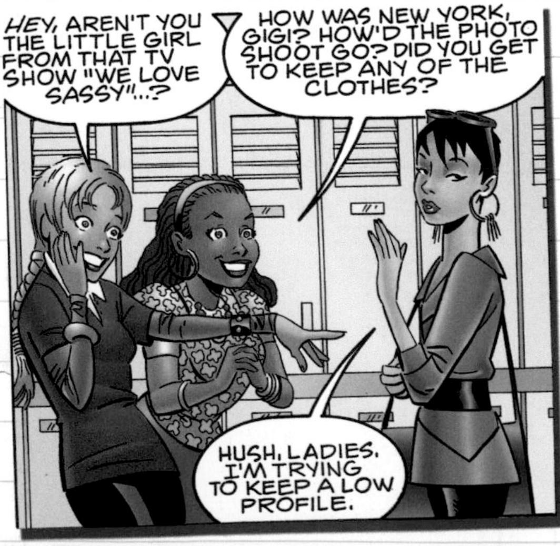
HEY, AREN'T YOU THE LITTLE GIRL FROM THAT TV SHOW "WE LOVE SASSY"...?
HOW WAS NEW YORK, GIGI? HOW'D THE PHOTO SHOOT GO? DID YOU GET TO KEEP ANY OF THE CLOTHES?
HUSH, LADIES. I'M TRYING TO KEEP A LOW PROFILE.

li'l jinx

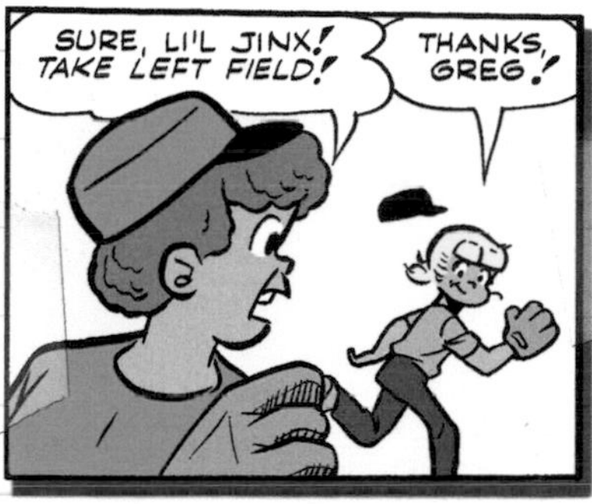

SURE, LI'L JINX! TAKE LEFT FIELD!
THANKS, GREG!

Li'l Jinx was so good at baseball, that as a little girl she would sometimes get kicked off the team for making all the little boys feel bad that she was hitting more home runs than they were! But even back in the day, friends like Greg would try to get the rest of the team to give her a chance!

li'l jinx & her dad

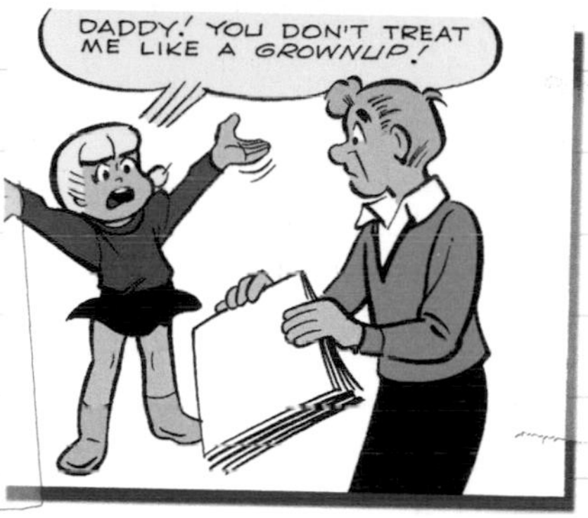

DADDY! YOU DON'T TREAT ME LIKE A GROWNUP!

Jinx will always be daddy's li'l girl -- but she's never been on board with the "li'l" part! Even as a child, Jinx wanted to be treated like an adult, and would often argue that case! Hap might have been easier to convince if Li'l Jinx's behavior didn't plant her firmly in childhood!

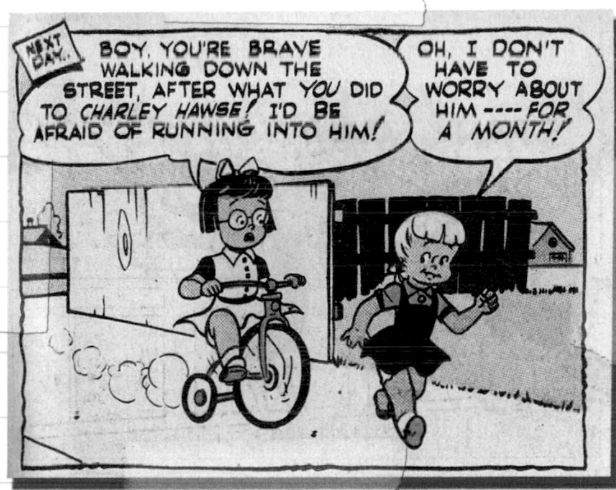

NEXT DAY.
BOY, YOU'RE BRAVE WALKING DOWN THE STREET, AFTER WHAT YOU DID TO CHARLEY HAWSE! I'D BE AFRAID OF RUNNING INTO HIM!
OH, I DON'T HAVE TO WORRY ABOUT HIM ---- FOR A MONTH!

li'l jinx & gigi

Gigi was one of the first of Li'l Jinx's friends to appear in the original strip. Pictured left, Gigi wasn't actually named when she first appeared, but the likeness would be hard to mistake (Gigi often wore glasses when she was li'l.) Eventually Gigi was named and developed the knowing attitude that makes her so very Gigi.

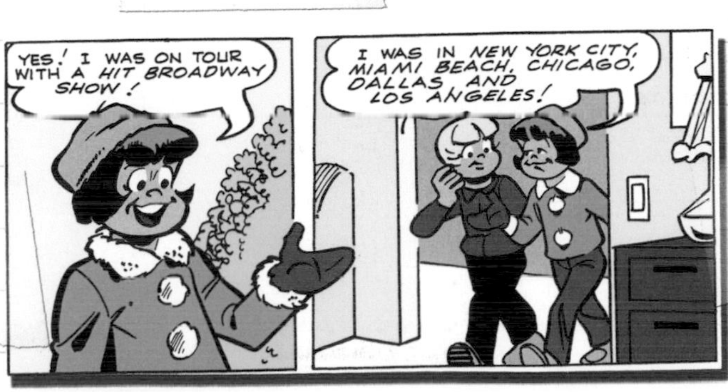

YES! I WAS ON TOUR WITH A HIT BROADWAY SHOW!
I WAS IN NEW YORK CITY, MIAMI BEACH, CHICAGO, DALLAS AND LOS ANGELES!

Pictured to the left we get a glimpse of the Gigi that's quite a bit similar to the one we've grown to know and love!

jinx, charley & greg

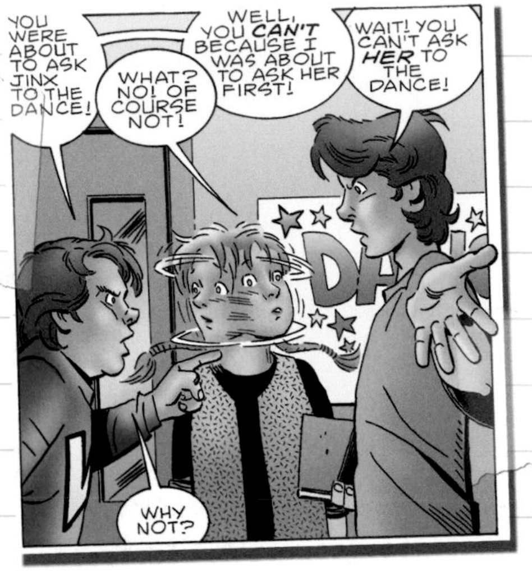
YOU WERE ABOUT TO ASK JINX TO THE DANCE!
WHAT? NO! OF COURSE NOT!
WELL, YOU CAN'T BECAUSE I WAS ABOUT TO ASK HER FIRST!
WAIT! YOU CAN'T ASK HER TO THE DANCE!
WHY NOT?

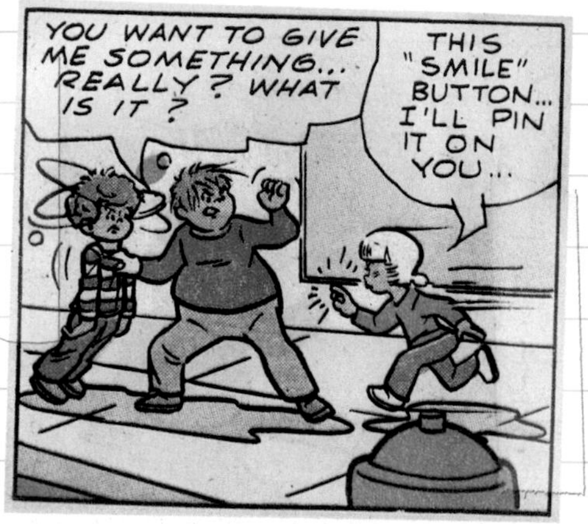
YOU WANT TO GIVE ME SOMETHING... REALLY? WHAT IS IT?
THIS "SMILE" BUTTON... I'LL PIN IT ON YOU...

Of all the original series characters adapted to the Jinx graphic novels, Charley has changed the most. In the Li'l Jinx comic strips, he was always bigger and taller than everyone else, and usually the bully. Sometimes he had a crush on Li'l Jinx -- probably because she was strong enough to hold her own against him, and smart enough to trick him out of bullying people.

Greg, on the other hand, was always friendly with Li'l Jinx. He was more likely to be her confidant than girls like Gigi and Roz. He didn't particularly seem to mind when Li'l Jinx rushed in to save the day for him, whether from bullies or on the baseball field, eviscerating his machismo with her sports ability, quick thinking, and wit that never needed to be cutting edge -- just sharper than Charley's!

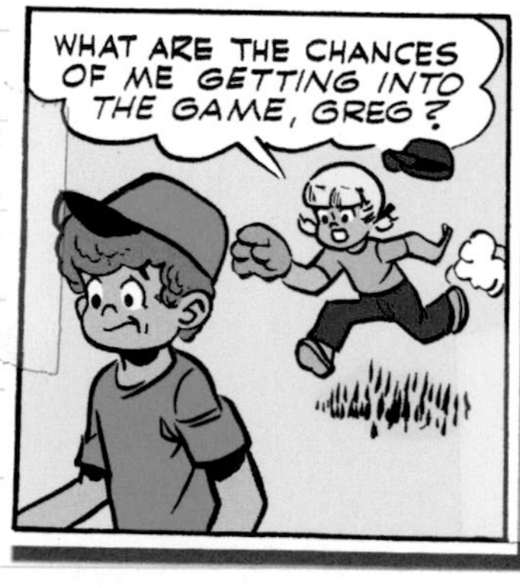
WHAT ARE THE CHANCES OF ME GETTING INTO THE GAME, GREG?

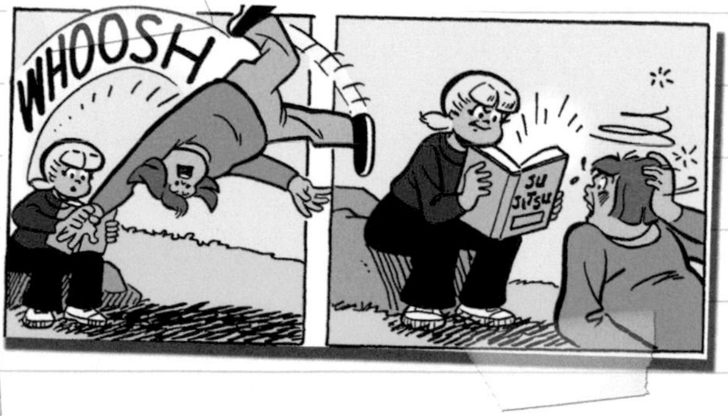
WHOOSH
JU JITSU

Many Li'l Jinx strips are published in Archie Comics Digest Magazines -- look out for them at the best comic shops and bookstores, or online at ArchieComics.com!

jinx and her mother

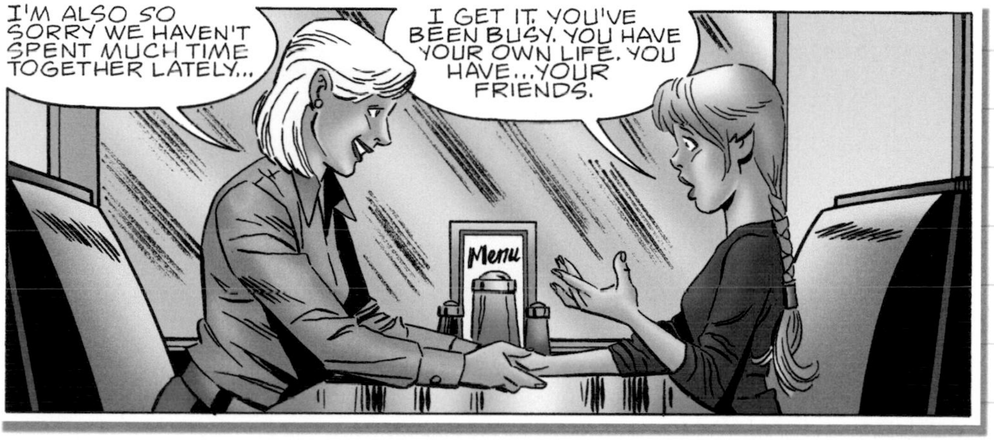
I'M ALSO SO SORRY WE HAVEN'T SPENT MUCH TIME TOGETHER LATELY...
I GET IT. YOU'VE BEEN BUSY. YOU HAVE YOUR OWN LIFE. YOU HAVE...YOUR FRIENDS.
Menu

Li'l Jinx comics usually focused on the interaction between Jinx and her father, but this wasn't always the case. In Li'l Jinx #1, printed in November of 1956, both parents played an equal role in the lead story. In fact, Mery Holliday appeared in every issue of the first year of Li'l Jinx's comic!

As one of Archie Comics' most popular characters, Li'l Jinx timeless appeal kept her title in print for decades. As time progressed, Mery appeared less and less in the stories. Eventually, a year would go by between stories that showed Jinx and her mother interacting. (Those stories usually involved Li'l Jinx playing with things that her father didn't own, such as high heels and hats covered in fruit.) Mery sightings were so rare that even hardcore fans began to doubt her existence!

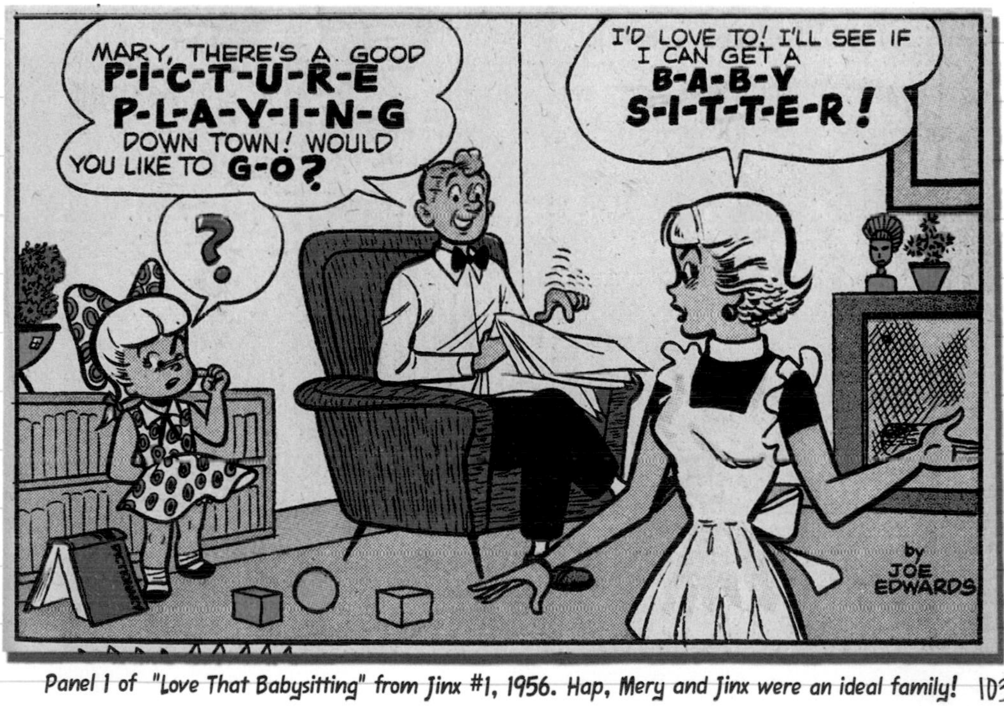
MARY, THERE'S A GOOD P-I-C-T-U-R-E P-L-A-Y-I-N-G DOWN TOWN! WOULD YOU LIKE TO G-O?
?
I'D LOVE TO! I'LL SEE IF I CAN GET A B-A-B-Y S-I-T-T-E-R!
by JOE EDWARDS

Panel 1 of "Love That Babysitting" from Jinx #1, 1956. Hap, Mery and Jinx were an ideal family!

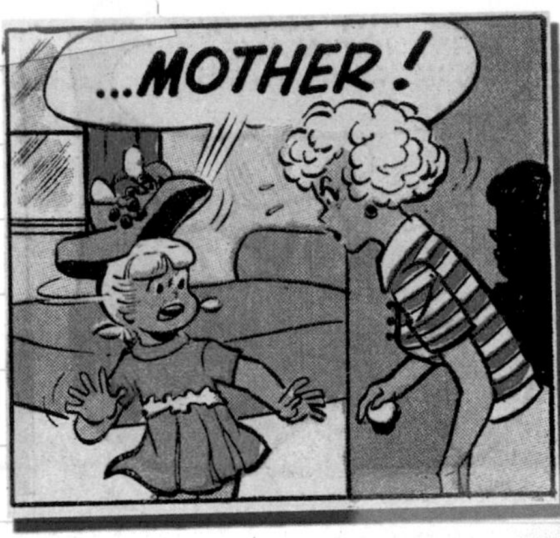
...MOTHER!

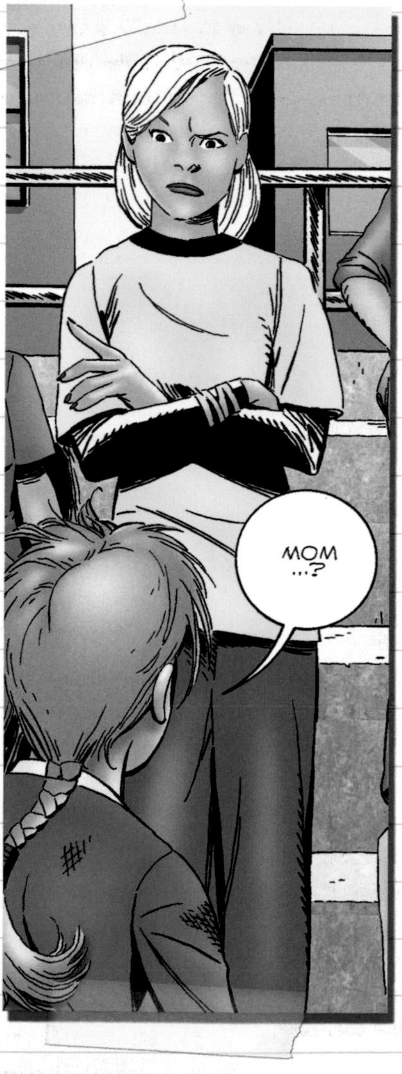
MOM ...?

The earliest incarnations of the Holliday family showed a happily formal married couple (he wore a suit and bow-tie, she an off-the-shoulder evening gown to a night at the movies in the Li'l Jinx #1 story "Love That Baby Sitting") with a little girl whose personality just ran against the grain of their perfectly manicured household.

Stories and characters change and evolve over time, and over the next few decades, Jinx slowly began to wear pants and a signature red t-shirt more than skirts and dresses, ditched the massive bow in favor of her signature pigtails, and not only brought all her problems to her father, but her need for affection as well.

It's not that Mery wasn't an interesting character. She was great! As Li'l Jinx's story grew, Mery just wasn't needed as much for her daughter's story to be told, and her appearances became rare. When she did show up, it was to fill a role in a situation that Hap absolutely couldn't.

Li'l Jinx's stories didn't suffer for this change. If anything, it allowed for her relationship with her father to be explored in some depth, as well as allowing the focus of her comics to include Greg, Roz, Gigi, Charley "Hawse," Mort the Worry Wart, and Russ. Rather than giving the Jinx creative team a difficult situation to explain, it gave us an exciting opportunity to tell a great story.

What happens when a teenager starts wondering if her own tomboyish nature is related to her mother's absence following a divorce? How will her own sense of identity be challenged when her mother comes out as a lesbian? The potential to tell a great story was irresistible -- and made complete sense as an adaptation of the well-established Li'l Jinx characters that the world fell in love with.

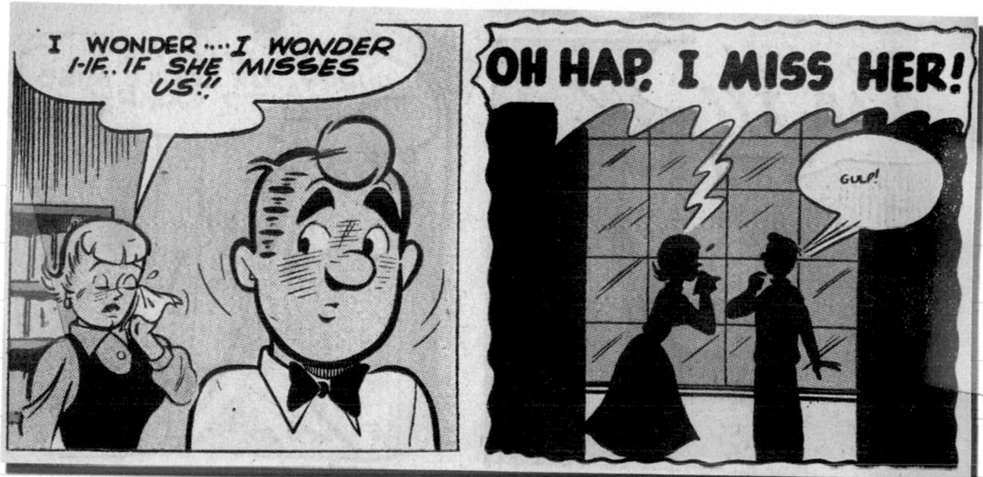

I WONDER .... I WONDER I-IF.. IF SHE MISSES US!!
OH HAP, I MISS HER!
GULP!

Compare the above clipping from Li'l Jinx #16, published in September 1957, with the below clipping from Li'l Jinx Laugh-Out #33, published in September 1971. Both stories are about Li'l Jinx going away to summer camp. In the first story, Hap is (ahem) happy to get his daughter out of his hair, while Mery misses her daughter more than either Hap or Jinx seem to mind the separation! In the second story, Mery isn't present at all. Hap takes the time to explain to Li'l Jinx about the fun things she'll learn!

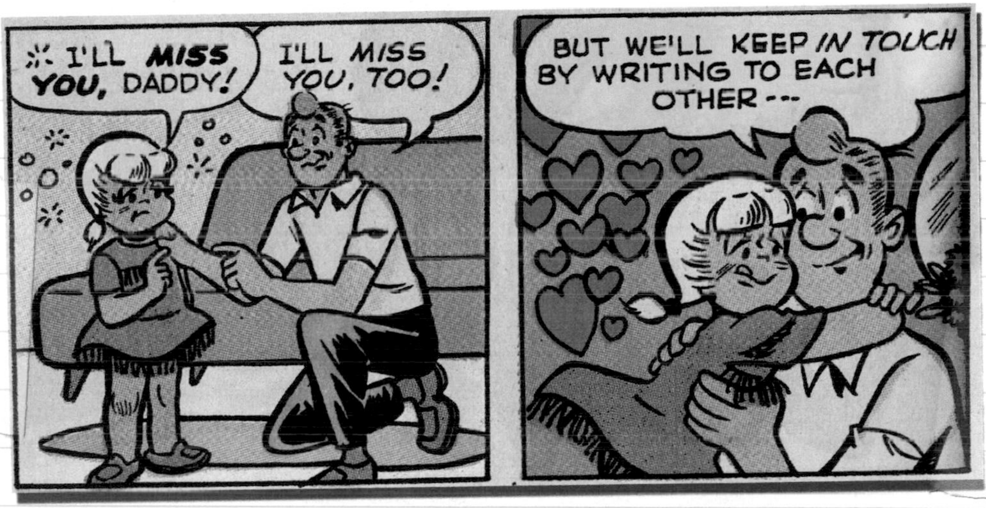

I'LL MISS YOU, DADDY!
I'LL MISS YOU, TOO!
BUT WE'LL KEEP IN TOUCH BY WRITING TO EACH OTHER ---

He comforts her in a way that her mother would in the original incarnation, and both of them are richer characters for it.

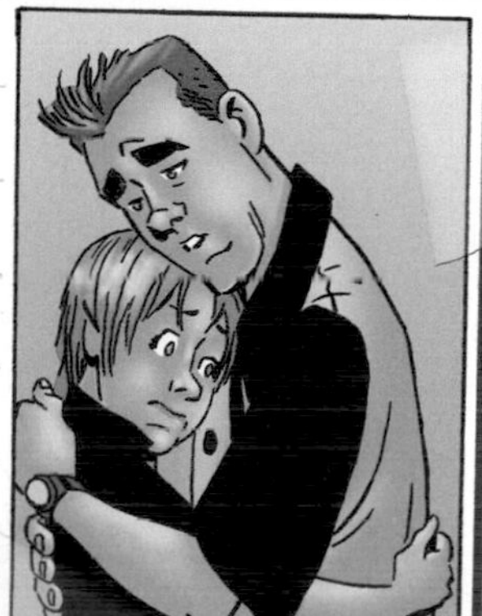

The relationship Li'l Jinx and her father shared gave these new Jinx comics (through the excellence of series writer J. Torres) a strong basis from which to build her relationship with father as a teenager. It's pretty easy to imagine a tomboy like Jinx to have spent at least some of her time growing up without her mother. (It didn't hurt that many of Mery's '70's appearances involved her in some way ignoring Li'l Jinx when her daughter was trying to catch her attention.) But real life never follows the 'easy' assumptions, and neither does Jinx ...

the concept art of Mery

We knew that Jinx's mother would be an important part of her story, so her character was set up during series development. As a nurse, her career would prevent her from seeing Jinx as much as either of them would have liked. As a divorced couple, Hap and Mery might not always get along, but do their best to make Jinx a priority over personal arguments. Jinx's father could be described as "long-suffering," so it was pretty clear that Jinx's "social graces" might have originated with her mother, who outs herself to her daughter in a way that she *could* have handled a little more delicately.

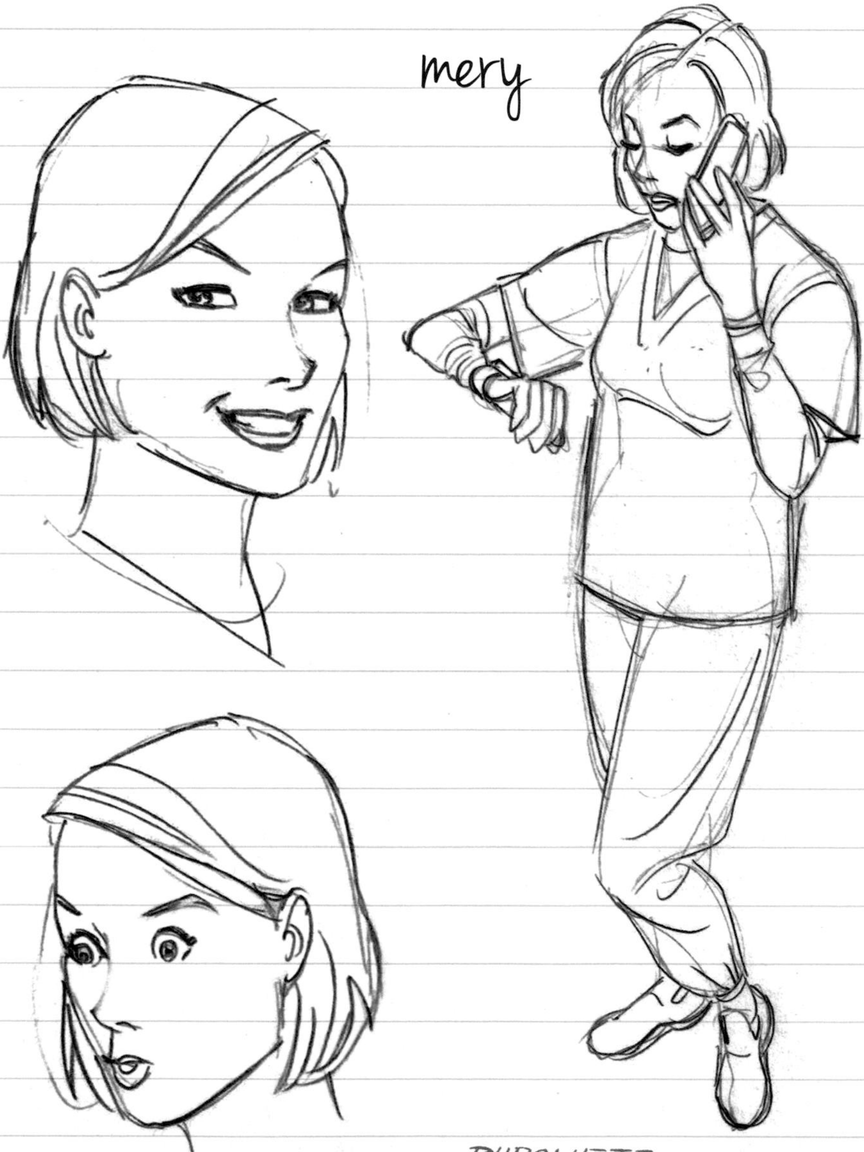

mery
BURCHETT

the concept art of Mari

While Jinx 2 was in development, writer J. Torres brought up the need to diversify the sexuality of the main characters of the Jinx cast. As soon as he said that, it was like a the last piece of the puzzle had been found in the construction of Mery Holliday's character, and the role that she played in Jinx's life. We then had one of the most exciting and fun tasks in comic book development: creating a new character!

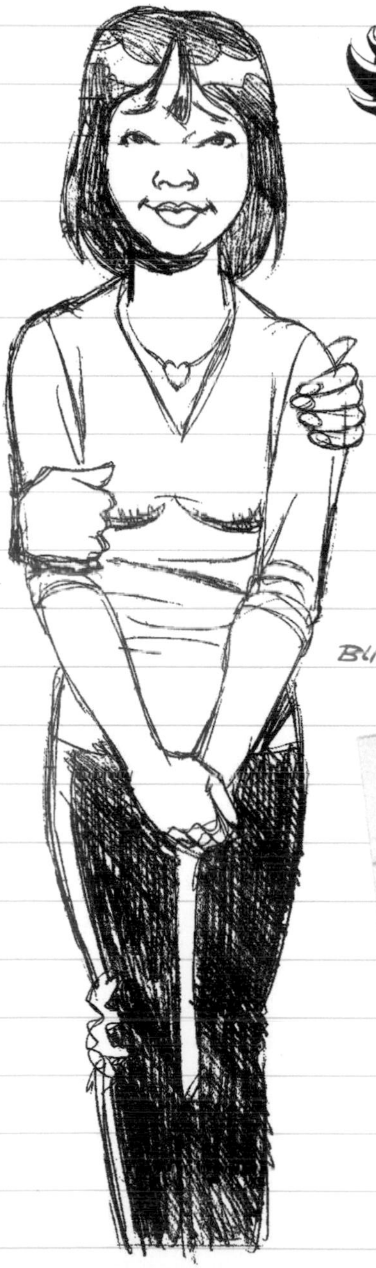

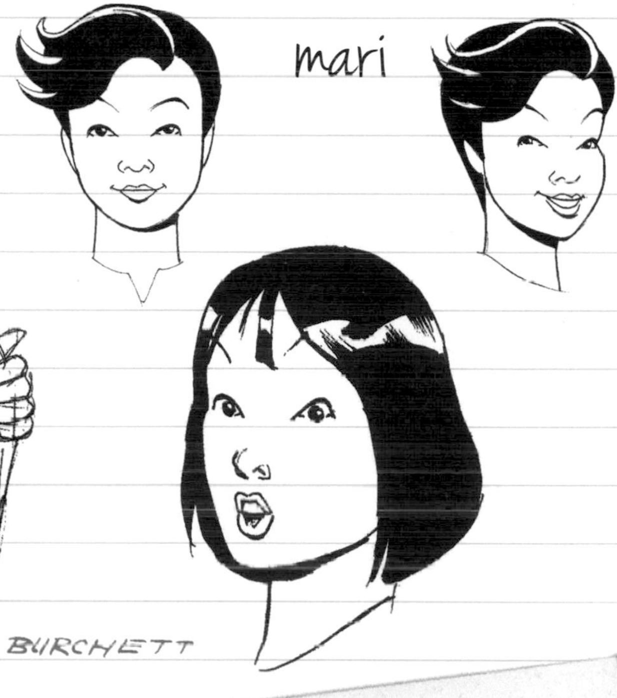
mari
BURCHETT

Did you know ..?

Maritess, Mery's Filipino girlfriend, went through multiple design stages before a final design was selected.

Deciding on her name took even longer, but Writer J. Torres and Editor Suzannah Rowntree eventually settled on Maritess, a name that could be shortened to 'Mari.' They couldn't resist a couple called Mery and Mari. You can take characters out of Riverdale, but you can't take Riverdale out of the characters!

behind the scenes with jinx covers

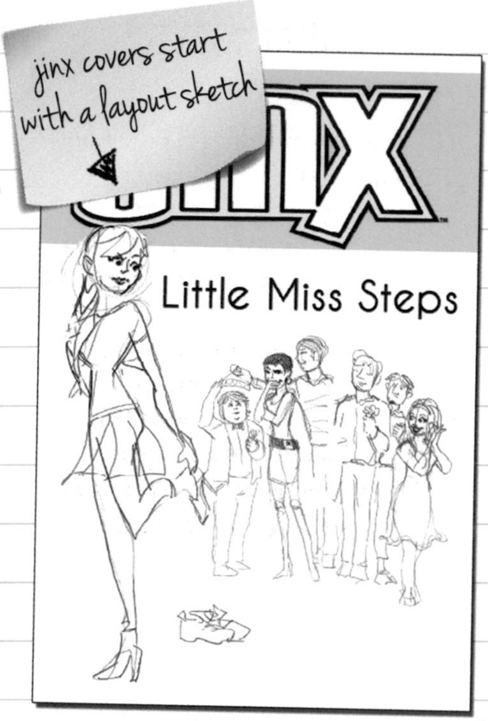
jinx covers start with a layout sketch
jinx
Little Miss Steps

laying out a cover

Jinx covers start with layout sketches. Here the editorial team visualizes the ways Jinx and her friends can be shown on the cover of a book. There can be any number of layout sketches at this stage of development, but sometimes everyone gets lucky and it looks good right away!

the artist draws

With a layout in hand, the penciller (in this case, the talented Rick Burchett) brings the sketches to to life! Once the layout is practically applied, it's easy to see what is working and what isn't. If it doesn't work, it's back to the drawing board!

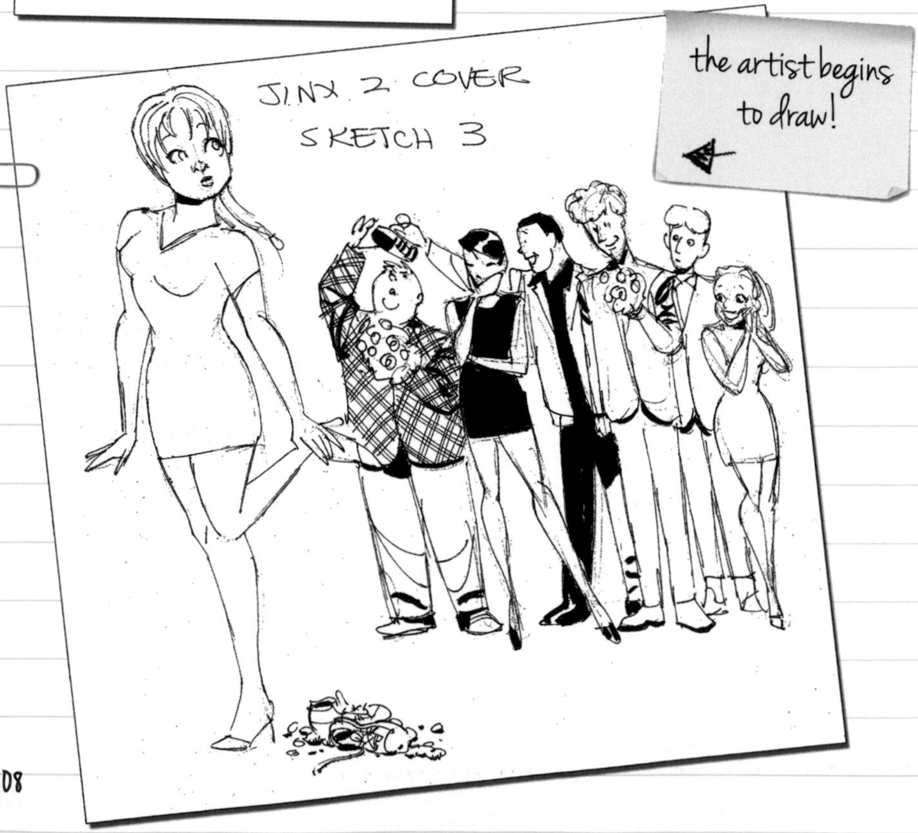
the artist begins to draw!
JINX 2 COVER
SKETCH 3

more art!

JINX 2 COVER 2 SKETCH

When the artist starts to draw from layout sketches, they are also encouraged to come up with additional concepts. (You never know when you're going to hit the jackpot.)

The two black and white sketches on this page are two of these concepts, developed by Rick Burchett. The sketch below made such a good impression that it was developed to be the back cover image of the book!

inks & colors!

WELCOME TO THE DANCE

With a great cover picked, the pencils are finalized and sent off to the letterer (if there is any text on the cover) and after that to the inker. The inker on Jinx: Little Miss Steps is industry legend Terry Austin! It's then scanned and colored in Photoshop.

this sketch is the back cover image!

and that's how a cover is made!

Once cover artwork has been digitally colored, it's dropped into a layout prepared by a graphic designer. You can see the the final version of the layout sketch that we started with on the cover of this book. As an added bonus, the back cover imagery (shown below) was also developed along the way!

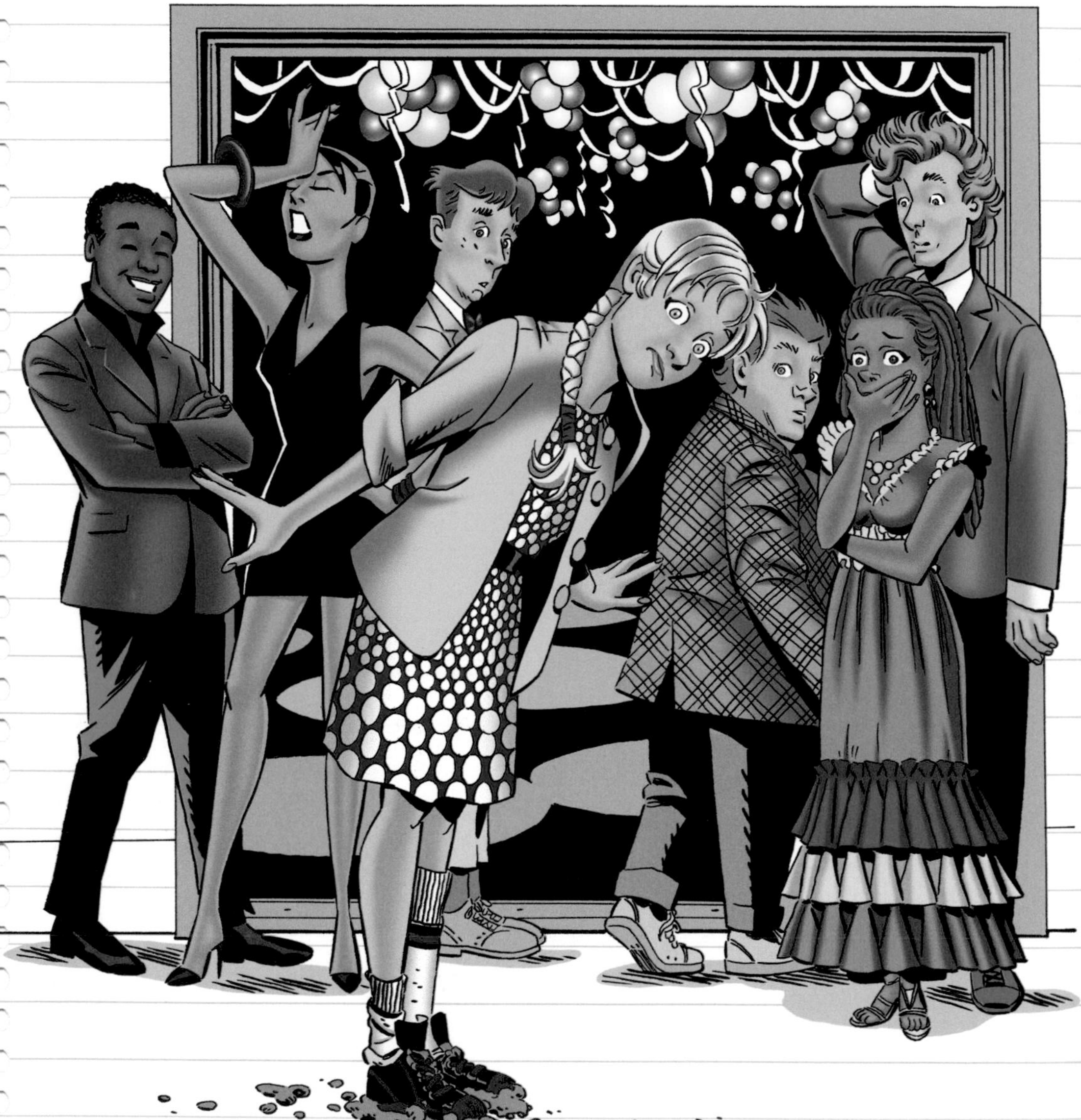

The best covers are created by a team of talented people! Pencillers, inkers, letterers, colorists, designers and editors work together to produce an image designed to show you the best of what the story inside will bring you!

the end

... for now!